First published 2019

First printed edition published 2024 by Drollery Ltd.

Copyright © Alice Coldbreath, 2019

ISBN 978-1-916736-06-1

More books available by Alice Coldbreath:

The Vawdrey Brothers Series:

Book 1: Her Baseborn Bridegroom

Book 2: His Forsaken Bride

Book 3: An Ill-Made Match

The Brides of Karadok Series:

Book 1: Wed By Proxy

Book 2: The Unlovely Bride

Book 3: The Consolation Prize

Book 4: Her Bridegroom, Bought and Paid For

Book 5: An Inconvenient Vow

Book 6: The Favourite

The Victorian Prizefighter Series:

Book 1: A Bride for the Prizefighter

Book 2: A Substitute Wife for the Prizefighter

Book 3: A Contracted Spouse for the Prizefighter

The Winter Palace, Aphrany

"Oh dear," fretted Mathilde as she took a step back and regarded her young friend, who stood swathed in one of her long white shifts. "Is this really going to work?"

"Course it is!" said Willard, rubbing his snub nose. "We're much of the same height."

"Yes," agreed Mathilde doubtfully. But she didn't really think people would notice his height anyway when he lay down in her bed.

"Too late to get cold feet now," scolded Robin, her other friend. "Now sit on this stool while I chop off your hair. Piers is standing watch down the end of the corridor. He said if your nurse returns, he'll hoot three times like an owl."

Mathilde obediently dropped down onto the chair. She held very still as Robin wielded the shears about her head.

"Don't take her ear off, Rob," cautioned Willard. He was laying his own suit out for Mathilde to don. She glanced at the bright particolored hose and short tunic and felt her heart quail. But Robin was right, it was far too late for cold feet. She had committed herself to this daring plan weeks ago. She watched in strange detachment as a pile of her long mouse-colored hair grew at her feet. A draft on her neck made her shiver. "Is it done?" she asked nervously.

"Just tidying it up a bit," said Robin with a frown as he capered about her, snipping with the blades.

"You need to tidy it." Willard snorted. "Looks like she visits the same barber as my uncle!" From his derisive tone, Mathilde could tell that was not a compliment.

Robin ignored him, frowning in concentration. He took a step back and tipped his head to one side. "Not too bad," he said at last, looking back over his shoulder at Willard.

"If you squint," agreed Willard.

"Now get those clothes on," urged Robin. "And I'll start tacking your hair to this." He snatched up the lace cap she wore to bed and started at it industriously with a needle and thread. Willard knelt on the floor and gathered up her fallen locks.

Mathilde caught up Willard's clothes. A roll of wrapped linen started to unfurl, and she made a hurried grab for it. "What's this?" she asked, holding it up in confusion.

Robin colored slightly. "It's for binding," he said and gestured to his own flat chest.

"Oh!" Mathilde glanced down involuntarily at the slight swell of her small bosom. She didn't think she'd have to worry too much about that aspect of the charade, but she was grateful to her young friends, who clearly thought of everything. "Thank you."

She disappeared behind a painted screen to change. The boys at thirteen she thought were too young to care about nakedness, but she was fully four and twenty, so modesty had to be preserved. Studiously avoiding the glass, for she did not wish to be put off by her shorn head, she hurriedly pulled on the white linen braies, followed by the woolen hose, blue leg first and then yellow leg. When it came to fastening the two together at the top, she struggled a moment, her fingers fumbling over the unfamiliar process. When it felt secure, she turned to unravel the strip of linen and wrap it around her chest area. In truth, she wasn't really sure she'd tied it tight enough.

Turning this way and that, she wondered if, in fact, it hadn't added bulk rather than not. Sure enough, her reflection was a slap in the face. She scarcely recognized herself and blinked in silent stupefaction at the strange-looking creature in the mirrored glass. The sight of her legs alone was enough to rob her of breath! Did she really have the nerve to go abroad with them on display like that? As for her hair… She gulped. It hung down no longer than her jaw. And she had worn it down to her waist since she was five years old.

"My lady?" called Rob from the other side of the screen. Doubtless he had heard her fall silent.

"N-nearly done," she stammered and sprang into action, the spell broken. Too late to worry now. She had made her bed, and an imposter was going to lie in it. She wriggled into the undershirt, followed by a bright green tunic and a leather belt. Pulling the laces at her throat tight, she made a knot in them. "I'm coming now," she said as she took a deep breath and emerged from behind the screen.

"Lord blind me!" ejaculated Willard in surprise. Both boys were knelt now, up close to the candlelight while they sewed her hair to the edges of her nightcap. They both stared.

When they did not speak, Mathilde nervously fingered the blunt ends of her locks. "Will I pass muster, do you think?"

"Not if you play with your hair like that," said Robin, clearing his throat. "You're a boy, remember."

Mathilde dropped her hand hastily.

Willard jumped up and approached her as Rob carried on sewing. "You got to change your mannerisms too, milady. S'no good, just your clothes and hair."

"I see," said Mathilde, nodding. She squared her shoulders. "Like this?"

"Better," he conceded. "But you got to have assurance. Like, you got to be reminding yourself in your head whenever you walk into a room. Don't creep in like a mouse. You got to think 'I'm every bit as good as the likes of you. And one day I'll be better. I know it, and so do you.'"

Mathilde's eyes widened. "I see," she said, listening intently to his advice. She rather thought that such a mantra *would* help with her confidence. "I think," she said suddenly, "that I should have a knife at my belt."

Willard grinned, pleased she was taking to her role. "Aye, you should," he agreed. "But my father gave me mine so…"

"I did not mean to take yours," she said quickly when he looked reluctant. "I can take the one from my dressing table…"

"That one?" asked Robin, nodding toward the jeweled dagger. "It would get stolen in a heartbeat on the road, my lady! Or others would think you stole it and we'd be hauled before the law."

"Oh," replied Mathilde, crestfallen.

"You can take mine," offered Willard.

"Oh no, I couldn't—"

"You can," he said firmly. "If you're to be a convincing boy, then you'll need one."

"Then you must take mine," said Mathilde, equally firm. She walked to the dresser and picked it up by the hilt. "When we meet again, we can exchange back. And this will be a token of our faith in one another." She passed it to him carefully, and he took it with a soft whistle.

"Where did you get it?" he asked, turning it over. The jewels flashed. There were two rubies decorating each end of the cross guard, and on the pommel was a large emerald.

"My first husband sent it to me as a betrothal token ten years ago. I used it for opening letters and cutting pages and such."

"Are you sure?" asked Willard, suddenly doubtful. "What if I lose it or—"

"Quite," she replied, cutting him off. "After all, it is my own to bestow." When both boys stared at her, she added awkwardly, "And it is not as though it has any sentimental value. I only ever met Lord Langdon once."

"I always forget that you're even married, let alone a widow," commented Willard.

"A widow twice over," she reminded him quietly. She couldn't really blame him. She'd never felt like a wife herself in anything but name. Hopefully that would all soon change. In a few short weeks she would face her current husband, Lord Martindale, in person. Then she would tell him that she wanted to be wedded in truth, as well as lawfully.

Willard passed her his own serviceable dagger in a leather sheath. She tucked it into her belt without examining the blade. After all, it was more about feeling the part than functionality. "And if I should lose your blade," she told him, "then mine becomes yours."

"Then I hope you do lose it," said Willard fervently.

"Well, in that case let us exchange now and be done with it."

"Truly?"

"Truly," she said. "After all, you are sure to run into some serious reprisals for your part in my flight. It is only right that I make you some gift in reparation."

Willard spat in his palm and extended his right hand to her. She wrinkled her nose. "Nay, you mustn't do that," he cautioned. "All men know this is as binding as a blood oath. Or as near to it as, damn it," he added conscientiously.

"A blood oath?" repeated Mathilde doubtfully. Spit might be a bodily fluid, but it was not blood.

"Is that not right, Rob?" Willard appealed to their friend.

"Aye," Robin flung at them over his shoulder. His needle flashed in and out of the light brown hair.

"Very well, then," Mathilde said, and raising her hand, she delicately spat into it. Willard rolled his eyes. Then she extended her hand and tried not to flinch at the feeling of his wet palm against her own. *Being a boy is disgusting!*

Some ten minutes later, she gazed down at Willard lying in her bed, wearing her nightgown and cap, with her long locks hanging about his shoulders. It was most extraordinary, and the impression made Mathilde feel quite light-headed. "Don't forget," she cautioned. "Speak in a whisper. I told Nurse my throat was sore, so she'll be expecting your voice to be scratchy and hoarse." Willard nodded.

"And huddle under the covers," added Robin. "Don't loll. You're supposed to be suffering from a chill and you've got to spin it out as long as you can to make good our escape."

Willard pulled a face of long-suffering and gave an exaggerated shudder. "Oh, I'm ever so ill, Nurse," he whispered pathetically. "I believe I shall not last till morn!"

"Don't say that for lords' sakes!" blurted Mathilde in alarm. "That would make her fetch my mother!"

"Only say that you're tired and need to rest," added Robin.

"Would you both stop fretting?" sighed Willard. "I shall be very well. 'Tis you who shall be late. Weren't you supposed to meet Gordon at the south gate on the stroke of midnight?"

Mathilde's and Robin's eyes met. "We'd better go, my lady." Impulsively Mathilde fell on Willard and hugged him fiercely.

"Mind my hair!" he said in a muffled voice. "It's not terribly secure."

"If they try to punish you, you must get word to me at the Martindale estate, which is called Acton March," Mathilde urged him. "And when the furor has died down, you must write to me—"

"Only if it seems safe," added Robin heavily.

"You have the purse of money I gave you—"

"Yes, yes," said Willard. "Stop fussing and go! All will be well. I'll get a hiding no doubt, but I daresay it won't be my last." He uttered this with such sanguinity that Mathilde's bosom was filled with admiration for her brave young friend. Truly, he was the role model she should take for her boyish ideal.

"I will never forget this, Will," she promised as Robin grabbed her wrist and started to pull her from the room. "I am forever in your debt."

"Oh aye," agreed Willard with a yawn. "And you said I could keep the knife, mark you!" He turned onto his side and tucked a hand under his cheek, his eyes drifting shut, as Mathilde quietly pulled the door closed behind them.

"He can't truly be feeling sleepy," Mathilde marveled as she and Robin crept along the shadowy lesser-used corridors on a tortuous route down to the south gate of the castle. He must have been dissembling for her benefit. After all, she felt like her own wildly beating heart would leap out of her chest given any excuse.

Rob snorted. "He could sleep the night before his hanging, that one," he murmured.

"Don't say that!"

Rob's hand closed tightly around her own. "Don't forget his uncle's a bishop," he reminded her. "He won't come to any harm. Besides, he'll tell them you made him do it. Like we planned, remember?"

"That's true enough," she consoled herself.

"Ho! You boys!" She and Robin both stiffened and turned to face a rather tipsy-looking courtier dressed in a virulent shade of puce. He beckoned imperiously, and Rob started forward. "Not you," the young man said with a frown, rocking back on his heels. "That one." He pointed at Mathilde. "A look of innocence still clings to his features. My lady love may be softened by it," he added sentimentally. Rob opened his mouth, but before he could utter a word, Mathilde hurried forward and stood before the young man. He blinked down at her a moment owlishly. "Have you ever been in love, m'boy?" he asked with a hiccup.

"Nay, my lord," she answered truthfully, then coughed. Should she have tried to lower her voice? It sounded sadly girlish.

"A pure high treble," he sighed with a sad smile. "Tell me, do you sing in the King's choir?" She shook her head. "A pity." He lapsed into melancholy silence as Mathilde gazed up at him expectantly.

"You have some commission for us, sir?" prompted Robin with an edge to his voice.

The young man gave a start and looked at Rob with disfavor. "Do you know who I am?" he asked, his gaze returning to Mathilde thoughtfully.

She hesitated. "I think... Are you connected with the Woodcote family?" He looked familiar, and she had a notion she had seen him about court with Viscount Woodcote and his cronies.

He nodded, looking pleased. "A quick-witted boy! I am Sir Edgar Hill, Viscount Woodcote's heir." Mathilde bowed, pleased with her improvisation. She was starting to enjoy herself. Sir Edgar Hill returned her bow with a flourish and then drew a folded paper from his doublet. "I would like you to deliver this letter unto the Lady Elizabeth Coton." He spoke the name with reverence, though he had lowered his voice and cast a furtive look around. "You must not let it fall into the hands of her kinsfolk at any cost. Do you understand?" He shot her an anxious look. She nodded. Then he withdrew a silver coin from his cuff. "This is for you, young master. For your pains and your discretion," he added meaningfully. "By the by," he said, reaching out and catching her chin in his gloved hand, "who are your people?" He screwed up his eyes. "I do not recall seeing you hereabouts. I should surely remember such a pretty boy."

Mathilde's eyes widened. *Pretty?* Then his words sank in. "M-my people?" she stammered.

9

Rob cleared his throat. "My young friend is an *associate* of the de Courcey family."

Sir Edgar's expression cleared. "Ah, I see." He clicked his tongue. "How oft does vice take the guise of virtue," he said regretfully. "I doubt the bloom of innocence will last long on that cheek. Not with that lineage."

"We'll take our leave of you," added Rob with meaning, and Mathilde dropped back to join him.

Sir Edgar waved a gloved hand, and Robin tugged Mathilde down a side servant stair.

"Should we be in here?" she whispered as they descended the perilously steep staircase.

"It won't signify," Rob muttered.

"What did you mean by claiming I was an associate of the de Courceys?" she asked curiously.

"De Courcey has a notorious number of bastards."

"Oh!" She blushed faintly in the darkness.

"When you say that," Rob added, gruffly apologetic, "people tend to stop asking questions."

"That was very clever of you," said Mathilde without rancor. "I had thought of a false name to travel under," she admitted. "But it was not a court name."

"No, you wouldn't want a court name for the road," Robin agreed without much interest.

"It's Leander," Mathilde told him proudly. Leander seemed to her to be a vastly heroic name.

Robin halted on the step. "That's too fancy," he said, shaking his head. "You want something plain like Smith or Jenkins."

"Smith?" she repeated with displeasure, but Rob was vaulting himself onto a window ledge to peer down at the courtyard below.

"Gordon's there waiting at the gate with the horses," he said with relief. "Come on."

2

Solstice Eve, Acton March

Guy Randall, Marquis of Martindale, dropped the gnawed meat bone with a clatter and pushed the empty platter away from him with a belch. He cast a jaundiced eye around the hall and wondered how long he would have to sit here and show willing before he could make good his escape. The company was starting to grow rowdy. The bride sat squarely in the groom's lap, and there was much laughter and jocularity, neither of which was to Guy's taste. A serving wench approached, and he narrowed his gaze at her. Her step faltered, and she held up the jug of ale to make plain her intent. *Oh*. He gave a curt nod for her to proceed, and she filled up his drinking vessel, sneaking looks at him out of the corner of her eye. He ignored her scrutiny, and she retreated, casting one last look back at him over her shoulder.

"Would it kill you to give the lass a smile?" rumbled Firmin, taking him by surprise.

Guy scowled at him. "When have you ever known me to smile at women?"

Firmin shook his head. "You're too young to be getting the reputation for a woman hater."

A woman hater? Guy grunted. After all, what did he care what people said? And if it stopped serving wenches from wasting their smiles on him, then it was all to the better.

"You'd think that big black beard would be enough to put 'em off," struck up Waldon, who sat on the other side of him.

Guy turned his ferocious gaze on him instead. "You've a beard yourself," he pointed out scathingly.

"Aye," agreed Waldon. "But not the reputation for hating women, or a wife." Guy braced himself for the moment when Waldon realized his blunder. Sure enough, he saw his friend stiffen and then look wide-eyed toward Firmin, who gave him a small shake of his head.

For Guy did have a wife. A wife that none was permitted to ever speak of. A money-hungry, thrice-wed, southern bitch of a wife, who even now paraded around the Argent King's court, bearing his title as if it were his own severed head. How he hated her, and all she represented. The desecration of all his boyhood ideals and dreams. The brutal awakening to the cold reality of his life. He slammed his fist down on the table but held himself back from speech. It took an effort.

"Guy…" started Firmin warningly, and he looked up to find the wedding revelers all staring at him fearfully. Clearly, they thought he was about to turn the table over and start bellowing. He passed a hand over his brow. He hadn't really lost his temper in a twelvemonth. His hand shook slightly as he reached for his drink before tossing it back. The musicians struck back up their tune, and a sigh of relief seemed to pass through the room at a potential disaster averted.

"One more jug of ale," he said in a low voice. "And I leave."

"None could complain at that," rallied Firmin. "You've been a generous overlord and done Temur proud."

"A right handsome wedding gift you gave them," joined in Waldon. "They'll get a good start in life with that."

Guy curled his lip in reply. All he had given them had been a purse of gold, and he had plenty of that. He disliked being

13

dragged from his hearth during Yuletide, when he wanted to be sequestered away from all celebrations and making merry. He glanced over at his young cousin, the groom.

"Poor bastard," he grunted, though even the most impartial bystander could see Temur was flushed and giddy with happiness and ale.

His new wife—Guy had not bothered to remember her name—had one shapely arm curved around Temur's neck and looked just as triumphant as the groom. He would not let a woman get so close to his jugular, he thought grimly. Temur was a fool. But at least Temur's bride had been of his own choosing, Guy acknowledged. That was more than his wife had been. He had been given the bleak choice of signing his fealty over to the southern king, along with half of his wealth, or face execution. The added bonus of being leg-shackled to a woman he'd never even met had been the crowning insult.

He'd been sat in a filthy cell when the papers had been placed before him with pen and ink. He had not even realized then how complete King Wymer's victory over his family had been. For with a wife he had married by proxy—a wife never actually given into his possession—his line had also effectively been severed. For how could he ever beget a legitimate heir to continue it or to inherit? On his death, his lands and his title would revert to the Crown. So really, he had signed away *everything* on that accursed day. Was it any wonder he was so bloody bitter?

He brooded over his cup for another half hour before taking his leave and heading back. Was it his imagination, or did the company breathe a collective sigh of relief at his departure? He wouldn't be surprised, for all everyone insisted his blessing was necessary, he was under no illusions that he was well-liked.

How the hells was anyone else supposed to like him when he absolutely despised himself?

Firmin insisted on accompanying him back, though Waldon stayed behind to celebrate the nuptials. It was a six-mile ride from the village of Acton Dymock to his sprawling estate of Acton March. The large manor house was mostly plunged in darkness on their return. Candles had been left alight in the wood-paneled hallway, but there were no other signs of life.

"Will ye take no supper?" Firmin asked when Guy immediately headed past him to mount the shadowy staircase to his private rooms. He needed no light to guide his way.

"Nay." He shook his head. He'd eaten a good supper at the wedding feast, but usually that would not mean he could not eat again. It was thinking of *her* that had made him lose his usually considerable appetite.

"I'll bid ye good night, then, Guy." Firmin hesitated. Guy stood a moment on the stair, then it struck him his steward was about to wish him a happy Solstice. He stared at him balefully, and Firmin gulped and gave a nod instead before turning away.

Firmin was a good steward, a good friend if it came to that. But Guy preferred his own company when he was feeling morose. As he undressed for bed, he noticed the driving rain that was starting to pelt against the windowpanes. It would be a cold, cheerless day on the morrow for all it was a feast day. In truth, he found it hard to remember a time when it had been any different.

He added a few more logs onto his fire and threw himself into his oversized canopied bed. The sheets were cold, and he cursed as he rolled this way and that, bundling himself up in the blankets. The wind was starting to howl outside. When the windows began to rattle, he realized that the rain had turned into hailstones. It was a filthy night. He spared a thought for any travelers abroad at this hour and was glad he'd left for home when he had. It might offer little by way of cheer or comfort, but it was shelter from the storm at least, if nothing else.

In his father's day, on nights such as these, the whole household would gather around the huge stone hearth in the Great Hall and someone would tell the old tales. Sometimes it was an aged servant, and other times a traveling bard, who might know different variations on the stories. But the most vibrant tales were told by Old Helga, who had been the local wise woman. Tales of the Wild Hunt and how the All-Father would be riding forth with his company of wolves and ravens. Woe betide any hapless traveler who strayed into their path. But the All-Father could be beneficent, when the mood took him, and if he found his quarry worthy of reward.

Guy wondered if Old Helga still lived. He had not heard any mention of her in years. He had not ventured along the path that led to the wood for many a long day. Doubtless her cottage still stood, even if it was empty, as it was in such a remote spot. Though on his land, she had paid precious little by way of rent or tithe. Her kind never did. *Witches*. He gazed sightlessly into the darkness, remembering that Yuletide many moons ago when she had foreseen his own demise. *What was it she said?*

He couldn't remember. He had only heard it secondhand, for his father would never speak of it. Whatever it was, it had been enough to get her thrown from the hall and denounced by his father. Folk whispered it was something about his downfall being tied with the Blechmarsh line. Well, if that was so, she had been right enough. The southern king had roundly defeated the north and united all Karadok under his standard. But the Lords of Martindale had always been loyal to the northern crown and had fought to the bitter end.

They had not gone down without a fight, and they had paid the price. Not as cruelly as some, he thought, reflecting on his neighbors the Kerslakes, who had their ancient castle razed to the ground, or the Pierces, who had lost all three of their sons in battle. But then, had their house not also lost all its sons? All their future sons that is, for he would be the last of his once proud line.

He stared out into the darkness. Had Old Helga really seen it all in the bones? If so, her warning had fallen on deaf ears. His father had remained stubborn and staunch to the very end. Luckily, he had died in his bed before the northern cause had folded and before his only son had been forced to marry one of the enemy. But who would have thought the war would wage for ten long years? Ten years and he had transformed from boy to man in that time—forged in the fires of bitter experience.

The rain beat against the roof, distracting him from his thoughts, and just as he was turning onto his side, he heard the loud three knocks against his fortified front door. Except, he couldn't possibly. Not from the vantage point of his bedchamber. Even as he told himself this, he sat up in his bed, his heart beating loudly. He somehow *knew* that was what he had heard. Someone had knocked at his door. For a moment, one of the old tales flashed into his mind. The tale of the disguised traveler, come to test the worthiness of the inhabitants on a cold winter's night. To see if a humble beggar would be offered shelter from the storm. Except, it was no beggar who stood before the potential host, ready to stand in judgment. He shook his head. It wasn't like him to be so fanciful.

The house was all in silence. It seemed the summons had stirred no one save himself. Grumbling, Guy reached for a robe and donned it. He craned his ears but did not hear another sound. Doubtless it was all in his imagination, he told himself uneasily.

17

He must have imbibed more than he'd realized, or else it was stronger than the usual fare.

He had just reached the top of the staircase when he heard another three bangs again on the door and almost jumped out of his skin. This time, he knew it was not mere imagination, for he heard faintly the kitchen dogs barking down below. They had been roused by it also. Snatching up a candlestick, he approached the door and began drawing back the bolts. As he swung the door open, he braced himself, but that did not stop his eyes from starting from his head at the sight that greeted him.

Flanked by two beadles and another he vaguely recognized as a representative of one of the wealthier merchant families from nearby Wickhamford town were two youths, soaked to the skin, their wet hair plastered to their heads and their stockings and boots covered in mud. Grimly, Guy ran his eye over them. They were not part of his household; he was sure of that.

"My Lord Martindale—" began the beadle, and at his words, the smaller youth let out an exclamation.

Guy's gaze snapped to him, and the little wretch had the nerve to stare back at him with open curiosity. "Y-you're Lord Martindale?" he stammered, through lips fast turning blue.

"I knew he were a little liar!" gasped the other beadle, seizing the lad's arm and shaking it. "Said you knew his lordship, didn't you, you little swine!"

The other lad sprang forward at this rough treatment. "Don't you touch him!" he yelled, only to be cuffed roundly by the other beadle.

"Now, now," interjected the merchant distastefully. "Let's not get overzealous in pursuit of our duty, officers." He looked back at Guy. "May we come in, my lord?"

"What business is this of mine?" Guy growled, even as he fell back to allow their entry.

His eye was drawn again to the smallest youth, who surely could not be more than thirteen or fourteen in years, unless he was severely undernourished. They trooped past him, dripping rainwater puddles onto the floor. Guy turned his head, hearing an inner door open, and saw two befuddled-looking servants peering around it. He guessed his household had probably been celebrating the season in his absence, and that must have been why they had been so hard to rouse.

"Light the fires in the main hall!" he barked and glanced at the shivering boy again. "And fetch blankets!" He did not know why he added the last directive. Doubtless the angelic face hid the soul of a hardened criminal. Still...for some reason, he did say it. He wasn't worried overmuch that anyone would accuse him of being tenderhearted. If they did, it would be a first.

The servants fled before him, and Guy led the way to the hall where they were hurriedly lighting the sconces. Bogdon nearly fell into the fireplace he was rekindling, and Jankin looked decidedly bleary-eyed as he brought in ale and blankets for their visitors. Obviously, he thought grimly, his servants had been making merry below stairs.

Guy pulled out a chair and gestured for his visitors to do likewise. He stared at the two boys a moment before nodding toward the fire which had been banked for the night but was now starting to put forth flames again. The bigger one took his meaning and dragged the smaller one toward the blaze.

19

"Hold!" ordered one of the beadles sternly. They were divesting themselves of their rain-soaked cloaks and hats.

"Let them stand with their backs to the fire," Guy found himself growling. At their astonished faces, he added in a surly voice, "You'll be cheating the hangman if you let them catch their deaths now." The merchant's son laughed, but the beadles both took their seats stiff with affront. Guy motioned for Bogdon to bring forth the ale jug, and his guests were served refreshment as the two boys stood huddled before the huge fireplace, far bigger than the both of them. The whole time, Guy was strangely aware of the huge eyes fixed on his face. Who was the boy to him? Could he be the offspring of one of his men? He raked his memory but could find no answer.

"Take a blanket," he barked, ignoring the reproachful gaze of the first beadle. "I can't hear myself think above the chattering of teeth," he added and looked up as more footsteps approached. This time it was Firmin, who had either not yet undressed or had delayed to redress himself.

He gazed about him in astonishment. "But what is all this?" he asked.

"Join us," said Guy. "I'm about to find out myself." He turned back to the men now seated at his table. "Well?"

"My name is Thurston, my lord," said the merchant when the two beadles sat in stony silence. "Today it was my civic duty to serve as a parish officer. These boys were apprehended earlier in Wickhamford town."

Instead of asking what that had to do with him, Guy found himself glancing back at the fireplace where the bigger boy was now vigorously rubbing a blanket over the smaller boy's head and mumbling under his breath. The smaller one stood patient as a lamb, as he was subjected to what looked like a thorough

20

scolding. *Could they be siblings?* There was precious little resemblance that Guy could see. The bigger boy had rusty brown hair and freckles whereas the smaller one was fine-boned and delicate, with skin that looked translucent in the flickering firelight.

Guy turned back to find all eyes on him. "What had they done?" he asked testily.

The first beadle bristled. "Assaulted a poor carter delivering his goods." Guy stared the man down. "My lord," he added hastily.

"Really? These two *boys*?" he asked scornfully.

"Don't be deceived by appearances, milord," piped up the second beadle. "They're a pair of devils the both of them. Poor man was covered in bruises, and that little one even *bit* him."

"Did they rob him?" Guy asked, his eyes returning to the small figure shivering in front of the fire.

"No," admitted the first beadle grudgingly.

"There was his horse," the second beadle reminded him.

The first beadle perked up. "Ah yes, they stole his horse, milord."

"You're saying they're a pair of horse thieves, then?" asked Firmin, shooting a puzzled look at Guy.

Thurston sucked the air between his teeth and frowned. "I think that's a bit much, indeed I do," he said gravely. "I couldn't support a charge of horse thievery, upon my soul."

"Now Master Thurston!" objected the first beadle. "What would your pa say, if he knew you wasn't a-doing of your duty?"

"He'd say a lot more if he knew I unjustly supported a hanging charge," Thurston responded with spirit.

"But what I say is this," interrupted Firmin. "What the devil has any of this to do with Lord Martindale?"

"*He*," said the first beadle, pointing at the smaller boy, "said as he knew Lord Martindale, who would stand as character witness for him."

The smaller boy's eyes had been drifting shut as he relaxed in the heat of the fire. They snapped open now and clashed with Guy's. "Boy, come here," Guy said firmly. The older boy's hand shot out to stay his friend, but he was gently shaken off.

"It's alright, Rob," he heard him murmur, then he walked around the table until he stood directly in front of Guy. To his astonishment, all Guy could see in those large hazel eyes was curiosity. No shadow of fear or trepidation showed in their depths. He returned the gaze, and instead of denouncing the little wretch, he found himself asking curiously: "How is it that you know me, boy?" Firmin's sharply indrawn breath showed how far he was acting out of character, but Guy did not break eye contact, and the boy gazed steadily back at him.

"Because, my lord," he whispered. "I am your wife."

3

Mathilde waited expectantly for Lord Martindale to react, but if anything, he only seemed to go very still in his seat.

"What was that the boy said?" rumbled someone. She rather thought it was the grizzled-looking latecomer, but she did not have eyes for anyone other than her husband at present. She was wholly engrossed taking in all his glory. He was tall and powerfully built with broad shoulders and strong limbs. He was clearly master here, with his rich, booming voice, yet he opened his own door, which she found strangely fascinating. Things must be vastly different here in the north, she thought.

Both her former husbands had been old men, but this one was young, even that black beard covering what she was sure was a strong jaw could not obscure the fact. She was wildly encouraged by his kindness to her and Rob by providing them with fire and blankets. He was clearly both thoughtful and generous, and her heart swelled to find him so. By some miracle, her mother had hit on a bridegroom who was not wholly past prayers.

Suddenly he came to his feet, staring straight ahead of him a moment. Then he spoke two words, "Follow me," and strode past her. Mathilde blinked and quickly followed, cries of "*My lord!*" and "*But where are you going?*" ringing in her ears. He paid no heed to them, so neither did she. He flung open a door on the opposite side of the hall and disappeared through it. Mathilde hurried after him. He did not look back over his shoulder, but instead plunged down a dimly lit corridor and then up some stone steps. She paused at the bottom of the steps, which were steep and winding, and felt a flicker of panic rise up, which she swiftly extinguished. Her days of fearing her own shadow were behind her, she told herself sternly.

She had traveled the length of the kingdom dressed as a man. She had hitched rides on carts. She had slept in common taverns, on hard wooden benches, and even once under a hedge. She had haggled over the price of a loaf, been cuffed round the ear by an irate stallholder, and that very morning she had been in her first fight in defense of the innocent. In short, she had earned her spurs. She was *not* about to fall at the final fence.

Steeling herself, she started up the steps, listening to the ring of Lord Martindale's—*her husband's*—boots against the flagstones. He took exceptionally large strides, and she wondered if he was scaling two steps at a time. Her fitness levels had vastly improved over the past month, but she was no match for him. When she finally reached the top, panting slightly, he stood, a shadowy figure next to another open door. It appeared he was expecting her to walk through this one first. She hastened to comply. He followed her through the door and shut it after him, turning a key in the lock. Then he stood a moment, leaning back against the door, regarding her through narrowed eyes.

Mathilde glanced around at the bare room, but there really wasn't much to look at. A bed was in the corner and a battered trunk under the window. Other than that, the only furniture was a small table and a rickety-looking chair. She turned back to Lord Martindale, who slowly folded his arms.

"Prove it," he said shortly.

Mathilde blinked, wondering how she was supposed to do that. "You did not send me a betrothal token," she said after a moment's hesitation. "My father's name was Lord Douglas Doverdale. But you probably negotiated the marriage terms with my mother."

He shook his head. "Wrong."

Mathilde stared at him. "Wrong?" She faltered.

"There was no negotiation," he said in a hard voice. "I signed the papers in a prison cell. And it was not the Doverdales who brokered the marriage."

Mathilde's mouth dropped open. "But—" She broke off confusedly. It was certainly true that it had been conducted far differently to her previous two marriages, she thought with unease. He didn't have one foot in the grave for one thing, and she hadn't been given any gifts. When she glanced back at him, she found he was still watching her closely. "Who did, then?" she asked in bewilderment. And when had he been imprisoned?

"Your King," he said as though the words left a bad taste in his mouth. Of course, he was a northerner, thought Mathilde. He would have supported the Blechmarsh claim to the throne. "Or rather, his advisor, Lord Vawdrey."

"Oh," she said, realizing this reaction was vastly inadequate. She shivered, feeling suddenly cold again. Her clothes were still damp, and there was no fire lit in the room.

"How do I know you're her?" he asked again, and Mathilde suddenly noticed that his glower was a little menacing. Doubtless it was the shadowy room, and the fact she was tired and had spent most of the day in a dark cell herself.

"I'm not sure how I can prove it," she said in a small voice. "You can ask me any question about myself, but..." She trailed off, not wanting to give voice to her sudden suspicions that he knew very little about her, and maybe cared even less. She bit her lip, willing it not to wobble, blinking hard. She was a boy, she reminded herself. Or as good as. She did not cry.

"Take off your clothes." Mathilde's head snapped up, and as she stared at him in horror, she watched some color creep into his cheeks. "I need to see that you're at least a lass," he said gruffly.

"Oh," she breathed out in relief. For a moment there, she had forgotten how manly and brave she had grown and had known a moment of paralyzing terror. She felt herself sway slightly on her feet as she tried to pull the damp tunic over her head. Her jailers had taken her belt and Will's dagger from her earlier. Her heart still beating painfully in her chest, she struggled until she had wriggled out of both tunic and undershirt.

Then she stood in just her braies and chausses and a roll of linen bandages wrapped round her chest. When he made no comment, she reached up with trembling fingers and started to unravel her bindings. Her entire body had turned to gooseflesh by this point and her numb fingers were making a poor job of it. She tugged and fumbled until the bandages lay pooled at her feet. Rounding her shoulders, she let her hair fall forward to hide her mortified face. Thankfully, it was just about long enough for concealment. For a moment, there was nothing but silence, and then he cleared his throat.

"There's blankets over there on the bed," he said. "Cover yourself."

She nearly tripped on her own feet, which felt like blocks of ice, as she turned to strip a blanket from the bed and wrap it around herself. It was rather prickly, but in recent weeks she had known worse. With her back to him, she managed to wipe a forearm across her wet eyes. She hoped the gesture went unnoticed.

"I want my knife," she said desperately as she turned back around to face him.

"Your knife?"

"They took it from me, and I need it back." Taking a deep breath, she launched into an explanation. "It's not really mine, but a friend's. If I lose it, then I will have broken faith with him."

He stared rather hard at that. "What friend?" he demanded, sounding like the words had been wrenched from him.

"Willard Peyton," she told him and had to stop herself from asking if he knew him. "His uncle is the Bishop of Hudde." She did not know why she was gabbling like this, but she was suddenly terrified that if she stopped, she might burst into tears. She was so disappointed in herself, she could cry. A month ago, walking across a crowded room had frightened her. Only this morning she had thought herself invincible. Then she had been bruised, arrested, and forced to strip in front of a stranger. She had a creeping suspicion that he meant to lock her in this room and keep her a prisoner before ransoming her back to her mother. The thought made her feel sick to her stomach.

"Come here," he bit out.

As she took a few reluctant steps toward him, he reached into his shirt and looked to be unfastening something. Mathilde's heart was in her mouth as he seized her and briskly started rearranging the folds of her blanket. His hands grazed her bare skin, but strangely she did not find herself flinching from his touch, as it was completely impersonal. She watched as he extracted a leather strap from around his neck and fastened that firmly about her waist to secure it. When she glanced down, to her astonishment, she saw that she once again wore a sheathed dagger on the narrow black leather strip.

"Now take off your hose," he said, glancing away. "They're soaked through."

27

Mathilde hesitated, but in truth, the blanket was now swathed about her like a dress, concealing her legs. She reached beneath her impromptu "skirts" and dragged the wet chausses down to her ankles. To her surprise, he knelt and helped her step out of her soggy boots and peel the damp fabric from her feet. His exclamation made her jump. He was looking up at her accusingly.

"What happened here?"

Mathilde glanced down at her bare feet. Did he mean the bruising? She hesitated. "The carter was very fat and trampled on me," she explained. "And then afterward, I got rather jostled in the jail." He stared up at her a moment. "After I got arrested," she reminded him.

He took a deep breath in and out. For a moment, his large warm hand covered both her feet, then he withdrew it and turned his face away from her. Mathilde watched him uncertainly. He seemed to be in the grip of some strong emotion, but she must be misreading him, for that could not be right. When he straightened up and stood before her, his expression was guarded and tense again, giving away nothing.

After a moment's pause, he unlocked the door and stood back. Mathilde realized she had done him a huge disservice. He had not been intending to imprison her after all! She felt almost dizzy with relief and beamed up at him as she scuttled back through. So elated was she that she scarcely felt the bite of the cold flagstones against her bare feet. She floated back down the steps, almost giddy, though that might have been due to the fact she had not eaten since the previous evening. She stumbled slightly on the last step, and he reached out and steadied her. Then, he seemed to notice afresh that she had no shoes or stockings and cursed under his breath.

28

"It's of no consequence," she started to tell him, but he was already gingerly gathering her up and lifting her into his arms. Mathilde held her breath. She had never been carried before. At least, not since she was an adult. She glanced nervously at him from the corner of her eye. In truth, his expression was forbidding in the extreme, but she found herself relaxing against him in spite of it. Appearances might appear to the contrary, but this husband of hers *was* kind and considerate. Once again, she felt the optimistic that there was still a chance she could claw herself some semblance of a winning hand from the paltry one she had been dealt.

4

Guy booted the door to the main hall open and strode through. He was incredibly angry, but the burden he was carrying in his arms right now meant he couldn't really let loose with his temper. Truth be told, he wasn't sure that it shouldn't be directed at himself. "I want my knife," she had said after he had forced her to strip to the waist. And he couldn't say he blamed her.

Everyone turned and looked as he made his way straight to the head of the table.

"My lord—?"

Someone dropped something, which clanged noisily against the floorboards. Guy set her down at the head of the table, straightening the skirts of her blanket-gown so she was decent. He was sure they got a flash of bare leg as he lowered her, for he heard a shocked hiss, and her friend suddenly appeared, crouching at her side with an agonized look on his face. He sent a look of pure hatred Guy's way. "I'll kill you," he choked out in a low, shaking voice, "even if I swing for it."

"Rob!" She—this woman who claimed to be his wife—reached out and seized the boy's hand. "All is well, I swear it." At his pointed look, she repeated, "I *swear* it." Guy realized he still had no idea what their relationship was. The boy had seized her upper arms and was staring into her face intently. After a moment he relaxed, then clasped her to him in an awkward embrace. "You scared me," he gritted out before thrusting her away from him as if she were some troublesome sibling. He was bright red now and scowling.

She reached out again and grasped his hand in hers. "I'm sorry, don't be angry," she murmured. He hunched his shoulders crossly but did not pull away his hand.

"What in the hells—?" spluttered Firmin.

"I vouch for these two," said Guy tightly. His angry gaze dared the beadles to dispute his right.

Thurston pursed his lips in a whistle. "So, *he's* a *she*," he murmured and grinned. Guy glared at him.

The first beadle cleared his throat. "You—er..." His eyes met Guy's and then dropped away. "I see, my lord," he said hastily. "I see."

The second beadle was still staring dumbfounded at her, as though she'd grown a second head.

Then the female piped up. "I want my horse," she said in a loud, carrying voice.

The first beadle gasped at her temerity. "*Your* horse?"

"Yes, mine," she agreed. "The carter said, 'If you want me to stop beating him, he's yours for a sovereign.'"

"You paid the carter a sovereign for his horse?" asked Guy, turning his head sharply.

"I did."

He turned to the beadles. "She paid for the horse," he said succinctly. "So why did you say she stole it?"

"Well," huffed the first beadle. "Seemed an unlikely tale. Some gutter urchin payin'..." He trailed off, realizing the flaw in his logic.

31

"Well, she's not a gutter urchin, is she?" said Guy coldly, driving the point home.

"Um…"

"It seems we made a mistake, gentlemen," said Thurston in a conciliatory manner.

"What about the assault?" asked the second beadle. "What about that?"

"Assault?" echoed her companion indignantly. "That swindler took our sovereign and then tried to take back the horse as well. *He's* the thief!"

"That's right." She took up the argument spiritedly. "We only tried to defend our own rightful property from that hateful man." She turned to young Thurston. "I trust you confiscated the animal?"

"I…believe so," he said, turning quizzically to his companions for confirmation.

"Then I should like it returned to me upon the morrow," she said promptly. The beadles both looked incensed at being ignored from proceedings but dared not say anything. They were quite purple in the face. "And I should like that carter clapped in the stocks," she added. "To teach the ruffian a lesson."

Thurston laughed, and it dawned on Guy that the young merchant in all likelihood thought she was some fancy piece, past or present. Perhaps he thought she had called in a favor from him when they had slipped out of the room. That, or performed him some service.

Guy clenched his fists. He didn't like the appreciative way the merchant was eyeing her. Far too boldly. But the fact was, there was a reason Guy had not announced her true identity, and it was a good one. He did not yet know how he was going to handle the sudden appearance of this alleged wife. He needed to play a close hand, and letting her claims be known to all and sundry would not be wise. The downside was that by not disclosing who she claimed to be, he was leaving her position open to speculation. But what else could he do? He had no intention of rashly saddling himself with her when he hardly knew what to make of her.

"I trust that concludes the matter," he said, facing everyone down. He chose to take the cough and the shuffling of feet that greeted his words as all the assent he needed.

"After the return of my property, of course," she chimed in, the only person who seemed oblivious to his foul mood. "You have my knife and belt, as well as my horse," she reminded them.

"It will be returned to you in due course," said Thurston smoothly when he realized his companions were momentarily quite incapable of speech.

She beamed at the young merchant, and Guy realized his mood could take a worse turn. As he saw his visitors out, he could feel Firmin's eyes boring into him and forced himself to turn and face his steward.

"Have fires lit in the south tower." He looked at him meaningfully. The south tower was fortified, and all the doors had locks. Firmin's frown grew deeper, but he nodded curtly and left the hall to see rooms were prepared for them. "Your name?" he asked, barely looking at her face. Still, he could quite plainly see her surprised dismay at his query.

"It's Mathilde, my lord." She hesitated, as if about to say more, but deciding against it.

"And I'm Robin Geddings, second son of Sir Edgar Geddings," said her friend, stepping to her side. His eyes were steely. "Lady Martindale's protector." The words were flung at him as if issuing a challenge. Guy just about managed not to react to the use of her title. For two pins, Guy realized this young buck would tangle horns with him, despite his youth. By his estimation he could not be above fourteen. Robin held his gaze, and Guy nodded with grudging respect.

"Robin is a good friend and true," Mathilde said hurriedly and laid her hand on her protector's sleeve in a conciliatory gesture.

"I'm sure," responded Guy, remembering the lad's dire threat to kill him. He smiled grimly. It seemed she could command respect from green inexperienced boys. But he was no child, and he would not fall such an easy victim to her wiles.

"We're sorry to rouse your household so late in the night, my lord," she said politely, once she realized he was not going to offer more by way of conversation.

Guy glanced about him. The two servants had made themselves scarce, no doubt to fetch them washing water and lay their fires. Only the three of them stood in the hall. Was she being sarcastic? Perhaps she thought, by rights, all the staff should be lined up to welcome her? "Tonight is the Solstice Eve," he growled unexpansively. "The household is abed."

"Solstice Eve?" she said, her eyes widening. "I had not realized. When one is traveling, one loses track of the days." She twisted her hands together nervously before continuing. "We celebrate the Midwinter in the south. Some of our customs are a little different I believe."

"Come, wait before the fire with me, my lady," urged Robin, taking her arm and drawing her away. He was clearly fuming at Guy's churlish behavior and refusal to play the polite host.

"It seems strange to hear you address me as 'my lady' again," he heard Mathilde say, as they retreated.

"You've always been my lady," said Robin, casting a look over his shoulder at Guy. "And I never forgot the fact."

As he waited for Firmin's return, Guy found his ears straining without conscious volition to follow their conversation. It comprised of her exclaiming over the dampness of Robin's clothing and urging him to remove his shirt and wear a blanket instead, as she did. At one point, he thought he heard Robin ask tersely about the dagger, but their voices were lowered now, and he could pick out only the odd word.

He found himself wondering if the boy would point out to her that she was being denied the use of her title or position thus far. He had no doubt the lad had picked up on that, even if she had not. Or was she merely feigning her blissful ignorance of the fact? He could not make her out at all, and it irritated him that she was putting him to the bother of trying to fathom her out. Guy believed in being up front and frank, laying one's cards squarely on the table. He had no time for the subterfuge and deceit that courtiers employed.

When he allowed himself to glance at them sometime later, both were huddled under a pile of blankets, conspiratorially close. He fancied someone's head rested on the other's shoulder, though he was not sure which. He tapped a finger against the tabletop as he coldly debated whether or not he could use this to his advantage, as a means to divorce her if by some miracle she turned out to be who she said she was. After all, she and the boy must have been each other's traveling companion for at least a couple of weeks now as they traveled north. The propriety was surely lacking, for she should have had female attendants. He found himself curious, in spite of himself, how they had ended up in such a sorry state. Had their original party been broken up?

Robin Geddings was clearly gently born, even if he was a second son. Boys had definitely been married and even gone into battle younger than he. The sneaking suspicion crossed Guy's mind that the lad would not cut up too rough, if he was required as a sacrifice to save her reputation. He was clearly devoted to her. For some reason, that thought annoyed him too. Footsteps approaching snapped him out of his unpleasant thoughts. Firmin had returned to inform them the bedchambers were prepared for the night.

"Have the Lady Mathilde taken hence, and Master Geddings also," he said with a significant look at his steward.

It seemed Firmin was still in the dark as to who she was, for he received this in stoic silence, merely gesturing with his hand for them to follow him. Mathilde scrambled to her feet and performed a surprisingly dainty curtsey, in spite of the fact she was wearing a belted blanket and, very likely, her feet hurt. Almost against his will, he found himself glancing at them again. He had no idea why it bothered him so much that her feet were discolored and bruised.

"You've provided them with plenty of blankets?" he heard himself mutter and glanced away shamefacedly at Firmin's startled expression.

"Aye," his bewildered steward answered, for Guy did not usually show any interest in household arrangements.

"And a supply of logs for their fires?" Guy added, unable to stop himself. After all, he told himself, they had been half drowned in the rain, and could very likely take their deaths.

"Of course," Firmin said, still looking confused by this turn of events.

"And...some repast," he said gruffly.

"That is very kind of you, my lord," Mathilde said warmly. "I would greatly love a cup of spiced wine, and Rob is no doubt famished. They did not give us anything to eat in Wickhamford jail, so we have not eaten since yester'een."

Guy started. "Not eaten?" he echoed. She shook her head, and he threw a startled look at her companion. Robin's mouth was drawn into a grim line, and he curtly nodded his agreement to this extraordinary statement. "Have supper taken to their rooms," Guy ordered.

Firmin rolled his eyes, no doubt remembering the fact that half the servants were worse for wear, and he would be hard-pressed to rouse anyone. "I'll see what I can do," he said. "But I'm not promising much better than bread and cheese."

"Oh, but that sounds wonderful," Mathilde said brightly, and if his thirty-one years had not taught him better, Guy would almost believe she meant every word.

That night, Guy lay awake for an exceptionally long time, and when he finally did fall asleep, he dreamt the Yule-Father had brought him a gift. A gift, quite frankly, that was a mixed blessing.

5

Mathilde woke every hour on the hour. She found she had not managed unbroken sleep since she had left her mother's quarters at the palace. On the road, it was hardly prudent. Here, everything was unfamiliar, the bed was hard, and the chimney smoked. It did not help matters that she had heard the key turn in the lock behind her the moment she sat upon the bed.

She had not been given any water to wash in and so had been forced to get into the bed still covered in travel dirt. At least she had managed to get warm. For a moment the previous night, she had wondered if she would ever feel warm again, for the cold had seemed to creep into her very bones. But when she had finally relaxed her shivering limbs, at last she had felt warm. As for the lack of a wash, she could not hold that against Lord Martindale, for he had been otherwise most solicitous for their comfort, she reflected. After all, had not he given specific instructions for their fires, blankets, and food? Her heart warmed to remember it. And truthfully, she was too excited to sleep. She had arrived on her husband's doorstep on Solstice Eve. It felt right, like a good omen.

She wriggled her toes, to which feeling had recently returned. They felt sore, so she stopped. Her thoughts turned to her mother at the palace. Today was a feast day. Doubtless her mother would not be feeling very festive. She would still be smarting at Mathilde's act of defiance. But Mother never *did* feel like celebrating, Mathilde thought, turning over and hugging the thin pillow.

Lady Doverdale was a sober, dour woman of middle age. Even when her husband, Mathilde's father, had been alive, she had rarely cracked a smile. Somehow, she seemed to drain the joy out of anything with her disapproving sourness. At any event, she was always the specter at the feast. Luckily, Queen Armenal esteemed her highly, and she held a great position at court as the Queen's Mistress of the Robes. Mathilde could only hope that matters at court would distract her mother from her own filial impiety. Perhaps with time, she would become reconciled to Mathilde's new life away from her?

She sighed and turned her thoughts to happier subjects. She wondered how Lord Martindale's household celebrated Midwinter—nay, what was it they called it here? *Yule?* Her impressions of the place from the previous night were a little hazy. They had arrived in driving rain and darkness, but she had been able to make out that the place was large and built on a grand scale. Inside had seemed imposing, full of dark wood and huge stone fireplaces. It had also seemed rather drafty, but doubtless she had been chilled to the bone by that point, so it might not be so cold as she had imagined.

As for Lord Martindale, he was a fine, if somewhat imposing figure of a man, she thought, conjuring his tall, dark form to her mind's eye. She bit her lip. It was true, she admitted, that her former self would have been reduced to a state of abject terror in his presence. It was no doubt a good thing, she told herself staunchly, that the last month had filled her with so much experience and bravery. Perhaps, after all, it had been fortunate that her mother had not permitted her to meet her husband four years ago. She would certainly have not been up to the task then.

But *now*, she thought, *now* she had lived as a boy, had traveled independently, bought her own horse, and even been to jail! *Now* she was a woman of the world and was equal to anything! The notion was a vastly satisfying one and silenced the niggle of remaining disquiet. While it was true that having to remove her clothes in front of Lord Martindale the previous evening had been a frankly awful experience, afterward he had redeemed himself. He had even, she remembered, made her the present of his knife.

The thought cheered Mathilde. She reached out of the bed for the plain black sheath and serviceable dagger which she had laid on a rickety old chair. While it was true, it was not as fancy as the one her first husband had sent her for a betrothal gift, this one was wickedly sharp and had a good balance to it. Robin had started teaching her how to whittle wood, and the one Willard had traded with her had become somewhat blunted.

She set this knife down on the mattress beside her and gazed at the gray light coming through the small window. It was doubtful that the jail would forward her horse and her knife today. After all, it was a special day and most folk would be making merry. However, if they did not appear upon the morrow, she would have to set forth to reclaim them, she thought determinedly. Her honor depended on it. Besides, the poor horse deserved to be treated well from now on, and she had vowed to be the one who saw to it. A man of noble character always kept his word and paid his debts, she thought. A noblewoman, she corrected herself. Her eyes were drifting shut again now, and a small smile played about her lips as she slipped back at last into sleep.

When she woke again, it was much later. She could hear footsteps on the stairs outside and sat up, rubbing her eyes. She heard the key turn in the lock and then a sharp rap on the door.

"Come in!" she called out and heard a thud outside, followed by a smothered exclamation. The next minute, the door opened, and a red-faced woman entered, carrying a large jug of steaming water and a basin. She had her lips pursed and a stony expression of disapproval on her face.

"Here's water for washing," she said abruptly and set them down on the table along with two large cloths she had over her

shoulder. The entire time, she kept her eyes averted from
Mathilde, as though she were somehow indecent. She turned
about and marched back to the door.

"Thank you," Mathilde called after her. "I don't suppose—"
But the door slammed shut and the woman was gone. *Oh*. Well,
at least she could set about her wash, even if she had no
clothing to don afterward.

Mathilde climbed out of bed, steeling herself against the brisk
chill in the air. No one had laid her fire this morning, and she
could see ice had formed on the windowpane. The water was
nice and hot though, and she sloshed around enthusiastically,
washing her face, neck, and hair using a small ball which had
been stuffed with soap leaves. She put off the inevitable
moment she would have to divest herself of her blanket as long
as she could. When she could delay it no longer, she shrugged it
off and completed a brisk soaping of her whole body. Then she
rinsed out her washcloth and washed off the soap lather.

Wrapping a clean blanket about herself, she made her way over
to the frozen window, forced it open with some difficulty, and
emptied the soapy water out of it. Then she refilled the empty
basin with rest of the water from the jug and dunked her whole
head in it to wash out the suds. Only then did she grope about
for the drying cloth and wrap it around her wet hair.

At least now her locks took a lot less time to dry, she reflected.
When it had hung down to her waist it had taken simply hours.
Hurriedly, she made her way back over to the bed and grabbed
another blanket to wrap about her shoulders. She felt clean for
the first time in weeks! Sitting down on the bed, she pulled the
headcloth away and started to run her fingers through her damp
hair in the absence of a comb. Another knock sounded on the
door, more hesitant this time.

"Come in," called out Mathilde, looking up. A dark head peered around the door, wearing a heavy frown. Her spirits rose. "Good morning, my lord!" she cried. "Happy Solstice! I mean, Yuletide," she corrected herself a little self-consciously.

Lord Martindale blinked, then he cleared his throat. "And to you," he said a little gruffly. Perhaps he was not one who rose in good spirits of a morning.

"Come in," Mathilde invited generously as he was still hovering on the threshold. His gaze flickered over her. No doubt she looked a little odd arrayed in blankets and drying cloths. Otherwise, she could not account for his hesitation. "I have just washed," she explained unnecessarily, but for some reason he made her nervous. Where once she would have sat as silent as a mouse, now her pride demanded she attempt to conceal this fact with empty chatter.

"Why is the window open?" he asked abruptly. "There's a gale blowing through here."

"I found the casement a little stiff to open," Mathilde said guiltily, springing to her feet. "Once I had opened it, I found I could not fully close it again."

"Why did you open it in the first place?" he asked, his frown deepening. He stared at the small trail of puddles of water that led to the window.

"To empty the washing water out of it," Mathilde explained, realizing she had made a bit of a mess of it. She wrung her hands. "I have not yet had the chance to—"

He held up a hand, and she saw he was staring at the unmade hearth. Flinging back his head, he yelled, "Firmin!" Mathilde jumped, then had to suppress the ignoble urge to hide under the bedcovers as the older grizzled man from the previous night

42

appeared in the doorway. "Send someone in here to light her—"
He bit off his words. "To light this bloody fire!" he roared.
"Then I want the wench who brought the washing water thrown
out on her ear!"

"Thrown out?" echoed Firmin in bewilderment. He shot an
accusatory look at Mathilde. "For what offence?"

"For not doing her bloody job!" Lord Martindale seemed to rein
himself in with effort. He stood a moment, taking a deep breath.
"Has anyone found her any clothing yet?" he asked in a voice
of ominous quiet.

"Not yet."

Lord Martindale turned back to Mathilde. "Get back into bed,"
he said shortly. "Your lips are turning blue." Then he turned
back to Firmin. "She needs woolen stockings and shoes. If
someone has to ride to Wickhamford, so be it."

"It's Solstice morn…" Firmin objected.

"And what does that signify in this house?" Lord Martindale's
voice was harsh and brooked no argument. Firmin huffed and
stomped off, shaking his head.

Mathilde crept back under the covers. She was truly tempted to
pull them up right over her head to block out the tension in the
room. For some reason, her husband had woken in a foul mood.
From the sound of it, he did not even believe in keeping the
feast day. Maybe he was annoyed she had mentioned it? She
swallowed and peeped over the top of the blanket. He gave a
muffled exclamation and strode over to the bed, scooping her
up, bedclothes and all.

"My lord!" Mathilde squeaked as he bore her out of the room.
"If—if there are no women's clothing to be had, I am more than

happy to dress in boys'," she suggested in a quavering voice. He muttered something, but she did not catch it.

Thinking it would be prudent, she lapsed into silence at this point. He was carrying her down a flight of stone steps with seeming little effort. Mathilde tried not to worry what anyone they came across would think of the peculiar sight she presented. However, any servants fled before them as Lord Martindale strode down a series of long corridors flanked with suits of armor, axes, and crossed swords adorning the walls. Mathilde was just wondering if Robin was already up and about when they rounded a corner, and she recognized the large arched doorway that led to the Great Hall. She blinked when he strode right through it and crossed the vast room, not stopping until he reached the fireplace she remembered from the previous evening. A fire blazed there already.

"Chair!" he bellowed, coming to an abrupt halt. There was a scuffle behind them and a scraping of something against the floorboards. Lord Martindale grunted, and then turned about and deposited her carefully into a chair.

"Fetch a small table and some repast!" he bellowed at the pale servant who was hovering nervously nearby. Mathilde reached for her slipping blanket, but he was there before her, tugging it up to cover her shoulders. "You'll get warmer presently," he muttered in a low voice.

"Yes, I'm sure. Thank you, my lord," she added, sinking back into the seat.

"Draw your feet up under you," he said gruffly. "You're small enough." That was true, thought Mathilde, for the chair was huge, but it was hardly dignified. With difficulty, swathed in so many blankets, she rearranged her limbs so her legs were folded underneath her on the seat.

A little table appeared beside her, bearing bread and butter, honey, and a soft-boiled egg. "Thank you." Glancing around, she saw that she had been given a selection of the items on the large table in the center of the room. "Will you not join me in breaking your fast?" she asked, looking up at her husband. He shook his head, and she saw from his expression that he scorned the practice. In truth, it was not a widely eaten meal, but she had been used to having it at court.

"I ate a rich meal last evening," he said grudgingly.

"Oh? Did you entertain for Solstice Eve?" she asked, reaching for a napkin and knife.

He snorted. "No." At her swift, enquiring glance, he added, "I attended a wedding." His grim expression stopped her from asking after the wedded couple.

"How nice," she said instead brightly. A heavy silence greeted her words. *Perhaps not.* To her surprise he did not move away, but instead stood a brooding presence at her side. Hastily, she set to buttering her bread. It was not white, like the loaves they served at court, but was much darker with seeds and grain embedded in it.

Feeling eyes on her, she let her gaze wander around the hall. A handful of servants straggled about the place, ostensibly fetching and carrying, but Mathilde could see her appearance had caused something of a stir. She was just dipping her knife into the honey when she noticed Robin sat tucking into a plateful over at the main table. She raised a hand in greeting, and he returned the gesture with raised eyebrows. She gave a faint shrug. There was no explaining away her current situation. *Clothing*, she mouthed at him. Robin glanced down significantly at the new burgundy tunic he was wearing.

45

Mathilde was just opening her mouth to explain she, too, had offered to wear boys' raiment when Lord Martindale growled out, "Eat your bread!" Obligingly, she lifted it to her mouth. The texture was rather chewy, but the flavor not unpleasant.

"Very nice," she said. He grunted again. She picked the shell from the egg and ate a bite of that. "About that servant," she started, tucking her hair behind her ears. For some reason, now that it was shorter, it seemed to have a very pronounced curl. When it had been long, there had been no suspicion of one. It was most strange.

"What about her?" Lord Martindale asked, seeming to come to a decision. He drew up a chair opposite her and sat sprawled in it, regarding her moodily.

"I do not think it quite fair to dismiss her like that. After all, it was I who could not shut the window—"

"She should have seen to it," he said, dismissing the subject abruptly. "What happened to your traveling party?"

Mathilde blinked at the rapid change of subject. "Traveling party?" she repeated doubtfully. He gave a short nod. "It consisted of just myself and Robin."

He looked frankly disbelieving. "I understood the Doverdales to be an influential family at your fancy southern court," he said flatly. "You can scarcely expect me to believe that."

No, that probably was expecting a bit much, Mathilde acknowledged, setting down her boiled egg. "Um…" She took a deep breath. "I…I decided that it was high time we met. After all, we have been married some four years now…" She looked up hopefully to see how he had received that news.

His black brows drew together. "You're saying," he said slowly, "that you took this step unsanctioned?"

Oh dear. "After all," she carried on desperately, "you are my husband, and does not your will overrule my mother's in this regard?"

Lord Martindale sat staring at her. "Do you mean to tell me—?" he started, sounding disbelieving, and Mathilde had just steeled herself against his thunderstruck tone when the door to the Great Hall burst open and two men walked in, one burly giant with gray streaks in his beard, and the other who was younger and blond, looking rather the worse for wear.

"Ah, here you are, Guy," boomed the first. "I was just saying to Temur…" But just what he was saying to his companion, they were not to find out. As he caught sight of Mathilde, the words seemed to freeze on his lips. Both newcomers stared at Mathilde, transfixed. She dabbed her lips with the napkin and turned expectantly back to her husband.

Lord Martindale gave an irritable shrug. "Aye?" he growled. "What is it? Can a man not break his fast in peace?" These words seemed to astonish them still further.

"Guy?" said the younger man in an uncertain voice. "Who's this lass?"

"That's what I'm trying to ascertain!" Lord Martindale burst out angrily. "But I'm plagued and beset all round with interruptions!"

Mathilde jumped at his words. *What does he mean?* she wondered uneasily. She had told him who she was. Did he feel some lingering doubts as to her identity? As if noticing her consternation, he made a brief gesture toward her. "This is the Lady Mathilde," he said abruptly. "You will treat her with the accord due to a guest in my house." *A guest?* Mathilde stared, crestfallen, as the two men bowed dubiously in her direction. *The Lady Mathilde?* She was the Lady Martindale—and his marchioness! The two men looked frankly unconvinced by her credentials. Casting her a warning look, he said briefly, "These are two of my men, Waldon and Temur."

"I'm happy to meet you," she said with as much bewildered dignity as she could muster. *What is going on?* Clearly, he did not want these men to know that she was his wife. They started exchanging some words, which Mathilde did not even attempt to make sense of. Her head was in a whirl and her eyes smarted.

She sat with her back very straight as it dawned on her that it was not just these men he wished to be kept in the dark. He had not introduced her to *anyone* as his wife. Not even last night. The realization made her gasp, and all three turned their heads in her direction. Quickly, she masked it with a cough, raising her balled fist to her mouth. "Excuse me," she said, attempting to scramble out of her chair, momentarily forgetting she was bundled in about ten blankets. She flailed around for a few moments before managing to find her feet.

"Where do you think you're going?" asked Lord Martindale harshly.

Mathilde did not answer him, for in truth, she had no notion. She just knew that it was imperative that she get away from him *this very instant*. She took a shaky breath and hurriedly started toward the table where Robin still sat in the center of the hall. Her view was blurry, as her eyes were full of embarrassing tears, and her chest heaved with the effort not to let them fall. Although she succeeded holding back her tears, she could not say the same about her blankets, which she seemed to be fast shedding with every step. She made a grab for the last one and was just stumbling over one flapping round her ankles, when she felt her upper arms seized firmly from behind.

"Hold!" growled Lord Martindale's voice in her ear. "What the hells do you think you're doing, disrobing in front of everyone?"

"Unhand her at once!" yelled Robin, springing up from his seat.

"Who's this young sprig?" muttered Waldon, turning to his companion.

Temur shrugged. "Think I must still be drunk," he said, scratching his head.

Mathilde gazed accusingly up at Lord Martindale. "I want to leave!" she announced in an injured voice.

"You've only just arrived," he pointed out tersely.

"Well, I'm clearly unwelcome!" she flung at him shakily.

"Keep your voice down! And stop wriggling unless you want to give everyone an eyeful."

Mathilde flinched and glanced over her shoulder at their avid audience. There were a good many astonished faces and open mouths. Turning back, she whispered, "But I don't understand." She was unable to keep the hurt out of her voice. With a frustrated growl, he suddenly heaved her up and over his shoulder. Mathilde was too astonished to make a sound. The blanket she had managed to hold on to was twisted awkwardly about her, and she could definitely feel a frigid breeze around her nether regions. Before she could so much as protest, she was being borne precipitately out of the Great Hall. Squeezing her eyes shut, she sobbed, little comforted by the knowledge that no one could see how utterly defeated she felt.

49

6

What the hells am I doing? Blood pounded in Guy's ears as he flung open the door to his bedchamber and tipped his fair burden, almost entirely naked he noticed now, into the middle of his own bed. She squeaked as she hit the mattress and scrabbled for her blanket which was currently wrapped around her left knee. Guy had to turn away, and after kicking the door shut behind them, he turned his attention to safer quarters, restoking the dwindling fire in the hearth.

Why was his heart thudding so wildly in his chest? *Why* he had reacted so strongly, he knew not. But somehow her words, nay not exactly her words, but her expression had affected him. Or perhaps it was some potent combination of the two? She was hurt. He had hurt her. Then, of course, there was the fact that *everyone* in the hall had been getting a glimpse of what belonged to him alone.

He cast a fulminating glance over his shoulder and found she had given up on the blanket and was disappearing under his bedcovers. The strong wave of satisfaction that broke over him at the sight of her in his bed took him aback. He struggled a moment with his thoughts. What was wrong with him today? Bringing her to his bedchamber was doubtless a mistake, a small, cold inner voice nagged at him. If he had any idea of somehow renouncing this female as an imposter, then this was clearly a misstep. There had been several witnesses to his demonstration of overbearing behavior. On the other hand, all but one were his own loyal men and true. None of them would ever bear witness against him. As for her companion, he was still incapable of growing a beard, let alone swearing a grown man's oath.

He brooded on this, watching the flames grow in the fireplace. When he had himself under a tighter rein, he turned to face her again. She was huddled under the top blanket, such a sad, woebegone look on her face that he was immediately on the back foot again. Were those tear tracks down her cheeks? *Why does she have to look so young?* He knew for a fact the woman he had married was supposed to have worked her way through two husbands before him!

"Why did you come here?" he asked, more harshly than he'd intended.

Her gaze flickered to meet his, but the expression of hopelessness didn't change. "It doesn't matter," she said bleakly. "I was mistaken. I thought… At least, I hoped…" She swallowed. "But I was wrong."

Her words were so quietly uttered he had to crane to catch them. She'd thought what? That she could twist him around her little finger? *My gods.* He let his eyes roam over that unruly mop of curls. What the hells had she done to herself? He felt a flicker of the concern he'd felt the previous evening. But she had assured him that nothing had befallen her on the journey. He frowned, except *clearly* something had happened, for no gently born female had seen the inside of Wickhamford jail! He sighed with frustration and rubbed his temples. He'd already heard her account of how that happened, precious little sense that it made. "Why were you dressed as a boy?" he demanded instead, and for a moment he did not think she would answer.

"I thought it would be safer to travel that way," she mumbled, still not meeting his gaze.

He frowned. With only another boy as companion, he supposed that made sense, but still… *I decided that it was high time we met* were the astonishing words she had uttered earlier. His brain whirled as he came to the realization of what she was admitting. That she had run away. Like a willful, spoiled child. She had left the safety of her parent's guardianship and put herself entirely at his mercy. *Little fool.*

He kicked one of the logs further into the fire. For some reason though, he left that harsh thought unspoken, and he wasn't used to considering other people's feelings. The problem was, she didn't look like a spoiled, pampered courtier. She looked like a little waif and a stray. Unbidden, the memory of her bruised toes swam into his brain, clouding his judgment. It annoyed him that he couldn't act rationally around her.

"I can leave on the morrow," she said tonelessly, her eyes still lifeless and dull. Why did she look like that? Not so long ago she had gazed at him with clear, wide eyes that had tied him in knots. Then her words sank in and struck him on the raw. "Oh, will you?" he asked, his own tone pointed and brittle. *Gods, these southerners.* They thought they could saunter into his life, wreaking havoc, and then dance back out again. It was about time she learned to fear him, as everyone else did. His expression hardened and he crossed his arms, regarding her with his nastiest expression. The one that made grown men quake in their boots.

"It would serve you right," he said coldly, "if I keep you prisoner here, until you give me a son." Let's see how she took *that*! *That will take the wind out of her sails no doubt,* he thought with satisfaction.

He heard the hitch in her breath and felt a sudden flash of regret. Why, he had no notion, he thought uncomfortably. Except, he would be a monster indeed to enjoy the tears of women. But when he looked at her, she had lifted her head from the mattress and an expression shone from her eyes that startled him. Naked longing and *hope.* Suddenly she was flushed with color, her lips parted. *What the hells? That* was what she

52

wanted? He felt his breathing coming fast. His baby? *It couldn't be?*

"Oh, my lord," she said and clasped her trembling hands together. He was confused. Doubtless she was about to beg him now for mercy, to let her return south. But her words were warm and seemed to breathe life into parts of him that he had quite forgotten even existed. She raised her eyes to meet his, and they were *shining*. "I would like that above all things," she confessed huskily.

Guy stared at her. She wanted his baby? He was reeling. *Doubtless for some nefarious purpose*, his brain shrieked at him, but his head wasn't ruling him right now. He felt like he was struggling to even breathe. "My son?" he repeated hoarsely. Surely, he had misunderstood her?

She nodded her head. "Oh yes. Yes, please," she answered, so politely that he was struggling to remember why the request was so outrageous. *Yes, please?* He gazed at her in amazement. She smiled back at him, a pretty blush spreading over her cheeks. She looked so entirely guileless that his survival instincts kicked in, overruling his pounding heart. *She's dangerous*, a voice whispered to his soul, dousing him like a bucket of ice-cold water. He could still feel the steady pulse of his groin responding to her with an almost painful intensity. He shifted on his feet. Could she tell the state she had reduced him to? Doubtless, she was well versed in the arts of appealing to men. She was certainly playing him like a strung lute. The way she had identified the one chink in his armor left him dry-mouthed with horror. Clearly, she was a master of this game of manipulation, and he was the mere novice here.

He blinked, feeling like a stupefied mouse in front of a snake. *How is she doing it?* He was amazed by her arts. She sat there with her sawn off, uncombed hair and, despite it all, had the

53

nerve to seduce him! He hadn't even looked at a woman in years, except with suspicion. More fool him, he believed in keeping his word, even when it had been given under duress. Some ridiculous sense of honor had kept him faithful to the empty marriage vows he'd uttered. He'd had no idea at the time, he thought as he stared at her, that the wife he was pledging himself to could be represented by *this*. If he had known…he had the terrible suspicion he would not have resented it quite so bitterly. *I must be out of my mind.*

Guy found himself descending the staircase a few moments later, his head still reeling. Firmin, Waldon, and Temur were waiting for him below. Feeling their keen gazes trained on him, he forced his thoughts away from the naked female he'd left in his bed and tried to focus instead on the quizzing he was about to receive. Holding up a hand to forestall them, he led the way wordlessly to his study.

"Who in the name of the gods is she?" demanded Firmin as soon as the door closed behind them.

Guy walked around his desk and collapsed into his chair. He passed a shaking hand over his brow and shook his head. "I'm not sure yet," he said grimly. "I need to be sure."

"Well, her brother's beside himself, poor little bastard!" muttered Temur. "He'd soon as run you through with a blade as look at you!"

Guy frowned. "He's not her brother," he answered shortly. For some reason, Temur's words annoyed him, though why he had no notion. A husband's rights far outstripped those of a brother, even if Robin Geddings did turn out to be some male relation of hers.

"You can't just go exercising feudal rights on a wench that's not even from round these parts," protested Waldon with a horrified expression on his countenance.

Exercising feudal rights? Guy dropped the hand from his brow abruptly. "What the fuck are you talking about?" he demanded, staring from one appalled face to another.

Waldon couldn't even meet his gaze. "It's not right," he muttered into his beard, staring miserably at his feet.

"Gods, surely you know me better than that?" Guy burst out indignantly. "No Marquess of Martindale has claimed that right in living memory!" He stared hard at them, one after the other.

Firmin cleared his throat. "Of course not, Guy," he said uncertainly. "It just looked a little…er…" Words failing him, he turned and nudged Temur.

"I wouldn't have invited you to my wedding feast if I thought there was a chance you'd claim Lettys's first night," Temur admitted frankly.

Guy spluttered incoherently.

"Then why did you do it, my lord?" piped up Waldon in puzzlement, scratching his bristly chin. "We all saw you strip the little maid and then carry her out over your shoulder—"

"I didn't strip her!" cut in Guy coldly. "She hasn't got a garment fit to be seen in…" He turned back to Firmin. "Did you send for clothing?" he asked irritably.

"Aye, I sent Roger, but he's not returned yet."

"Well, when he does, I want it sent straight up to her." He hesitated a moment. "She's in my bedchamber," he added, throwing a challenging look their way.

"Your bedchamber?" repeated Firmin sounding stunned. The three of them exchanged uneasy glances, which Guy ignored.

"Waldon, Temur, you're dismissed," said Guy in clipped tones. "Firmin, you stay."

The other two did not look best pleased to be sent away, but Firmin was his most trusted man, and Guy wanted to keep his cards close to his chest on this one. Temur sent him a dark look over his shoulder as he disappeared out the door.

"She didn't look that sort," mumbled Waldon unhappily as he pulled the door closed behind him, and for some reason, Guy felt the tips of his ears turn red.

"What's going on, Guy?" asked Firmin in troubled tones. "This isn't like you." Guy waved toward a chair, and Firmin grabbed it and dragged it over to the desk.

He took a deep breath. "She says she's my wife," he said heavily.

Firmin sat up abruptly "Your wife?" he echoed hoarsely.

"Aye."

Guy watched Firmin's eyes widen with shock. He sat stock-still for a moment or two, then seemed galvanized into action. "Nay, that she cannot be," his steward said firmly, shaking his head. "Not after the manner she arrived in last night. No gently born lady would ever have borne such treatment."

Guy shrugged. "It's what she claims."

"A horse thief? Marchioness of Martindale?" Firmin sounded appalled.

"She said she paid for that horse," Guy found himself saying. *What the hells?* He gave a quick shake of his head. Clearly, his thoughts were still addled from earlier. Luckily, Firmin didn't seem to notice his slip.

"She's lying through her pretty little teeth," his steward answered confidently.

Guy clenched his fist. "Thought her pretty, did you?" he asked in an odd tone.

Firmin looked pained. "Nay! Her teeth only I noticed," he hastened to explain. "She had them all," he added lamely. "And they were white and straight and even." Guy breathed out again. "You need to have a care, Guy," his friend was saying earnestly. "Who knows what this wench is up to? She clearly moves in criminal circles and could even have been sent by your enemies—"

Guy looked up with a frown. "What enemies?"

"The enemies of the north, of course," said Firmin. "The Argent King himself!"

Oh. "To what end?" asked Guy listlessly. The truth was, he had grown heartily sick of such talk in the last few years. In all honesty, the so-called southern king was now King of all Karadok. The north had surrendered and the last of the northern royal bloodline had been taken. There were endless rumblings and treasonous toasts drunk to the lost princess, the so-called rightful heir.

As for Guy, he had renounced all thoughts of plots and daring rescues after one fateful night five years ago when he had met the Princess Una. Nothing had prepared him for the pale girl with tired eyes who had begged only to be left in peace. Far from chafing under the yoke of King Wymer's imprisonment, she seemed to view her would-be deliverers with actual dismay.

"You see, unlike my father, I do not believe in the divine right of kings," she had murmured apologetically. "I never have." He had been profoundly shocked as every tenet his father had instilled in him from childhood had crumbled around his ears. *The last of the Blechmarshes did not even believe in the northern cause.*

"It could be lots of things." Firmin was waxing lyrical now on the subject. "Those southerners are equal to anything. They may want to cheat you somehow. To send a false bride and then accuse you of breaking your marriage vows."

That seemed a little far-fetched to Guy, but he just nodded absently. After all, what did he know of the woman he'd married? Precious little. Maybe she wanted to remarry? By all accounts, old men were her preferred quarry. She certainly wouldn't get her hands on any more of Guy's fortune now. Maybe she'd already spent her way through the gold he'd been forced to relinquish? His mouth twisted bitterly. That would mean the female upstairs was some creature of hers, which might make more sense.

He'd expected his thrice-married bitch of a wife to be some conniving harridan, not some waif with big eyes and an exquisite little body. So maybe she *was* an imposter? He leaned back in his chair, trying the thought out and rolling it around in his mind. There was something to be said for it. He ignored the faint bitter aftertaste it left him with. Luckily, he was far too jaded to have allowed himself to seriously believe that little temptress upstairs was his true marchioness and fate. If his thirty-one years of experience had taught him anything, it was that he was just not that lucky.

"What will you do?" asked Firmin.

Guy hesitated. "I'm not sure," he said slowly. "Bide my time, I suppose."

Firmin huffed and shifted in his seat unhappily. "And nurture a viper in your bosom, until you can be certain?" he asked with disapproval.

Guy shrugged. It was hard to think of her as a viper. He judged it best not to say this aloud in case Firmin got the impression she had already ensnared him.

"I had heard," Firmin started cautiously with a look back over his shoulder at the closed study door, "that Kerslake is back."

Guy shrugged a shoulder. "He generally turns up every few months."

Firmin hesitated. "You know what they say…"

"Yes, I know what they say," responded Guy swiftly. Everyone in these parts whispered that Tristan Kerslake was an active spy for the north.

"Then, he may know of her…the real one, I mean. He may even have caught a glimpse of her. *On his travels*," said Firmin with meaning. "Which means he could identify this one as an imposter."

"I doubt very much that Kerslake's travels took him anywhere near the southern court," Guy replied dismissively.

"You never know," said Firmin mysteriously. "Anyway, it couldn't hurt to ask."

"I suppose he may," Guy conceded grudgingly. Seeing Tristan always reminded Guy of Tristan's sister, Julia. They looked very alike with their auburn hair and good looks. Generally, Guy avoided having to think about Julia Kerslake—or Julia Allworthy, as she was now known by her married name. Firmin shot him a sympathetic look, and Guy smarted that his past disappointment was public knowledge. Still, it was all water under the bridge. He wasn't eighteen anymore with a head full of dreams. That boy was long gone. It seemed a lot longer than thirteen years ago.

Guy stared into the distance. Sometimes, he thought, it would be nice to get away from it all. His responsibility. His people. His past. But that was something he could never do, no matter how weary he grew of both his burden and his privilege. This new complication simply added another stick to the donkey's back. He had to find a way to counter this possibly hostile move, to minimize the damage this female could inflict on his reputation. Already, the scene that had played out this morning in his Great Hall would likely be doing the rounds in the servants' quarters. He had never brought a woman into his home before this. If he wasn't careful... He drew in a sharp breath. For all he knew, the servants could be drawing the same conclusions as Waldon and Temur.

He needed to act fast. But how could he separate her from his own household? He thought fleetingly of the Dower House. But placing her there would also give rise to gossip. She was no kinswoman of his, so there could be no legitimate reason for settling her there. *Think, Guy, think!* And suddenly it flashed into his mind. He remembered the old hunting lodge deep in the forest. He hadn't thought of the place in years.

"The old hunting lodge," he said aloud. "The one my father built."

"Aye," said Firmin cautiously.

"It still stands?"

Firmin gave a short nod of assent. "It does," he said gruffly.

Guy brooded in silence a moment. "What if I were to take her there," he said slowly, speaking his thoughts aloud. "And keep her sequestered there, away from everyone. Until I'm sure of her. Until we have proof either way."

Firmin gave him a searching look. "There could be some merit to your suggestion," he said, clearing his throat. "We certainly don't want her here," he said sourly. "She's sown nothing but discord this morn."

Guy felt an inexplicable burst of irritation with his steward. "If her claims are true," he retorted, striving for a mild tone, but even he could hear the edge to his voice, "then she has every reason to be here."

Firmin gave a wave of his hand. "Her claims are preposterous, Guy!" he spluttered. "Nay, I'll never believe such a thing." He paced over by the window, and Guy found his thoughts turning once again to the enticing little maiden with her fair skin and curling hair. Firmin was right. It was preposterous to think she could be his marchioness. "I would like that above all things," she had said of bearing his baby. *His baby.* His breath quickened. How she had the nerve to sit naked in his bed and say such a thing was beyond him. To a man such as *he*? She ought to be cringing and terrified at the idea of such a great brute touching her tender little body. Not giving him an open invitation! Again, unbidden, he thought of her bruised feet. "The carter trampled me," she had said matter-of-factly. He wanted to kill that fucking carter. *Slowly.*

"Guy?" Firmin was speaking again. Guy turned his head quickly. "You have every right to be angry at her deception," his friend cautioned. "But we must ensure no harm befalls her, or you'll doubtless pay a high price." It seemed Firmin had misinterpreted his angry looks, imagining it was directed toward the small female. The idea brought him up short. Firmin's words were annoying him, but hers hadn't. Hers had stopped him in his tracks.

61

"Perhaps you're onto something," Firmin continued slowly, oblivious to Guy's conflicted mood. "Maybe removing her to some remote spot is a good notion. After all, only servants have seen her so far. None have heard her false claims save yourself. It would be unwise to allow her to remain here, stirring up trouble for us all." Again, despite the fact Firmin only echoed his own thoughts, Guy found himself having to fight down a stinging retort. Firmin was his most trusted friend and advisor. Right now, his every word grated on him. Why was that?

"The hunting lodge is remote enough," he forced himself to say. "Though probably in some disrepair. She'll need a servant or two to accompany her there."

"She can take her young friend with her," said Firmin in a generous tone that annoyed Guy, considering the lad was not part of their household to bestow.

"He's not a servant," he pointed out sharply. "He'll likely have to return to his own people soon."

"His people?" asked Firmin, looking up with swift concern.

"He's the son of a knight. Sir Edward Geddings." *Or was it Edgar?* Guy wasn't sure.

Firmin looked a little taken aback, but quickly rallied. "I would take every word that falls from their lips with a pinch of salt," he said, curling his lip. "They're a pair of liars."

"Firmin," Guy said with sudden curtness. "Watch your step." Firmin opened his mouth, but Guy stopped him with an abrupt gesture. "If there's even a remote chance she could turn out to be who she says she is…"

Guy had left his warning unspoken, but Firmin hesitated and colored slightly. "I take your meaning," he said a little stiffly.

Guy sat back in his chair. "Leave me now," he said in dismissal. "Send Waldon back to me."

Firmin shot him an incredulous look. "You'll need me here in order to plan," he protested.

"No." Guy had made up his mind. "I'll oversee this personally."

He made a great show of opening and closing the drawer to his desk, ignoring the heavy silence before Firmin took his leave. Doubtless Firmin's nose was out of joint over the business, but he'd get over it. Guy just knew he couldn't listen to his overt hostility toward the wench. For some reason he found it intolerable. He had to remain cautious and on his guard, but he expected everyone else to treat her with deference. For now.

Moments later Waldon shuffled in, a wary look in his light blue eyes. Swiftly Guy outlined his plan to take the Lady Mathilde to the old hunting lodge. He did not specify who she was to Waldon, but likely the man had his own suspicions. "We'll need provisions," he said. "The place has been shut up for at least four years."

Waldon nodded. "Aye," he agreed. "And covered in a thick coating of dust, likely as not." Guy murmured some agreement. "Has she her own attendants?" Waldon asked, scratching his neck.

"No," Guy said with a shake of his head. "Her companion, the boy, goes with her. But she'll need a servant. Can you get someone from Acton Dymock?" Guy asked, naming the nearest village.

Waldon's eyebrows rose. Doubtless he thought it odd that Guy could not spare one of his own. To be honest, Guy was torn. On one hand, a trusted servant of his own might be better as they would not talk. On the other hand, *all* servants talked. If it was one of his own household, no doubt it would spread like fire throughout all those in his employ. But then, an outsider might spread gossip to…well…*outsiders*. He sighed.

"What about Prudence Eddard?" suggested Waldon with a sudden smirk.

"Who?"

"Sour-faced wench you dismissed this morn."

"Heard about that, did you?" Guy asked, giving him a sidelong look. He'd already forgotten, and see what had happened? It was common knowledge!

Waldon shrugged. "Would serve her right," he said with a chuckle. "She's a stiff-necked scold and not much liked. It's not as if she'd have a lot of choice in taking the post," he added. "Her father's lately remarried and won't want her back at his table."

Guy grunted. "Can you see to it she's ready to leave by noon?" he asked, glancing at the window.

"She's already packing her things to leave," Waldon reminded him. "She'll likely jump at the chance not to have to return home in disgrace."

"See to it," Guy said shortly. "And Waldon, see that she understands the post requires discretion." To his discomfort, Guy couldn't quite meet his eyes as he spoke the words. Waldon murmured some assent. "And we'll need foodstuffs— salted meats, flour, you know the sort of thing. Enough for a small household, for at least a month."

Waldon's eyes widened, but he kept his mouth firmly closed. He gave another brief nod. "I'm to have it all ready for midday?" he said, starting up out of his chair.

"Yes. And Waldon?" The other man paused in the act of crossing to the door. Guy hesitated. "These arrangements are between us," he said, motioning with a finger between the two of them. "The fewer people know, the better."

This time it was Waldon who kept his eyes averted. "Aye," he said with a jerk of his chin, and he was gone.

7

Mathilde was dressed in her new green wool dress and matching cloak with brown fur trim. On her feet were scarlet stockings and a pair of brown leather ankle boots, and on her hands she wore knitted mittens of dark red to protect her against the biting cold. She watched with great interest as the cart was loaded up with the last of the various wares they were taking for their sojourn to Lord Martindale's hunting lodge. She was especially interested to see a basket with five hens in it. They squawked and flapped as they were placed next to a large cheese and a keg of wine. Her only objection came when her husband went to lift her up onto a fine bay mare saddled in red leather.

"This is not my horse," she pointed out. She was a little shocked to find she was expected to ride astride. Of course, this past month she had done so on many an occasion, but she had not been dressed as a female then. She swung her one leg over to the other side of the saddle, and Lord Martindale helped drag her skirts down over her suddenly exposed scarlet stockings.

"It will have to do for now," he said a little gruffly and started to turn away.

"My lord?" she said impulsively. He paused. "I would rather reclaim my own horse and my own knife before we journey away from home."

He gave a quick glance to his attendants and then seemed to consider her words. "We're only traveling three miles further into my estate," he pointed out with a frown. "And I have provided you with both a new horse *and* a new knife."

Mathilde bit back the hasty retort that sprang to her lips. She wanted her own dear horse that she had rescued and her own knife that Will had given her! But she was a wife now, and wives were supposed to be meek and conciliatory. "And very nice they are too," she acknowledged brightly. In truth, both were probably far superior to her own belongings in every way, except sentiment. "But I still want my very own," she added with quiet firmness. Lord Martindale frowned at her, no doubt thinking her both stubborn and ungrateful. "My own horse has been much abused," she added appealingly. "And I promised him he would be safe in his new life with me."

"And your knife was gifted to you by your friend. Yes, you told me," he said dryly.

"I will fetch them for you on the morrow, my lady," said Robin obligingly as he swung himself up and onto the saddle of the tall chestnut horse he had been provided. "I'm sure I can find my way back to Wickhamford easily enough."

"Oh, would you, Robin?" she cried.

Lord Martindale announced simultaneously, "You will do no such thing, boy." They both turned and looked at each other.

"But—" Mathilde started.

"I will see to it in my own good time," Lord Martindale ground out.

Feeling eyes on her, Mathilde turned her head to find Waldon watching their exchange with interest. Not so, the woman standing by his side, who was staring stonily ahead. She looked vaguely familiar to Mathilde. Noticing the direction of her gaze, Lord Martindale said: "You've already met Waldon. This is your new maid, whose job it will be to serve you while you're at the lodge." His tone was strangely pointed, and Mathilde looked back at the maidservant with curiosity. Two spots of pink had appeared in the maid's rather sallow cheeks.

"Her name's Prudie," rumbled Waldon with a lopsided grin. The smile transformed him, and Mathilde realized that despite the gray in his beard, he was probably numbered no more in years than thirty-five or thereabouts.

"Prudence!" the maid corrected him with a sideways glare in his direction before bobbing a hasty curtsey. "Milady."

"I'm glad to meet you, Prudence," Mathilde murmured politely. Prudence had long passed her youth, and looked to be about thirty years in age; she had black braided hair and very straight beetling brows. She gave a tight, humorless smile and stooped to lift her pack of belongings to add them to the cart. Mathilde was pleased to see Waldon pluck it out of Prudence's hands and sling it on for her. Before Prudence could protest, Waldon turned and lifted her with seemingly little effort and swung her up onto the cart as well.

"I could take the reins," Prudence said quickly, but he ignored her and clambered up beside her. Mathilde noticed the maid's color grew even pinker and she bit her lip with vexation. Prudence seemed a very capable woman, but perhaps not the best tempered.

"Have you looked your fill?" Lord Martindale growled. He was seated now on his own horse, a magnificently large white beast.

Mathilde's gaze darted to meet his. "Prudence seems familiar to me," she admitted. "Yet I can't quite…"

"She was the maid who failed to serve you this morning," he said shortly.

"Oh, *of course.*" She remembered now. She beamed at him. "You did not turn her out after all."

He gave her an odd look. "This pleases you?"

She nodded. "I'm persuaded it was all simply a misunderstanding."

He snorted. "Pull up your hood. There's a chance of more snow later."

Mathilde gazed up at the sky, which was very white. She could well believe it was full of snow. With a slight shiver, she pulled her hood up over her hair and realized she had lost the linen square that had been serving as a veil. Where had that gone? She looked about distractedly. Maybe it had gone down the back of her cloak. Now her hair was too short to braid, it was extremely difficult to affix pins to it. Dressing as a woman again had not seemed familiar at all. Then again, that might have been because the clothes she wore were nothing like her court wardrobe. Even her petticoats were thick and woolen, and the head veil she had been provided with had been a serviceable navy blue before she had lost it. Mathilde had never worn anything save the purest and gauziest of whites upon her head. As a snowflake brushed against her cheek, she glanced up at the sky again. Possibly the ladies dressed this way here because of the extreme cold. It seemed only sensible that fashion should become a secondary consideration.

The horses had started forward, and Lord Martindale took the lead with her close behind. The cart followed them, and Robin brought up the rear. As they left the main approach toward the sprawling manor house, Mathilde noticed her husband shoot her several assessing glances. They were cantering at a brisk pace now, and she fancied he was weighing up her seat on a horse. Luckily, she had nothing to worry about on that score. Her mother had been scrupulous in her education, and she had been able to ride well from a young age, though she had not lived on a country estate since she was very small. Both her parents had been courtiers through and through, and the running of their estates had been largely left to others, though her mother kept an iron grip on the accounts.

When it came to feminine accomplishments, Mathilde knew her strengths and weaknesses only too well. She excelled at the tapestry loom and with the needle. She enjoyed drafting out designs and patterns to execute, and she enjoyed reading poetry, ballads, and tales of adventure and romance. All of these, however, were solitary pursuits. When it came to courtly pursuits such as dancing, singing, playing, and, worst of all, polite conversation, she was woefully inadequate, despite the many excellent tutors her mother had engaged over the years. She simply hated to perform in front of an audience.

Eyes on her caused her to freeze. Under the keen eye of her mother, her steps would falter, and her fingers would fumble. A roomful of people wittily conversing made her stomach churn and her palms sweat. In social situations, all she wanted to do was stare at her feet and pray for invisibility. She knew she was a sad disappointment, but the truth was that from infancy, she had been both shy and awkward. Perhaps it would not have been so bad if she had been given any siblings to deflect the hawklike maternal gaze, but she had none. As such, her dissatisfied mother had decided her child was simply not fit to live her own life. Instead, she had arranged things so that Mathilde would remain at her skirts for an eternity, where her shortcomings would have no consequence. It did not matter if Mathilde could not dazzle at court or secure her own admirers. Instead, her mother had arranged a succession of older husbands who did not require anything from their bride, except a few legal ramifications. In her own way, Mathilde supposed her mother was trying to shield her from a world she considered her child to be ill equipped to negotiate.

But with each passing year, her position had become steadily more unbearable. She wanted—all the time—to *live*. She had no relationships independent of her mother, except, that is, for her relationship with the palace pages. And if Nurse ever caught wind of that, she would report back to Lady Doverdale and that, too, would be summarily stopped. So much of the time, she felt so very *alone*. In truth, it had not seemed so very bad, until she had made friends with the Countess Vawdrey. Fenella was her very first court friend, and while she had felt so proud that Fen had even felt her worthy of befriending, it had opened her eyes to the half-life she was enduring. She had been embarrassed that when they made arrangements to meet, she was always accompanied by her childhood nurse. Fen was too kind to even raise an eyebrow, but for the first time Mathilde had felt the keen sting of embarrassment. She wasn't stupid, she knew people laughed up their sleeves at her at court, but that hadn't mattered somehow. But Fen was her friend, and her opinion did count. Fen treated her like an equal, but strangely enough, it was that very fact that made Mathilde realize she *wasn't* one. Not in semblance or plain fact.

And then there had been the magical day when she had held Fen's nephew, baby Archie, in her arms. Her heart had swelled so hard, she had thought it would burst. The baby had looked right into her eyes, almost as if he could see into her soul. By some miracle what he had glimpsed there did not put him off. He had not found her wanting in any way. Instead, he had burrowed into her arms for comfort, had laid his head on her breast, had turned to her. Mathilde had rocked him in her arms. She had dried his tears and sung him a lullaby. And in that instant, she had known. She wanted so much more from this life. She wanted to be a mother. It was from that very moment that she could trace the point in time her sleepwalking had ended, and her heart truly started to beat. From that minute, she

71

had looked about her critically at the gilded cage she had been living in and started to make plans for her escape.

"You ride well." The words were almost an accusation and startled her out of her reverie. Lord Martindale's critical gaze was sweeping over her again.

"Thank you." They were approaching a thick wooded forest now. The bare trees were covered in glittering snow.

"Surely," he said with a frown, "as a highborn lady, you would have learned to ride sidesaddle?"

"Yes," Mathilde said. Then she noticed his hard stare. "This last month though—" she began, but he cut her off.

"Of course," he said. "I might have known, this last month has been enough for you to adapt."

Mathilde darted a surprised look at him. Why did he sound so skeptical? "After all, it's much harder to ride sidesaddle," she pointed out.

He seemed to consider this and, after a moment, gave a shrug. He twisted back in his saddle to check on the progress of the others. "There's a track down here that's wide enough for the cart. It will take us through the wood," he said, raising his voice so the whole party could hear him.

It was hard to make out any track under the snowfall, but it seemed that her husband knew well the lay of his land. They made good progress, but Mathilde was surprised at how long the ride through the trees took them. It was a good hour before she began to see light breaking through and saw they were approaching a clearing. "This is surely further than three miles," she hazarded, glancing at Lord Martindale.

"We could not take the direct route, due to the wagon," he replied.

"Oh!" Mathilde sat up straight in her saddle. "I think I see it!" She pointed in excitement. "There! Is that it?"

He was watching her with a hooded gaze. "Yes," he said, his eyes still on her.

Mathilde turned back to it with delight. The hunting lodge was a timber-framed building of brown and white with a pointed tiled roof and latticed windows with wooden shutters. Mathilde had lived nearly all her life, certainly as long as she could remember, in magnificent royal palaces of imposing gray stone. The rustic hunting lodge enchanted her. The idea of living in such a place, however temporarily, filled her with a giddy sort of pleasure. She would have clapped her hands if she weren't already holding her horse's reins.

"It's not been used in recent years," Lord Martindale was saying. "Since the war."

"Oh." The smile was wiped off her face and she nodded. "I see." *The war.* She kept forgetting that in these parts the outcome was not a celebrated one. "I'm sure it can be set to rights in no time," she said and glanced back at Prudence, who had a sour look back on her face and seemed to be muttering under her breath. "I can help," Mathilde offered glibly. After all, it did look like a lot of work for one servant. She felt her husband's eyes on her again, but when she turned to meet his gaze, he had already looked away.

8

Guy was no nearer to exposing the wench. Just when he thought she had given herself away, a niggling doubt would cross his mind again. No lady of noble birth, he told himself, would roll up her sleeves and join in so wholeheartedly with the cleaning. Then he noticed how spectacularly bad she was at it.

Her attempt to sweep a floor merely seemed to be an exercise in moving the dirt around it. When she dusted, she got more cobwebs on herself than on the cloth, and when she tried to clean a window, she put her foot through a woven stool and tore her stocking. In the end, he simply scooped her up and set her down next to the newly lit fire in the kitchen. "Sit here," he barked, placing her next to a large pile of freshly chopped wood he and Waldon had fetched in.

"Should I feed logs to the fire?"

"Don't touch it!" But he was too late. She had already smothered it with an ambitiously large piece of wood.

"Oh dear!" She gazed down at the extinguished fizzle of smoke with dismay. She was so fucking useless that Guy was starting to think she must be a lady born and bred. *Where the hells did she get that large smut of dirt across her cheek?* Every time he turned his back to her, she seemed to stumble into some new misfortune. "Um…" She snatched up another log and seemed to be trying to fan the nonexistent flames. "Perhaps if I just—?"

He took the chunk of wood out of her hand. "Sit still," he said sternly and crouched down next to the fire. She bit her lip and collapsed back down on the low stool, looking so crestfallen, he found himself relenting. Why, he had absolutely no idea.

"Watch what I do," he said in a low voice. Immediately, she perked right back up, tucking her hair behind her ears, and scrambled forward to watch his attempts to rekindle the abused fire. He watched her covertly as he set about rebuilding it. No one could have been more impressed than she when the flames started to lick about the kindling.

"You did it!" she cried, turning to him triumphantly.

What it didn't explain was his almost overwhelming impulse to lean across and kiss her firmly on her pretty mouth. Would she draw back? Reproach him for such familiarities? Glance at him beneath her lashes? Employ one of a hundred such feminine tricks that those well versed with entertaining men used? He forced himself to consider the likelihood she was deliberately playing with him.

Worryingly, he wasn't even sure such behavior would put him off. He reminded himself that he heartily detested artifice and coyness in the opposite sex. Then again, she had acted far from demure earlier that day, when she had told him outright she wanted his babe. His heart pounded. Perhaps she would be bold in her desire for him to bed her. He shivered. *My gods*. Did he want that? He gave his head a quick shake to clear it. Admittedly it had been a few years since he had bedded a woman, but he had never had such tastes before. Then again, prewar Guy seemed like a wholly different person in his memory. Perhaps the last five years had warped him.

He must be mad to let her twist him round her finger like this. This little dab of a female! He gave her a sidelong look. Why was he even letting her affect him this way? He straightened up and turned from her, clearing his throat. He wanted to appear icily detached and forbidding. To let her know that he, Guy Randall, Marquis of Martindale, was nobody's fool. Men feared him, and women, frankly, made sure to stay out of his way. She must be mad to try to provoke him like this!

The truth was, though, that he felt far from detached. He felt edgy with… He paused. What even was it? Some weird *need*. Almost a yearning to possess what was rightfully his. He swallowed, his throat suddenly dry. Why the *hells* was he thinking of her as his*?* The thought stunned him. But when he tested it, he knew that was exactly what he was doing. It could be the only explanation for why every word Firmin had uttered earlier had pissed him off. She wasn't his wife, he reminded himself angrily. He was almost certain of that. There was no rational reason for him to be having these feelings for her. So why was he? Distractedly, he stared out the window, trying to marshal his thoughts. He wasn't used to his thoughts and impulses being so out of accord. *What am I doing?*

In vain, he reminded himself he was tucking her away in this hunting lodge for perfectly logical reasons. Even Firmin had agreed with the notion in principle. Why then, was he suddenly so filled with unease and self-doubt? He felt his face heat. He knew full well why, he berated himself savagely. Underneath his actions had been another motivation entirely, a selfish one he had refused to acknowledge. The hunting lodge had been a place of escape and release. When he had come here, first with his father, and later with his friends, it had been in the pursuit of leisure and relaxation. Had he set his little false bride up here because he thought of her in those terms? As an illicit pleasure, for him to enjoy in secret?

The hand that stroked his short beard trembled slightly. *You selfish bastard*, he told himself bitterly. *You stupid, selfish bastard. You're playing right into your bitch of a wife's hands because you can't resist this poisoned chalice she's sent you.* He glanced back over his shoulder at her. He wanted to take her upstairs, is what he wanted to do. He didn't care about the fact she had a smudgy face and was likely covered in dirt. Or the fact she was likely an accomplished little play-actress. *Does she have no sense of danger?* he wondered, breathing hard.

She sat there so serenely, gazing at the fire with a smile on her lips, while he was aching and trembling with the effort to contain himself. He ought to dump her here, in the middle of the woods, and run like hell. But that wasn't what his every impulse was clamoring for. He drew a frustrated breath and ran his fingers through his hair.

A footfall behind him made him turn. Waldon had come through the door, dragging a large mattress for his bed. *For her bed*, he corrected himself harshly. Guy crossed the room and grabbed the other end. He looked back over his shoulder. "Don't touch that fire," he warned her direly. She nodded and hugged her knees. *Dimples*, he noticed. *She has dimples in her cheeks*.

He and Waldon bore the mattress up the stairs and set it down in the master bedroom. The whole time Guy strove to get his rioting senses under control. By the time they had set the mattress into the bed frame, he wasn't shaking anymore. The familiarity of the lodge soothed him a little. He had forgotten how much he used to love the place.

The main bedchamber was a large one, with a huge vaulted ceiling of sloping exposed beams and a good deal of antlers and horns strung up around the walls. His father hadn't been exactly known for his subtlety. Come to think of it, neither was Guy. He just hoped she—Mathilde, as she insisted on being called—didn't feel like a cornered doe up here. Frowning at his own fancifulness, he regarded the canopy above the massive dark wood bed. It was of a faded scarlet patterned with gold. The bad-tempered servant had driven all the dust from the room, but it still seemed dark and masculine, and entirely wrong for the female he'd left below stairs.

"The boy will be down the hall in the end room," Waldon said, interrupting his thoughts. "And the maid, Prudence, has already set her things up in one of the attic rooms."

Guy grunted. He crossed to the window and looked out at the small garden. Robin was down there rigging up some temporary fencing for the hens. *It will need to be more substantial than that*, Guy thought with a glance at the encroaching woods, *if it is to keep the foxes out.* "You'd better help the boy set up a run for the fowls," he said. "Or they'll all be carried off in the night, like as not."

Waldon came to his side and looked down with interest. "You'd almost think he'd never done such work before," he said, shaking his head.

They both made their way back down the stairs, and Guy directed Prudence to go now and make the beds up with sheets and blankets. Waldon went outside to help with the chickens, and Guy settled himself once again across the fireplace from Mathilde. He stared at her broodingly. "You see yourself being comfortable here?" he asked abruptly.

"Oh yes," she replied readily enough. "In fact, I think it's a particularly good notion of yours, my lord. For this way we can quite get to know each other, can we not? In more intimate surroundings."

His throat instantly became dry. *Intimate.* It was a suggestive word. Was she telling him her bedroom would not be barred against him? Even more importantly, did she not realize that she was already failing in her mission to discredit him? He was installing her in a separate household to his own. That was not something one did with a wife. It was something one did with a mistress. Her employer, his wife, would no doubt be furious at being outmaneuvered. "Of course," he said aloud. "You realize I've many demands on my time. I've an estate to run. It will be several days until you see me again."

Instantly, her expression turned to seeming dismay. He tensed, waiting for her to argue or complain at such treatment, but she did not. "I see," she said slowly. "Well then, I will simply have to make the most of things when you are here." She smiled at him again, and Guy felt robbed of his breath.

Footfalls were heard on the stairs. "The beds are made, milord," announced the maid, Prudence, in her rather grating voice.

"Tell your mistress, not me," he replied, his eyes still on Mathilde.

"The beds are now done, milady," Prudence said after a moment's heavy pause.

"Thank you, Prudence," Mathilde replied, holding his gaze steadily, if a little shyly.

Was there an invitation in her eyes? If she knew how long he'd been without, she wouldn't be issuing it so glibly, he thought grimly. Guy did not allow himself to dwell overlong on the idea. That way lay disaster. He jumped to his feet. "I'll take my leave of you, my lady."

"Mathilde," she corrected him swiftly.

He cleared his throat. "Mathilde," he said, trying it out. He noticed she didn't look remotely uncomfortable about laying claim to it as her own. She was a cool piece. He needed to watch his step around her. In truth, he should probably stay the hells away from the conniving little madam.

"I hope we will see you very soon," she said, clasping her hands together.

I bet you do, he thought harshly and cursed himself for a fool when he felt how his pulse had quickened at her words.

9

Mathilde was enchanted with her new abode. As soon as her husband left, she took herself over the lodge. She wished he had given her leave to call him Guy, but he had not. Still, you could not rush these things, she told herself as she peeped into Prudence's attic room. She did not want to invade her maid's privacy, so instead she poked around the vacant room next door to it. They were both decent sized, and this second room seemed to have been used for storage of bits and pieces of furniture in varying states of repair. There was a third attic room which was a good deal smaller than the other two and had a low truckle bed in it and no window at all. She supposed in the past it must have been used for the lowest-ranking servant, and felt heartily sorry for them, stuck in that poky little hole.

On the next floor down, she found Robin's room to be a very pleasant room, of middling size with a large tapestry depicting a hunting party decked out in outfits of blue, with many dogs and horses and attendants with golden horns. She inspected the stitches with interest. Whoever had worked this piece had been highly skilled and master of some techniques Mathilde was not familiar with. She turned the edge of the tapestry to look at the back. While she was here it would be good to pick up some new methods, she thought. What a pity that her husband's household seemed to have so few women. She should have asked him to send her some tapestry supplies, she thought, biting her lip. That had been remiss of her. Back at court, working with the loom and needle was generally how she filled her days.

Leaving Robin's room, she walked down the hall and found her own bedchamber, which was huge and handsome, yet seemed delightfully airy and open. She loved how *light* the interior of the lodge was, doubtless because all the walls between the beams were painted white. The manor house had been filled with dark wood paneling and furniture and seemed rather oppressive and gloomy. She pulled up her uncomplimentary thoughts of her husband's home quickly. No, that wasn't fair. She had seen only a little of Acton March Manor. She had not been given a tour. Still, she knew which property she preferred.

The bed canopy and curtains of red with gold leaves were perhaps a little faded, but she liked the overall impression of rose gold it gave now, possibly more than the flaming scarlet it would once have been. Ten of her could fit comfortably in that massive bed. She wandered over to the window, past the bench with the matching cushions and the large dresser with mirror. The view was over the garden below, which was overgrown and straggling and would need a good deal of work come spring. Would she still be here? she wondered idly. Or would she have taken her official place as Marchioness of Martindale by then?

She found two further rooms on this floor, one of which appeared to have been used as a sitting room but was still covered in a thick layer of dust. This, too, had a large tapestry which entirely covered the back wall and depicted a large wood, filled with beasts including stags and bears and wolves. The more you examined it, the more animals you spotted. Birds in the air, and even fish in the stream. Once it was dusted, Mathilde was sure it would be a pleasure to behold.

She opened the door next to it and had no sooner spotted a long table for formal dining than Prudence's head bobbed up from where she was sweeping out the fire. "I've only just started in here, milady," she said warningly. "It's not fit for occupation."

"Oh, of course, Prudence," Mathilde answered. "Could I help at all?"

"Certainly not!" Prudence sounded shocked. "Begging your pardon, but you would only be in the way." She closed her mouth tight and looked very fierce.

"Well, I wouldn't want to be a hindrance."

"Thank you, milady." Prudence sounded relieved. "Perhaps you could check on that young man of yours." She frowned. "I dread to think what mischief the young scoundrel could be getting in."

Mathilde regarded the maid with surprise. "Oh, Robin is very mature and responsible," she answered. "You may rest easy on that score. He has my complete and utter confidence."

Again, Prudence's lips screwed up tight with disapproval. "If you say so, milady," she muttered.

Mathilde took a deep breath. "I do say so," she said. When Prudence's eyes darted to hers, Mathilde smiled a kind, but firm, smile. Then she shut the door behind her and made her way downstairs to finish her exploration. Most of the ground floor was taken up with the large kitchen with its two fireplaces, pots and spits, and a large functional table with a worn surface. The other rooms were a large store and pantry area and a buttery. These were full of implements that had not been used in a long time, and the shelves and containers were mostly bare and empty where once they would have been well stocked and heaving with provisions. The things they had brought with them had been placed tidily away, she noticed, catching sight of the large round cheese and a salted ham. Doubtless Prudence's work. She was industrious, even if she was a little abrasive. Leaning toward a draughty window, Mathilde caught sight of Robin moving about the garden and made haste to join him there.

As she shut the door behind her, she was immediately reminded of the bitter cold. Mathilde shivered as she picked her way along the path, which was slushy from the number of boots that had traipsed up and down it already. There had been more coming and going this day than any time in the past few years, she reflected, wondering if the place had felt as neglected as it looked. She had left her gloves somewhere inside, so she rubbed her hands together, as she looked around to find her friend. He was hanging over the side of an enclosure. As she hurried to join him, she realized he was feeding the chickens.

"This looks very impressive," Mathilde said. "Did you make it yourself?"

Robin looked modest. "I had some help," he admitted. "And this area was clearly used for this same purpose in past times." He passed her a chunk of bread, and noticing how he was crumbling his own up and scattering it for the fowls, she did the same. For a few moments they stood in harmonious silence, listening to the clucks and squawks of the chickens as they gobbled up the breadcrumbs. Robin finally broke it by pointing at the largest hen and saying, "That one's name is the Prioress," he said. "She holds sway over all the others."

"So she does," agreed Mathilde. "And she looks like she is clad in a black and white habit." She watched the other hens a moment. "That one's name is Intrepid," she said, pointing to a gray speckled hen. "See how she refuses to bow down, despite how the others are trying her?"

Robin nodded. "That one is Fussy and that one is Feisty," he said, pointing at the two brown hens who looked practically identical although their behaviors were quite different. Fussy spent most of her time scratching in the snow and looking dissatisfied. Feisty spent most of her time squaring up to others and flapping her feathers in challenge. "That leaves one more

84

for you to name," Robin said, nudging her in the side. Mathilde cocked her head to one side and eyed the remaining nameless hen. She was mostly white with a very red comb. "And you're not allowed to call her Snowy," said Robin.

"I wasn't going to!" Mathilde protested hotly. "How about Valiant? Val for short."

Robin rolled his eyes. "You and your names. Valiant is nearly as bad as Leander! Why do they have to be so grandiloquent?" he complained.

"Because," Mathilde said, slipping her arm through his, "they are aspirational. It's important to aspire to things."

"Very well, but I shall call her Val, and likely think of her as Valerie."

"That is fine," said Mathilde. "For she and I will both know her real name. And so will you, deep down."

"Aye, my lady," he said with an eye roll.

"You called me 'my lady' again," sighed Mathilde, missing the easy camaraderie of the road.

Robin shrugged. "Of course. Anything else isn't really proper." At her disappointed expression, he scratched the back of his neck. "Maybe in private…" he started gruffly.

"Oh yes!" Mathilde agreed readily. "In private you must still call me Matty."

Robin grinned reluctantly at that. "That's a boy's name. I only called you that in front of other people to be convincing."

"Well, I like it," she insisted. "Besides, you refused to call me Leander, like I wanted."

"Leander!" he repeated scornfully. "I should say not! I'd never be friends with anyone called Leander."

"What's wrong with the name?" asked Mathilde. "If I were ever to have a son…" She broke off wistfully. "Well… It's a very good sort of name."

Robin snorted and tilted his head back to look up at the sky. "It's snowing again!"

Mathilde brushed away the flakes that were settling on her eyelashes. "Snow!" she breathed reverently. "It's a sign!"

"Sign of what?" asked Robin curiously.

"When it snows," she replied softly, "everything is covered over, including the past, and made crisp and new again." They gazed a moment in silence at the falling flakes.

"You don't need to be made over," Robin said abruptly.

"No," agreed Mathilde. "Because I already have been, by the adventure of our journey north." Feeling Robin's curious gaze on her profile, Mathilde turned to face him. "Thank you for accompanying me, Rob. You're an exceptionally good friend to me. In truth"—she hesitated—"you and the Countess Vawdrey are my best friends in all the world."

Robin flushed. "What about the other pages?" he asked, looking away.

"They are good friends to me," she acknowledged. "Very good friends. Willard, Gordon, Piers—I'm very fond of them all. You boys were my first friends. But you and Fenella are my very best."

Robin cleared his throat. "We should probably light some more fires. We will need to keep the house warm."

"Why don't we just sit around the kitchen fire?" Mathilde suggested. "It's cozy there and welcoming. It seems foolish to use up all the firewood Waldon chopped for us by lighting fires in all the rooms. Especially," she added, "since we are a household of only three."

Robin brightened at the idea. "That's not half bad," he said. "Of course, I can chop us more logs as we need them."

"Of course," agreed Mathilde. "But there is no point in creating additional work where it is not needed. Should we shut up the chickens in their basket?" she asked, looking at the crate which had been filled with straw.

"Maybe we should leave them to choose, until it grows dark?" Robin shrugged. "They can make up their own minds till then."

"Very well, but we must not forget, we are very close to the edge of the wood," Mathilde said with a shiver, "and you never know what predator might emerge under cover of night."

Robin nodded in agreement, and they made their way, still arm in arm, to the warm, bright kitchen where the fire burned merrily in the hearth.

10

"No," said Guy, his patience wearing thin. Almost he was tempted to bring his fist crashing down on the tabletop, but he restrained himself. Just. "I do not want the pick of the confiscated horses," he said scathingly. "I want the horse that was brought in with my—with the two young lads the day before yesterday," he corrected himself hastily. What the hells had he been about to call her? He had slept badly the previous night, dreaming about foxes and chickens and the gods only knew what. He needed to pull himself together. Through gritted teeth, he elaborated. "The horse the carter claimed was his after the affray."

The jail official gazed back at him unhappily. He was not one of the beadles who had accompanied Mathilde to Acton March. It irked Guy to think of her by that name, but she had given him none other, so it would have to suffice for now.

"But, my lord," the man bleated, spreading wide his hands, "the carter likely took the beast with him."

"You mean he has been released?" barked Guy, looking suddenly furious. The bastard should have had a spell in the stocks at the very least! "There was also some personal property that needs to be released to me. A belt and a knife taken from the smaller boy."

The official quaked. "If you would wait here for one moment, my lord," he said, lurching to his feet. "I will go and make enquiries."

Guy bit back his retort, which was to enquire rather acidly, why the fellow had not done so in the first place. He gazed around with dissatisfaction at the surroundings of Wickhamford jail, which was a gray stone structure of rather bleak aspect. The holding cells were below this floor in the cellars. The air was dank. He found it hard to believe it would be any more congenial on the floor below. When he thought of Mathilde being dragged here, he had a strange acrid feeling in the pit of his stomach. Hearing footsteps in the corridor outside, he turned his head to see reinforcements had been brought this time.

"My lord!" cried a large jovial-looking man who looked vaguely familiar to him. He gave a hurried bow. "Your servant, sir, your devoted servant. My name is Bernard Thurston. We have met previously on several civic occasions." Catching sight of the expression on Guy's face, he added, "Right sorry am I to hear there has been such a confounded mix-up around this matter!"

"Thurston," Guy repeated in clipped accents. "I believe your son played a part in this debacle."

Thurston flushed. "He—er—he was performing his duty that night here," he answered cautiously. "And gave an account of it afterward that ensured we did not release the animal into the carter's possession when he left us."

"The horse is still here?"

"It is, in the courtyard below, my lord. It has been awaiting your collection."

Guy felt himself relax in spite of himself. He cleared his throat. "Well, that's something at least," he conceded. "What about the carter?"

Thurston cleared his throat. "He was released, my lord," he confessed apologetically. "In truth we did not have any charge to keep him here."

"Well, I have plenty," Guy countered aggressively. "We could start with assault and theft."

The merchant gazed back at him unhappily. "My lord—" he started, but Guy cut him off.

"If you did not believe this, then why did you not release the horse to him?" he asked with some belligerence.

Thurston gave a small cough. "In truth, my lord, because my son made it plain that if we did so, we would incur your considerable displeasure."

Guy drew in a deep breath. "I see," he answered once he had recovered his temper. "It seems I owe your son a debt."

"I'm sure he does not see it in that manner," Thurston murmured, "and was only too glad to be able to perform some small service for your lordship."

Guy lapsed into brooding silence. "What of the items confiscated from the two boys?" he asked after a moment.

Thurston turned and motioned to one of his companions. It was the same melancholy-looking fellow from earlier. He held a small wooden trunk, which he made haste to bring forward, setting it on the table before Guy. The small key was still in the lock. Guy turned it and flung back the lid.

Inside were two coiled brown leather belts and two sheathed daggers. One must belong to Robin, he supposed. Both knives looked perfectly serviceable and bore neither embellishment nor crest. He gave a short nod. "I will take these with me."

"Of course, my lord. Edwards will come downstairs and accompany you to the stables."

Guy wasn't that surprised when they reached the stable yard and found the horse to be a broken-down old nag, without even a bridle. Somehow, Mathilde's words had prepared him for this eventuality. He cast his eyes heavenward and then ordered it to be brought out and a halter and leading rein attached.

Temur was awaiting him in the thoroughfare outside and eyed the animal with interest. "I take it the lady has not much of an aptitude for horses," he commented wryly.

"Actually," Guy rumbled, "she's a very fair rider." He kept his eyes straight ahead when he felt Temur's surprised gaze on his face. He had attached the horse to his own, and it was following along behind placidly enough.

"Not much of an eye for horseflesh though, has she?" Temur rallied.

"I believe this horse was acquired for altruistic purposes," Guy forced himself to respond. "Can we drop the subject?"

Temur shrugged. "Are we headed back to the manor now?"

"I've a few other things to pick up," Guy said shortly. "Did you place the orders I gave you?"

"I did," said Temur. "Though you gave me no measurements for the tailor. Luckily one of his daughters was there and looked to be of a muchness, so I told him to take her for a guide."

"Good thinking."

"I was at a loss at the cordwainer's though," Temur confessed, scratching his head. "And I doubt very much you measured her feet."

"I know exactly the size of her feet." Guy frowned, pulling on the reins to halt his horse. He held up his hand. "From the tip of my middle finger to here," he said, pointing a finger to his wrist. "Measuring this much in width, at the widest point." He held his thumb and index finger up to illustrate.

Temur blinked. "Well—"

"In which direction is the shoemaker?" Guy asked, turning in his saddle.

"We're going back?" Temur glanced up at the sky. "It looks like we'll likely have more snow before midday."

Guy sent a scornful glance at his companion and turned his horse about. "Which direction?"

"This way," sighed Temur, urging his own horse to turn. "It's over yonder," he said, pointing to a distant sign of a wooden shoe. They started forward.

"How's that wife of yours?" Guy asked abruptly. "What was her name again?"

"Lettys. She's well, my lord," Temur responded cautiously. Guy grunted. He could feel Temur's curious gaze still on him. "She's ruffled my father's feathers a bit," Temur added after a moment. "Maybe us moving her in with the old man was a mistake, but he couldn't manage the place on his own and it seemed the obvious move to make."

Guy listened to this with knitted brows. "How is your father? I don't think I saw him at your wedding," he said. He was sure that was right, but in truth he'd paid scant attention to the personal lives of his men over the past few years. Really, he should have done better, especially with Temur, whose father was some sort of cousin of Guy's mother, a few times removed, which made him his kinsman. They had a large place over at Acton Dymock.

"He was not there, my lord," sighed Temur. "He took my mother's death hard. He gave us his blessing to wed but could not face the celebrations. It's been over five years now since my mother died. The house needs a lot of work, and Lettys can't

92

wait to be the new broom that sweeps all before it. But Father's resistant to change and well…" Temur coughed. "There's been a few sharp words on both sides."

"Hmmm." An image of Guy's own father flashed into his mind's eye, and he could well imagine what his sire would have had to say about him installing Mathilde at the hunting lodge. "It can't be easy," he said heavily.

Temur could not have looked more astonished if he had fallen off his horse. "No, my lord," he agreed. "And that's putting it mildly."

Guy shot a sidelong glance at him. He didn't want to sound too interested in how Temur was negotiating married life. After all, his own situation was not the same at all. This imposter wasn't his wife, despite what she said. She couldn't be. Aloud he said, "How long were you courting Lettys?"

If anything, Temur looked even more alarmed by this turn in the conversation. "Some three months, my lord."

"Three months? That's not long." Guy frowned.

"Couldn't see the point in putting it off." Temur shrugged. "I wanted her; she wanted me. What was there to delay about?"

What indeed? Guy thought back fleetingly to his own broken betrothal. He and Julia Kerslake had been promised for over five years. It had all counted for naught in the end. For most of that time, he had been embroiled in the war. They had spent precious little time getting to know one another. Sometimes he thought he had never really known her at all. Perhaps, after all, there was something to be said for short betrothals.

"My lord?"

Guy gave a start. "What is it?" Had Temur been speaking?

Temur pointed up at the sign of the shoe, speckled with snow. "We're here."

11

Mathilde had been excited on her third morning at the lodge to hear a knock on the door. *He's come!* she thought, bounding out of her seat. *At last!* But she was only halfway down the stairs when she heard Prudence's waspish accents drifting up to her.

"What now? And don't go traipsing those wet boots on my nice clean floor!"

She'd never dare take such a tone with her master, Mathilde thought, her shoulders drooping. It must be more supplies. Her steps slowed in her descent. Over the past two days they had received a bewildering amount of items for their store cupboards: cereals, vegetables, dried herbs, and spices. She had thought this was a temporary arrangement for her to be living separately to her husband, but perhaps Lord Martindale intended it for the longer term? It was rather a lowering thought.

She watched from the bottom step as two burly men rolled a large barrel before them through to the pantry and guessed it must be ale. Leaning against the banister, she swallowed down her disappointment. It seemed her husband did not share her keenness to grow acquainted. Abruptly, Mathilde sank down onto the step. She pulled her woolen mantle tighter about her and propped her chin on her hands, her elbows resting on her knees. Maybe she was just destined to be always alone. The thought had no sooner formed in her mind than she dismissed it as contemptible self-pity. Lord Martindale had a vast estate to run. She was just one of many people he had to deal with, she told herself roundly. This attitude of melancholy would do her no good. Perhaps she had been too long cooped up against the cold weather?

Her eye strayed to the wintry scene outside the window. It wasn't actually snowing at this instant. Should she go for a walk? Perhaps Robin would join her. She mustered a smile for the delivery men, who were both goggling at her over their shoulders as they disappeared out of the door. She cast a quick glance over herself to make sure nothing was amiss. What had caught their attention so? Not finding anything, she stood up from the step and went in search of Robin.

"The young master's outside, milady," Prudence said and folded her lips. She was up to her elbows in flour and seemed to be making some sort of pie. Mathilde beat a hasty retreat before she could incur Prudence's displeasure. Drawing on her cloak and boots, she, too, ventured out of doors.

Robin was crouched down over the hen house this morning and appeared to be collecting eggs. Mathilde waited as he gingerly picked them out of the straw.

"Three out of five," Robin said, looking up to find her watching him. "That's not bad."

"It's very good," Mathilde agreed, though she knew nothing about keeping hens.

"What do you say to us getting a cow?" Robin asked, stepping over the fencing.

"A cow?"

"For milk and cheeses." Robin nodded toward a structure at the bottom of the garden. "It looks like they might have had one here before."

He held out the eggs for her inspection. "Very nice," said Mathilde approvingly. "Are not the horses we rode here being stabled in there presently?"

"Aye," agreed Robin, "but there's easily room for a cow. Or possibly a goat," he added, screwing up his nose.

"Perhaps you should ask Prudence, as she would be the one expected to milk it?" Mathilde suggested.

Robin pulled a face. "I can already tell you what Miss Curds and Whey would say."

Mathilde laughed. "She might surprise you."

He snorted. "I very much doubt it."

"What do you say to our going for an exploratory walk this morning?"

Robin's gloomy aspect brightened. "I'll just take these into the kitchen," he said. "And we can set forth at once."

"Don't forget your mittens and hat," Mathilde called after him and started making her way carefully down the garden path. The fresh powdery snow was perfect for walking on, but the churned-up snow on the path had frozen hard and was treacherous indeed.

She had only just reached the edge of the wood when Robin came crunching through the snow after her. "Wait for me!" he puffed, his orange hat slipping down over his eyes. He paused to adjust it to a jaunty angle.

"Which way shall we go? I vote this path." Mathilde pointed to a thin trail leading in the opposite direction to that from which they had come. Robin nodded in agreement, and they set off at once. "How was your bed last night? Did you sleep well?"

"Aye, very well. Yourself?"

"Very comfortably, though my bed is four times as big as the one I am accustomed to."

"My room is much better than my usual quarters. Old Sir Avery is a penny-pinching curmudgeon," Robin grumbled about the knight he served at court.

Mathilde's footsteps halted. "Robin!" she cried.

"What is it?"

"I never even thought about Sir Avery! Will you not be in very great trouble at abandoning his service?"

Robin shrugged, unconcerned. "Probably."

"But will not your people be very cross, after he agreed to take you to squire?"

Again, Robin showed supreme indifference. "My *step*father will doubtless cut up a bit rough," he admitted. "But Mother wanted me for the church anyway. She hates knights and combat, ever since my father was killed in battle."

Mathilde looked at him doubtfully. "Is that something you would be interested in pursuing?"

Robin grinned. "No. My older brother, Gregor, is more suited, in truth."

"But—"

"If old Sir Avery throws me off, all the better. I wasn't learning anything from him anyway, except different ways to tie your garters." Robin pulled a face. It was true, Mathilde reflected, that Sir Avery was an elderly knight who spent most of his days attending different ceremonial functions at court. Certainly, his jousting days were long since spent. "He only agreed to take me as my father was his godson," Robin continued, picking up a stick and inspecting it. He started swishing away with it as if it were a sword.

"I suppose we ought both to write, explaining where we are," sighed Mathilde guiltily.

"There's no hurry." Robin frowned, performing a side step, kicking some imaginary foe.

"Mind out for that tree root—" Mathilde started before Robin took a spectacular tumble and slid two feet in the snow. "Rob! Are you alright?"

"Ouch." He sat up, rubbing his shin. "That's the trouble with all this snow—" He broke off, staring into the trees. "Did you see that?"

"What?" Mathilde turned to look in the direction he was looking fixedly.

"That old crone?" He pointed. "She was right there!"

"I saw no one." She turned back to see Robin still sat there staring. "Do get up, Robin, the snow will soak through your cloak."

He clambered to his feet and started off at a slow jog in the direction he had pointed to.

"Robin!"

He beckoned to her. "Come on!"

"We'll get lost!" Mathilde warned. "You're leading us away from the path."

"We'll find our way back!"

"Robin!"

He stopped and turned back to look at her. "Mathilde," he said in the same challenging tone. "Your nurse isn't here now. This is our chance. One more adventure." He crooked an eyebrow at her. "Matty would seize the opportunity."

She laughed. "Oh, very well, but only because you called me by my boy's name."

He grinned, and Mathilde made haste to follow him. As they hurried on, she looked about with interest to see if she could spot the jay who was calling through the trees. Doubtless he was retrieving some acorns he'd buried in the autumn, but even though she kept a sharp lookout, she could not catch sight of the buff feathers or flash of white on the rump that often gave the bird away. She was surprised he could hide so successfully among the bare trees.

Robin muttered, "I swear I caught a glimpse of her skirts..." or "Just there!" whenever Mathilde suggested he must have lost sight of their quarry.

"What was she wearing?"

"A sort of pale blue," said Robin. "Or maybe gray."

They had been walking a good twenty minutes when Mathilde caught sight of the large raven watching them with interest from a nearby oak tree. As she watched him, he tipped his head to one side, opened his beak, and emitted the jay's haunting scream. "Oh!" she said aloud.

"Do you see her?" asked Robin, wheeling about.

"That raven," said Mathilde. "He's impersonating a jay."

Robin screwed his eyes up, waiting for the raven to do it again, but the bird merely returned their gaze impartially. "Everyone knows ravens are tricky," he said at last.

"But he let me see he was doing it," Mathilde answered. "I wonder why."

Robin gave a startled yelp. "Look!" He pointed to a curl of smoke to the left of the raven's oak. "There must be a dwelling nearby." The raven nodded indulgently. "Come on!"

Mathilde shivered and tried to shake off the unnerved feeling stealing over her. With one last glance at the raven, she followed after Robin, setting her own feet directly in his footprints in the snow.

The curling smoke came from a chimney set in a curious shack of stone and mud, with a thatched roof. They came upon it suddenly, as though the clearing sprang up out of nowhere, but in fact, the cottage was set on the very edge of the wood next to a small stream. In truth, if it had been placed in a village or hamlet, surrounded by other similar houses, it would not have seemed unusual at all. It was the location alone that made it startling.

"Look!" whispered Robin hoarsely, but Mathilde had already spotted the flash of faded blue at the window. In the next instant, the wooden door opened, and an upright woman with long hair of iron gray stood in the entrance. She was dressed in a woolen gown, which would once have been blue, but had been washed so many times since that it was now an indeterminate shade somewhere between blue and gray. Flakes of snow still clung to her skirts, and she wore no mantle or cloak to guard her against the bitter cold. Without a word, she turned and walked back into the house, leaving the door open for them. While Mathilde hesitated, Robin took the unspoken invitation and followed her inside.

"Wait for me!" Mathilde hurried after them, shutting the door behind her. Inside the shack, Mathilde had to take a moment to adjust her eyes from the dazzling snow outside to the gloom within. To her surprise, Mathilde found there was a cow standing sedately against one wall and several chickens scratching around on the dirt floor around her. "Oh, excuse me," she murmured to a little black hen who was staring up at her beadily.

"Light me a fire, boy," the old woman said suddenly, making Mathilde jump. She had sat so still, Mathilde had not caught sight of her at first. She sat cross-legged next to a hearth, which was in the center of the room and comprised of a large metal bowl on three legs. Over this stood three poles lashed together with a pot hanging down from them on a chain. Mathilde was startled to see nothing but cold ash within the bowl. What had caused the plume of smoke then that had caught their attention from the wood? She darted a look at Robin, but he seemed to find nothing amiss with the woman's request and was already hurrying outside to fetch twigs and branches for her fire. "Come, child, and sit beside me here," the old woman continued and patted the floor next to her.

"Should I not help gather some wood for the fire?" Mathilde asked, but the old woman shook her head. Mindful not to seem ungrateful for her hospitality, Mathilde crossed the floor to join her and sank down onto the floor next to her. "I hope you do not mind our intrusion. My friend caught sight of you in the wood and we followed."

A shadow passed over the already darkened room, and Mathilde gasped as something blocked the only available light from a small window. A loud swoosh was heard and a flutter of feathers, and in the next instant the large raven sat on the old woman's shoulder.

"Just in time for introductions," cackled the old woman, "though it seems you have already met Tancred?"

"Oh yes, in the wood," said Mathilde, gazing on the glossy blue-black plumage. The bird stared fixedly at the far wall, refusing to acknowledge their acquaintanceship. "I am

102

Mathilde, and very pleased to meet you." The bird's eye darted to her a second before he looked away. "Tancred. That's a very handsome name."

"Don't mind him," wheezed the old woman. "He's always standoffish at first. I am called Old Helga in these parts." She made a curious gesture, placing her thumb on her chin and touching her index finger to the tip of her nose. Mathilde was not familiar with the salute but did her best to replicate it. The old woman gave a delighted chuckle. "You have other names?" she asked, turning her head to look at Mathilde with interest.

Other names? Mathilde flushed with embarrassment. Was that what the action meant? But after all, did she not? She had traveled for almost a month under a boy's alias and was on her third married name. "Oh yes," she said quickly, recovering herself. "I have had at least four."

The old woman nodded appreciatively, her eyes darting over Mathilde's face. "The magpies foretold your coming two days ago," she muttered dreamily, almost as though to herself. "For a moment, I thought I saw four for a boy. My old eyes played tricks on me, for when I looked again there were only three. Three for a girl."

Mathilde started in surprise. "I was dressed as a boy," she confided in a rush. "So that would be why you saw four at first."

"Is that so?" Helga asked, looking completely unruffled by this news. "Doubtless you had your reasons." She nodded sagely, and for some reason, her total lack of curiosity put Mathilde immediately at ease. Rob entered the shack with an armful of branches and set about laying out the fire. Mathilde and Old Helga sat in companionable silence until the flames caught. Mathilde noticed a cat creep forward out of the shadows to get closer to the source of warmth. She sat up straight, her tail whisking, but as the larger logs started to spit and flare, she closed her eyes and seemed to settle, hunkering down onto her belly. In one corner, a goat bleated, making Mathilde jump. Her eyes could make out a heap of hay or straw in another corner, but she wasn't sure if that was the old woman's bedding, or food for the livestock.

"I'll chop you some logs before we leave, Granny," Rob said politely and settled down beside them. "Your stores are low."

Helga nodded. "Good boy." She rearranged herself so that she hugged her bony knees and stared into the flames.

"Have you no blanket for your shoulders, Granny?" Rob asked, glancing around. "You must be cold. Your dress is likely damp from the snow."

Old Helga looked surprised. "Cold? Not I. I have too many companions to be cold."

Mathilde glanced at the hem of the old woman's dress and was astonished to see that the white flecks she had taken for snow, in fact, were a woven pattern in the fabric. A slight movement to her right made her turn her head, and to her shock, a large gray wolf sat there silently, staring into the flames. She gave a stifled exclamation and saw Rob reached for his knife, only to find he did not have it. The wolf flicked him a contemptuous glance with his fierce yellow eyes.

"Do not anger Maven," Old Helga warned mildly. "All who sit at my hearth are bound by a sacred truce."

Rob shifted uneasily. "So long as we all abide by it," he said grimly.

Tancred winked one wicked black eye at Mathilde and gave a mirthless cackle. Helga reached to her belt and unknotted a small cloth bag which she held out in front of her at arm's length and then turned upside down. Several flat stones tumbled to the floor. Helga glanced down at them and grunted. Tancred also craned his head to look. It seemed to Mathilde that there were scratched symbols on their surfaces, but they were not lettering as she knew them.

"This is you," said Helga, pointing to a small blue stone. "The traveler on his quest. The hero." Mathilde's eyes went very wide. She was the hero? She felt her cheeks flush with pleasure.

"This here," said Helga, pointing, "is your foe."

"My foe?" Mathilde squinted down at the large shiny gray stone with the rough surface.

Helga nodded slowly. "A wise hero knows his true foe."

Mathilde frowned. *The carter?* she wondered. She could think of no other enemy.

"With a man like yours," Old Helga said suddenly, "you need to give all of yourself over. Hold nothing back."

Mathilde started. "My husband?" she blurted in surprise, her breath coming fast. "He's not my enemy!"

Helga paid no heed to her outburst. "His past has left him suspicious and bruised. You must needs shower him with your affections."

Mathilde's heart was beating so loud now that she could almost fancy she heard it pounding in her ears. "I can do that," she said eagerly. "I, too—" She broke off, looking across at Robin. Was it suitable to speak of such things in front of him? "I have plenty to give," she said in a stifled voice.

Again, Helga continued without acknowledging Mathilde's response. "He tells himself and everyone he does not like tenderness, that he does not need it. But that is a lie." Helga nodded. "Deep inside, he craves it desperately." She shot a look of challenge Mathilde's way.

Mathilde clasped her hands together. "I—I can do that. I will!" she vowed. "What else, Granny?" she said pleadingly, addressing her in familiar terms as she had heard Robin do. On the road, Robin had addressed all women as "Aunty" or "Mother," and all old ladies as "Granny." Often it had earned him an extra spoonful of stew, a soft word, and kindly advice.

Helga opened her mouth as if to speak and then hesitated. Both women turned as one to look at Robin, who was staring fixedly at the ground, a wooden, uncomfortable look on his face. This was no conversation for him to hear, thought Mathilde awkwardly. Helga gave a quick gesture of one hand and the cat sauntered forward from its position in the circle and butted its head against his knee.

"Hey, pretty girl," murmured Robin, lifting her onto his lap. As Mathilde watched, he grew wholly absorbed in fondling the cat's ears and whispering to her.

"Men. So easily distracted by the female of the species," said Helga with a wry chuckle.

Mathilde leaned forward. "Please continue with your advice, Granny," she whispered. "I am listening."

Helga gave a considering nod. She reached down and ran her fingers lightly over the other stones where they lay. "Each time you water the dried-up seeds of his affections," she carried on in a low voice, "fresh shoots will burst forth." She gave a short laugh. "He will not be able to help himself. Already…where all was shriveled, near-deadened, now is *pulsing* with sap." Something about the old woman's words made Mathilde's cheeks redden. She was glad Rob was not listening. Old Helga shot her a keen, assessing look. "You're sure you know what you're doing?" she asked, screwing up her eyes.

Was she? Mathilde bit her lip. "I am," she said, raising her chin. After all, everyone knew fortune favored the bold. The trouble was, practically everyone she knew thought her timorous in the extreme. "I am twice a widow," she bluffed, "and no child."

Old Helga angled her head as if sharply assessing her words. She was watching her closely. "Twice widowed…" she repeated, as if trying out the words on her tongue and finding them puzzling. With a frown she reached down and quickly gathered the stones, throwing them down again. Mathilde held her breath. "You do not lie in word," the old woman agreed, "yet they are twisted in meaning." She shot a knowing look at Mathilde, who flushed scarlet. Helga's gaze narrowed. "You have traveled a long way," she mused thoughtfully, "and I do not speak of distance." She screwed up her eyes. "The traveler has been tested," she said dreamily, "through many trials and learned many things."

"I have," Mathilde agreed earnestly. "I have learned many, many things. How to whittle, swear an oath, swagger like a boy—"

"Those lessons will not help you now, child," said Helga dismissively. "You need to learn some new tricks, and fast."

Mathilde's face fell, and she darted a quick glance at Robin, who was now playing with the cat and a piece of string. "Can you teach me, Granny?" she asked humbly.

The old woman shook her head. "I took another path and know nothing of such things. But perhaps I can help point the way," she mused, tapping her chin. She sat up straight, and then held her hands palms out to her sides, muttering under her breath. Mathilde craned her ears, but still could not make out the words, which sounded guttural and coarse on the old woman's tongue. "Fetch me that sack from the corner," she said suddenly, and the change of tone was so abrupt it was almost startling.

Helga pointed, and Mathilde obediently climbed to her feet and retrieved the dusty hessian sack. It had something in it from its weight, although it was not heavy by any means. She handed it obediently to the old woman, who reached inside and pulled out a book. All the animals in the circle turned to look with interest, but none of them looked as astonished by the appearance of the leather-bound volume as Helga herself. She stared at it as if she had never even seen one before. Then she shrugged and handed it to Mathilde.

"Thank you," Mathilde said politely, though in truth it felt a little anticlimactic. She turned the book over in her hands. In the murky interior she could not make out the words contained in its pages. "I'm sure it will be very instructive."

"Buggered if I know," said Old Helga dismissively. "I never read one."

12

"What did she give you?" asked Rob curiously as they made their way back to the lodge. Mathilde had surreptitiously stolen a look at the title page as soon as they had left Helga's cottage.

"It's a copy of *The Tales of Sir Maurency of Jorde*," said Mathilde brightly, trying to hide her disappointment.

Robin blew a raspberry. "That book's dull as ditchwater!" he hooted, swishing at the trees with yet another imaginary sword he'd picked up on the way home.

"It's very popular at court," Mathilde argued, which was true enough. Her own nurse had read it to her several times. It was also very worthy with its tales of chivalry and virtue. Rack her brains as she might, she could think of no lesson in its pages that could teach her on how to secure her husband's affections. Unless, she thought doubtfully, she was supposed to read it to him as a bedtime story?

"Well," said Rob judiciously, "we can't say she robbed us, for we gave her no coin."

"I'm sure she gave me very sterling advice," Mathilde insisted stubbornly. "I just need to reread this, and I'm sure it will make more sense in light of what she said."

Rob made another rude noise, and Mathilde ignored him, going over the thrilling words that Old Helga had uttered about Lord Martindale. *Each time you water the dried-up seeds of his affections, fresh shoots will burst forth.* Her heart thudded at the idea that she, Mathilde, could achieve such a result. Could she truly earn the love of her husband as she yearned to? She clasped the book tight in her hands. Oh, how she longed to do so! If he would only turn to her, she vowed she would be the absolute best wife in all the kingdom! If only, she thought with niggling uncertainty, she knew exactly what men wanted from their wives.

In her mind's eye, she flitted through the various couples she knew of at court. The King and Queen, she thought, biting on her lip, were the most famous examples, but in truth, she had seen little sign of genuine affection between them. They spoke to each other fair, of course, but she had seen them only in public life. Behind closed doors, for all she knew, they might act completely differently. Her own parents had always been scrupulously polite and courteous to each other. She could never remember an occasion where she had seen them embrace or even raise their voices at one another. She frowned. Somehow, she felt convinced that was not how she would encourage fresh shoots to grow from Lord Martindale's heart.

Then another image flashed into her mind. Her dear friend Fenella with her husband, Earl Vawdrey. They acted very differently to the other couples she knew. Indeed, before Fenella had come to court, Mathilde had been convinced that Oswald Vawdrey was a very sinister and terrifying personage. Of course, his reputation as the King's spymaster preceded him, and she had been frightened of her own shadow in those days, so practically everyone she came across had been an object of fear. But Earl Vawdrey, with his thin smile and cold eyes, had truly brought her out in a cold sweat. And yet... *And yet*, thought Mathilde slowly, he was quite different with his wife.

At the royal banquets, Mathilde had seen Oswald Vawdrey touch his wife's hand, had seen him feed Fenella from his own plate. Mathilde had tried not to stare, of course, that would be rude, but it was fascinating to see how they were with each other. When they conversed, you could be in no doubt that Fenella had his undivided attention. When Fen crossed a room, his eye instinctively followed her.

Mathilde had once, in the Queen's audience chamber, seen Earl Vawdrey reach across and fleetingly touch his wife's cheek. The look on his face showed he had not been able to stop the impulse despite their surroundings. Mathilde had caught her breath to see that private moment when their eyes had met. Seeing them together, she could be in no doubt that what was between them was an accord, an intimate bond which was sacred and true.

Mathilde had known instinctively that such a thing was exceedingly rare. She had never dared hope something like that could ever lie in store for her. At best, she had hoped her husband would allow her the role of wife at his side. Other than their union being blessed with a child, she had not raised her hopes further than that. But Helga's words had hinted at something more. That Lord Martindale could grow fond of her. She pressed one hand to her hammering heart. If she could carry on being brave, maybe, just maybe, she could win something more precious than mere acceptance from her husband. The thought made her feel quite giddy with longing. But to be a wife, she needed *new tricks*, Helga had said. She puzzled, wondering where she could pick them up.

Feeling a few flakes of snow, she glanced up at the sky, wondering if Lord Martindale would come for supper tonight. She had not seen him in four days. Should she try to send word to him? She could always send a message back with one of the many deliveries he had sent to the lodge. They seemed to be daily occurrences at the moment.

"We're being followed," said Robin suddenly.

"Pardon?" Mathilde swung round and saw the little cat trailing after them. When she saw she had been spotted, she sat down on her bottom and started licking her paw, as if she had not

111

been slinking in their footsteps at all. "Now she's ignoring us," she observed. "Pretending it's a coincidence."

"Why don't we take her back with us to the lodge?" suggested Rob excitedly.

"This morning you wanted a cow," Mathilde reminded him. "I did not realize you were so very fond of animals."

Robin shrugged. "Neither did I. But she is a very superior sort of cat," he said wistfully.

Mathilde scrutinized the cat, but to her it looked to be a very ordinary sort of tabby, not so hugely different to the many palace mousers, except perhaps smaller. "You seem determined to accumulate a menagerie these days," she commented. "She is a witch's cat, though, and belongs to Old Helga."

"She followed us for a reason," Rob insisted. "Perhaps she's tired of spells and potions. I could tell Prudence I saw a mouse in the pantry," he mused. "I bet she'd beg me to get a cat then."

"Very likely," she agreed absently, and they both lapsed into their own thoughts again. Rob kept casting satisfied glances over his shoulder, so she guessed the tabby still followed. It seemed to take them a lot longer to get home than it had taken them to get there. They must have taken a wrong turn or two, Mathilde suspected as they finally emerged from the trees. "Thank goodness," she breathed, catching sight of the lodge. "I can't feel my feet."

"We've got visitors," said Rob as the cat suddenly ran into the clearing and took a running jump into his arms. "Clever girl," he crooned, immediately absorbed in soothing the cat.

Mathilde turned her head and saw the horses poking their heads out of the shed. "Oh!" she squeaked and ran forward. "Oh, Rob, look! It's my horse! My very own dear horse!" Not waiting to hear his reply, she hurtled forward, very nearly losing her footing as she flung her arms around the neck of the horse that had got her arrested. As he rubbed his face against her, and pushed his velvety nose into her hood, Mathilde promptly burst into noisy tears.

13

Where the hells was she? It was starting to snow again, and the servant, Prudence, had no bloody ideas on the subject. They had been waiting now for well over an hour. Guy paced restlessly across the floor. What if she's decided to run off again? The maid swore she hadn't gone far, but where was the wench? Maybe she had already received orders for her return. Or she'd taken umbrage at being left neglected for so long?

"Perhaps we should come back tomorrow, my lord?" suggested Temur. "She's likely gone to visit with a friend or some such thing…" He trailed off lamely, catching sight of the angry look Guy cast his way.

"She knows no one around these parts, apart from myself," he retorted acidly. Guy was just debating setting out to look for her himself, when out of the corner of his eye, he caught movement outside the window. Turning quickly, he saw her launch her small figure to hang around the old nag's neck. "There she is," he said with suppressed fury, heading for the door and ignoring his overwhelming sense of relief at her reappearance. Instead, he stoked his righteous indignation as he hurried down the stairs and wrenched open the front door.

"My lord," Temur cautioned behind him, hurrying in his wake. "Now don't say aught you'll regret if you don't want to frighten the lass!"

Guy ignored him, striding out into the snow, his expression grim. She was going to have to learn to fear him if it meant her staying where it was warm and dry and not catching her death of cold! Just then, she turned her face toward him, almost stopping him in his tracks. Her eyes were streaming, her face swollen and red. He checked midstride, pausing a moment before closing the distance between them. "What's happened?" he burst out in concern, and to his surprise, he found he moderated his angry tone without conscious thought. "Are you hurt?" He cast an eye over her but could see nothing obvious.

She shook her head, her face screwing up again and fresh tears spilling over. "What is it?" But she only pressed her face into the horse's nose and hugged him tighter. Her slim shoulders shook with sobs, and torn between frustration and alarm, Guy stooped down and plucked her up in his arms. She pressed her fists into her eyes, openly bawling now. Guy shot a look at Robin, who looked completely unconcerned, brushed past them, and headed toward the lodge. Uncertain of his cue, Guy followed him into the house, walking straight past Temur, who was waiting at the door, open-mouthed.

"I told you not to upset her," Temur muttered, shaking his head. Guy cast a quelling look his way and started up the stairs, still carrying Mathilde in his arms. To his astonishment, halfway up the staircase, she twisted in his grasp, and flung her arms around his neck. He very nearly dropped her.

"Is it your ankle?" he asked in gruff bewilderment. "Did you fall in the snow?"

She made no reply, only buried her face in his chest and huffed there a minute as Guy made his way into the upstairs sitting room, making straight for the wooden bench next to the fire. When he moved to set her down, she made a dissenting sound, so instead he lowered himself gingerly onto the cushions, with her on his lap. He was too worried about any possible harm she'd done to herself to think about Temur gawking at him from the doorway. Reaching to unfasten her cloak, he carefully untangled it from her, running his hands up and over her arms, checking for any possible breaks or injuries. She sat quietly, letting him ease off her boots and dispose of her cloak over the back of the chair, sniffling and swiping at her eyes.

"What happened?" he asked softly.

She took a series of deep breaths, calming herself. "We went for a walk," she said in a wobbly voice.

"Yes?" He fought to keep his tone calm.

"And then... And then..." Her face crumpled again, and she sobbed aloud.

"Then what?" Guy barked in alarm. He heard Temur tut in disapproval behind him but forced himself not to react.

"Then I saw D-Destrian," she said brokenly and peered up at him through tear-filled eyes.

"Who?" Guy asked sharply.

"My horse," she whispered tremulously. "You brought me my horse!" The look of devout gratitude she sent him made his mind go blank. "I'm so h-happy!" she wailed and collapsed again onto his chest. He froze to the spot, feeling a damp spot grow across his tunic. Casting an agonized look of confusion over the top of her head, he saw the door softly closing. Temur had made himself scarce. Guy had no idea where the boy, Robin, had gone. What was he supposed to do? The tears showed no sign of abating. If this was how she behaved when she was happy, what the hells did she do when she was sad?

Gingerly he placed a hand on her middle back and patted her gently. "There, there, now," he ventured. She drew in a shuddering breath. "All will be well," he said, wishing he didn't sound so uncertain himself. She exhaled noisily and peeped up at him through watery, red-rimmed eyes. "Feeling better?" he ventured.

116

She hiccupped. "Sorry," she said softly. "I just feel so relieved that we're reunited." She smiled at him, and Guy stared. She was talking about the horse, he reminded himself savagely, not him. There was absolutely no reason for him to have this strange, breathless feeling in his chest. *But she said you had made her happy*, a stunned voice in his head pointed out. No one had ever said such a thing to him before, much less thought it! Even at this very moment, she sat in his lap as naturally as if she belonged there. Guy waited, dry-mouthed, for her to spring from him in horror, realizing her position, but instead, if anything, she leaned further into him. "I'm tired and cold," she confided shyly. "I think we got a bit lost on the way back."

Instead of scolding her roundly for her reckless behavior, Guy found himself rubbing her upper arms. "You stayed out too long," he said, but even to his own ears, his rebuke lacked the sternness it should have. *What is happening?* She nodded and crowded further into him with a soft whimper that scrambled his brain. Guy felt his throat go dry Suddenly, he felt very aware of the fact he had a scrap of soft femininity pressing against him in all sorts of dangerous places.

"I should put some more logs on the fire," he said huskily, putting her bodily from him before he embarrassed them both. For a moment, he thought she looked disappointed, but that couldn't be right. He rose off the chair and, approaching the fireplace, threw on four or five logs and turned back to find her watching him. There was not a shadow of calculation in those hazel eyes, he thought. If he didn't know any better, he could almost have imagined they were roaming over him with maidenly admiration. Her eyelashes trembled and she glanced away. Her face was already so red from crying that he could not tell if she blushed or not.

He cleared his throat. "You should eat something. You're likely hungry. Then perhaps a bath and early to bed."

117

"Will you stay?" she asked eagerly. Then she must have caught something in his expression, for she added hurriedly, "For a meal, I mean."

He knew he was in trouble when he felt the wild disappointment that flooded him at her words. He only hoped his expression did not reflect it. "Of course," he said woodenly with a shrug. "If you wish it."

"Oh, I do!" Her face was shining and earnest now. It made him think of that other occasion. When she had said she wanted his baby above all things.

Swallowing, Guy turned away. He would put that from his mind. He had to. "I'll tell them we're staying," he said gruffly and left the room.

The meal was an awkward affair. Guy sat at the head of the table and Mathilde next to Robin on his right. Temur sat on his left. Prudence served a tasty meal of game pie and winter vegetables. Robin and Temur set about consuming their food with a single-minded purpose that did not allow for conversation. Feeling the weight of Mathilde's expectant gaze on him, Guy cudgeled his brain for some safe topic of discussion. The only thing he could think of was horses.

"You'll still need to keep that mare from my stables with you," he said, clearing his throat. "That horse of yours—I mean, Destrian," he amended, coloring slightly and avoiding Temur's eye. "He isn't really fit for anything but retirement."

"Oh, but I shall still ride him for short journeys," Mathilde replied quickly. "He's a very excellent horse and most keen to be in my keeping."

Guy regarded her doubtfully. She had far too good a seat to have a broken-down dray horse for a mount. Still, he didn't

118

want to upset her further with brutal truths right now. "Anything further than a short ride, you must take the bay." His tone was mild but brooked no argument.

"I would be very pleased to keep the bay mare," Mathilde agreed. "She's a lovely horse. It's only…" Her expression grew wistful. "One does grow so very fond of one's own horse. And Destrian has such a beautiful nature."

"I'm sure," Guy said briskly, disliking the way Temur was now taking interest in their conversation.

"Yes, and after all, *he* chose *me*," Mathilde carried on.

"He chose you?" Guy repeated without much interest. Temur was definitely hanging on their words now, curse him!

"Yes. There I was, waiting for Robin outside the alehouse, when Destrian just placed his head here." She patted her shoulder. "He had such a gentle expression, and I knew at once that we were kindred spirits. He had a fresh scar down the side of his dear face, but he let me stroke him and made that sort of whickering noise that horses make. You know the one?" Guy nodded. "We were getting along quite famously when that brute came shambling out and set about him with his stick." Her face darkened. "That was when he made that comment about my buying the horse if I did not like to see the way he treated him. Naturally, I reached into my purse at once. You will scarcely credit what that villain did next," she said indignantly.

"Pocketed the coin and tried to take the horse as well?"

"Yes!" agreed Mathilde, her eye kindling at the memory. "Naturally, I protested."

"How did you protest?" burst out Temur, who looked like he couldn't hold back his curiosity any longer. Guy sent him a quelling look, but Temur was enjoying the tale far too much to pay him any heed.

"Well, I seized upon his arm and bade him take his hands off my horse," said Mathilde reasonably. "When he refused, I was forced to take more direct action."

"The direct action you should have taken," said Guy darkly, "was to call for assistance. Loudly."

"Oh, Rob came running out as soon as he saw us scuffling," Mathilde assured them. "And hurled himself into the fray."

"I'm sure," said Guy dryly as Robin nodded his agreement, his mouth too full of stewed leeks to verbally concur. Guy turned back to Mathilde. "And was that the point when you bit him?" he asked coolly. Temur gasped, staring at Mathilde.

"Oh, you heard about that, did you?" she asked, looking a little disconcerted. She fidgeted a moment in her seat. "I do understand that was not quite proper conduct for a fight, but you see, he was four times my size, and I did not bite him until I found myself knocked to the ground."

"Knocked to the ground?" repeated Guy carefully. He placed down his knife.

"She bit his ankle," said Robin, swallowing down his mouthful. "And didn't he roar?" He grinned.

"I sank my teeth in as far as they would go," said Mathilde, nodding with quiet pride. "I spat out a mouthful of blood after. Mind you," she conceded, "some of it might have been mine, for he kicked me off so violently, my teeth rattled in my head!" They both laughed, and Temur joined in, but Guy pushed his plate away, his appetite suddenly gone.

"Would you recognize him if you saw him again?" he asked grimly.

"Oh certainly," said Mathilde, dabbing her mouth delicately with a napkin. "So would Destrian. He's a vastly intelligent horse."

"I wouldn't," admitted Robin regretfully. "Though both his eyes are likely still blacked." He inspected the knuckles on his right hand.

"Good lad!" said Temur, pushing the ale jug toward the boy.

"And when the carter started shouting 'Stop, thief!' at the top of his voice," Mathilde continued, "Destrian kicked him into the street, which only goes to show how clever he is. If only the beadles had noted who he took for his true owner, then we need never have been put in a jail cell at all."

"A jail cell?" spluttered Temur, plunking down his cup. Between them, Robin and Mathilde explained their unjust arrest. Temur's mouth was practically hanging open by the end of it.

"I often say beasts are more intelligent than people," Temur said at the conclusion, stroking his short blond beard. He started telling a long rambling tale about a mule his grandfather once owned. Mathilde and Robin were vastly entertained by it, but Guy lapsed into a seething silence. He found it hard to recover so quickly from the account of her assault and detention. It had happened practically on his own land! If he had known the full extent of what had happened, he would have had every man in that jail hauled over the coals, irrespective of station. The officials had been almost as culpable as the carter himself. If it had not been for that merchant's son performing his civic duty, then the story could have taken a vastly different turn that night. What if she had been flogged? His blood ran cold at the idea.

121

"Guy?" He looked up to find Temur regarding him with some concern.

Unclenching his fists, Guy reached for his ale cup. He would stay another half hour and then leave. Being around her was dangerous. He was feeling all kinds of unaccustomed things. She was churning him up inside. "Is there anything stronger in the house?" he asked, holding up his empty cup.

Prudence had just set down a bowl of fried battered apples and a dish of cheese.

"There is a fine large bottle of mead, milord, which was brought over to be used for a hot winter punch," she admitted with a frown. Clearly, she had meant to make it last for quite some time, thought Guy, seeing her reluctance to fetch it out.

"Bring it, and I don't want it mulled," he said, seeing she was quite capable of watering it down with fruit and spices. "I'll drink it as it comes."

Prudence ducked her head, he suspected, so that he should not see her vexed expression. He did not know what Waldon could have been thinking to suggest such a displeasing wench. The bottle was a large one, and once uncorked he realized of a particularly good vintage. He drank deeply of the first cup and offered it around. Everyone else declared themselves well pleased with ale.

As Guy refilled his cup to the brim, he heard Temur describing his wife Lettys's fondness for wine made of the wild plum. As the others chimed in in relaxed conversation, Guy drank deeply. He needed to be easy, not coiled tightly as he was, and ready to spring. Another cupful would do it. Another cup and he would be able to relax his face from its tight, grim expression. To loosen his rigid, hard body from the grip of this terrible tension that had overtaken him. Another cup. Another cup would do it.

14

Mathilde gazed admiringly at the broad, muscular back in front of her. She had been a little shocked at first, when Temur had stripped her husband right down before pulling the blankets over him the previous night. But perhaps, after all, that was how husbands slept in their beds? Temur was a husband, so he should know. Instead of gaping at the spectacle, she had busied herself tidying away Guy's boots and clothes as Temur had thrown them over his shoulder. She had to try very hard not to ogle the astonishing body that was revealed to her in tantalizing glimpses.

After that, Temur had bid her a hurried goodnight and taken off into the night, explaining that Lettys would be expecting him at home. Robin and Prudence had gone to their own beds. Mathilde had noticed Rob had the cat cradled in his arms as he disappeared down the passageway. Mathilde had slowly washed and undressed down to her shift. Then she had hesitated. Did wives sleep in their shifts as unmarried women did? She had no clue. At first, she had blown out the candle and climbed under the covers with her shift on. But as she lay on her back, her hands folded over her stomach, the darkness seemed to reproach her for a faint heart.

It stood to reason that if husbands were naked, then wives should be too. Biting her lip, she reminded herself that she was no longer the weak and pitied little mouse about court that she had been. She was a woman now and brave as a tigress. Sitting up in bed, she had pulled the shift up and over her head and discarded it over the edge of the bed. Then she had settled back down, her heart thudding in her chest. Turning her head, she made out his bulk in the darkness beside her and listened to his breathing. In truth, the bed was so large, there was no reason why their nude bodies should collide at all over the course of the evening. However, she found herself considering the possibility. The thought of it made her quake with both anticipation and fear. He was so *big*. She was so little. Would she not be squashed like a flea by that large golden body?

Her cheeks burned as she thought of the well-turned muscular limbs and the strange smattering of hair she had seen, which covered him in unfamiliar places. She traced the smooth skin under her own belly button. He had seemed to have a trail of hair leading down from his. Her breath quickened. If only she could have had a better look! It had been fascinating. Daringly, she recalled the fleeting glimpse she had seen of his actual manhood and caught her breath. If she was not terrified of waking him, she would have liked to turn the sheet down and take another look at it. Doubtless Temur had thought her well acquainted with it already, she thought wistfully. She should be, of course, as his wife of four years!

She had dozed fitfully all night, keenly aware of his presence in her bed. A handful of times, she had woken to find she had inched forward or rolled right into him. Whenever this happened, she lay breathlessly a moment or two, thrilled by his nearness, savoring the amount of warmth his big, hard body threw out. She was acutely aware of the fact his bare skin was in direct contact with her own. Where they touched, she tingled. Could he really not feel it?

But Lord Martindale had not woken once, alas. Indeed, he had seemed entirely oblivious to her company. Perhaps that was the mead. It must have been strong, for it had felled him entirely. Then again, he had scarcely eaten a thing for his supper. Such a big man should have a matching appetite, she would have thought, listening to his deep, steady breathing. Reluctantly, each time, she had retreated from him to her side of the bed. He did not reach for her once and did not change his position all night. She felt a slight pang at that, but the important thing was that he was here, and that finally she was in the marriage bed!

She sighed and looked around the large bedchamber with satisfaction. This is how it felt to be a wife, waking up next to your spouse. She wondered if she could edge closer to him without disturbing his sleep. Feeling greatly daring, she drifted closer to him under the covers. She could feel his heat even from this distance, and she shivered, though not with cold. What would he do if she plastered herself up against his back? Would he wake? Would he—*turn to her*? Her pulse raced. She ached to touch him. Would that be wrong?

Tentatively, she reached out a hand to trace his shoulder blade. His breathing hitched a moment, and Mathilde froze. Then the steady breathing started back up again, and she relaxed. She would not touch him. She would simply lie huddled close by, feeling his body heat. He was so wonderfully warm, even from this distance. He groaned and muttered something she could not catch, shifting against the mattress. Mathilde held her breath.

Then, suddenly he rolled over, and she found herself engulfed in a big bear hug and caught between a hard body and a firm mattress. Lord Martindale's face was pressed into the space between her neck and her shoulder. There was not an inch of her that wasn't draped in muscular male. For a moment, she did not even breathe, as her senses went crazy. She could feel him *everywhere*! Pressed up against her in all sorts of places. She fancied she could even feel *that*, his—his manroot, heavy and strange against her thigh. If it wasn't that, then she wasn't sure what else it could be. She lay there stunned, and blinking, hardly daring to draw breath. How he could still sleep was a mystery to her. She wriggled and found to her relief that she could still draw breath.

Doubtless, she thought with trepidation, he would wake before long. Something stirred against her, and Mathilde stifled a gasp. What was that? Her brain raced. It was definitely in the same area as his manroot. She forced herself to exhale. Everywhere else he was still as a statue. Was that—was that his body *reacting* to her? Her education in such matters was vague, to say the least, but she had some hazy notions how everything worked. If it *was* his body recognizing that hers lay beneath him, was that not a good and positive thing? Strangely, Old Helga's words about pulsing sap flashed into her brain, and she flushed. But maybe, by lying with him like this, she was watering his *seed* somehow. If his sleeping body could recognize her as his wife, did it not make sense that his waking mind would soon follow suit? She felt quite giddy at the notion.

Forcing herself to steady her shallow breathing, she noticed with consternation the alarming degree that her sensitive nipples had hardened against his chest. His chest hair almost seemed to be stimulating them. They must be poking right into him! Her stomach fluttered strangely too. And lower. She gulped as the trembling in her body seemed to extend out from those areas. Was this her own body reacting to his proximity? Truly, the human body was a wonderful thing! Biting her lip, she forced her eyes to close and her breathing to continue with its steady rise and fall, content to glory in the feel of his embrace.

It must have been about a half hour later that Lord Martindale's head lifted from the crook of her neck, and he gazed blearily down at her.

"Good morning, my lord," she murmured, blushing rosily.

The expression in his eyes went from blank to shocked in an instant. He levered himself up and off her, rolling to the side. Mathilde turned her head to watch with interest as he sat on the

126

edge of the bed. How was his skin so tanned, she wondered, when the north was so bitterly cold? As if he could feel her eyes on him, he turned to look at her over his shoulder. Mathilde gave him an encouraging smile. He cleared his throat and looked hastily away. Why did he look like that? she wondered as her heart sank. He looked, quite frankly, appalled.

"Is anything wrong, my lord?" She faltered, with sudden misgiving, and sat up, clutching the blankets to her to preserve her modesty. It seemed waking in the marriage bed was a vastly different experience for Lord Martindale than it had been for her. He had a black scowl on his face now as he turned to look at her.

"I don't remember," he said grimly. "I was sotted."

"Aye, you were," she agreed, wondering at his accusatory tone. After all, no one else had encouraged him to empty the bottle.

He raised a hand to his brow and stared distractedly at the door and then back at her again. "This was not what I planned," he said. "I would never have slept here in my right mind."

Mathilde flinched as though stung. "Where else would you sleep?" she asked with an edge to her voice that surprised her to hear. She had been so happy when she woke this morning, yet he was churlish and rude. "We are husband and wife, are we not?" He gave a harsh crack of laughter at her words and shook his head. Mathilde gripped the sheets tighter. "I did not force you into my bed, if that's what you mean, any more than I forced you to guzzle a whole bottle of mead!"

He turned and gave her a hard stare. "Tell me the truth for once," he said in a harsh voice. "If you're capable of it."

127

"What do you mean?" Mathilde's voice rose with indignation. Was he calling her a liar now? She saw him glance down at his lap and then back at her speculatively.

"Nay," he said, shaking his head again. "I'll not believe it." He stood up from the bed, naked and glorious, walking across to the nearby chair where his clothes were folded. He stooped and pulled on his braies. Mathilde realized she was staring wide-eyed at him and forced herself to look away and give him some privacy. "If I'd forced ye last night," he said in a low rumble, "you'd not be able to walk."

For a moment, she was so shocked by his crude words, she could not even speak. Then her brain scrambled to her defense. Suddenly it was imperative that she wiped that look of skeptical arrogance off his handsome face. *Oh, he thinks me a pathetic little thing, unfit for purpose, does he?* She blinked rapidly to dispel the bitter tears. He was like everyone else. Judging her and finding her wanting. She took a deep breath.

"Oh, you didn't force me," she said brightly. "And you seem to forget you are my *third* husband. I'm an old hand at beddings." She sat very still as he absorbed her words.

"You—" he breathed, taking an involuntary step toward the bed.

Mathilde sat up straighter. "Yes, why don't you come back to bed, husband?" she said in the same sweet tone and patted the spot next to her. "You'd be most welcome." How she wished she truly were a woman of the world, she thought, quaking inwardly at the dangerous glitter in his eye. One who no man would resist. Instead of a foolish, thrice-married virgin!

He seemed to struggle a moment for speech, and watching him, Mathilde felt a sort of wild elation to have turned the tables on him. However, she didn't want to push things too far. Instead, she concentrated on relaxing her hold on the bedclothes, which she was gripping so tightly her fingers were white. She had no idea how she was going to get from the bed to her clothes, without exposing her nudity. She felt stupid and vulnerable sitting here naked, while he flung about looking like a thundercloud. If she wasn't careful, she'd end up blubbering again like she had yesterday, though then her tears had been happy ones.

Striding wordlessly to the wooden dresser, Guy snatched up a jug of water and started drinking it straight from the pitcher. She watched water trickling down his chin and onto his bare chest. He seemed to have a raging thirst, and her eyes opened wide to see it. Then her eyes dipped down further, and she gave an involuntary exclamation. His tented braies did not hide the fact he was hard. *For her.* She stared, rapt. Perhaps she wasn't so hopeless after all.

Once again, it was Old Helga's words that sprang into her mind. "You'll need to learn some new tricks," she had said. New tricks. "Are you sure you're up to it?" she had asked shrewdly. Mathilde nodded slowly. But she needed help. Where was that book Old Helga had given her for guidance? In truth, it had not looked promising, but she was desperate enough to try anything.

The jug thunked down on the dresser, and Lord Martindale dragged his forearm across his mouth. He stood there panting a moment. When he spoke, his voice was gravelly and deep. "I'll not believe it," he said gruffly, not quite meeting her eyes. "I've never broken a vow in my life."

What vow? wondered Mathilde, then inspiration struck. She had once seen Queen Armenal yawn elegantly at some edict the King had made. Somehow, even a little goose like her had recognized instinctively that the Queen had done it purposely,

129

in order to needle her spouse. King Wymer had turned quite purple with chagrin at the time.

"As you wish, husband," Mathilde said as nonchalantly as she could manage and faked a yawn, stretching back languorously into the pillows. When she glanced up through her lashes, to see how he had taken *that*, she saw it wasn't her face he was staring at. Glancing down, Mathilde found her full-body stretch had exposed her naked breasts to his view. Snatching at the sheets, she covered her front, hoping she hadn't ruined the sophisticated tone she had been trying to set.

Her husband raked his face with his hand. "You'd better call me by my given name," he said, his voice husky and deep.

Her eyes flew to meet his. "Very well, Guy." Speaking his name made her breathless. It felt dangerously like progress. Was she getting somewhere?

"You still want me to call you Mathilde?" he asked in a pointed tone.

What else would he call her? She frowned. "Of course, Guy."

He snorted, cast a rather cynical look her way, and started pulling on the rest of his clothes. "I'll get a bath sent up for you."

"Thank you."

By the time she'd bathed and dressed, he had already left.

Right, thought Mathilde grimly. *I've had enough of this. Where was that book?*

15

Guy was a sweating, roiling mess. Only part of this, he thought, his hands trembling as he threw his horse's reins to one of the grooms, could be attributed to the quantity of strong drink he'd swallowed the night before. The rest was all down to her. *Seductive little minx!* What the devil did she mean by arching her back like that? Displaying herself to him and giving him a flash of her perfect tits. True, he'd seen her naked before, but both those times her nudity had brought out his protective streak, not his lust. This time though… He swallowed convulsively. This time it had been different.

The setting alone gave it an altogether different flavor. She had been on a bed in front of him. And she had not been shy. He groaned, remembering how she had patted the bed, invited him to join her in it. He closed his eyes. But when he did that, his mind's eye presented him with the image again. That exquisite little body. The one she had assured him was ripe to give him an heir. He caught his breath. Could she…could she possibly be his *wife*?

Mounting the steps up to the main entrance, he turned over what he knew about that lady in his mind. Precious little, in truth. He had not wanted to commit to memory anything that dark-eyed devil had said to him, as he had coolly laid out the terms of his capitulation and disgrace. He had wanted to blank the entire shameful episode from his mind completely. The dishonor of being forced to take a southern bride to wife.

His cheeks flushed even now as he thought of it. He knew she was a widow though, no blushing virgin for him. As he had scanned the documents that Vawdrey bastard had placed before him with his bland smile, he had caught sight of the fact he was not her second, but her third husband. He remembered neither name nor rank of those who came before him. But for both to have died before she even reached twenty, they must have been elderly, he thought with a curl of his lip. Old and infirm, like the man Julia had broken their betrothal to marry. *Old and rich.* Unless, he thought with a start, they had been killed in the war.

Once inside, he made for his own rooms. "Send me up fresh drinking water and a bath," he barked to a passing servant, then started up the stairs. His heart gave a slow, steady thud as it occurred to him that he might have done his wife a disservice all this time, to think her mercenary and grasping. Maybe, just maybe, she had been as much a pawn in this as he.

If this female really was who she said she was, it was hard to imagine that pretty little face hiding any guile or cunning. He thought of the way she'd bawled her eyes out the preceding day. All over the return of some horse she'd lost her heart to, and barely even owned! Even the way she cried seemed honest and wholehearted. By way of contrast, he thought of Julia when she had rejected him so prettily, dabbing her eyes with a kerchief and making a great play with her damp lashes. Even at the time, he had a sneaking suspicion that Julia was enjoying her role and play-acting to the hilt. And he had thought himself in love with her at that point.

Throwing back the door to his bedchamber, he flung himself across the room, staring down out of the window at the courtyard below. Could this woman truly be who she said she was? And if so…if so, would that be so very terrible after all? If she *had* been as much a victim as he, then blaming her was unjust. After all, she could not help in which part of the kingdom she had been born.

Could she have married at seventeen and then lost her first husband on the battlefield? If so, who was he to judge her for remarrying? He was not naive enough to imagine that most noblewomen were given much choice when it came to matrimony. She was young and beautiful. His throat was suddenly dry at the thought of how lovely. Even her hacked-off, chin-length hair could not obscure her loveliness.

He rubbed his stubble, wondering how she would look in clothes that actually fit her. Not a fraction as good as she did naked, he'd wager.

Could he really have spent the night in a bed next to her? There had not been so much as a stitch of clothing between them. He cursed his drunkenness for his lack of recall. But if he'd been sober, a little voice whispered in his ear, he would never have climbed into the bed beside her at all. And never seen that little catlike stretch when she'd arched her back and bared her lovely bosom to him. That really didn't bear thinking about, he reflected, as a servant entered with water pitcher and goblet. She set it down and scurried back out again. He poured himself a cup and tossed it back. He was parched, a sure sign of the way he'd spent the previous evening.

"I did not force you into my bed," she'd flung at him. Then he winced, remembering his own crude words. She had gone very pale at that, then very flushed. He wondered if that blush had covered even more of that sweet little body. What would he have done if she had bared even more of it to his devouring eyes? He shook slightly as he refilled his glass.

Would he have fallen on her like a starving man? He groaned and pinched his eyelids. He couldn't possibly have had her. Life could not be that cruel. To have possessed something that delectable and then forgotten it completely. *But didn't you do that already?* the same cool voice whispered within. When he'd married her by proxy that cold February morning? He'd secured his release from Wymer's dungeon, and then ridden away back home to lick his wounds, without even a thought for the bride he'd left behind. If she was his bride in truth, then he'd owned her for the last four years and never laid claim to what was rightfully his.

A knock on the door made him jump. "Your bath, m'lord."

A troop of servants carried in the tub and started filling it with jugs of water. He remembered that was how he'd left her that morning, to bathe. If she'd told the truth about their night together, then right now she'd be washing away the evidence of his pleasure between her legs. He turned back to the window. Could she have spoken the truth? Could he have had her when his defenses were lowered? When drink had swept away his reservations, resentments, and suspicions? Had his resolve been weakened to such an extent that his needs and wants had come to the fore? He wouldn't be the first man to be weak to temptations of the flesh.

He was going round in bloody circles. Then a fresh thought struck him. If he *had*, then that meant the decision had been taken out of his hands. What was the point in crying over spilt milk? If he'd succumbed, then so be it. What was the point in holding himself aloof from an unwanted wife if he'd shown that deep down he actually *did* want her? His breathing quickened. After all, what was there left to agonize over now?

He bathed, redressed in a clean set of clothes, and spent an hour going over estate business in his study. A welcome sense of calm had overtaken him. He may have acted rashly, even ignobly, but at least he could now stop torturing himself. It was almost a relief. And she had made it clear that he was more than welcome in her bed. For some reason, that was the fact that stayed uppermost in his consideration. If she *was* his wife, then he had accepted a former enemy into his life. If she was *not* his wife, then he had broken his vows and taken a mistress. A mistress who was possibly working against him in some plot.

Either way, he had chosen which bed he wanted to lie in, and it was hers. Whoever the hells she was.

*

Mathilde settled herself into the window seat, pulling a warm woolen mantle tight around her shoulders, tucking her feet up under her. She settled the book in her lap and took a deep breath. Right, there had to be some hidden meaning among this flowery set of knightly tales, she thought grimly, and she was going to find it out! Turning the book over in her hands, she noticed what a handsomely bound copy it was with its red leather cover and gold clasp. It seemed a little funny that Old Helga should have such an expensive-looking book in her keeping when she didn't read. With a shrug, Mathilde let the book fall open at a random page.

Glancing down, she noticed it was an illustrated page and then froze. *Wait one moment. Is that…a naked woman?* Mathilde's eyes nearly fell out of her head as she beheld the image of a female figure flaunting her nudity before a knight reclining nearby on a bed. *She appeared before him arrayed in a gown so thin, that it hid nothing of her feminine splendor*, she read in astonishment. Indeed, in the picture, the lady's shift was entirely see-through.

Mathilde blinked. She certainly did *not* remember this episode from Sir Maurency's tales! Gazing at the picture, Mathilde's scandalized eyes could clearly see the female's nipples and the feminine hair between her legs! *What manner of book is this?* She flipped back to the beginning of the book, seeking the title page. "*The Tales of Sir Maurency of Jorde*," she read. So her eyes had *not* deceived her yesterday. Mathilde frowned. From what she could remember, Sir Maurency was a saintly individual whose dealings with women had been blameless in the extreme.

135

Perhaps, she thought, in this version there was an additional tale, where some wicked woman tried to tempt the pure knight? If so, whispered a little voice in her head, maybe she *could* learn some new tricks from this book. Mathilde caught her breath at the thought of it. Then her face fell. But Sir Maurency was bound to resist. He was such a moral paragon. With a sigh, she flipped to the first page, anticipating what she remembered of Sir Maurency's exemplary childhood. From what she could recall, it involved much gentle persuasion to all and sundry to see the error of their ways through his own shining example. Mathilde's nurse had been very fond of stories of saintly children. She had hammered them home to the infant Mathilde on a regular basis.

The Seduction of a Virtuous Knight by a Lusty Wanton Widow, she read for the first line and stopped abruptly. *What?* Her heart thudding, she scanned the rest of the page. Even from the first few paragraphs, she could see this was *not The Tales of Sir Maurency of Jorde*. It was a different story altogether. Clearly, the binding cunningly concealed an entirely different book beneath its cover! The title page was to mislead people as to its contents. She exhaled a pent-up breath and thought back to Old Helga's query if she was equal to her task and blushed vividly. Had Helga deduced, correctly, that she was entirely clueless in womanly wiles? Or had she guessed that Lord Martindale might need some enticement to perform his duties? Either way, it was a little embarrassing. She bit her finger. Still, she was right; there was no point in being proud. She needed all the help she could get!

Glancing around furtively, Mathilde opened the book again and flipped the pages to find another illustration. This one made her mouth fall open in astonishment. The virtuous knight had been surprised in his bathtub and the wicked widow was straddling him with her sturdy thighs. *Sir Pelomon tried in vain to resist her lures*, she read. *But alas! The weakness of the flesh overcame him once more and he was lost to the sinful pleasure.*

Mathilde's fascinated gaze returned to the seated position of the lovers. She had no notion that coupling could be achieved this way! Sir Pelomon's head was flung back, and his eyes closed as though in ecstasy. His cheeks were tinted a ruddy red. She could well believe he was lost to some mysterious pleasure between the widow's thighs, but it was the idea that it was the female who took the lead in their encounter that was both thrilling and shocking to Mathilde. *I am a widow*, she thought faintly. A widow twice over! What would Guy think if she approached him while he was in his bath? Her cheeks burned bright red at the notion. She would never have the nerve to clamber over the side and lower herself onto his lap! Would she?

Unbidden, an image rose in her mind of Lord Martindale's head flung back in ecstasy, his cheeks flushed, his eyes sparkling. How would that feel? she wondered, biting her lip. To know that she was the cause of so much pleasure? She daydreamed breathlessly a moment, though she could not get a clear enough picture in her mind's eye. Too much of it was an unknown entity to her, she mused sadly. She may well be a widow, but she had never actually been a *wife*!

She looked back at the image doubtfully. Would it really work that way? When Nurse had reluctantly described procreation to her all those years ago, it had involved a darkened bedchamber, a lawfully wedded couple, and a husband's rights. When Mathilde's subsequent marriages had involved elderly and absent husbands, Nurse had been greatly relieved on her behalf that she was to be spared such unpleasantness. But this widow was actively seeking out the act. Perhaps she, too, wished for a baby, pondered Mathilde. After all, the text had not mentioned her motivation thus far.

She leafed back toward the beginning of the story. *Sir Pelomon was the fairest knight in all the kingdom, with fine white limbs and curling locks of pure spun gold.* Mathilde automatically substituted this for strong muscular limbs and dark brown hair and continued reading. *Many was the maiden who sighed for his favor and tried in vain to catch his eye. Sir Pelomon was not to be swayed from his chosen path. He was dedicated to the higher pursuit of knightly virtues of chivalry and valor.* Sir Pelomon was a little dull, thought Mathilde, but even this piqued her interest. After all, usually it was the female characters who were consumed with virtues.

Another few pages followed regarding Sir Pelomon's purity of heart and single-mindedness. *When does the widow come into it?* wondered Mathilde. She dutifully turned the pages until Sir Pelomon's quest took him to an enchanted forest where he challenged a wicked giant and defeated him in honorable battle. With his dying breath, the giant bade him to return his sword to the widow of a man he had mercilessly slain some years previously. *"She awaits a husband who will never return to her,"* the giant confessed and then expired. *Aha, enter the widow*, thought Mathilde.

Of course, Pelomon considered himself honor-bound to return the sword. As soon as the lonely widow clapped eyes on the fair Pelomon, she was overtaken by illicit desire for the fair youth. She must have reconciled herself to the fact her husband had been dead for a while, thought Mathilde, somewhat taken aback. For she had barely batted an eyelid on learning her absent husband's fate!

The widow set about seducing innocent Sir Pelomon at once but was astonished at his unworldliness and purity. Her propositions barely seemed to register with him, and as such, she was forced to take increasingly drastic action to spark his interest.

Mathilde sat up. This was the point at which she needed to pay special attention. This morning she had intimated to Lord Martindale that the deed had already been done, but that was far from true. She needed to make it fact as soon as possible. Maybe she should take notes? She glanced about but could see no writing paper in the room. Impatiently, she dismissed the idea, vowing to commit the tips to memory instead.

The widow started out by wearing her gowns cut indecently low, revealing her abundant charms to the chivalrous knight, hoping to incite his lust. She sat at meals with him, spilling out of her gowns, with her hair loose, *shooting him many lascivious stares, until he could not fail to notice the whiteness of her bosom or the redness of her pouting lips.* Mathilde pondered this a moment. Her bosom was more pink than white, and it certainly wasn't abundant. It had never spilled out of any gown she'd worn, and she doubted it ever would, even with the lacings half undone. As for her lips, they weren't red either, but more of a middling color. She sighed. Unluckily for the widow, Pelomon was so dense he did not pick up on these cues either, so the lusty widow was forced to step up her campaign to another level.

Mathilde turned the page eagerly. This time, she started parading herself to him in his bedchamber, only half-clothed and making feeble excuses for her presence there. Mathilde frowned. At least she already had an excuse to be in Guy's bedchamber. The widow was really scraping the barrel with the reasons she came up with, in her opinion. A mouse had scared her, she had a tangle in her long golden hair that her maidservant could not free. To all these excuses to get close to him, Sir Pelomon seemed impervious.

Then finally, on the third night, the widow had a portentous dream. She cried and wailed, and Sir Pelomon was roused from his slumbers and forced to try to comfort her in her distress. She

139

twisted and turned in his arms, wrapping herself around him like a snake. In the confusion, her shift "fell off." Sir Pelomon found his limbs entwined with those of a naked woman. Finally, his cast-iron virtue faltered, and quicker than you could say "knight errant," his chastity was a thing of the past.

So, her own instincts had been half-correct the previous evening, Mathilde thought with faint pride. She had been right to discard her shift. According to this book, strong men were weakened at the sight of the female form. But what she should have done was pressed her flesh against his as much as possible, instead of keeping to her side of the bed. She frowned. Her own forays over to her husband's side had been far too timid. She should have been bold like the lusty widow!

Mathilde examined the subsequent illustrations with fascination. The page was quartered into four, and in each of the frames, the couple was arranged in some different licentious position. The first one was much as she had imagined, with Sir Pelomon on top of the widow, her legs and arms wrapped around him in a tight embrace. Mathilde flushed at the position of the widow's hands which gripped Sir Pelomon's buttocks with shameless abandon. The widow's back was arched as though she tried to mesh their bodies as tightly together as humanly possible. Sir Pelmon's face was buried in the widow's neck in an attitude that reminded Mathilde of that very morning. Guy had lain like that atop of her. If she had wrapped her legs around his back and grasped his buttocks, would he have submitted to desire like Sir Pelomon? An image of his backside when he had walked across the bedroom floor that morning flashed into her mind, and she nearly gasped aloud. Would she ever have the nerve to do such a thing?

Mathilde gulped, her eyes wandering over to the second picture where Sir Pelomon sat upon the bed and the widow knelt at his feet. Her face was pressed into his lap, Mathilde noticed with consternation, and Sir Pelomon appeared to have steam coming out of his nostrils. *What on earth…?* Giving up on that one as a total mystery, Mathilde moved to the next where the widow was back on the bed, on her hands and knees this time, and Sir Pelomon was pressed up behind her, his hands grasping her waist. *Surely not?* A suspicion entered her mind, but she dismissed it almost instantly. Surely a man would never do such a thing? A beast was one thing, but never a man! She frowned over the image. It certainly looked like it though.

The fourth picture was remarkably similar to the one she had already seen in the bathtub, with the widow astride Sir Pelomon. But this time, she was the one with her head flung back, and Sir Pelomon appeared to have his face buried betwixt her breasts. Mathilde stared. *He certainly seems to have taken to fornication like a duck to water,* she thought. Maybe if you got past a certain point then instinct took over. She certainly hoped so. A sound at the door startled her, and she slammed the book shut guiltily and flung it from her. It landed in the middle of the floor with a heavy thud.

"Milady?" It was Prudence. "I was wondering if you was expecting any *visitors* this evening?" she asked, pursing her lips and staring at some point past Mathilde's left shoulder.

Mathilde licked her lips and glanced furtively at her discarded book which lay between them. "I, er, dropped my book," she said weakly.

Prudence frowned and took a step forward, as if to retrieve it for her.

"No!" Mathilde burst out, springing from her seat, practically throwing herself on top of it. "I have it! Do not trouble yourself," she panted, scrambling to her feet. She pushed the hair from her face and cleared her throat. "Wh-what was it you were asking me?"

Prudence stared at her now as if she were quite mad. "For supper, milady," she said sharply. "Are you expecting guests, or will the leftovers of the game pie do?"

"I hope my husband may call around," admitted Mathilde wistfully. "But he may not." Prudence gave a start. "H-he may be too busy," Mathilde explained and wondered why the maid was staring at her like that.

"Lord Martindale?" asked Prudence in an odd tone.

"Yes, was that not what I said?" Mathilde gave herself a small shake. She needed to pull herself together. "I fear I got a little lost in my book," she explained, hoping that would explain her scattered wits. She hugged the wicked book to her stomach.

Prudence gave a short nod. "I'll make a new pie, milady. Right away."

"Oh, but you needn't trouble yourself," Mathilde said hastily. "It may well just be Robin and me for supper. I would not want you to needlessly—"

"No trouble, milady," said Prudence loudly. "I hope as I always know what's due to my own mistress." She dropped into a spontaneous curtsey that took Mathilde entirely by surprise. Now that she thought of it, she didn't think she'd seen Prudence curtsey once since they had been introduced.

Returning to her window seat, Mathilde took up her book to find out what happened next with the lusty widow. She was a bit disappointed to find that the next morning, Sir Pelomon heartily repented his actions. Had she been expecting him and the widow to live happily ever after? It seemed this was not that sort of book. Mathilde read on. Sir Pelomon determined to leave the widow's castle the very next morning, and the lady seemed to accept his decision with equanimity. Riding resolutely away, the widow waved him off with her handkerchief from the highest tower. Sir Pelemon vowed he would ne'er fall prey to such wickedness again, but alas his soul was now besmirched, and it almost seemed as though others could tell.

At the next tavern, the ruddy landlady slipped a hand in Sir Pelomon's breeches, fondling and telling him how *"well-built and mighty a member he possessed."* As Sir Pelomon struggled to contain his no longer innocent reaction, the landlady bent over his bed, hitched up her skirts and invited him to slake his lusts on her ample body. Her own husband was sadly incapacitated, and she longed for the touch of a man.

Clearly from the illustration, Sir Pelomon was fired up from the view afforded him between the landlady's generous thighs, for he fell upon her with ravenous, awakened appetites. Mathilde's eyebrows rose. Now that he had sampled the forbidden fruit, it seemed it would never be as easy for him to live a blameless life again. Once again, in the aftermath, Sir Pelomon bitterly reproached himself, but Mathilde was starting to suspect that a pattern was emerging.

Biting the side of her mouth, Mathilde found herself wondering if Sir Pelomon was really the victim as the book portrayed him to be. Should he not be firm in his resolve and simply barricade his door against all these wanton women? On the next page there were several illustrations of him bending the cushiony body of the landlady over every stick of furniture in his bedchamber and even rutting her upright against the wall. The landlady's mouth was wide open as though she yelled her pleasure for all to hear. The positions of their couplings were varied. Mathilde's cheeks burned red.

A sneaking suspicion entered her mind, and she flipped quickly through the rest of the pages. Sure enough it looked like the rest of the book consisted of Sir Pelomon's many various amorous adventures. In amazement, Mathilde wondered just how many times a virtuous knight could be seduced. Slowly she closed the book. She fancied she was too much of a beginner to be reading the advanced stuff. She needed to stick with the basics for now. It seemed to her that the first story was the one that would prove the most useful to her present circumstances.

Now, what devices had the lusty widow had at her disposal? *A very fine see-through shift.* Mathilde thought of the only one she owned at present and frowned. It was of a rather coarse linen, and she doubted very much that anything could be seen through it. *Low cut gowns a-plenty*, she remembered, thinking back to the story. Well, again, at present all she had was the gown she was wearing which was more designed to keep one warm than desirable. Mathilde tapped her chin thoughtfully. It seemed she was badly in need of some new clothes. *Tangled hair*, she thought, remembering the story, *a misplaced mouse.* Well, her own hair was so wavy these days it often knotted, and she could always feign a mouse's presence. *What else?*

She reopened the pages and turned back to the beginning. A quick scan told her the only other discernible factors were the widow's own unquenchable wish to seduce Pelomon and a desirable female form. While Mathilde was confident of her own burning desire to be a true wife to her husband, she was a tad less certain that her body was the sort men lusted after. She glanced down doubtfully at her own small figure. No one had ever mentioned it if it was.

She thought of court, her only frame of reference. Lenora Montmayne was widely considered the most beauteous maiden in all Karadok, but she seemed to inspire courtly admiration over anything else. Mathilde had never heard tell of even a whiff of scandalous rumor about her conduct with her suitors, who all tended to be eminently respectable. Besides, Lenora was likely very well chaperoned when she was escorted.

Helen Cecil, on the other hand, was not so respectable and said to be the King's current mistress. She was perhaps a little earthier in her appeal, Mathilde considered. Helen had a bold, appraising way of looking men in the eye when she spoke to them, and she threw back her head when she gave her full-bodied laugh. Mathilde had seen her reach out and touch a sleeve fleetingly when she stood conversing with powerful men. She did not hang on to their words in a fawning manner, it was more an appreciative look in her flashing eyes. She liked the company of men, and she did not care to hide the fact behind a demure expression or modest gaze. Sometimes, she threw her words at them like a challenge, by turn mocking and then admiring them. She kept them on them on their toes. Men probably found Helen Cecil seductive, Mathilde thought with sudden conviction. She bet Helen knew a few tricks to incite a man. Maybe she had even used them to ensnare the King's favor? She had never really considered such things before.

In truth, Mathilde had not much cared for Helen. By the same token, she was sure Helen herself had no good opinion of Mathilde. She would have dismissed her as a total nonentity. Helen was not the sort to have female friends; she did not join in with the tapestry circles, or the various friend groups that appreciated the arts. Mathilde did not think she had ever seen her much about with any women, apart from her sister, Jane, who by contrast was rather quiet and had recently become one of the Queen's ladies-in-waiting.

Would Guy think Helen Cecil was attractive? Mathilde wondered with a pang. She fancied she already knew the answer. Biting her lip, Mathilde devoutly wished she had spent more time observing the bold Helen, instead of looking away from her bright flame. But Mathilde had always kept to the

145

quiet corners at court, creeping about like a little mouse. To be honest, she wasn't sure such tricks would work for one such as she. With a sigh, she wondered where she could hide *The Seduction of a Virtuous Knight by a Lusty Wanton Widow*. It would not do to have anyone come across such a book by accident. Climbing the stairs to her room, she hid it in one of the many sections of a large carved chest at the foot of the bed. It had certainly given her plenty to think about, she reflected, sitting back on her heels. But did she have the nerve to put any of it into practice?

16

I will not go to her, Guy resolved grimly. He had been distracted all day, and he wasn't the only one who had noticed it. At midday he, Firmin, and Temur went to pay a series of scheduled visits on his estate. He could feel Firmin and Temur casting furtive glances at him all afternoon. Finally, on their ride back from an outlying farm, they plucked up the courage to tackle him about the cause.

"You didn't seem much interested in what Hapland suggested about passing the tenancy to his son-in-law," Temur piped up. "Did you have someone else in mind for that end plot?"

Guy shrugged and noticed them exchange looks. "I've nothing against his proposal," he answered grudgingly. "Johnson seems capable enough."

"You barely spoke to him," Firmin pointed out with a frown.

"What's there to say?" Guy growled. "Hapland said he was willing to teach him. Why should I gainsay it? It makes no odds to me."

"It's not like you not to sound someone out," said Temur. "That's all. Usually, you take these things so seriously."

Guy gave a huff of irritation. "I took the both of you along," he said pointedly. "If you had any doubts, you should have spoken up!"

"I've nothing against young Johnson," Firmin admitted slowly. Guy turned in his saddle to look at Temur.

"Me neither," he said, glancing away.

"So why are you quibbling about my decision, then?" demanded Guy.

"You just seem a little out of sorts," said Temur cagily. "Not yourself, that's all." He looked as if he wanted to say more, but after darting a glance at Firmin he seemed to think better of it.

"I can't believe you went to her last night, Guy!" Firmin burst out furiously, as if he could no longer contain himself. "Everyone's whispering about you staying out all night, taking a kept woman!"

Guy pulled up on his reins and stepped into Firmin's path, blocking him. "What did you say?" he asked in a low, angry voice.

"Did you really think it would remain a secret? It's the talk of the place!"

"I never said anything!" Temur interjected in alarm, but Guy ignored him. He already knew neither Waldon nor Temur would have gossiped.

"She's the enemy and you know it!" Firmin shouted, grabbing at his own reins to control his skittish horse. "Some emissary of your southern bitch of a wife, or worse!"

"If I can keep a civil tongue in my head when it comes to her, then I'm damned sure you will, Firmin," Guy roared.

"A civil tongue? You took her to your bed last night!" Firmin spluttered as his horse slipped on the icy path. "And soon everyone will know of it!" he added bitterly as his horse righted itself.

"I don't give a damn!" spat Guy, wheeling his horse about. "Let them know of it! It's my business and no one else's."

They stared at each other, breathing hard. Their breath hung about them in icy clouds.

"If your father only knew! A southerner at Acton March," Firmin spat. To his surprise Guy found the words no longer held the sting they should.

"We lost the war, after ten long years of fighting," he said tightly. "Call him the southern king all you want. Wymer's colors fly over all Karadok now. The Blechmarshes are done. My father's dead. You'd best wake up to the fact, Firmin. You surrendered along with the rest of us."

"The princess still lives!" Firmin stated hoarsely.

Guy fixed a steely gaze on him. "Una's been Wymer's prisoner some five years now. You know what happened that night at Sandysford as well as I. She refused the chance of escape with myself and Ulverston. It was her last chance. It's a miracle they haven't executed her already."

"Maybe they have," said Temur, breaking his silence. "And they're just southern lies about her being under house arrest."

Guy shrugged. "We played our cards in the whole debacle," he said, feeling suddenly tired. "And we lost. That hand is played out."

Firmin struggled a moment with words, then seemed to lose the will to speak. He sagged in his saddle, looking defeated.

They were approaching the house now. One of the servants ran down the steps to take the horses, but Guy did not dismount as the other two did. Strangely enough, Firmin's words had only cemented his earlier thoughts, that it was pointless resisting the inevitable. If his guilt was already decided, then why should he continue to fight his own will? Feeling the weight of a burden lifted, he tugged the reins, turning his horse about.

"I'll be back on the morrow," he flung over his shoulder and started off for the woods at a gallop. He thought he heard Firmin call after him but did not turn back. The fresh snowfall had obliterated any tracks through the woods, but his horse picked his way through the trees surely enough, remembering their previous path. He wondered fleetingly about the reception he would find. He hadn't exactly done himself credit the last time, getting drunk and then insulting her on the morning after. His brain skipped over the night he'd spent in her bed. He could not remember it and could only hope he had been a considerate lover. It had been so long since he'd lain with a woman, the possibility that he had not been gentle weighed heavy with him. She was so small and delicate. And he, decidedly, was not.

He needed to make reparation for his previous uncouth behavior. He wished he had some gift or peace offering to bring her. Would any of the clothes he had ordered for her in Wickhamford have been delivered yet? He had told Temur to specify the lodge for their delivery and to impress on them the need for urgency.

On arriving at the lodge, he led his horse into the now-snug lean-to, where Destrian and the bay mare—he had no idea if she'd named her yet—were stabled. They whinnied in welcome as he backed Bayard into a vacant stall. He rubbed him down and tethered him, noting someone had not been neglecting their duties as the floor was clean and fresh straw had been put down.

Letting himself in through the kitchen door, he encountered Robin at the kitchen table sketching out a plan on a piece of paper, with a tabby cat upon his knee. Both turned to look enquiringly at him.

"My lord," greeted Robin.

"Robin. Where is your mistress?"

150

"I laid a fire in the upstairs sitting room for them. She and Prudence are in there, adjusting some gowns."

Guy paused halfway through the door. "She had a delivery from the tailor then?"

"Aye, my lord. Gowns and shifts and cloaks aplenty," Robin assured him.

"And none of it fits?"

"Not to her liking." Robin shrugged.

Guy supposed he should not be surprised. After all, a provincial tailor from Wickhamford would likely not be up to all the latest fashions. "The stable looks good," he said, eyeing the boy. "You've been busy."

Robin nodded. "Oh, I know how to take care of horses," he said sagely. "As a squire, it's part of my duties. Fowls, however," he said with a frown, "are another matter."

"What's amiss with them?" Guy asked.

"One nearly got carried off last night," Robin said darkly. "Did you hear nothing?" At Guy's startled denial, Rob nodded his head. "Mabel woke me, but it seems the rest of the house slept on through the racket." He stroked the tabby, and Guy deduced she was Mabel. "I opened my window and heard a terrible squawking and flapping. There was a fox. He'd got over the fence and was trying to prize the basket open."

"They are cunning," Guy agreed, remembering his own dream of a couple of nights ago with sudden clarity. He had been the fox. Mathilde, the little unprotected hen. "If he'd got in the basket, I doubt he would have stopped at one."

"I threw a bowl down at him," Robin confessed. "A blue one that was on my shelf. It smashed all to pieces. I hope it wasn't

151

valuable." Guy shrugged. "I thought I'd raise the whole house! In any event, the fox ran off, and I fetched the hens in for the rest of the night."

"Fetched them in?"

Robin nodded. "They slept in there," he said, nodding toward the buttery. "Prudence didn't half make a fuss about it this morning," he grumbled. "But most folk in the country live under the same roof as their livestock," he said plaintively. "So, she had no cause to take on so. I daresay she'd have been mad as fire to wake up to the prospect of no eggs!" He pointed to the paper he was so busy over. "I'm designing them a new home," he explained. "But until I've built it, they'll have to sleep in here of a night."

Guy murmured some agreement which seemed to appease the boy, then started up the stairs in search of Mathilde. Outside the door, he paused a moment, hearing Prudence's scandalized voice.

"Oh, you've cut that ever so low, milady!" she protested. "T'isn't decent, indeed t'isn't!"

"Oh, well," Mathilde answered airily. "I daresay it is a *little* low, but I shall only wear it at home, when entertaining my husband, so it shan't signify overmuch."

Guy gave a soft knock on the door and then opened it. Mathilde sat on a sofa with a gown of scarlet across her lap and a needle and thread in her hand. "My lord!" she said in startled accents, as if he was the last person she had anticipated seeing. All around her were strewn various garments, and on the floor at her feet lay many scraps of multi-colors. It looked as though she had taken her shears to practically every item of her new wardrobe. He blinked.

152

Prudence was crouched with a mouthful of pins nearby. She also had a guilty, surprised look on her face, as if she had been caught doing something she oughtn't. She spat out the pins and quickly gathered them up. "I'll go and fetch some refreshment," she said hurriedly, jumping to her feet and scurrying from the room.

Guy watched the door close behind her with bemusement and then turned back to Mathilde, who seemed to be trying to stuff the scarlet dress behind a cushion.

"The—uh—garments I ordered were not to your liking?" he asked awkwardly as he came further into the room.

"Oh no! It wasn't that! The fabrics were just lovely and the trimmings very tasteful," she assured him tactfully.

"Then…?" He raised an eyebrow as his gaze swept over the devastation surrounding her.

"'Tis only that as a *married* woman," she stressed, "I would wish to have them cut in a style with a little more sophistication."

"I see."

"You do not mind?" she asked anxiously.

"No," he said, rounding the nearest chair and dropping into it. "They are yours to do with as you please."

She smiled nervously. "Thank you." He opened his mouth to try to apologize for the manner in which he had left her that morning, but she forestalled him. "Did Rob tell you about the chickens?" she asked.

"He did."

"And to think," she marveled, "we none of us heard a thing!"

Guy nodded, clearing his throat. "It is surprising it never woke any of us," he agreed.

Mathilde nodded. "Will you have your supper with us this evening?" she asked brightly.

"Aye."

She fixed an intent look on him. "You did not bring Temur or Waldon with you?"

He shook his head. "Mathilde, about this morning…" he started hesitantly.

"I think I might just change for dinner," she blurted, leaping up from her seat. Seizing the scarlet dress, she practically fled from the room.

Guy was just wondering if he had seriously offended her when the door opened again, and Prudence appeared with a jug of ale and some plum juice. She set down the tray and immediately started gathering up the scraps of discarded fabric which littered the floor.

"It will just be you and my mistress for supper," she said briskly. "Master Robin means to eat downstairs and finish his plans for the hen house."

"I see." He glanced over at the log pile. "I'll go down and fetch more wood in." He felt far too ill at ease to just sit there idle.

"Thank you kindly, milord." Prudence surprised him by looking grateful for once. "It will give me chance to set all this to rights," she said, glancing round at all the pinned gowns and garments that were littered over the backs of chairs.

He nodded and made his way downstairs, where he found Robin frowning over his sketches. His cat sat on the low footstool in front of the fire now, washing her face.

154

"Where did you find the cat?" Guy asked. He didn't remember seeing one at the lodge before.

"She followed us back from Helga's hovel," Robin said absently. "I wonder if a hinged roof would work better?" The last was muttered, almost to himself.

"Old Helga?" Guy asked sharply. *How strange.* He had only thought of the old crone for the first time in years a few days ago, and here was mention of her again.

"Aye, we stumbled on her cottage while walking in the woods," Robin answered, his mind clearly elsewhere.

"She still lives close by then," Guy muttered to himself as he passed out into the garden and picked up the axe to start chopping up the logs. The little cat followed him outside and watched him awhile, before growing bored and jumping up onto the window ledge, mewing for Robin's attention. The boy soon hurried to let her back in.

He cast an anxious look up at the darkening sky. "I'll have to get the hens in before ere long," he observed. Guy glanced over at the hens, who looked none the worse for their recent ordeal. "I told Prudie you agreed they could sleep in the buttery until their new house was ready," Robin said furtively, glancing back over his shoulder. "So, if she says anything to you…" Guy grunted as he swung the axe. Robin took this as agreement and headed back inside with a satisfied nod.

As soon as he had a sizeable pile, Guy gathered an armful and took it inside. First, he stacked up a good pile next to the kitchen fire where Robin and Prudence would be sitting this evening. Then he carried up armfuls to the sitting and the dining room, unsure where Mathilde envisaged them spending the majority of their time. He knew which room he wanted her to entertain him in, but it wasn't either of those. Hesitating a

155

moment, he fetched another armful up and tapped on the bedroom door.

"One moment!" He heard hurried footfalls and then the slamming of a trunk. "Come in."

Guy opened the door and found Mathilde swathed in a woolen mantle. "Are you cold?" he asked in concern.

"N-no, I was just trying on my new shifts," she said, her cheeks flushed. "They are rather thin, so…"

"I'll light the fire in here," said Guy with a frown. "And get it warmed up for you."

"Thank you," she said and hovered nearby while he laid the wood. "Do you, er, do you think it might be as well to have a small table set up in here for us to eat our supper?" she asked breathlessly. "As it will only be the two of us. It seems foolish to have so many fires lit in the house…" Her words trailed off.

Guy shot a look at her. She was practically wringing her hands. Why was she so anxious? The unpleasant thought occurred to him that it might be down to him. He was just worrying that it could be due to his behavior the night before, when her words finally registered with him.

"That would be most agreeable to me," he admitted gruffly as it sank in that she actually wanted him in her bedchamber with her. A warmth spread throughout his body, and he relaxed slightly. He couldn't have been so very terrible a bedfellow, he thought with relief. Not if she was willing to have him in there with her again, so soon after.

He was just coaxing a flame when Prudence and Robin carried in a small round table and two chairs, setting them down before the fireplace. Mathilde flitted around it, placing down knives and spoons as Robin carried up the dishes and Prudence fetched him water to wash.

Guy set about his ablutions as Mathilde took a spill from the fireplace and lit candles on the table. Noting she was still bundled up in blankets, he frowned.

"The room should soon warm up," he said as he dried himself with a cloth.

"Oh yes," she agreed absently and started pouring wine into a goblet.

"No wine for me," he said hastily, and she poured him ale instead.

Rob came in with a dish of vegetables and set them down next to Prudence's pie. "I think that's everything," he said, scratching his neck.

"It looks ample," Mathilde said with a quick smile.

"Shout for me if you need anything, but I'm going to fetch the hens in now," he said over his shoulder as he departed.

Prudence entered with a dish of breads, cheese, and butter which she set down gingerly on the table. "If that's everything, then I'll take myself down to the kitchen fire, milady," she said with a small curtsey. "I mean to turn my hand to some of the alterations we made this afternoon."

"Of course, but pray do not strain your eyes," Mathilde bade her. "Candlelight is not always the best for needlework."

Glancing up, Guy was surprised to see the maid smile at Mathilde as she closed the door behind her. "Prudence seems quite changed from the crosspatch of a week ago," he commented as he crossed the room and sat himself down at the table.

"Indeed, she grows more agreeable by the day," Mathilde concurred. "She is proving most invaluable."

He mulled on this as Mathilde cut into the pie. The only conclusion he could draw was that her mistress's winning manners had won Prudence over.

"Is this a large enough slice?" Mathilde asked him, looking up. He nodded, and she loaded up his plate. Guy watched her covertly as she selected him the largest of the roasted root vegetables. She judged his appetite fairly accurately, he recognized, with a flicker of surprise. Though at this precise moment, it wasn't really for food. He took the plate she handed him and set it down in front of him. She passed him a cup of ale and raised her own goblet of wine. "To a hearty meal, in good company," she said a little self-consciously, as though she had never made a toast before.

Guy lifted his own cup in acknowledgment and then took a tentative sip before remembering it was from his own stores. Knowing he would not grow sotted on ale, he relaxed back in his chair.

"Have you had a pleasant day, my lord?" she asked politely as Guy wondered at the fact he found it so charming to be in this intimate setting with her, exchanging small talk. Maybe it was the novelty, he pondered. Otherwise, he could not account for it.

"Aye," he rumbled, then remembered his manners. "Have you?"

She made haste to swallow her mouthful of pie in order to answer him. "Oh yes," she said, and reached for a napkin. Rather than dabbing her mouth with it, she fanned her face. "I can definitely feel the warmth of the blaze now," she said with a nervous laugh.

"Maybe you should take off your blanket?" Guy suggested, seeing her cheeks were quite rosy now. A pained look crossed Mathilde's face.

"Er, yes," she agreed. "I will presently." Reaching for her wine cup, she took another swig.

He wished she was not still so skittish around him. Should he say something about the previous night? He didn't want to shatter the pleasant mood by mentioning his boorishness.

"This gravy is very flavorsome," he commented instead, and he was just kicking himself for his own blandness when Mathilde rewarded him with a grateful look.

"Isn't it?" she said with a pleased smile.

Gods, she was pretty. He stared at her a moment like a lovesick swain. She had left off a veil again today, and her waving hair framed her face, reminding him of a stained-glass window he had seen once at the cathedral at Great Naunton. He could not remember the subject, doubtless some saint or ethereal figure. Then, biting her lip, she shrugged off her blanket and all thoughts of divine beauty fled. Guy's jaw dropped. *Holy hells!* He stared like a fool at her exposed shoulders and décolletage. The scarlet gown seemed barely to cover her nipples. Was she even wearing a shift underneath it? He swallowed and reached for his ale with a hand that shook.

"Is that one of your new gowns?" he asked in a croak. No wonder she said they all needed alteration! They were scarcely decent! He could feel his eyes starting from his head.

"Yes," she answered breathily. "Do you like it?"

Guy could not answer for a moment. His head pounded. His throat was dry. Unbidden, the image of her perfect, high breasts rose in his head, when she had afforded him a glimpse of them

159

that very morning. Her little nipples had been a dusky pink. He gulped a mouthful of ale.

"There's not much to it," he answered raspily. Her face fell. He was a fucking idiot.

"Oh, well…" Her words trailed off. "At court some ladies wear their necklines like this," she said self-consciously. She placed a hand across the swell of her breasts, and Guy made an involuntary sound of protest in his throat. She looked up quickly. "Perhaps if I was wearing a necklace it would look a little more acceptable," she ventured. "I can—"

"No!" he objected when she started to rise from her seat.

She turned slightly. "I don't have any jewelry with me, but perhaps a scarf—"

"Don't cover up on my account," he said gruffly and almost swore. She sank back into her seat, staring fixedly down at her plate. He closed his eyes briefly as his mind raced with how to make reparation for his ineptness. He was so badly rattled at this point that he could only think of honesty. "You're very beautiful," he said abruptly. "I'm just not used to such company. In truth, I'm overwhelmed by it."

She gasped and looked up at that, their gazes clashing. Whatever she saw in his eyes seemed to embolden her, for she squared her shoulders and smiled again, her dimples flashing at him from her cheeks. *Gods, that smile.* He felt dazzled and befuddled by it. He longed to kiss that mouth, those pretty lips right now. He had never wanted anything so badly before in his life. She would taste of wine and sweet, sweet woman, he just knew it. He'd never craved sweet before. He'd never had sweet. He couldn't remember now what kind of women he'd squandered his youth chasing, but they had been the wrong sort.

They had never made him feel like this, such savage longing and *need*.

He glanced down at his half-consumed plate with a frown. He didn't want food. How the hells was he even going to get through this meal? He had no earthly clue. Suddenly she gave a squeak and jumped up out of her seat.

"What is—?" He didn't even get the chance to finish his sentence before she dropped down into his lap. He drew a shocked breath.

"Oh, Guy…" She trembled almost violently in his lap. "I—I think I saw a mouse."

He stared at her uncomprehendingly. Her words barely registered. He just knew her sweet, fragrant, practically *naked* little body was pressed against his, her hands resting lightly on his chest, her flowerlike face turned up to his. He gazed at her lips, just inches from his. He needed a taste. Just a swift, fleeting taste. She would not refuse him, a starving man. She was far too kind.

With a moan, he pressed his lips to hers, his hands landing on her waist and gripping her there, convulsively. She gave a muffled sound of surprise, but then surged forward with an enthusiasm that stole all breath from his body. Her arms wound around his neck, and she clasped him to her with a willingness that made his mind go blank. When his brain stuttered to a start again, moments later, he found they were both still melded together, their lips sealed in a kiss such as childhood sweethearts might share. He felt himself quiver, though how such an innocent kiss could fire up his blood to this extent, he knew not at all!

Her lips were so soft, it made his insides turn over. Her eyes drifted shut and she sighed against his lips. He felt himself tense. She *liked* this. She wanted more of this. In that case, he needed to steel himself to give it to her. No matter how much he hungered to deepen their kiss, to swipe an arm across the table, clearing it of its fare, and throw her down on it and devour her instead! Instinctively he knew she was not ready for that. She would be scared by his desire if she knew how it raged inside him. He needed to rein it in and take it slow.

She shifted on his lap, and he winced. He had been hard since she shrugged off her damn blanket, but he needed to put her needs first. He was damned lucky she was even letting his clumsy hands touch her precious little body. He forced himself to relax his grip on her waist, then cursed when his hands shifted down to trace the flare of her hips as if they had a will of their own. Abruptly he wrenched back his head to draw a ragged breath. She gazed up at him through half-closed eyelids.

"Guy," she whispered. "Please."

"Anything," he found himself answering shakily.

"Please don't stop."

He swore filthily, and she didn't even murmur a reproof. Just stared at his lips in unspoken invitation.

"I don't know how long I can do this," he confessed, his voice raw. Already without conscious thought, his hands were sliding down around her sweet little rounded backside. He wasn't good at sweet. He squeezed her buttocks through the silky scarlet fabric, wondering what her bare skin would feel like there. He already knew it would be soft and plump, a pleasing contrast to her slightness elsewhere.

"Just a while longer," she pleaded, and unable to resist, he crushed his lips to hers. *Already, gentle is going out of the window*, he thought with a regretful pang. She moaned against

162

his mouth but didn't part her lips. *Gods*, he wished she would. He had thought only moments ago he would pass out from the sweetness of her lips alone, but now he wanted a taste of that mouth. Like the filthy beast he was, he drew his tongue along the seam of her lips and felt her gasp all the way through his body. Her open-mouthed surprise was too good an opportunity to miss. His tongue sought out hers, and when he found it, the kiss exploded. *Gods*, this was all that mattered.

This was his. He reveled in the sensation, his body reeling at the pleasure that flooded him. Her arms tightened about his neck, and for a moment, he paused to check there was no hesitation, no alarm on her part. Then he felt one hand slide up the nape of his neck and tangle in his hair there, gripping him tight. No, she wasn't asking to be let loose. *Thank the gods.* He ravished her mouth, and the kiss turned carnal. He stroked his tongue against hers, no longer coaxing, but demanding. She shuddered and angled her head the other way.

With a jolt of shock, he realized she was now squirming in his lap in such a way that was exciting him beyond all reason. Would she move like that on his cock? *Gods!* He could scarcely imagine the pleasure that would give him. He felt almost wild at the notion.

Seizing her hips, he dragged her across his lap, to where such movements would maximize his pleasure. She stilled a moment and drew back her head, her eyes very wide. They regarded each other, panting hard.

"Is that—?" she ventured. Words seemed to fail her.

He cleared his throat. "Should we stop?"

Her answer was a swift cry, "No!"

"Mathilde—" But she forestalled his words by grabbing one of his hands between hers and lifting it with great daring to her bosom. He sat very still as she placed his large paw over the rapid rise and fall of her breasts. Now *he* lost the ability of speech as he closed his hard, callused hand upon the soft swell of flesh there. "My gods," he whispered.

She stared into his face breathlessly, as if unsure what happened next. He bit back a pained smile and slid his fingers beneath the scrap of silk defending her modesty there. Her little nipples were hard as beads. He dragged the fabric down to her waist, exposing the pink tips to his greedy gaze.

"Gods!" he whispered again and, adding his second hand, cupped her perfect little breasts, trapping her nipples between his fingers and squeezing them gently there. Mathilde arched her back and closed her eyes with a breathy moan. As soon as her questioning gaze was extinguished, Guy bent his head and traced her nipples with a swirling tongue. Mathilde cried out again, and he drew them into his mouth, one after the other, sucking greedily. She shivered at that and started to move again in his lap. He drew a shaky breath. Did she realize how much she was stimulating him?

Unable to resist, he dropped his hands down to her thighs, clasping her there and pulling her roughly where he needed the friction. After only the tiniest hesitation, she started to grind against the hard swell of his cock, and Guy gritted his teeth to withstand the fierce pleasure it gave him. *If we were naked, I could be inside her right now*, he thought with a shudder. Imagining the tight clasp of her body had him almost spending in his breeches.

17

Something clicked into place inside Mathilde's brain. Now *this* position was almost like the one where the lusty widow sat astride Sir Pelemon! So, when Guy pulled her flush against his… Her mind paused, unsure of the vocabulary. *The evidence of his arousal*, she supplied in lieu of anything else, and *urged* her to move against it… It was almost as if they were mimicking the act, but with their clothes on! She flushed at her deductive reasoning and bit her lip. If only she wasn't wearing the remnants of the scarlet dress, she thought ruefully, glancing down at where it puddled at her waist. The tops of her arms and breasts were entirely bare. Wickedly, she had removed her shift earlier and was completely naked underneath it. How could she make this work?

Guy's hot mouth was at her breasts again, tormenting and teasing her. She didn't know how to move to the next stage, and after the thrilling baring of her breasts, he did not seem to be in a hurry to bare anything else. She trembled violently.

Oh, how she longed to unlace his tunic at the strong column of his neck and slide her hands against his naked chest. But her stupid tight sleeves were shoved down to her elbows, trapping her upper arms to her sides. She could almost weep with frustration. Earlier, she thought, when she had wound her fingers into Guy's hair and pulled at its roots, she had been able to guide him to deepen their kiss. She flushed hot at the memory of the giddy rush of power she had felt. But with her arms trapped she couldn't maneuver him at all, and he seemed entirely riveted to her exposed bosom.

Her nipples were so sensitive now, she could hardly bear it. With a gasp, she remembered that morning, when she had felt his crisp chest hair against them. It had felt so good.

"Guy, please," she moaned. "Remove your tunic."

No response. With a gasp, she felt the graze of his teeth. If she did not hurry things along, she thought, biting her lip, she would be engulfed in flames and burnt to a crisp! She felt instinctively that some crisis was approaching, and she had not managed to move things along to their logical conclusion as she should have. The lusty widow had simply *fallen* out of her shift, but sadly it was not proving as easy for Mathilde. She could not remember precisely how the widow had managed to get Pelomon out of his clothing. As for Guy, he still had all his clothes on!

Then suddenly, she remembered the lusty landlady at the hostelry. Her seduction method had been a lot more direct than the widow's, Mathilde remembered. She had simply slipped her hand between Pelomon's legs and fondled him there. Mathilde could still move her lower arms. Did she have the nerve though?

Abruptly she stopped wriggling in Guy's lap and, ignoring his grunt of displeasure, dropped her hands to tentatively trace the hardness at the juncture of his thighs. The shape was bewildering. *Where is the end?* At that, he lifted his head from the valley between her breasts and tipped it back to look at her with glinting eyes.

"Don't!" he said thickly. "I won't be answerable—"

When she squeezed him there, he sucked in his breath, and she thought for an instant she had hurt him. Then he spoke, and she barely recognized his voice it was so deep and gravelly. "*Gods*, take it out. Take it out," he practically begged her.

Mathilde fumbled at the lacings. It didn't help that she couldn't see what she was doing. "Lean back," she appealed. Suddenly, he released her breasts and shoved her hands away. She was about to protest, but then she realized he was deftly unlacing himself.

"Sit astride me," he rumbled as he shoved braies down over his hips. Mathilde gasped, staring down at the hard angry-looking flesh that curved away from his thighs toward her. Finding her too slow, he started shoving up her skirts, and Mathilde felt her first pang of trepidation.

"Um, Guy," she panted. His hand seized her roughly behind one knee, urging it up and over his lap so she sat astride and facing him. "Guy!" His gaze snapped up at the panic in her voice. "I don't know about this. You're too big!" she blurted.

He followed the direction of her panicked gaze. "Was I not the same size last night?" he asked, not unreasonably.

Belatedly, Mathilde remembered her lie that morning. "Um, about that—" she started, but he cut her off.

"Still sore?" He looked pained, Mathilde thought.

"Guy—"

Hearing his sharply indrawn breath, she looked up to find him gazing intently between her legs.

"Oh gods." He shuddered. "Let me—let me just touch you, then."

Mathilde nodded, cursing herself for a coward. Her thoughts raced. Why had she lost her nerve now? Doubtless she was built the same as other grown women. This balking at the eleventh hour was pitiful. Underneath her brave new character, was it possible she was still a shrinking, timid creature after all? It was only rather hard to believe that they would…well, *fit*, she thought with trepidation, eyeing his unwieldy appendage. Fondling it, and telling its master how well-built he was for

167

pleasing a woman was the very last thing she felt like doing! Still, this was the new fearless Mathilde who shied away from nothing.

Taking a deep breath, she said, "But only if I can touch you too."

Guy's gaze returned to hers, and he blinked a few times and then swallowed. "Aye," he said hoarsely. "But you'll have to mind me, though, and do as I say."

Nothing could suit Mathilde better, since she scarcely knew how to do it in a way that would please him. The book had not been terribly specific. Greatly emboldened, she stretched out her hand to him and ran it tentatively down his length, from the tip to the root. He hissed between his teeth and held himself very still. She felt his rigid flesh jump beneath her fingers. It almost seemed to vibrate with its own life. Curving her fingers around its girth, she gently squeezed its pulsing breadth.

"Lightly," he gritted out. "Not so…firm," he rasped.

"Does it pain you?"

"Gods, yes."

She loosed her grip immediately, but the look on his face was far from relieved. If anything, he looked wildly disappointed.

"Are you sure?" she asked hesitantly. "Only…"

"I'm too close."

"I'll be gentle, then," Mathilde insisted. "I can be gentle."

She set her hand down very tenderly on the broad, swollen head and fluttered her fingers over the warm skin there. He cursed. She wasn't deceived though. His involuntary impulse was to strain toward her touch.

"It's very sensitive here," she whispered. And why was it wet? She dropped her gaze to stare in fascination at the bead of moisture at the tip. She felt wet between her legs as well. Was this their bodies readying themselves for their union? To ensure they would fit? She felt a flicker of optimism return. Perhaps their bodies knew better than she did.

He groaned raggedly. "You should probably stop."

"I like touching you, Guy," she said truthfully and watched the play of emotions across his face. He did not speak, only squeezed his eyes shut as she ran her moistened fingers around the velvety crown. "You're…" she hesitated. "Very well formed. Here as well as everywhere else." Her tone was admiring. *Maybe the landlady had been right after all.* His coloring was different here too, a deeper pink. She found it fascinating. "What do I call it?" she asked him suddenly curious. "I don't think anyone ever…" *Manroot* was what Nurse had called it, but she didn't want to say something hopelessly outdated.

"I'm not sure what you should call it," he admitted, his color hectic and flushed.

"What do you call it?"

He hesitated again. "My cock," he rasped. "But…"

"Cock," mused Mathilde. *Like a male hen?*

His deep blue eyes snapped open at that, his breathing ragged. "*Gods.*" He licked his lips. "I'll spill in your hand if you don't stop right now." His voice was husky, the look in his eye slightly panicked.

"Would that be bad?" she asked, genuinely unsure. She didn't want to stop.

169

"Move your hand down," he rapped out. An order this time. "I'm too sensitive."

With a sigh, she ran her hand caressingly down his hard length, reveling in the breathy groan he gave, the way his hips bucked, jolting her on his lap. At the base was crisp dark hair and nestled in them something Nurse had *never* referred to. She stroked them tenderly.

"And these?" Mathilde asked.

"My ballocks." His voice was strained.

That was an odd name, Mathilde mused. No wonder Nurse had not uttered it. She fancied she had once heard Piers threaten to kick Will in his ballocks. Now she knew what he had meant. Considering how extremely sensitive Guy was, she thought, listening to his shallow breathing, that would hurt *a lot*. She cupped them carefully in her palm, and he gave a harsh groan. She no longer thought she was hurting him though. Without thinking, she slid her hand back up his length and touched a tentative finger to the fluid bead at the tip.

"Mathilde!" He jerked upright, batting her hand away, and took himself in hand, wrapping his fingers around and squeezing the head of his angry cock, swearing furiously.

She winced. That had to hurt. "Why are you doing that?"

"I can't take any more torment," he panted unevenly. "It's my turn now. Open your legs wider."

"Torment?" Mathilde repeated blankly. "Did I not treat you very nicely?"

"Aye, too nicely," he growled. "And now I get to return the favor."

In truth, Mathilde could scarcely hold her legs open any wider, as she was fully astride him. Instead, she leaned back, resting her hands against his knees. He bunched the skirts further up from around her thighs to her waist.

"Gods," he said throatily. "You're as perfect here as everywhere else. *Exquisite.*" The last word was breathed as he dragged his thumb down through the light curls covering her mound.

Really? wondered Mathilde, biting her lip. She hadn't realized it was anything special. Then his thumb dipped lower, robbing her of all breath.

His eyes snapped up to meet hers, and he breathed out raggedly. "Sweeting," he said, and his voice broke over the word. "Gods, help me, you're so *wet.*" His words were uttered reverently, so Mathilde did not have a chance to be embarrassed at the fact.

His thumb passed through her folds and seemed to settle on a spot that zinged through her entire core.

"*Oh! Guy!*" Her trembling cry made him sit up. A look was dawning in his eyes that she scarcely recognized, his nostrils flaring. Had she inspired that look? For a moment, he looked torn, irresolute about something.

"I could almost swear," he said thickly, "that you're as close as me."

Mathilde stared back at him. She could barely think with his fingers playing between her legs. Her eyes drifted shut as she concentrated on the fluttering sensation in the pit of her stomach. The feel of his fingers, swirling around that spot that seemed connected to every impulse and sensation in her body.

"I want to—to put my mouth on you," he said unevenly. "Can I?"

"You m-mean to kiss?" Mathilde stammered, opening her eyes. Or did he mean to lick and suck her breasts again? She felt a frisson of alarm, even as her pulse raced at the idea. How was she supposed to withstand both?

"Sort of," he said oddly, and releasing her waist, he swept his arm along the table surface behind her, pushing all the plates and dishes to the edges.

Mathilde thought she heard something hit the floor, but it sounded muffled and from a good distance away. Then he was lifting her, placing her on the edge of the table and laying her back onto its surface. Mathilde blinked up at him in confusion. *What is happening now?* Instinctively, she went to close her legs, but he prevented her, hooking his arms around her thighs and holding them firmly in place.

"Guy?"

This hadn't happened in *The Seduction of a Virtuous Knight*, so she wasn't prepared for any of this. Maybe she should have read on further? She glanced down and found her exposed breasts heaving, her dress hanging around her waist in tatters. *Oh my gods!* In trepidation, she sought to meet Guy's gaze, but he was sat back in his chair, devouring her splayed figure with his eyes, his expression ablaze.

"I'm going to consume you, utterly," he rumbled with intent.

Mathilde just had time to utter "Pardon?" when he surged forward, his head dipping between her legs. She drew in a shocked breath, then felt his hot breath upon her in the most disquieting place. Her eyes widened in foggy comprehension. Surely, he did not mean to…?

"Guy!"

She gave a strangled cry, but his mouth was on her, lascivious and devastating. She bucked and struggled, but his arms were like steel bands around her thighs, holding her open to him. His tongue coaxed and dipped into her, exactly like he had when he kissed her mouth, and sent her mind reeling. All the breath squeezed out of her body, and she shuddered as he alternated between gently tracing her with his tongue and then sucking and lapping at her as if she were the most delicious piece of fruit he had ever savored. Choked sounds fell from her lips, tears started from her eyes as she lost herself in a maelstrom sensation and—yes, pleasure. Wicked, wicked pleasure that licked along her veins like wildfire from every place his tongue stroked and plundered.

Torment. That was what he had called her touch, and she understood now, as her back arched, and her fingers twisted in his dark hair, pulling and clasping, but never deterring him from his purpose. But it seemed her own torment was not to be withstood. It built and built and suddenly she went hurtling right over the edge with a startled yell. The next thing she knew, she was being dragged off the table, back into Guy's lap. More specifically, onto his—*what had he called it?* His cock.

She winced as she felt its broad head nudging into the heart of her, and then gave a gave another yell as she felt a sharp pinching sting deep within her, which was more than being simply stretched by its huge size. Her maidenhead had been breached, she realized, as Guy groaned and surged right into her. Mathilde sucked in a painful breath, feeling his large hands shift fitfully over her hips, urging her to sink right down onto him, feeling his hard flesh forging up into her until their crisp nether hair met and tangled together.

"Gods," she heard him mutter roughly into her hair. "I've never felt anything so…" He bit his words off precipitately. "Mathilde?"

173

She didn't answer. One of his big hands was rubbing up and down her lower spine, but it didn't feel soothing, more like he was trying to urge her to something. She was just getting a nasty suspicion that he expected her to do more than simply try to keep breathing, when he suddenly jolted, and she felt the strangest sensation of his cock pulsing inside her.

"Umm…" She lifted her head from his shoulder.

"Hold still!" he groaned. "I can't—" His head fell back, and she watched an agonized expression pass over his face. "*Fuck!*"

Mathilde sat very still as he gripped his fingers into her buttocks and shuddered against her. His whole body seemed deep in the throes of some kind of turn. She held her breath, then suddenly, she felt something very strange, and Guy gave a long, rasping groan and dropped his head onto her shoulder. Mathilde blinked. So earlier, when he had said he *was close*, he had meant to this crisis point. When he spilled his seed inside of her.

Oh. She sat quietly, contemplating the act she had just partaken in. She was no longer a thrice-married virgin, she thought, her spirits fluttering and reviving. She was, in deed and truth, now a *married woman!* Her face flushed with triumph, even though she was feeling at this moment rather sore and in some discomfort accommodating him. Presently, though, she was sure he would recover himself and withdraw from her. *In his own time.*

In the end, she wasn't sure how long they remained like this, but suddenly, she found herself swung up and carried over to the bed. She made a noise of objection, mostly because both of her arms had gone to sleep. He laid her down carefully and started trying to disentangle her from the remains of the scarlet dress, without much success. After struggling a moment or two, she heard him curse under his breath, and then he just grabbed it

174

in both fists and ripped it along one of the seams. Mathilde's eyes blinked open, but she didn't make a noise until he lifted one of her arms and then she cried out.

"What is it?" he asked with alarm.

"It's gone to sleep," she told him in a small voice. "The sleeves were stuck halfway down…"

He examined her closer, then swore. "Your skin is all marked here, you should have told me the dress was cutting into you."

"I didn't want you to stop," she explained simply.

He hesitated. "Next time…" he said warningly.

"Next time, I'll tell you," she promised obediently and he set about freeing her other arm.

"You need to get cleaned up," he said in a low voice. "I'll go down and get you some hot water."

"There's no need. Prudie left two clean pitchers of water for us to wash."

He paused. "You wouldn't prefer warm water?" he asked solicitously.

She shook her head. "No, it's fine," she said, rolling to one side and clambering off the bed. Her legs felt a little wobbly, but she walked to the basin and poured some clean water into it. Then found the soap leaves and started scrubbing her face and neck.

He cleared his throat. "You'll need to wash between your legs," he told her, then after an awkward pause. "Where can I find you a clean shift?"

Mathilde passed the cloth between her legs and then swilled the cloth in the bowl. There were only a few drops of blood by her

175

reckoning. "If you're sleeping naked, then so will I," she said, frowning. Married people slept naked after all.

He was quiet a minute. "You want me to stay, then?"

Mathilde turned around with a sharp inward breath. "Of course!" she said, staring at him. He looked, she thought, a little taken aback. What was wrong with him? She frowned. Why was he hovering there, looking all awkward, after he'd just been inside her body? Did he still think he'd hurt her unduly? She wished she had not yelled out so loud now.

She sent him an encouraging smile. "All is well."

She carried the basin over to the window, unfastened the latch, and emptied it out. Returning it to the dresser, she put a fresh cloth next to it and poured in the rest of the clean water. She could feel his troubled gaze on her the whole time.

"Come, Guy, come and wash." She patted the cloth. "Here's clean cloths for you."

Looking back over her shoulder, she saw him avert his eyes guiltily. He looked flushed and...*oh. Aroused.* Again. Already. That did give her momentary pause. She'd had no idea that men were so quick to recover. It wasn't all the way up like it had been before, but it certainly wasn't lying harmlessly between his legs, that's for sure.

"If I stay," he said, flushing, "I'll want you again."

"Well, and what of it?" she answered pragmatically. He looked stunned by her answer, so she tried again. "My maidenhead is now gone," she pointed out.

He rubbed the back of his neck. "I'd not expect you to part your legs a second time for me this night, lass," he said gruffly. "I only meant to prepare you for the fact this will be poking through the bedsheets all night."

Mathilde laughed. She couldn't help it. He looked even more abashed than anything. "I don't mind," she said.

"And you don't want a shift?" he asked with a frown.

"That would hardly be much of a barrier," she answered lightly. Besides, she'd be falling out of all her new ones, she'd modified them so indecently.

Leaving him to wash, she crossed the room to the bed and climbed on, a small smile playing about her lips, even though she ached in strange places. She had done it! She had seduced her husband, and now she just needed to keep doing it until he was convinced he could not do without her at his side.

18

Guy rode back the next morning as dawn was breaking. He felt strangely conflicted. The female he had left soundly sleeping was *not* his wife. He now knew that beyond all manner of doubt. Twice widowed women on their third marriage were *not* virgins.

It had been a wrench to leave her there, naked beneath the sheets, but he had steeled himself to do it because he needed to think. And there was no way in hells he could think straight lying next to her. He'd barely had a wink of sleep all night. His body had thrummed with awareness of her. His desire to enfold her in his arms was almost overwhelming. He'd promised himself that, as soon as her breathing evened out, he would give in to it and draw her body to his. If she was fast asleep, then his erection would not be an issue, as she would be oblivious to its rude presence.

Then she had surprised him by scooting over and snuggling into his side. His involuntary stiffening had not seemed to deter her. She had elbowed him, thrown a leg over his, and cozied right up to him. As he had lain breathless and stunned, trying to rein in his rampaging emotions, she had drifted off to sleep as if she had not a care in the world!

He thought now of her matter-of-fact manner as she had wiped her blood and his seed from between her legs, and how she'd laughed at his scruples. It seemed she was a lot more realistic than he about their new respective roles. For she *was* undoubtedly his mistress now. Acting in any other way was, frankly, foolish.

He supposed he should be angry. But when he examined his feelings in the cold light of day, he found no anger present.

How the fuck could he be angry when she had given him the most pleasurable experience of his life? His every impulse now was to cherish her. Even now, he was half inclined to turn his horse back and return to her. Had he been too rough? The choice of position had been ill suited for a virgin. He felt guilty for making her take him like that. How would she feel, waking alone after what they had done the previous night? Would she be scared? Sore? In need of comfort? He felt a pang and cursed himself for a fool. If anything, she had seemed vastly pleased with herself after the act, he remembered and had to bite back a smile. What was wrong with him?

She was undoubtedly a liar, though not a skillful one, as he had not believed her story from the outset. Not really. Her claims had made no sense. Was that why he did not resent her duplicity? There was something else though, something he did not really care to acknowledge. Underneath the jubilation there was a current of...sadness. Even of faint disappointment. The smile faded from his face. He frowned as he stabled his horse and walked back toward the house, shaking his head. Underneath it all, had he really hoped she was his marchioness? *Fucking hells.* He must be a bigger fool than even he had realized.

Now he was just left with the question of who she really was. Strange to say, a full confession about who sent her and with what aim was *not* his most pressing concern. After all, he already knew it must be his true wife at the bottom of it. That seemed glaringly obvious. Oddly enough, he found his top priority was to know her real name. He *ached* to know it. How could they have shared their bodies, when all the time he was calling her by another woman's damn name? He ran up the steps to the entrance hall and passed a servant hovering there.

"My lord!"

179

Reluctantly he halted in his tracks and turned back. "Yes? What is it?"

"A rider came by last night with a letter for you."

"Oh?" A deep sense of unease washed over him. Was this a mere matter of coincidence? Or was his true marchioness about to show her hand? His throat tightened. "Where is it?"

"In your study, my lord. My lord!" the servant called after him as Guy had made straight for that room. "The rider said his journey had been much delayed due to the snow! The letter is two weeks late in reaching you!"

Guy reached his study moments later and found the missive lying in the middle of his desk. With an unpleasant jolt, he recognized the crest as that of Sir Cecil Allworthy. Why the hells should Julia's husband be writing to him, he wondered, breaking it open and scanning the contents. He soon found out. It was apparently time for Julia's annual pilgrimage back to the land of her forbears. Which was odd, thought Guy, as she normally did not venture north until the spring, when the weather improved. Suppressing a sigh, he supposed he would have to meet with them and attend some damned reunion feast. What a bloody nuisance!

It was only as he reached the last paragraph that he realized the dubious honor of hosting fell to him this year. *Fuck.* Surely it was not his turn? Counting back the last three visits, he supposed grudgingly that it was. Strethneal had hosted them last year and Kirkby the year before. It was damned irritating, but there it was.

Cecil Allworthy was a quiet sort of fellow; he did not care for sport or entertainment and could occupy himself very well in the library. As for Julia, she enjoyed an audience and would generate a steady stream of visits and visitors. However, that was her affair. She could hold court by herself in one of Acton March's sitting rooms and receive all and sundry there. Guy was damned if he'd be drawn into the rigmarole. He would not act as escort either, he vowed. If Cecil was not up to squiring her about the neighborhood, then Firmin could do it.

He usually found Julia's attitude a little galling, in truth. These days, he found he could only tolerate her company in short bursts. Julia, whom he had vastly admired at eighteen, he did not find so pleasing in his early thirties. She was accustomed to speaking to him gently, with a melancholy, tender aspect, as though she did not wish to hurt him or give him false hope. Clearly, she still thought him the enamored youth who was keen to indulge her every whim, but that boy was long gone.

She was also prone to extreme nostalgia about the land of her youth, and the memory of Kerslake Castle, a place she complained heartily about when she actually lived there. He cast the letter down with disgust, and then his servant's words sprang to mind. What was that he'd said? Something about the letter having been delayed? Uneasily, he picked up the letter and scanned it looking for a date of arrival. *The seventh*, he noted with displeasure. That was in four days' time! With a muttered profanity, he scrunched the letter up in his hand and went in search of Firmin.

It was a good couple of hours before Guy simmered down again. Firmin showed a regrettable tendency to keep popping up with questions about their visitors and how to accommodate them, until in the end, Guy was forced to bark at him that he did not need to be troubled with the arrangements, which were a matter of indifference to him. Firmin had seemed shocked, but Guy had stared him down, until his steward retreated with his lists. Guy entertained precious little, and it was well known that he hated to socialize, so he did not know what Firmin could be about bothering him with such things!

In the end though, his black mood lifted. Even the imminent arrival of the Allworthys could not dent his sense of well-being overlong. He was supposed to be checking over an inventory, but instead his thoughts turned pleasurably back to his Mathilde. No, that was wrong. She was not his Mathilde. She was the delightful little jade who had tricked him into breaking his wedding vows. Except she hadn't really. Any flicker of resentment he might feel over her lies was replaced almost instantly with the fierce pleasure of knowing that she would only ever be his and his alone. She was a little liar, but for all he knew, his real marchioness could have some sort of hold over her, compelling her to this charade. She would have little choice in being treated like a pawn.

Her uncertainty, her innocent overtures the night before had all been real, and he would swear an oath to it. He could not regret taking her for his own, though it was the only knowingly dishonorable thing he'd ever done; his marriage vow, the only vow he'd ever broken. How could he regret it now? He had no idea what the end game was of the plot she had found herself entangled in. But when he thought about her being sent to him, the way she had been, vulnerable and unprotected, his blood boiled.

On her way to him, she had been assaulted, and she had been thrown in jail. In his heart he swore vengeance against his greedy bitch of a wife who would use her like that. *She must be some minor scion or connection of the Doverdale family*, he ruminated. She could not be a servant, as she was just too unworldly. Unless her whole personality was a complete ruse, but he did not believe that anymore. He couldn't.

He was restless at supper. Would she have expected him to ride over today? Twice, Temur was forced to repeat himself, as Guy was not keeping up with the conversation at the table. Firmin confined himself to one comment about the impending

Allworthy visit before Guy's sour expression curtailed that topic altogether. Then Waldon started talking about his visit that day to Wickhamford town. Guy was unheeding at the beginning of the tale, but soon realized all eyes were now on him.

"What was that?" he said, lowering his cup.

"I said he asked after you, and 'your young friends,' most particularly."

"Who did?"

"That young master Thurston, the merchant's son."

"Did he, be damned," muttered Guy, whose mood took a turn for the worst. He slammed down his goblet.

Waldon scratched his ear, looking abashed, Firmin merely disapproving.

"Wasn't he the one as stopped the carter from taking the Lady Mathilde's horse?" piped up Temur, not at all sensitive to any shift in mood.

Guy glared at him. "He was," he said brusquely.

"You should have put him in his place, Waldon," said Firmin, pressing his lips together thinly. "He'll be dragging Guy's reputation through the mud."

"It's a rare tale," said Temur. "If you only knew the half of it! Why, that—"

"That's enough," Guy interrupted him with a frown. Then he leveled a look at Firmin. "I'm not concerned about my reputation." And he wasn't. The fact he had a mistress was bound to get out. He wasn't going to fret overlong about it. Skulking around in fear of discovery would turn something sweet into something sour, and he wasn't about to ruin everything. Not when it was the first taste of sweetness he'd had in years. He wasn't that fucking stupid.

In truth, Temur was right. He owed Thurston a debt. He just didn't like the fact the young merchant was so interested in his affairs. He remembered the younger man's bold gaze and evident amusement when he realized his captive was a female. Perhaps he should pay Thurston a visit and make plain to him how things stood. Mathilde was not anyone else's business, save his own. Looking up from his plate, he saw all eyes were still trained on him and cleared his throat.

"Waldon, you'll need to get over to the lodge at some point tomorrow to help young master Robin execute some plans for a hen keep," he said. "They nearly had a fox break in last night."

"Oh, aye," said Waldon easily enough, but Guy could see Firmin was startled at him raising the lodge so casually at table. He'd best get used to it, he thought grimly. He wasn't going to lie about where his interests lay.

"How's that old nag of hers?" asked Temur.

"Destrian," Guy corrected him unthinkingly. Temur guffawed and Guy glared at him. "It's his name," he enunciated belligerently.

"You should hear what they've called the chickens," said Waldon with a grin.

19

Mathilde glanced out of the window again as Prudie cleared away the table. Night had fallen, and Guy clearly wasn't coming. *Again.* She looked down ruefully at the low-cut blue gown she had donned for supper. For modesty's sake, she had thrown a scarf around her shoulders to spare Robin's and Prudie's blushes. She had slashed the neckline to the point of outrage.

The only decent dress she owned now was the original dark green wool gown she had been given. She had taken to wearing that in the day, then for supper she would don one of her scandalous numbers and sit in the vain hope Guy would appear. It had been some three days since she had last seen him. Waldon had been over and helped Robin secure the hens and restock the log pile. Another delivery had been received by Prudie, of spices this time, and sugar. Mathilde had received a parcel of soft leather shoes and embroidered slippers with long pointed toes from a shoemaker in Wickhamford. Their fit had been surprisingly accurate.

Otherwise, she had spent her time mostly in the kitchen, which frankly held the fascination of the unknown for her. She had never actually spent time in one after all. She would sit next to the kitchen fire with a book or a little needlework that Prudie had supplied her with as her maid busied herself with household chores in the background. Sometimes Robin's little cat would keep her company, but mostly she was left to her own devices. Really, Mathilde needed a loom and some tapestry work to keep herself occupied, but she had no supplies and felt a little lost without her usual pastime.

She took daily rides through the woods, slowly on Destrian and briskly on the bay mare she had named Sabrina. Strange to say, she had never managed to find Old Helga's hovel again, though she could have sworn she had hit on the same route she and Robin had taken once or twice, she never ended up at the clearing. It was most strange.

Mostly she longed for her husband to make an appearance. Where was he? Why had he not ridden over since their night together? Had it not been as pleasurable for him as it had for her? She considered this possibility. He had seemed pleased, but perhaps he had been simply humoring her? Or perhaps, she thought anxiously, the novelty of an inexperienced virgin soon palled on a man? Ought she to return to Old Helga's book and consult Sir Pelomon's adventures for some further advice on the matter? The widow had taken good care to give Pelomon a constant reminder of her charms, lest he forgot them, but how was she supposed to do that when Guy was in another residence?

She worried her lip and bade Robin a good night as she mounted the steps with a heavy heart. It was growing heavier by the day. He could not want her as she wanted him, she thought despairingly. *Then you must make him want you*, a little voice told her. *You must find a way. You are not the shrinking maid you once were!* Fleetingly, she remembered her friend Willard's advice to her. To remind oneself that you are fully equal to everyone else. Nay, to tell oneself that you are better! *You are bold*, she told herself as she rounded the top of the stairs. *You are a fully-grown woman and a wife. You are the mistress of your own destiny!*

Now where the hells was that book? Robin had lit a fire in her room before supper, so her bedchamber was warm and cozy. Casting off her scarf, she hurried over to the chest at the foot of her bed and flung the lid open. It was filling up now with all her new possessions, and she was just lifting out a bunch of multicolored stockings when she heard the discreet knock on the door. "Who is it?" she called out, casting around for her discarded shawl. She didn't want to embarrass Robin with her breasts spilling out of her tight bodice.

"It's me," rumbled back a voice that most definitely was *not* Robin's.

Mathilde gasped and let the lid of the trunk fall back in place.

"Guy!" she blurted as the door squeaked open tentatively.

"Are you decent?" he asked politely before his eyes fastened on her scantily clad self.

Not really, thought Mathilde, straightening up and casting him a smile she hoped was both warm and inviting.

"I'm so glad to see you," she enthused, hurrying around the foot of the bed and approaching him as he slid through the door. His eyes were fixed rather lower than her face, she noticed, so her smile might not actually have registered with him at all. He leaned back against the door as she bore down on him, hands outstretched. When she reached him, he clasped her fingers between his and squeezed them, clearing his throat.

"I've missed you," she said as she gazed up at him and saw his eyes flare.

"You have?" he rasped.

"Oh yes." She blinked up at him expectantly.

"I've been…very busy," he responded after a heartbeat.

"Oh, of course," she said with a quick smile. "I'm sure."

"You…you've been well?"

"Yes," she said enthusiastically. "Only—" She broke off.

"What is it?" The swift look of concern in his eyes heartened her.

"I don't have all that much to occupy my time," she confessed. "The snow means I can't spend as much time outdoors, and—"

"What do you need?"

Her smile wavered. To ask for a tapestry loom now would seem churlish in the extreme after all he had given her. "Just—just to see you a little more?" she suggested. At his frozen expression, she laid a hand on his arm. "I don't mean to be demanding, I fully realize that your time must be precious—"

He gave a sharp breath, and then Mathilde found herself gathered up in his arms and plastered to his chest. His lips came down on hers, warm and compelling. She gave a muffled exclamation, and then threw herself into the kiss, wrapping her arms around his neck, sighing against his lips. To her surprise, she found herself almost immediately thrust back and set on her feet.

"Your pardon," he said stiltedly. "I did not mean to—"

Mathilde gazed up at him. He did not mean to kiss her? She fancied her disappointment must have been palpable as she struggled to get a hold of herself.

"Of course not," she said blankly. "How stupid of me."

"Mathilde—" A sharp rap at the door interrupted them. They both sprang guiltily apart, and Prudie entered the room bearing a tray of refreshment. She kept her eyes downcast as she placed it on the small table and then made a swift departure.

"Thank you," Mathilde called after her, one hand fluttering over her exposed bosom. *I must be quite scarlet*, she thought, cursing her awkwardness.

188

"I know I've shown up at an advanced hour," Guy started in gruff tones. "But I don't want you to think I expect you to entertain me in your bed," he said, flushing red. "'Tis only that I was not at liberty to come any earlier than this." He huffed out a breath. "I want you to know that I do not mean to neglect you in daylight in the future."

Mathilde digested this in silence. "Oh," she said cautiously and moved to the table to pour them both a drink. "I see." She could feel his eyes on her as she filled the cups. After a moment's hesitation, he, too, approached the table and lowered himself stiffly down into a chair. "Perhaps we could take a ride together on the morrow?" she suggested tentatively.

He gave a brief nod, accepting the goblet from her, and raising it to his lips. "If you like."

"Unless… Are you injured or in some discomfort?" Mathilde asked, noticing the awkward way he was holding himself.

"No," he answered quickly.

"Are you sure? Only—"

"I'm well," he said, clearing his throat and tossing back his drink.

"So, you are at liberty in the morning?" she asked. "And won't need to depart at dawn?"

He winced faintly at that. "I could come back in the afternoon, if 'twould be more agreeable to you?"

"I mean you do need to leave at first light?" she ventured, vowing to rise with him this time, instead of slumbering through.

"Mathilde." His voice was heavy. "I do not presume—" He broke off. "That is, I am aware that I have not done anything to warrant—"

"Oh, but you will spend the night here with me?" she asked anxiously. That definitely got his attention.

"Do you want me to?" he asked, staring intently at her.

"Of course!"

He plunked down his cup and gave a small cough. "Then I will," he said.

Why does he look so serious? Mathilde wondered. *And why is he at such pains to make it clear he does not expect his conjugal rights?* She wished devoutly she had taken the chance to scan the book again before he arrived. As it was, she would have to simply do her humble best to please him. Without thinking, she tugged on the neckline of her gown, trying to provide a bit more coverage. Then she remembered she was supposed to be seducing her husband.

"That, er, gown." Guy frowned.

"Yes? Do you like it?" she asked hopefully.

His black brows snapped together. "It, er, the fit…" His words trailed off. "It's rather warm in here," he said in a surprising change of subject.

"Do you want me to open a window?"

"Gods no, it's snowing again. Only lightly," he added, and then she thought he cursed under his breath.

"Guy—"

"What is your real name?"

"Pardon?" She frowned. "We spoke at the same time," she said apologetically. "What did you say?"

He huffed and stretched out his legs before him, staring down at his booted feet. "I want you to trust me," he said in a low voice.

"I do," she said in surprise.

"Do you?" His voice was strangely heavy. "I want you to know, that—that I understand you are under the power, the sway of another. But if you would only trust me. I want nothing more than to be your protector."

The power and sway of another? Mathilde puzzled. Did he mean her mother? Unsure how to respond, she simply repeated, "I do trust you, Guy."

He tipped his head to one side and regarded her a moment. "And you have no other name for me?" he asked softly.

Other name? Mathilde knew herself to be hopelessly floundering now. "Um. My middle name is Therese," she said, unable to think of anything else.

"Therese?" he repeated.

"But no one calls me that."

"Would you permit me to?" he asked, and his tone was very strange.

She stared at him. "But I don't want you to," she answered honestly. "I prefer Mathilde." She wouldn't even want him to call her Matty, as she had urged Robin to. When she looked at him again, he looked conflicted.

"Very well," he said, but he looked strangely disappointed.

"Do you not want me to call you Guy?" she asked uncertainly. Was that what this was about?

"Of course you should call me by my given name," he answered shortly.

Unable to think how else to respond, Mathilde simply took another swallow of wine. They seemed to have become mired in confusion all of a sudden, she thought.

"Perhaps I should go," Guy said, straightening up in his seat.

"Oh, please don't!"

"I can return first thing in the morning," he carried on as if he had not heard her. "I should not have come at this hour."

"Why should you not?" Mathilde sprang from her own seat and moved as though to bar his way to the door. "I don't want you to leave!" He gazed at her, looking rather conflicted. "Please stay." In the end, he gave a short nod and sat back in his chair. Clearly, he did not mean to take her to bed, she thought, casting about. Conversation between them was only muddying the waters this evening.

"Shall we play cards?" she suggested brightly. "I found some in the drawer earlier. It might be a way to while away some time?"

He grunted, not looking exactly enthusiastic. "What games do you know?"

"I know lots," Mathilde told him excitedly and received a rather hard look in return. "I always play cards with Robin and my friends."

"Your friends?" Guy asked casually.

"Piers, Gordon, Willard. They all taught me how to play cards."

He said nothing at that, but feeling his scrutiny, she looked up from the drawer where she was retrieving a hand-painted pack of cards with hunting motifs. "These," she said and carried them over to the table, placing them down. "I am not familiar with this precise deck, but they look similar to Huntsman Bold."

Guy picked up the deck and untied the string binding them together. "I remember these," he said. "They were my father's." He was silent as he shuffled through the deck. "It's called Hound Takes Heron." He went through the rules of the game, and indeed it was terribly similar to Huntsman Bold, to Mathilde's way of thinking.

He dealt, and Mathilde arranged her cards into groups. She thought she had a fairly decent hand. "Ten of hounds," she said, discarding her first.

They quickly went through the first round, which Mathilde won, though she had a suspicion he allowed it. Then she shuffled, and they started a second round. It seemed to Mathilde that every time she raised her eyes, Guy was watching at her. It really wasn't so surprising, she thought critically, that she was winning the game hands down. "Should we introduce a wager?" she suggested. That might keep him focused.

Guy's eyebrows rose. "Do you bet money with Piers, Gordon, and Willard?" he asked.

Something about his tone made her look up sharply, but his expression was bland enough. "We gamble, but not with money," she answered, shaking her head. "They are always short of funds."

He was silent a moment, absorbing this. "What sort of things would you wager?" he asked.

"Myself? Usually my mending skills," she admitted with a smile. "Or a penny, or a clean handkerchief."

"What about a kiss?" he asked.

Mathilde frowned. "None of them ever asked for that," she admitted.

"I meant for me."

"Oh!" She blushed. "Of course, if that is what you want."

"I do. And what about you? What should I wager?"

"A kiss, of course," she answered promptly.

He gave a startled laugh. "So, if I win, you give me a kiss, and if you win, I give you a kiss."

"Exactly."

He smirked. "We could just forget the cards and kiss, Mathilde."

She caught her breath. It just would not have sounded the same if he had called her Therese. "We could," she admitted. "But I like the idea of finding out the difference."

"The difference?"

"Between me kissing you, and you kissing me."

His eyes seemed to darken at that. He cleared his throat and gathered up the current hand. "Very well, let's start a new hand."

*

Guy watched as, flushed with triumph, Mathilde laid down a winning hand. He was not going to withstand much of this.

"I claim my kiss," she said, clapping her hands together.

Whose stupid fucking idea had kissing been? he wondered as he braced himself to withstand it without exploding. To his consternation, she jumped out of her chair and rounded the table to sit on his lap. Immediately, his brain leaped to the last time they had been in this position. He flushed, and that was before he noticed her practically bared breasts in his face. *Gods.* Tipping his head back, he nearly jolted out of the chair at the feel of her breath on his lips. He couldn't believe she would even *want* to kiss him after the way he had treated her last time, like an ill-mannered brute. He remembered sweeping the remains of their supper onto the floor and spreading her out on the table before him, and his throat went dry. Sadly, she chose that moment to lift her face back from his and frown at him.

"What is it?" he rasped.

"This may sound odd but…" She hesitated.

She didn't want to kiss him. He swallowed down his disappointment. It was hardly surprising. "What is it?"

"Can you—can you take your tunic off this time?" she asked wistfully.

Guy stared at her. "My tunic?" he repeated blankly.

"So I can feel your bared chest against mine. When we kiss," she explained. Her face was red as a beacon now. "I really wanted to the other night, but you kept your clothes on." When he didn't move at once, she added hopefully, "Please, Guy."

What? He gulped and started unfastening the laces at his chest. His fingers felt like thumbs, and she had to help him maneuver the garment over his head. He had no sooner discarded it over his shoulder than her hands were running over the expanse of

195

his chest. He had to bite back an exclamation at the feel of her hands skimming over him.

"You're so well-built," she murmured admiringly. "I like this."

He glanced down. His chest hair? Is that what she meant? He watched her lightly scratch her fingers through the dark scattered hair and felt speech was beyond him. Her gaze flickered up to meet his, and then slowly, deliberately, she inched forward and pressed her mostly exposed bosom to his wide, muscular chest. Guy held his breath as she expelled hers in a dreamy sigh.

"I knew it would feel nice," she said, then placed her hands gently on either side of his face. "I'm going to kiss you now," she said, perhaps realizing he needed a warning. He gave a short nod, his eyes dropping to her mouth.

Then her lips were against his so soft and sweet that Guy's world tipped sideways. He breathed in through his nose and willed himself to lightly return the pressure of her lips *and not do anything else.* Then he felt it. Her little tongue licked along his bottom lip, and Guy's eyes shot open. *What? Surely, she did not mean to deepen the kiss?* Then she did it again. He gasped, and Mathilde's tongue darted into his mouth. Guy's brain shut down altogether.

One of her arms was tight around his neck. Her fingers tangled in the hair at his nape. She was whimpering into his mouth, and the world just did not exist for him outside of the hot, wet slide of their kiss. The soft swell of her cleavage gently rubbing against his chest was not enough. He managed to insert one hand between them and grabbed Mathilde's already plunging neckline, dragging it down until he could feel those pink little nipples against his chest. Mathilde gasped, but even his lust-addled mind could tell it was with pleasure and not shock.

196

"Yes, Guy," she moaned, dragging her hard nipples through his chest hair. This was what she had wanted? *Nice* was not a strong enough word for it.

He was just considering how much of a wrench this gown would need to rip it clean off her when she drew back, her eyes unfocussed and her breasts heaving. "Time for the next hand," she quavered and went to lift off his lap. His hands tightened at her waist, preventing it, keeping her squarely in place. "Guy?" she asked uncertainly.

He drew in a deep breath. "Next hand?" he repeated blankly.

"Of Huntsman Bold," she reminded him.

It wasn't Huntsman Bold, but at this precise moment he couldn't remember the exact name. Instead, he licked his lips, still staring at hers in unspoken invitation. "You want to play cards?" He all but growled the words.

"Don't you?"

Slowly, deliberately, he shook his head. "No."

"Oh, then..." She lowered her voice. "You want to carry on...kissing."

He shook his head again.

"No?" she squeaked. "What then?"

"Can't you tell?" He rocked his hips. She had to feel it. His cock underneath her was like a steel bar.

"But you said you didn't want to bed me," she pointed out breathlessly.

"I lied."

"Oh!"

"What about you?"

"I…yes, of course! Though…" She hesitated, and Guy steeled himself for some condition. "If you could kiss me too, that would be nice."

"That I can do," he said, swinging her up as he lifted out of the chair.

"Where are we—?"

He hefted her in the direction of the bed, leaving her in no doubt of their destination. Once he'd dropped her onto the mattress, he started unlacing his crotch. "Take it all off," he directed, looking her over. "Unless you want it in rags like the last one. I want you naked this time."

Mathilde bounced up onto her knees and started at her own lacings, which were on either side of her bodice. "It would be a shame to tear it," she gabbled nervously.

He shoved his braies down over his hips and stepped out of them along with his chausses. Naked now, he joined her on the bed and started helping her lift the dress off. She was actually wearing a shift tonight, so that swiftly followed suit. Once she was naked, he allowed himself a good, long look at her. What he saw took his breath away. "Gods, Mathilde, but you're beautiful," he said in a voice so gravelly he barely recognized it as his own. She gave him a wondering look at that. "Lie back."

She sank back obediently onto the bedcovers, her gaze still holding his as he stretched out carefully beside her, bracing himself over her so that he did not crush her much smaller body beneath his. Far from looking alarmed at his bulk caging her in, Mathilde smiled trustingly up at him, and he felt something between a pang and a tug deep in his chest. His cock lay heavy against her belly, refusing to be ignored, demanding attention.

Instead of shrinking from it or resenting its impudence, Mathilde reached down to carefully pet his length. "Is this good?" she whispered when he hissed through his teeth.

He gave a short nod. "This is how we should have done it the other night," he said hoarsely. "If I'd known you were untouched, I would not have sat you on my cock like that."

She frowned slightly. "Is that a more advanced position then?"

He blinked down at her. "What?"

"Not for beginners," she elucidated.

Just then, her thumb stroked him down the ridge of his cockhead, making her words undecipherable to him. He groaned. "Part your legs, love. I want to touch you too."

At his urging, she drew her knees up and opened herself to his gaze.

He sucked in a jagged breath. "*Gods.*"

A rosy blush covered her whole body. "Do you really think—?"

He lifted his head. "What?"

She bit her lip. "It doesn't matter."

"Tell me."

"That I'm—well—*beautiful?*" Her words were stilted, embarrassed even.

"You're the loveliest thing I've ever seen," he answered promptly.

Her mouth fell open. "I…but…" She trailed off, then took a deep breath. "You truly think so, Guy?" Her gaze was shy but met his squarely.

He gave a short, decisive nod. "Yes."

Her mouth opened on a silent *oh* and she stared up at him. Unable to hold himself back any longer, he put his hand between her legs. She bit her lip and arched her back when he parted her slick folds and slid his fingers between them.

"Oh, Guy!"

Again, she was wet, so wet just from his kisses, he marveled, and lowered his head to take her lips again. As he coaxed her tongue with his, his fingers teased and toyed with her, until he slid two fingers deep inside her, making her tear her lips from his and cry out. It wasn't discomfort that caused it, though she still felt very tight, for he felt her body tremble all around him in a spasm of pleasure.

"Keep your legs open, Mathilde," he warned when she tried to close them around his fingers, "I've something else for you shortly that you can hold on to." Her eyelids fluttered, though he was trying hard not to be crude and refer directly to his throbbing cock.

"I want it now," she said, shocking the hells out of him. "Please, Guy."

"You're not ready," he gritted out. "I don't want to hurt you this time."

"You won't!" she insisted breathlessly.

"Ah, but I'll expect you to do more than just accept me this time, sweeting," he said in a deep voice, brushing his thumb against her pearl and making her jump and gasp.

"Such as what?" she panted, her eyes drifting shut as she tried to withstand the stimulation.

"I'll want you to fuck me back." Now that *was* crude, but he was too far gone to regret it. She gasped, but not at his offensive words. Feeling her tighten and shake around his fingers, he pushed them deep and watched through half-closed eyes as she quaked and whimpered through her climax. How could she *not* know she was beautiful, he wondered dazedly, as his thumb circled her bead, and her breathing grew less ragged.

"*Now* you're ready," he told her with satisfaction and dropped a kiss on the tip of her nose as he swiftly rolled over her. He concentrated hard on listening to her breathing as he eased into her, by small degrees until he was lodged deep inside her, where he needed to be. "Wrap your legs around my waist," he urged. She did, crossing her ankles behind his back. "How does that feel?"

Her eyes fluttered open, and she regarded him a moment. "Deep."

"Does it hurt?" He frowned.

She shook her head. "Just burns a little."

Burns? He swallowed. That wasn't good. "We'll stay like this until you say we can move."

Again, her face registered surprise and uncertainty. "You didn't move last time."

He blushed. "No, last time was— " He found himself at a loss for words. "It'll get better, I promise."

"Did you think last time was bad?" she blurted.

"Gods no! But I was…very inconsiderate."

"I don't think you were."

He gave a pained smile. "That's because you don't know any better."

"Oh." She appeared to mull this over before rolling her hips and making Guy grunt. "Sorry. I was just checking."

"Does it still burn?" His voice shook slightly.

She screwed up her face. "Not really?"

She didn't sound too sure, but frankly, Guy wasn't sure how much longer he could hold out. He was already hard enough to hammer wood, and conversing with a woman while he was deep inside her was proving surprisingly stimulating. Who would have thought he'd enjoy that? Certainly not him! "Try again," he suggested. Mathilde did it again, and Guy shut his eyes, breaking off a curse.

"Does it hurt you when I do that?" Mathilde asked curiously. "Or…"

"It feels good. *Really* good," he said thickly.

"Is that…how you want me to move?" she asked shrewdly.

"Yes," he groaned.

"And what will you be doing?" She sounded a bit nervous.

His eyes bore into hers. "Do you want me to show you?"

She nodded her head, and Guy gave a tentative thrust of his hips.

"Oh," she moaned softly. "That's not so…bad."

"I want to do it harder than that," he admitted and felt himself breaking into a sweat. "But I can do it gently, until you're ready for hard."

She nodded again, completely trusting every word he said. "Should we try moving at the same time?"

He had to breathe in and out a few times before he answered. He could do this. "Yes."

He wasn't sure how long he labored above her, giving only shallow dips of his hips, concentrating on keeping his weight on his forearms and not crushing her, listening to her sighs and the hitches in her breathing as his cock throbbed in her tight channel. He couldn't concentrate too hard on the sinuous roll of her hips or the rigid control he was exercising right now would snap. The effort she made to match his easy rhythm nearly undid him, along with the frown of concentration on her face. Would she strive to match it, if he fucked hard like he wanted? Probably not. He imagined her digging her heels into the mattress and throwing herself into his pounding strokes. How would her face look then? A trickle of sweat ran down between his shoulder blades. He wanted to know. Badly.

"Guy?"

"Yes, sweeting." He swooped down and kissed her jaw.

"I'm ready now."

"Ready?"

"For hard."

He caught his breath and stared down at her. He should ask if she was sure, as there was no way she was. He didn't though. Just started rocking his hips in earnest between her thighs. "Tell me if you want me to slow down," he gritted out.

She nodded, her eyes very wide. He could see gold flecks in the depths of her eyes. Or was he just seeing stars? His vision was starting to distort. There was no way he could withstand this much pleasure. It was too *good*. She uncrossed her legs, tightening them around his hips, her fingers digging into his shoulders.

"Guy," she breathed, arching up into him.

Oh gods, she wanted him gentler? Exerting control he didn't know he possessed, he slowed to a stop and paused, shaking with the effort to continue more sedately.

She gave a disappointed cry. "No, don't stop!"

He nearly collapsed on top of her, but just about managed to hold his weight off her. "Just give me a minute," he wheezed. "I can make it slow."

She twisted beneath him, inhaling sharply. "Not slower!" Adjusting the grip of her legs, she wrapped them back around his waist to urge him closer. "Faster, Guy. *Harder*."

Harder? He stared down at her. She writhed beneath him and gave a frustrated sob. She was close? She wanted it faster and harder? Hardly believing his ears, he surged forward, plunging into her. She cried out sharply, but even in his inflamed state, he could tell her cry was one of gratification. *Thank the gods.* He allowed himself three, four more hard strokes and then felt her coming around his cock. He could hardly believe it. Her pleasure seen to, he allowed his own needs to come to the fore and finished, brutally hammering between her thighs like a beast.

*

They slept in late the next morning. Guy did not awake until he heard low conversation in the room. He cracked an eye open to find Mathilde and the servant, Prudence, pouring water into the washing basin. They shared a few quiet words, and then the maid withdrew. Guy lay still, reluctant to admit he was awake.

He felt an incredible sense of contentment that he could not remember feeling in, well, forever. Even before the war he had not felt anything like this. The sun was shining through the window and slanted across the room, adding to his general sense of satisfaction. A thaw must surely be setting in. He could hear the rustle of cloth and splash of water as Mathilde washed. Lifting his head, he could see she was wearing a shift this morning, though she had slept naked in his arms all night. She turned her head and saw him watching her. "Good morning," she said with a smile.

"Morning," he rumbled in reply.

"You did not leave at the crack of dawn," she commented, drying her hands.

"This time you're the one who rose too soon," he said, placing his hands behind his head.

"You said we could go for a ride today before you return," she reminded him.

"So I did."

"Are you still agreeable?" she asked cautiously.

"Even more so."

"Really?" Eagerly, she spun round, and he watched her approach the bed wreathed in smiles.

"Come here first though." He drew his hands from behind his head and sat up. At her approach, he reached out, caught her hands, and drew her in close to him.

Mathilde waited patiently for him to speak, and when he did not and simply gazed down at her upturned hands in his, she frowned. "Is this where you ask if I'm too sore for horse riding?" she asked shrewdly. Guy looked up, his face coloring hotly. "I'm a grown woman," she reminded him. "And you do not need to keep worrying as to my welfare."

"Of course I worry," he said swiftly. "You are my concern." He raised one of her hands to his mouth and kissed the palm, then the other, and kissed her wrist. "I don't suppose I can convince you to come back to bed for a while?"

She gave a gurgle of laughter at that. "I'm wide awake and raring to go."

"So am I," he growled, heaving her onto the bed. Mathilde shrieked and giggled as he tickled and pinned her to the mattress. Finally, he rolled to his back, taking her with him so she was lying across him. They lay like this for several minutes, neither inclined to disentangle from the other. In truth, he wished he could stay like this all day.

After breaking their fast, the two of them took a ride through the woods and up to Braeburn Heights. Mathilde rode the bay mare she now called Sabrina, and they galloped along past the tor, basking in the sunlight, which was quite dazzling against the snow. He had been right; she had a good seat and was a more than competent horsewoman. He pointed out Braeburn caves where many a poor soul had wandered in and perished, unable to find their way back out again. Mathilde had shivered gazing at the bleak rock face, despite the fierce sunshine and blue sky. Still, it was cold, and he noticed Mathilde's nose and ears turning pink despite her hood. Reluctantly, he realized after an hour or so that they must turn back. Her face fell when he said so, and for whatever reason, it warmed him inside to know that she took the same pleasure in his company. They did not hurry on their return journey, and on entering the woods, Mathilde exclaimed and turned in her saddle.

"Look!" she said eagerly, pointing to a curling plume among the trees.

Guy glanced in the direction her gloved finger pointed. "Aye," he said and frowned. "I believe it must be the old crone's cottage. I can think of no other dwelling hereabouts."

"Old Helga?" asked Mathilde excitedly. "Robin and I tried and tried to retrace our steps but could never find it again." She peered through the trees. "How odd now to simply stumble across it like this."

Guy shrugged. It did not seem so odd to him. "You and Robin are not yet familiar with these woods," he pointed out.

"Can we visit with her?" Mathilde asked. "Please, Guy?"

Guy considered her eager expression. "You're cold," he objected. "I need to get you back in front of a warm fire."

"Old Helga has a fire."

Guy's resolve faltered. "This would please you?" She nodded. "Very well, then." If he wasn't careful, he'd be dancing to her tune like a lovesick fool. Why was he not more bothered by the notion? Unaware of his thoughts, she smiled at him, and their horses picked their way through the trees toward the cottage. For a moment, Guy could have sworn the place looked abandoned, despite the glimpse of chimney smoke.

"You say you met her previously—?" he started when suddenly a large raven croaked in his ear, spooking his horse. When he had Bayard once more under control, he turned and found Mathilde dismounting.

"Good day to you, Helga!" she called, and turning his head, Guy was surprised to find the old woman stood in her doorway.

"The traveler returns, I see," Helga responded, looking not one whit different to when Guy had last seen her, some seven or

207

eight years ago. Her back still ramrod straight, her long hair still plentiful and iron gray, her eyes sharp. "How goes your quest?"

Guy did not catch Mathilde's response, for she had walked over to the woman, and they had clasped hands. Surprised to see them on terms of such familiarity, Guy swung down from his horse and approached. "Mistress Helga," he greeted her guardedly. He never was sure how you addressed witches. *With extreme caution*, his father had always recommended. Guy saw no reason to ignore the advice.

"Well met, my Lord Martindale," Helga responded, her beady eyes alighting on him keenly.

"It has been many a year since last our paths crossed," he ventured.

"Indeed." She squinted her pale eyes. "I see they have treated you kindly, in the main."

A few weeks ago, Guy would have found fault with these words, but now he was surprised to find, not so much. He grunted in agreement. "And you," he added belatedly. She hardly seemed to have aged a day, although in truth, it had always been hard to determine her years.

"I see the Yule-Father has brought ye a fine gift this year, my lord," she added slyly, her eyes cutting to Mathilde.

Guy flushed and shot an uneasy glance at Mathilde. She stood politely, listening with an alert, interested expression. He cleared his throat. "You could say so," he agreed.

Helga laughed, a throaty chuckle. "Will you come in and sit awhile before my fire?" She led the way inside, not waiting for their reply. Mathilde followed at once, so Guy was forced to do likewise. Helga sat upon a low stool and gestured to a spread fur for them to sit upon.

"Have you no"—he floundered a moment for the right word—
"follower to help you keep house, Mistress Helga?" he asked,
staring around the gloom of the room. There was barely a stick
of furniture about the place, though animals milled around, and
a straw mattress lay against the far wall.

"Follower?" Helga repeated with a dry crack of laughter.
"Chance would be a fine thing. Girls nowadays," she tutted.
"All they want is babies and husbands. No, no," she said
briskly, "I'm better off with my animal companions." She
glanced at the wicked-looking raven that sat upon her shoulder.

"Why not a male apprentice?" suggested Mathilde cheekily.
Guy glanced at her in alarm, but mercifully Old Helga answered
this with a wheezy chuckle.

"Why not, indeed?" she cogitated. "Maybe I'll give it some
thought, Mistress Impertinence. By the by, how's that young
friend of yours? The cat thief."

"Oh, Robin's well," Mathilde answered, looking unperturbed.
"He didn't really steal her, you know. She followed us home."

"Hmmm." She shrugged. "She always was a willful hussy, that
one. But maybe she has learned her lesson."

"Robin insists she possesses uncommon intelligence."

Helga snorted. "She's so sharp, she'd cut herself."

"We did try to find our way back, but somehow, before today,
we could not."

Helga glanced back at her bird. "Is that so?" she said. "The cat
could find her way back if she chose to."

"I was not sure," Guy put in, feeling he needed to uphold his
part in the conversation, "that you still lived here."

209

"Oh yes," Helga muttered. "I can still be found here. When the occasion demands it."

Which was a funny way of putting it, Guy thought, but then again, what else could you expect from her kind?

She pushed a basket of nuts before them, by way of hospitality. Mathilde took a walnut and cracked it neatly, fishing out the two halves. "My friend Will taught me how to do it that way," she confided. "It was his father's steward that taught him the trick."

Guy frowned over the mention again of these male acquaintances of Mathilde's. When she had spoken of them playing at cards with her, he had thought them perhaps manservants or retainers. But if this Will had a father with a steward, then perhaps that was not the case? He shifted his position uneasily. A dry crack of laughter startled him from his thoughts, and he found the old witch's piercing gaze resting on him with evident glee.

"A penny for them," she suggested softly, a glint in her eye. "Whatever they are, they are turning your blue eyes quite green."

Green? Guy glanced at her warily, unsure of her meaning.

"Does Tancred not eat nuts?" Mathilde interrupted them suddenly. Guy noticed the bird was now perched on the bowl and staring down at the nuts curiously.

Old Helga regarded her a moment. "Why don't you offer him one betwixt your fingers, dearie?" she suggested.

Guy's hand shot out to catch Mathilde's before she could even reach for it. "Never fear," he said darkly. "He'd have her fingers off, soon as look at her."

Old Helga went off into a peal of laughter, slapping her scrawny thigh. "Tancred's mellowed some since you last saw him, my lord."

"I highly doubt that." Guy eyed the malevolent-looking bird, who gazed steadily back at him.

"He's a very fine bird," said Mathilde, who was clearly no judge of character.

"Aye, that he is." The old woman nodded, selecting a nut, and passing it up casually to Tancred. He cracked the shell between his beak in an instant and devoured the tasty nut.

"Don't squander it," said Old Helga suddenly in a different voice this time, low and portentous. Guy started, his skin breaking out in goosebumps. When he looked at her, he found her regarding him steadily. He shot a quick look at Mathilde, but she was absorbed watching Tancred, who had now jumped down from the witch's shoulder to select another nut.

"The road has forked," Helga continued in the same heavy tone. "And you have a chance to deviate from the path that was laid out before you by another man's hand."

Guy's eyebrows snapped together. "I don't follow your meaning, old woman."

"Your kind never does. Until it's almost too late." Her retort was sharp, annoyed even. She wasn't using her seer's voice anymore, but her regular one. *What man?* pondered Guy. The King's man, Oswald Vawdrey, who had forced his hand and made him sign that marriage contract? Or his father? "Just the same as the old one," she said bitterly. "Just as stubborn. He never listened." She threw him a sharp look. "Did he tell you why he banished me from Acton March?"

"My father?" he asked, startled. "Nay."

She gave a brief nod. "Didn't like the reading I gave him. Didn't want the truth." She huffed.

Guy regarded her warily, remembering what he'd been told. She had prophesized something his father had not appreciated. "What did you tell him? That the north would fall?" he guessed shrewdly.

She gave a crack of laughter. "Even I would not be so foolhardy as to tell a zealot that his cause was a lost one."

"What then?" He was genuinely curious.

She gave a small smile. "What if I told you it concerned the fate of his precious son and heir?" she asked.

"*My* fate?" She nodded slowly. "I survived the war," he said pointedly. "He should have been contented with that. Many from these parts were not so fortunate."

She shrugged. "Discontented men are seldom grateful."

He looked at her sharply. Did her words contain a rebuke for *him*? He shifted again uneasily. "Any ban from our hall is hereby revoked," he said firmly. "You have been missed on feast days." He flushed slightly, thinking of his own lack of celebrations. His tenants and household had perhaps reason to feel hard used these past few years since he had taken over the reins. He needed to do better.

She inclined her head slightly in acknowledgment of his words. "Fairly spoken," she muttered. "May you never regret your words."

Why should he? Guy frowned, but already Helga had turned back to Mathilde.

*

The rest of the afternoon passed far too quickly. Guy escorted Mathilde back to the lodge and reluctantly returned home before supper. He had managed, for the most part, to push from his mind the fact his unwanted houseguests were arriving today. Still, he supposed he ought to be present for supper at least, though the thought gave him little pleasure. *Because you'd rather be at the lodge*, a small voice whispered in his ear. *With her.* He didn't even bother denying it to himself. Leaving her was starting to be a wrench. The truth was, he would rather neglect his duties playing truant with his mistress than dutifully take up the role of host to his guests. The thought unnerved him; he had always put duty first in the past. His father would have been appalled at such behavior.

He made his way through the manor quickly, intent on escaping anyone's notice before he was ready. By some miracle he managed to reach his study without anyone hindering him. Swinging back the door to his safe haven, he received his first unwelcome surprise. Someone had invaded his private space. Guy checked on the threshold. Julia Allworthy stood at his window, gazing out, showing her perfect profile with its straight nose and high, pure brow. Silently he cursed Firmin for not warning him she was in his study. Even as he started to back out of the room on silent feet, she turned suddenly, catching sight of him.

"Guy!" she cried in her full-bodied voice. "How wonderful!" She took several impetuous steps toward him, before halting, biting her lip, and looking him up and down in seeming admiration. "How *well* you look!"

She clasped her hands in front of her like a nun at prayer. Nothing else about her was remotely nunlike. She wore a plum velvet gown with gold trim and her rich auburn hair was dressed high on her head and studded with jeweled pins and a gauzy veil which did nothing to conceal her long swanlike neck.

Guy turned around wondering who else was in the room to benefit from this display, but he was the only other occupant. Had she always spoken so loudly? If she were a man, you would say she had a booming voice. He wasn't sure what you called it in a woman. Julia advanced even closer, her voice turning intimate and confiding.

"You needn't fear, we are quite alone," she said in a low voice that vibrated with emotion and extended a hand toward him to kiss.

Guy frowned at her. "Why should I fear seeing you in company?" he asked, pressing a perfunctory kiss on the back of her hand. For some reason there was a floaty scarf dangling pointlessly from her fingers that distracted him a moment. "You're a guest in my house."

Julia gave a delighted laugh. "How droll you are, Guy. I see you have not changed." She sighed. "How comforting that is to one such as I, displaced and in exile."

Guy stared at her. "Is something amiss with Allworthy House, then?" he asked in some bewilderment. The letter had not mentioned as much.

Julia gave him a look of sweet reproach. "Allworthy House will never be my true home, Guy," she said sadly. "And I think you know that." She turned and made her way over to the window seat, elegantly arranging herself there.

It was on the tip of Guy's tongue to point out that a wife's home was wherever her husband lived, but then he remembered his own circumstances. He didn't want to add hypocrisy to his ever-growing list of transgressions. "I, er, have a few things to be getting on with before supper, Julia," he said briskly.

She smiled indulgently. "I'm sure you know me better than to think I will interrupt you when you are busy with your estates," she responded archly.

Guy eyed her warily as he rounded his desk. She had no needlework or anything to occupy her, he noticed with irritation. Julia had never been a peaceable woman. She was the sort who expected to be entertained, and lavishly. Ignoring her, he opened his ledger and started checking the entries before totaling them up for the month. It was exactly two minutes before Julia interrupted the peace.

"How this takes me back," she declared huskily. "Was it not ever thus, between us?" Guy's frown deepened. He didn't remember her as being quite this annoying, in truth. "True accord," she continued when he did not respond. "Is when you can sit in perfect silence with another person and feel no obligation to speak."

"Quite," said Guy tersely. He dipped his quill in the ink and returned to his columns.

"Alas," she sighed, "that I cannot spend my every day thus employed. How vastly contented I would be!" She paused expectantly, clearly expecting some rejoinder from him.

Why the hells would she want to sit all day watching someone about their business? "Where's Cecil on this visit? He does not accompany you?"

"Cecil?" She sounded surprised.

"Your husband," he reminded her.

Her smile faltered. "Poor Cecil, he will never feel as we do about the north." Guy shrugged and returned to his page. "Do you remember, Guy," Julia asked, pressing a hand to her breast, "that summer I turned eighteen?"

Guy suppressed a sigh and laid down his pen. "We are the same age," he pointed out. "So, of course I do."

"And the words you said to me, down at the hollowed oak?" she asked, casting down her eyes demurely, raising the floaty scarf to her cheek. "I will never forget them. *Never!*"

Guy thought a moment. Was that where he had proposed to her? He had some vague recollection of it.

"How you must hate me!" she flung at him passionately, making him start. "For the way I trifled with your heart, fool that I was! How—" She lowered her voice again. "How I hate myself for the wretched mistakes of the past." Her bosom heaved; she raised her stormy violet eyes to meet his. "Can you—can you ever forgive me, Guy?" she asked tremulously.

Guy blinked. What the hells was all this? He had seen Julia several times since her marriage, and she'd never subjected him to such a scene.

"Of course, Julia," he said stiffly. "Don't distress yourself."

For one horrible moment, he thought she was going to rise off the window seat and fling herself at his feet in impassioned entreaty. Jumping up from his chair to forestall her, he made some excuse and beat a hasty retreat.

"Firmin!" he bawled as he strode down the corridor. He heard Firmin answer him from the long gallery and made in that direction. He spotted him at last instructing one of the underservants next to a portrait of the fourth marquess. "Why the fuck didn't you tell me Lady Julia was lurking in my study?" he fumed as Firmin hastily dismissed the servant. "I do not want to be left alone with her for the duration of her stay, do I make myself clear? And I want it made very plain my private rooms are strictly out of bounds to guests!"

A soft chuckle from the other side of the gallery made him wheel around. On a cushioned bench there lolled her brother, Tristan, resplendent in a purple doublet, his auburn locks gleaming about his shoulders. He looked very like his sister. Guy wondered waspishly if they had deliberately dressed in matching colors. "Kerslake," Guy greeted him coldly.

"Guy," Tristan greeted him effusively. "Well met! It must be some fourteen months or so since I last saw you."

Guy nodded brusquely. "Or thereabouts," he agreed.

"It seems my sister is making herself at home," Tristan murmured, a gleam of unholy amusement in his eye. "How she loves these trips back to the land of our forebears. I vow each time she grows more nostalgic and waxes yet more lyrical than the last." Guy glared at him resentfully. "I daresay you've noticed she has now recast you in her memories?" Tristan gave a gurgle of amusement. "You are no longer the disappointed suitor," he explained with relish, "but the man from whose arms she was torn, by cruel circumstance and an indifferent fate."

Guy glowered. "She jilted me in favor of Allworthy, as I remember it."

Tristan tutted. "Tsk, tsk, now that just won't do, Guy! That just won't do! She'll get very hurt if you don't fall in line and play along in the role she's assigned you."

"I've no intention—" Guy started hotly before another thought crossed his mind, and he turned back to Firmin. "Get Temur to bring that wife of his up to the house," he said shortly. "She can keep Julia company for the duration of her visit."

Firmin bridled. "Lettys?"

"Aye, that's her. Well remembered."

217

"I doubt very much her company is refined enough—" Firmin started, but the expression on Guy's face halted him. "Aye," he muttered. "If that's what you want, Guy."

"It is! And she's to dog her every step, mind!"

Tristan laughed again softly as Firmin departed, vibrating with disapproval. "Julia will hate that, you know. She heartily despises the company of women." Guy shot a startled glance at him. *She did?* "She won't put it that way, of course." Tristan yawned. "She'll simply tell you, oh so sadly, that other women are *unkind* to her, and she has *no idea* why." He pulled a face. "That's your cue to explain it's all down to jealousy on their behalf."

Guy regarded Tristan uncertainly. "How long are you staying?" he asked in an abrupt change of subject.

Tristan grinned lazily. "She mentioned a month, but who knows? Last spring, we stayed with the Earl of Strethneal for three. His wife was practically tearing her hair out by the time we left." Guy struggled not to utter an expletive. "Alas," sighed Tristan, "I am wholly dependent on my brother-in-law's purse strings and must dance to my sister's tune. Luckily, for some considerable time now, I have been dead to all shame. Otherwise, the life I live would be quite simply unbearable."

Guy regarded him sourly. "Why does Allworthy not accompany her this time?" he demanded.

Tristan's eyebrows rose. "He's practically on his deathbed, poor old sod. Why else do you think Julia's so keen to do a head count of her old suitors?"

"I'm married," Guy pointed out abruptly. He had never been grateful for the fact before.

"Well, yes," admitted Tristan, inspecting his nails. "But you've never abided under the same roof as your marchioness, now, have you? Likely, my dear sister is thinking that after four years, you may be able to petition for an annulment." *Hells.* Tristan smiled. "Quite so, my dear Guy," he murmured. "Quite so."

He did not find Tristan so easy to shake off as his sister and ended up in his company for the next hour before dinner, catching each other up with news of mutual acquaintances. Guy bade a vintage, full-bodied wine to be opened, which the two men cordially shared. When they went into their supper, they found Julia awaiting them with her most gracious smile. Guy noticed that the table had been set up informally, so they were all up the one end of its vast expanse. A lavish arrangement of hard-boiled eggs covered in saffron and flavored with cloves was set down in the center of the table. No doubt this was in honor of their guests, as usually only plain food was served from their kitchen.

Guy frowned and set himself at the head of the table; Julia sat at his right and Tristan at his left. There seemed only three covers laid.

"Cruel creatures." Julia pouted. "You have been neglecting me as a mere female, while you talk of your horrid men's business."

Guy eyed her with surprise. Had Julia always been so coquettish in manner? She was thirty-one now, and he thought such behavior ill suited her.

"Guy has been bringing me up to date with our old neighbors," Tristan said mildly as they were served the first course of sturgeon cooked in parsley and vinegar.

219

Guy turned to Jankin, who was hovering nearby. "Where is Firmin?" he demanded. "Tell him to come and be seated. He always takes his meals in here of an evening." Jankin ran off to find the steward.

Julia cleared her throat. "Perhaps he thought the occasion demanded a more intimate setting for the reunion of childhood friends?" she suggested sweetly.

Guy did not deign to answer this, just looked up at Firmin's approaching footsteps. "Sit down, man!" he bade him sternly, and Firmin made haste to do so. "From tomorrow night see to it that Temur, his wife, and Waldon are also seated here for dinner."

Firmin bobbed his head, though he looked a little taken aback. "Yes, my lord, I merely thought—"

"Well, don't," Guy interrupted him. "I don't pay you to anticipate my wishes." Which wasn't strictly speaking true, but he did not trouble himself too much about that. "Inform the kitchen," he ordered over his shoulder. "We are four of us dining." Jankin made haste to fetch another setting.

"I was thinking," Julia began, reopening conversation, "of taking a ride tomorrow afternoon." She threw him an ingratiating smile. "I remember that pretty bay mare you lent me the use of last time. I feel sure she will remember me."

"I no longer have her," Guy answered shortly. "I gave her away." He thought of the bay mare stabled next to Destrian at the hunting lodge currently. What was the name Mathilde had called her? *Sabrina.*

Julia's face fell. "Oh, what a shame! Whatever induced you to part with her? She was a beauty."

"You should not be so indiscreet, sister," Tristan drawled, setting down his goblet. At her questioning look, he elaborated. "Clearly Guy has bestowed the mare upon a lady he thought worthy of her."

"Nonsense!" she said with confidence and threw a look at Guy to corroborate. When he merely cleared his throat, Tristan laughed, and Julia looked extremely taken aback.

"You see?" said Tristan. "You must allow my knowledge of men to be far superior to yours, Julia."

"Well, if she was there for the taking, I wish you had given her to me," she complained. "She was far superior to the mounts Cecil keeps for my use at Allworthy." Guy said nothing, but Julia was clearly not going to let the matter pass. "I feel sure," she said with a superior smile, "that this mysterious *lady* cannot be as good a rider as I."

Guy considered this a moment. "From what I have seen, she is easily your equal," he said, remembering how recklessly Julia would set a horse at a hedge.

Tristan laughed again, but Julia's expression grew tight. "You cannot be speaking of the Countess of Strethneal at any event," she said with determined lightness. "For I well remember his grace telling me that I have far better hands than she." Guy refused to rise to the bait and gestured for his ale to be refilled.

"For some reason," Julia carried on plaintively when no one spoke, "the countess is quite cold toward me these days, I find. I wonder why that could be?" She looked around the table. Tristan rolled his eyes, and Guy took a hearty draught of ale.

"Did you trouble to write to her since we stayed with them last?" Tristan asked lazily. "People tend to find it quite rude when you do not formally thank your host."

221

Julia tossed her auburn hair. "'Twas the earl who was our host and not his wife, who is not even a true northerner," she said with a curl of her lip.

Guy allowed his thoughts to wander as the second course came out of stuffed capons, accompanied by a dish of cooked onion salad and braised fennel. He wondered if Mathilde would be at her bath now. She had spoken of her intention to take one as he had left her. It was a distracting thought.

"How wonderful it is to be back," Julia exclaimed, clapping her hands and jolting him from his ruminations. It was all he could do not to glare at her interruption to his thoughts.

"We are most fortunate, my lady, to accommodate your visit," said Firmin politely when Guy did not speak.

Julia frowned slightly, and for a moment Guy thought she would ignore his steward's words. Then suddenly she turned a radiant smile on Firmin. "You are very kind," she said. "I remember you from a previous visit. Firmin, is it not?"

For the rest of the course, to Guy's relief, she turned the full force of her charm on Firmin, though from time to time he felt her gaze trained on him. The next course was a large venison pie decorated with an edible depiction of the Kerslake heraldic beast, the dolphin haurient. "Good grief," Guy uttered.

Julia looked gratified. "Your kitchens have outdone themselves, Guy."

"Don't look to me. Firmin must have put the order in."

Firmin blushed. "I merely thought, for a sense of occasion." He gave a small cough. "For the next course we will be having a particolored jelly representing the Kerslake colors of blue and white."

"Quite the homecoming," drawled Tristan. "I've never seen the old coat of arms represented in jelly."

"I haven't seen you wear Father's signet ring in an age, Tristan," Julia commented with some disapproval.

"Father and Miles both had such fat fingers," Tristan complained. "Damn thing keeps falling off."

"The dolphin is very well represented in pastry," Julia praised, though to Guy's eye it was plain the cook had never seen one.

"Looks more like a pike," he commented.

"Really, Guy!" Julia tutted. "I'm sure we are fully sensible of the honor done to us."

"Well, to my mind the compliment is all mine," Tristan pointed out. "After all, you're an Allworthy now."

Julia's expression turned grave. "I assure you, brother, I will *always* be a Kerslake."

Guy muffled a yawn as the aforementioned jelly was served, along with fruit stewed in rose water. He couldn't go back to the lodge this evening…could he? He shot a look out the window. Night had fallen, but he could easily find his way back there in the dark. He felt his heart race, even as he dismissed the idea. No, he had given her his assurance that he would not repeatedly seek her out under the cover of dark, expecting to share her bed. It was important to him that he treat her always with respect. That was the only way he would win her trust and her real name; he was sure of it.

"Don't look now," Tristan murmured under the cover of his sister's animated conversation with Firmin, "but my sister is trying to make out the considerable change in you. She is sadly puzzled by it."

"Change?" Guy repeated blankly.

"You no longer seem affected by her allure," Tristan mused. "And that's putting it mildly."

Guy shot him a look. "I've no time for such things," he said abruptly, and to his annoyance found himself coloring hotly at the lie.

"And yet…the fine bay mare," muttered Tristan.

Guy glared at him, and Tristan laughed softly. He'd forgotten what a damn knowing bastard Kerslake could be.

20

Mathilde woke at first light and slid her hand along the mattress, but there was no warm body in the bed next to her. *He didn't come.* She huffed out a disappointed breath and reached under her pillow to don her shift. Now the fire had died down, the room was chilly. She bundled herself in her blankets and drifted back to sleep.

She wasn't sure how much later it was when she heard something bounce off the windowpane. *Could it be falling acorns?* she wondered sleepily. No, for the trees were all bare. She sat up and rubbed her eyes as she heard another ping against the glass. Throwing back the covers, she padded over to the window. Something rattled hard against the pane this time. Mathilde unfastened the casement and threw it open, peering down into the garden below.

It was *Guy*!

She felt her face break out into a smile. "What are you doing?" she called down softly.

"No one's about," he answered, not much louder. "Come down and let me in. The door's fastened."

She hurriedly complied, pausing only to catch up a woolen mantle to drape over herself and the embroidered slippers for her bare feet. Creeping down the stairs, she wondered at the fact that every single step seemed to creak. How was it that she did not hear Prudie every morning? You would think her tread would be lighter as she was so much smaller. Drawing back the bolt, she dragged the door open and found herself caught up in a strong pair of arms.

"Guy!" she breathed and wound her arms about his neck, kissing his cheek, and when he turned his head, his lips. He leaned back against the door, shutting it fast behind him. "You're very early this morning," she commented before his lips descended once again on hers.

"Aye," he rumbled in agreement. "I could not keep away."

She smiled, letting him see her pleasure at his admission. "I'm glad you came," she admitted. "When I first awoke, it was chilly without you."

"You were cold?" he said with a frown.

"Only because the bed's so large and—well, I slept naked in case you came," she answered truthfully. "I had to don my shift in the early hours."

His mouth opened and then shut again. Then he cleared his throat, and to Mathilde's disappointment, he gently released her so that she stood on her own two feet, dropping a kiss on the top of her head. "Let me light the fire down here. We'll get you warmed up."

"We're not going back to bed, then?" Mathilde asked, glancing back at the window. It could not be long past dawn.

He cast her a quick look but was already reaching for the kindling wood. "It won't take me long," he said, his eyes not quite meeting hers.

Mathilde sighed. There was a definite nip in the air down here in the kitchen. Still, she supposed Prudie would be pleased to find the kitchen fire all lit and ready when she rose. Then she had an idea.

She turned impulsively toward Guy. "How would it be if we were to arrange everything down here?" she said excitedly.

"Toast the bread and fetch in the eggs and everything before Prudie and Rob come below stairs." He eyed her curiously, and she suddenly felt a little childish for suggesting they play house together in such a way. "Of course, if you'd rather not..." she said hurriedly, giving him an excuse, but he shook his head.

"Any distraction would be welcome," she thought he muttered, though she wasn't sure of it. He was leaning forward now and blowing onto the small flames he'd started.

"I'll fetch in the eggs," she said, turning toward the door, but he reached out an arm to forestall her.

"Wait for me," he said. "I don't want you setting a foot out there alone. It's not fully light and you're not even dressed."

"No one will see me," she pointed out.

"We'll do it together." His tone didn't brook any argument. "You'll need to change your shoes," he added firmly. "And put on a cloak. The snow may be thawing, but it's still cold and wet underfoot."

"There's boots by the door and my cloak."

"By the time you're wrapped up, I'll have this fire going."

Mathilde nodded and stuffed her feet into her ankle boots, casting a furtive look his way and hoping he did not notice she had no stockings on. He was nearly as cautious as her old nurse! She drew on her cloak and fastened the ties. By the time she pulled the hood over her curly hair, wishing she had thought to draw a comb through it, he had straightened up and was holding his hand out for hers. She took it and then opened the door and led him up the path to where the hens were still shut up in their makeshift home.

"You draw the flap back here—you see how it is secured with these leather ties?" He looked over her shoulder. "It was entirely of Robin's own design," she told him proudly.

"Ingenious."

They found four eggs among the straw and released the clucking hens into their run. "One each!" Mathilde exclaimed. "Rob wants a goat next, for milk," she told him merrily as they returned to the kitchen. "How shall we cook our eggs?"

"Boil them?" he suggested after a moment's pause.

"Oh yes, of course," Mathilde agreed brightly. For some reason, he seemed strangely watchful as she poked among the pots, looking for a smaller pot to place above the fire and boil the water. He had to help her attach the pot to the chain, as she couldn't quite figure out the clasp. Then she burned her finger, and he immediately plunged her whole hand into a water jug.

"Keep it there awhile," he growled at her when she went to remove it.

"But I want to slice the bread."

"You'll cut your finger off next."

Mathilde's face fell. "I haven't done it before," she mumbled, feeling embarrassed.

Whatever he had been going to say died on his tongue as his expression softened. "Count to fifty," he said. "Then you can take your hand out of the water." Mathilde nodded. "Where's the bread?"

"Prudie baked a fresh batch yesterday. There should be loaves in the pantry."

He walked into the adjoining room, and Mathilde sighed, drawing her fingers out of the cold water. One looked rather pinker than the others but otherwise seemed none the worse for its experience. She dried her hands on a cloth and went to find a knife. Usually, when dressed in her practical green gown, she wore the knife he had given her still at her hip. But today she was not fully dressed, so she needed to find one of Prudie's. She heard Guy's footsteps as he returned with a round loaf.

"The water's boiling," he said, peering over the edge of the bubbling pot. Mathilde looked back at him blankly. "That means you can add the eggs," he told her, then smiled and shook his head.

"What is it? Why do you look like that?" she asked as she fetched the eggs from the side.

"No reason. You need to lower those eggs into the water on a spoon," he recommended. "If you drop them in, you'll crack them on the bottom of the pot."

"Oh." She went in search of a spoon, instead of a knife. "I'm glad you're here, or I would be making a sad mess of this. How is it," she asked slowly, "that you know so much about cooking?"

"Soldiering campaigns," he answered shortly.

"Oh." She was always stumbling onto the sore subject of the war, she thought with a wince. Shooting a sideways look at him, she found he was still observing her as she carefully lowered an egg into the water. "Like that?"

"Perfect."

She smiled at him, pleased with herself. "Three more to go," she said cheerfully.

"Where does Patience keep the butter?"

"Prudence," she corrected him. "The pantry again, I would have thought. She doesn't give me free rein," she admitted.

"I wonder why," he murmured as he went in search of the butter.

She gave the matter some consideration. "I can't think," she admitted, "for I like it here in the kitchen very much."

"Doubtless it's the novelty." His tone was dry.

"Maybe I should ask Prudie to teach me how to make bread. It would help while away the time when you're not here."

He paused in the act of crossing the room. "What pastimes are you usually employed with?" he asked.

"Oh, tapestry, mostly. I have my own loom."

"Why did you not say? I could order you one for here."

"Oh, would you?" In truth, she did not feel terribly enthusiastic about returning to her usual occupations. Somehow, learning new things had been much more exciting. The second egg precipitately rolled off the edge of her spoon and thudded hard against the bottom of the pan. "Oh!" She looked up at Guy in some trepidation. "What happens if I crack it?"

"You'll soon see."

Gazing down, Mathilde watched white ribbons escaping from the edges of the cracked shell into the boiling water. "Oh bother! That one can be mine," she said guiltily.

Unexpectedly, he laughed. A squeak on the stair alerted them someone else was about. They both turned and saw Prudence on the stairs brandishing a poker. Seeing it was them, she exhaled a sigh of relief.

"I thought we had intruders, milady!" she exclaimed. "Why, whatever are you—?"

"We're relieving you of your duties for an hour," Guy interrupted. "While I teach the Lady Mathilde how to boil an egg."

"Whyever should she need to?" Prudie asked, bristling.

"Lord Martindale is teaching me some of his soldiering skills," Mathilde said, keen to soothe any ruffled feathers.

"Oh," the maid said, looking slightly mollified. "I see." She eyed Guy suspiciously.

"Do sit down, Prudie. We've lit the fire and fetched the eggs," she added. "What else must we do?"

Prudie looked from one to the other. "Fetch the water from the well," she said promptly. "And set the water on to boil for washing."

"We will all wash after we've had eggs," put in Guy firmly.

Prudie pursed her lips but said nothing. Mathilde stuck her tongue out of the corner of her mouth as she concentrated on adding the eggs to the bubbling water. "I did it!" she said happily, turning a blind eye to the white mess that was the second egg.

"What the devil…?" murmured another voice from the stairs.

"Morning, Rob!" sang out Mathilde. "Do come and join us!"

Robin yawned and approached warily. "It's early," he pointed out. "Why aren't you abed?"

"Lord Martindale woke me throwing stones at my window."

Prudence and Rob both turned to look at Guy with interest.

He cleared his throat. "Mathilde, fetch the toasting fork," he said. "I've cut the bread."

Mathilde stared down at the blackened implements next to the fire. "Which…?"

"The double-pronged one." He anticipated her question. She picked it up and he helped her spear a hunk of bread. "Now hold it out to the flames, but not so close as to burn it." Placing his hands on her hips, he adjusted her stance to the correct distance from the fire, then returned to the shelves in search of bowls.

"I'm doing it!" Mathilde said excitedly, turning to Rob.

"Look out, it's getting charred at the edges," he recommended, reaching down to lift his cat to his knee.

They all turned at a soft knock at the door, and to Mathilde's surprise, Waldon appeared in the doorway. He gave a slight start when he saw the kitchen full of people.

"Ah, Waldon," said Prudence loudly. "Did you bring the, uh, salt I requested?

Waldon appeared to recover himself. "Oh…yes," he said after the slightest pause, though he did not produce any.

"We haven't enough eggs," Mathilde lamented at the new addition to their ranks. "Unless you've already broken your fast?" Waldon looked a little discomforted.

"I expect he thought he'd get it here," Guy said impassively. "Come in, man, and sit yourself down."

"There's two eggs left over from yesterday, milady," Prudence piped up. "In the pantry."

"Oh good! Guy…" She turned to address him, but he was already heading in that direction to retrieve them.

"You'll need to take out the first egg." he said over his shoulder.

"The first egg?" Mathilde peered doubtfully at the four eggs in the pan. She could only recognize the disastrous second egg. "Umm, I'm not really sure…?"

Guy returned and glanced down at the pot. "The speckled one," he said.

"Oh, well done!" She found the spoon and fished it out with the utmost care. "Who shall have the first egg? Prudie!" she decided before anyone could speak. Guy passed her a bowl, and she slid the egg into it, added the toasted bread and brought it to the kitchen table, setting it down before her maid.

"Thank you, milady," Prudence said briskly.

"Here's butter," Mathilde added, sliding it toward her. "And let me see, what else do you need? Salt!" She turned to Waldon. "Perhaps…?"

"We have salt we have not yet finished," Prudie interrupted her hastily. "In that box," she said, pointing to a shelf.

Mathilde fetched it, surprised to find it full to the brim. She set it down and watched Prudence crack the egg open with her knife, before turning back to pick up the toasting fork. Guy was retrieving the soggy mass of the second egg.

"I'll have this one," he said.

"There's a spare now, so you need not."

233

"I'm sure it will taste fine," he assured her. They finished preparing the rest of the food together, and presently all five were seated around the table, elbow to elbow.

"Very nice," Prudie pronounced, finishing first and pushing away her bowl. "Food somehow always tastes better when someone else prepares it."

Mathilde wondered if that was true. She was taking great enjoyment from her first self-prepared meal, but perhaps as Guy said it was the novelty of it that appealed to her. She turned to find him watching her. "How was your spoiled egg?"

"Delicious," he answered promptly, his eyes roaming over her.

"Is my hair a terrible mess?" she asked in a lowered voice when his gaze rested on it. "I did not think to tidy it before I came down." He shook his head. "It didn't used to be so curly before it was cut."

Underneath the table, his hand sought hers. "No?" he asked softly.

"No, it was practically straight."

"Perhaps it was the weight of your long hair pulling it down," suggested Rob helpfully. "When it grows long again, it may correct itself."

"I like it curly," Guy said unexpectedly. "Besides, it's not short now. It's fully to your shoulders."

"Only when I pull on the ends," Mathilde said ruefully, tugging on the curly strands.

"Curls aren't fashionable at court," Rob said with a shake of his head. "Not for a long time. Though they do say the King's first mistress had a head of yellow curls. The one who would only wear red velvet and kept a retinue of matching pages."

Prudence gave a sharp exclamation. "You mean to tell me the southern king keeps his leman in his castle?" she said incredulously. "No northern wife would stand for such a thing!" Mathilde found her face turning pink. No one publicly talked of such things, though it was widely known, of course, who was currently receiving the King's favor. Prudence pursed her lips. "Disgusting!" she sniffed.

"Funny, I heard your northern princess had a brace of bastard brothers," said Rob sarcastically. "I did not realize such things only happened in the south." A shocked silence greeted his words. Mathilde noticed Guy's face had colored.

Mathilde cleared her throat. "If it's more than a passing fancy, the King will usually set them up in their own household," she said hurriedly. "I had heard he's bought a country estate for the Lady Helen," she said, naming the King's latest paramour, Helen Cecil.

Her ears burned. If her mother could hear her speaking openly of such things she would be appalled! But somehow the dreadful silence had to be filled with something, even if 'twas only gossip. She did not want talk of north and south to split up the camaraderie of their morning meal.

"Oh aye, Kinnerton," Rob agreed. "A vastly pretty estate. He didn't buy it for her, though, it used to belong to his mother, the old queen."

"Oh," said Mathilde. "I had not heard." It always seemed surprising to her that people purported gossip was a woman's realm. Men seemed to be allowed to speak much more freely about such things, where women were forced to whisper and then judged ferociously for it.

Robin nodded. "They say he's given it to her in place of a titled husband."

"The wages of wickedness," tutted Prudie distastefully. "Fancy giving his own mother's place to his strumpet!"

"In truth, I do not believe King Wymer was very close to his mother," Mathilde explained quickly with a glance at Guy. "I do not think royal children are often raised with their parents. The young prince does not even reside at court, but safely in the country with his own household of servants and guards. Did you never hear the story of the King's coronation?" she babbled on desperately. "They say he cared not a rush for anyone truly, save his old nurse, Bathilde. There he sat on the golden throne, waiting for the bishop to put the crown on his head, when he looks up and sees they've removed his old nurse out of the front row to make way for a bunch of nobles. 'Be damned to them,' he cried. 'I care not if it's the Queen herself who makes way. I'll not be crowned without my nurse there to see it!'"

Mathilde noticed uncomfortably that Waldon and Prudie were listening intently to this story of the King who'd beaten their own forces into submission. Was this perhaps not the sort of story she should be telling? Guy still held her hand under the table, though, and had not squeezed it in warning or told her to stop talking. Doubtless this was a vastly different side to the warlike King Wymer they'd all be aware of. She thought briefly of her own dear old nurse, deaf and rather shortsighted, who likely would have had palpitations when she'd found an imposter lying in her charge's bed. Her eyes misted over, and she felt a pang of guilt, though she did not think her mother could possibly blame Nurse for her disobedience. Someone cleared their throat opposite. Mathilde looked up. It was Waldon, fixing her with a stern glare.

"And did they?" he asked gruffly.

"Pardon?" asked Mathilde.

"The King's old nurse. Did they bring her back to see him crowned?"

"Oh yes, of course. They would not dare disobey the King. Bathilde had the seat of honor."

He gave a short nod of his head, seemingly satisfied with this. "Loyalty's an important quality in a man," he said heavily. "Be he king or be he beggar."

"What about loyalty to his mother, the Queen?" asked Prudie tartly.

"A mother is as a mother does," he retorted sternly. "I doubt it was the old queen who wiped his arse!"

Rob nudged her in the side. "You shouldn't use that word," he said reproachfully. "Not now you're wearing skirts again."

"What word?" Mathilde asked startled. It wasn't her who had said *arse*.

"*Damned*," Rob elaborated.

Mathilde blushed. She had been so carried away with retelling the story that she had not noticed the slip. "He did say it though," she said, wondering who present she wasn't supposed to offend.

"You let your mistress alone, lad," Waldon interrupted, shaking his head. "We're not so mealy-mouthed around these parts."

Mathilde turned to Guy and was surprised to see him watching her with a small smile playing about his lips. He leaned down, closing the gap between them. "Now the snow is melting fast," he said quietly. "What say you to a ride into Wickhamford today?"

21

"That's where I first set eyes on Destrian," said Mathilde excitedly. She squeezed his hand and pointed to a tethering post.

Guy stared at the spot, an image of her being knocked to the ground flashing through his mind's eye. When he saw her wince, he realized his pressure on her fingers was too hard and released them at once. "Was the carter's accent from round these parts?" he asked casually.

She wrinkled her nose. "I'm not very good with accents," she admitted.

"If you ever see him again…" Guy had to struggle with himself to keep his tone even. "I want you to point him out to me."

She turned her head and looked at him curiously. "Rob already blacked both his eyes," she reminded him.

"You were thrown in a jail cell due to his false witness." Even he could hear the bristling hostility in his voice. "He kicked you." He had trouble even speaking the words.

"Only to dislodge me from his ankle." He turned incredulous eyes on her. "I could forgive him that, for I was biting him at the time," she carried on fairly. "But I will never forget his ill use of Destrian. He was a cruel man."

"He struck you. A woman." He spoke the words with loathing.

"At the time, I was dressed as a boy," she pointed out, and seeing hot words spring to his tongue, she raised his hand to her mouth and kissed his knuckles. "But you're right. He was loathsome. I wanted them to clap him in the stocks at the time if you remember."

"They released him the very next day," Guy growled angrily.

"How do you know that?" Her tone was surprised.

"I made it my business to know." At her startled look, he added, "I asked when I went to fetch the—to fetch Destrian for you," he corrected himself painstakingly. They were walking now along the thoroughfare. He kept a firm hold on her through the mulling crowds. Wickhamford was busy on market day, and the streets were covered with melting snow.

A small smile played about her lips. "Would you have had him put in the stocks?" she asked hopefully, giving him a sidelong glance.

"I'm not sure what I would have done," he admitted. *Was it a hanging offense?* In his book it was, but possibly not the lawmakers'. *Would that have mattered?* He glanced down at her and found her watching him with a funny expression on her face. Did she find him too bloodthirsty? He cleared his throat. "Shall we walk through the marketplace?" he asked to lighten the mood. Immediately, she was all smiles.

"Oh yes! Let's. When I was here before with Robin, our money was almost gone, and we couldn't buy a thing."

Immediately, an image rose up of her bedraggled and hungry. He drew in a sharp breath. "I'll buy you whatever you want."

"A glazed pastry," she said promptly, bringing a grudging smile to his lips. "There was a stall that had them, and they were fashioned like horns and filled with dried fruits." She screwed up her face in remembrance. "It was on the cathedral side, I think."

"Then it's this way." He tugged her hand, turning to the left.

"Can we take some back for Rob and Prudie?" she asked excitedly.

"You're sure Prudie would not take mortal offence?" he asked dryly. "At the notion a street hawker could make pastry preferable to her own baking?"

"Oh no. For did you not notice this morning how she said that food made by another always tastes nicer?"

He grunted, a little surprised that she had remembered such a thing. Though, in truth, her servant had been rather outspoken that morn. He remembered Prudence's disapproving talk of lemans. She did not seem to reflect on the position of her own mistress when freely voicing such thoughts. Luckily, Mathilde had barely seemed aware of the irony of her own maidservant holding such moralistic views. She had simply started chattering away with gossip about the Argent King's proclivities.

Apparently, wherever she and Rob sprang from, they were well aware of such talk. Guy had frankly little interest in such things, but he had noticed with surprise that Waldon had been hanging off every word—and even asked for more detail! He remembered, too, that Temur had reacted similarly on a previous occasion. It seemed it wasn't just him who was affected by her winning ways. Perhaps he should have let Firmin spend some time with her before he'd carted her off to the hunting lodge. Then his steward might not be so hostile in his outlook.

He bought a bag of pastries, but before they had even left the stall, Mathilde was passing them out to beggars. "I thought you wanted them for Robin and Prudence," he reminded her wryly.

"I swear Rob and I wore the same expression on our first visit," she murmured, prompting him to turn back and purchase more.

They strolled among the rest of the stalls, Mathilde nibbling on her pastry. "It looks better than it tastes," she admitted at last and threw it to a passing dog, who wolfed it down with a snap of his jaws. "Although if I were truly hungry, it would no doubt taste delicious." His had tasted fine, but he did not deceive himself he had a discerning palate.

"Did you ever have a nurse when you were a child?" she asked suddenly. At his frown, she added, "That woman there made me suddenly think of mine." Following the direction of her gaze, he beheld a plump-looking dame with a double chin and faded blue eyes. Turning back to Mathilde, he saw her own eyes had misted over. "I do hope she's well," she said guiltily. "Poor old thing. It must have come as a terrible shock to her." She sighed.

When he realized nothing more was forthcoming, he answered, "I'm sure I had a nurse. In fact…" He frowned. "If memory serves, a succession of them."

She laughed. "Were you very badly behaved, then?"

"I always had a bad temper." He shrugged. "But it was more to do with my father. Servants were always falling out of favor." He coughed. "If he thought anyone was too soft on me, too…sentimental, or I'd grown too attached, then he'd get rid of them." At her startled look, he added, "He didn't want me to grow up soft."

She squeezed his hand again. "I don't think you have a bad temper," she said, lifting her chin.

He cleared his throat. "I do though," he admitted. "And I bear grudges." Why was he admitting all his faults like this? he wondered uneasily. To the very person he ought to hide them all from! A little wildly, he cast about to distract her from his confession. "You were fond of your own nurse?"

241

"Oh yes, she was a dear creature. Although…" She broke off, avoiding his gaze. "I don't think I should have been her charge for as long as I was." He wondered why she looked so uncomfortable. "When I was a small child," she burst out confidingly, "she used to tell me fairy tales with the same characters to teach me my lessons. The angelic Lady Tilda and the naughty Lord Matty." She gave a nervous laugh. "Lady Tilda always abided by the rules and lived a life of virtue and fear." She smiled sadly. "Around every corner lurked a pitfall for her to plunge headlong into. Even seemingly innocent things were waiting to trick her from the righteous path. Ogres lurked behind every bend in the road." She gulped. "For a long time, too long, I tried to be like Lady Tilda, but—" She broke off her words distractedly.

"The one I really loved was Lord Matty. You see, Lord Matty always recklessly strayed from the path, he was just too full of joy and curiosity to live in fear. Of course, he reaped the rewards of the wicked. He was punished at the end of each tale, soundly whipped, and sent to bed without any supper. But here was the point that struck me the most." Mathilde paused. "His *resilience*. You see, he *never* learned his lesson, Guy. Next story time, who should come along, whistling a merry tune? Lord Matty." She gave a small shaky laugh. "The story didn't really come alive until he appeared. I used to *long* for him with bated breath. He was a breath of fresh air. Lady Tilda was just…unspeakably dull." She threw him a look of appeal. "Does that make sense? I once tried to explain to Nurse that he was my favorite, and she was quite horrified." She sounded so woebegone that Guy, who had been letting the story wash over him as he led them through the crowd, paused.

"I'm not horrified," he assured her, though it did cross his mind that he was not paying attention as he should. The bustling

242

crowd was distracting him. He didn't want anyone treading on her toes.

"I'm glad," she said gratefully. "You see"—her voice lowered—"one terrible day, I gazed into a looking glass and realized that it was Lady Tilda who was staring back at me." Her voice was choked now. She blinked her eyes rapidly. "It was very…upsetting."

Her distress got through to him, though the story's significance escaped him. "You could never be dull," he said firmly and crowded her to one side to avoid a donkey.

"I'm happy you think so," she said in a wobbly voice. "Though I fear many would disagree."

He wrapped an arm around her shoulders, drawing her in close to his side. "Mathilde, did you not notice how Waldon lapped up your story this morning? How Temur loved your tales the other week?" He paused, letting his words sink in. "*No one* finds you lacking here. Least of all me."

She gazed up at him, the color blooming in her cheeks. "I'm glad," she whispered, her arm slipping around his waist. They had come to a halt now as the crowd jostled and bustled around them. "Oh!" He turned his head to see what she was staring at. A broad, mean-faced man was loudly haranguing a stallholder, his expression twisted in spite. He raised a meaty fist to shake it in the woman's face.

"Guy," said Mathilde uncertainly. But he already knew what she was going to say. "That man—*he's* the carter."

22

Guy could feel the throb in his knuckles as he changed his tunic for dinner that evening. Two were bruised, and one even split. He winced faintly as he fastened his buttons. If anyone had told him he'd be brawling in the marketplace that morning, he would never have believed them. But he'd held on to his temper, just. Despite the fact he wanted nothing more than to beat that man to a bloody pulp, he'd allowed himself a few blows only and dragged him to the jail where he'd been apprehended. At this very moment, the carter would be in the stocks and on the wrong end of a lot of moldy, rotten fruit and vegetables. Mathilde had followed along jauntily behind them and told her story of horse thievery and assault in a clear voice. The carter had protested hotly and loudly that he'd never met the maid before, but he'd been cuffed around the head for his impudence and thrown in a cell all the same. She had not seemed unduly traumatized by the experience, although he'd had to assure her the villain would not hang and would be freed from the stocks after the third day of punishment to return home.

On their return to the lodge, Prudie and Robin had received the bag of much nicer almond cakes that had replaced the pastry horns and listened to the tale with relish.

"I know where I'm off tomorrow," Robin had announced. "Can I borrow Sabrina?"

"I'm coming too," Prudence had chimed in quickly. "There's an overripe turnip that would be just perfect for throwing at the knave."

Guy smiled to himself as he fastened the laces at his cuffs, though in truth, his relaxed frame was starting to tense up even before he'd left his room. Another whole evening of the Kerslakes stretched before him like a life sentence. And it wasn't even the last of them! How long was he expected to put them up? He had thought that by avoiding their company by day, he would find their visit more bearable. But somehow, after Mathilde's company, theirs seemed an even worse prospect than before. He didn't want to part from her. He allowed himself fleetingly to imagine being sat opposite her at the supper table and felt his heart thud in his ribs.

Although the circumstances today had taken a violent turn, their day together in Wickhamford had made him realize that he would gladly spend his every minute with her. He remembered Julia's absurd claim from before as she had sat in his study. That she would be vastly contented if she could only sit thus every evening. He had thought it ridiculous at the time, but now… Would it annoy him if Mathilde sat at his window seat and proclaimed herself well content in his company? No, he realized, no it would not. He would even go so far as to say he would like it.

He no longer even seemed bothered by the fact she laid claim to another woman's name so easily, he thought with faint surprise as he descended the stairs. It seemed he had absolved her of any blame for the deception. He had decided that either her upbringing was at fault, or she had been coerced into this role. Whatever the truth of it, he was sure now that she was not faking her pleasure in his company. Her spontaneous affection undid him. He hardly knew what to make of the warm expression in her eyes when they turned on him. He just knew he liked being the recipient of her smiles and, certainly, her favor.

As for Julia, naturally he had been disappointed when she had broken their betrothal eight years ago to marry her much older husband. But even then, he had at some level acknowledged it

245

was for the best. He had been actively involved in a war at that time. The idea of Julia remaining in the north, when it became apparent that Wymer's forces were marching their way, had never made sense. When Miles, her older brother and Guy's best friend, had approached him hesitantly and told him of the southern lord who admired her and offered her a safe haven at his side, Guy had conceded the field with good grace. He had no time for a wife and no place at his side at that point. His father had been disgruntled, it was true, but Guy had not suffered unduly at the end of it all between them.

It was only later, after the war was ended when Oswald Vawdrey forced an unwanted marriage on him, that Guy's resentment had festered. It was his time in jail, the death of his father that had turned him bitter and angry, not the loss of his intended. On several occasions over the last few years, inwardly he had felt almost *relieved* that beautiful, tempestuous Julia was not his. He had, of course, quickly dismissed such thoughts and not examined them. But now, he considered it a moment. In the cold light of day, he was forced to admit that he and Julia were not well matched, and probably never had been.

What had brought this realization to the fore? Immediately, it sprang to mind. *Mathilde.* He wished he knew her real name. Soon, she would trust him enough to confess her charade and then he would start to plan their future together in earnest. Perhaps, he could even fall in line with whatever it was his devious bitch of a wife wanted? For the quiet dissolution of their union, there was not much he would deny her. Gold, jewels, he would hand it over with small protest, as long as... *What?* He could keep her little pawn. For that was what it boiled down to. Wealth, property, he could part with both so long as it did not touch his estate which had been in his family for generations.

What he could not part with, he realized with surprise, was this little female who had, with shocking rapidity, become so essential to his own happiness. He frowned. Could she really have secured her place in his affections so very quickly? There was no question in his own mind. She had. He could not do without her now. She was…in his heart. He touched his chest lightly. There was no shadow of a doubt. Even if he could not marry her, there was no question of the place she occupied that was rightfully hers.

Marriage. That brought him up short. Had he just connected that institution with his mistress? The beat of his heart sped up. He had. *He must be mad.* To be considering, even fleetingly, the possibility of conferring his proud family name on a nobody, a female of frankly dubious origin, of linking his own fate inexorably with hers. *Oh, but if she was yours in name and by law*, a voice whispered in his head, *the things you could do*. The possibilities it opened up for them. He could place her at the head of his table. Call her his in front of any man. He could beget his heirs on her. His mouth went dry at the thought. He stood very still at the foot of the staircase. My gods. For that pleasure, there was not much he would not sacrifice.

He allowed himself to imagine her a moment, carrying his child. She had said she wanted that. True, she could have been playing on his feelings at the time. That line could have been a rehearsed one. But he would never forget the look in those hazel eyes when she had spoken of a baby. They had been alight with emotion, awash with longing. She had not lied when she spoke of wanting children, he would swear an oath on it.

How strange, he reflected, that reflecting on Julia should open his eyes to his true feelings regarding Mathilde. It was a strange world. For now, though, he needed to focus on the present. He had to wait until his true marchioness showed her hand. Who knew when that would be? Until then, he had to be patient and

247

not expect his own Mathilde to be overeager to trust him. No matter how he longed for her to be honest with him, he had to expect some reluctance on her behalf. She would expect his anger, his outrage at her deception. How surprised she would be when he evinced little of either! In truth, the fact he had come to terms with it so gradually was probably a good thing. There would be no explosion of wrath or indignation on his behalf that might drive a wedge between them or cause her to try to flee him. He went cold at the very thought.

She was his. If not by right, then by the sheer force of his desire for it to be so. He almost looked forward to the point where their current situation was torn asunder. While he cherished his every moment spent with her at the lodge, the realization that he wanted more, so much more from her, seemed to have awoken in him a desire to move forward with their situation, to progress. And what way was there for them to do this other than by official sanction?

I want to marry her, he realized, feeling dazed by the idea. He wanted her for his rightful bride. Only then, he thought dry-mouthed, could he truly prize her as he longed to do, by giving her the full accord of his status. A mistress could only be lavished with wealth and affection, but a wife could be given so much more, a title and social status. A place that was truly at his side. And that was what he wanted. He wanted to give her his *everything*. His name, his title, his servants, and his every worldly possession.

And the truth was, he had never felt that way about Julia. Not once. He could not even imagine her as a mother. Julia liked to be the center of attention at all times. He imagined her handing the child over to a nurse at the earliest opportunity. But Mathilde, his own Mathilde would be quite different, he knew it deep down inside himself. She would love their children. She would love him. She would be the wife of his heart and the mother his children deserved.

The realization rocked him. It was at this moment that his ears were assailed by Julia's melodious tones.

"Ah *there* you are, Guy," she announced, swooping down the staircase toward him. She paused on the first landing, almost as if giving him the opportunity of taking in her appearance in her burnished copper-colored dress and the matching headdress. "I must needs have a word with you," she said and glanced back over her shoulder. "This *creature* you have set on me cannot be borne!" she hissed. Guy glanced up the stairs and saw Lettys, Temur's wife, hanging back, clearly keeping Julia in her sights. He watched as Lettys turned to contemplate a gloomy portrait of Guy's great-grandfather with seeming absorption. He had almost forgotten his notion that she should be set on Julia's heels. He would have to tell Temur that he approved of his choice of wife after all.

"You brought no chaperone of your own, Julia," he pointed out. "So, I have provided you with one. Lettys has obliged me by agreeing to stay at the house for the duration of your visit. Incidentally, she is by way of being a kinswoman of mine through marriage, so I would expect you to keep a civil tongue in your head when you speak of her."

Julia's fixed smile wavered slightly. "I did not know," she said with a toss of her head. "She seems scarcely..." She broke off her words with a moue of distaste. "But anyway, regardless of her suitability, I have not needed a chaperone since I was a girl!"

"How you conduct yourself elsewhere is your affair," he answered coolly. "But in my house, you will abide by my own notions of respectability."

249

She gave a short, shrill laugh. "I had no idea you were so old-fashioned in your notions, Guy!"

"Didn't you?" He was bored of the conversation and didn't bother to disguise the fact.

Two red spots of color appeared in Julia's cheeks. She gave a tight smile. "There can be no impropriety, surely? We have known each other since we were children. I would beg you to reconsider this wholly unnecessary—"

"If it does not suit you to abide by my rules," Guy cut across her words, "then I will understand if you feel obligated to cut short your visit." She gave a faint gasp at this. "The choice is yours, Julia," he said as he turned on his heel and strode into the Great Hall, leaving her staring after him. It was ill mannered in the extreme for him not to have escorted her to the table, but for the life of him, he could not at that moment have offered her his arm. Not when he could even now still feel the press of Mathilde's hand there.

23

Guy sat slumped in his seat, trying not to resent his role as host. He'd bet that Mathilde and Robin were partaking of a far more pleasurable meal right now than he, certainly a far less formal one. He glanced across at Lettys, who Julia had thus far ignored for the entire meal. Temur's wife seemed to be bearing her duties stoically enough, despite the fact her husband had not joined them for supper. Temur was seeing to business for him in the nearby city of Helesport and would not return until the morrow. Lettys's heavy gold braids were coiled around her ears and peeked out from under the square of navy blue cloth she wore on top of her head. She was a handsome heavyset young woman with a determined chin. She was now tucking into a hearty meal, seemingly oblivious to Julia's resentment of her presence.

"And how have you passed the day, lass?" he asked her. "Temur tells me you've set his father's house to rights this last month or so."

"Well enough, my lord," Lettys answered cautiously, crinkling her brow. "It's as well to give my father-in-law the time to miss me, now he's got used to some order about the place."

"If your father-in-law will miss you, then you must make haste to return, of course," Julia said condescendingly.

Guy opened his mouth to point out it was not Julia's decision to make, when Lettys forestalled him.

"Oh no, my lady. In truth, I'm glad of the change of pace. And Father will likely realize all the things I do to make his life more comfortable when I'm not there to do them for him," she said with a satisfied nod.

Julia shrugged a shoulder peevishly and promptly lost interest. Guy made some effort to engage Lettys in some conversation around her father-in-law's property, which was a large farm at the very edge of his estate. "In truth it lies closer to Acton Dymock than Little March," Lettys told him, and Guy reminisced about a country fair that used to be held at Acton Dymock every spring.

"And still is, my lord," Lettys enthused. "For last year saw its first return since the war. Temur took me and lost a purse full of pennies while we were listening to a minstrel's tale. Right wonderful it was how he could spin a yarn. Temur said as how he likely had an accomplice in the crowd who cut his purse strings when he was distracted, but I think it was just a regular sneak thief," said Lettys with a contemptuous sniff. "It's a good thing Temur's got me to take care of him, that's what I say." Guy laughed, and Lettys cast him a look of curiosity, doubtless thinking him much changed from her wedding feast.

"Tell us then, how a good wife would prevent her husband falling victim to an opportunistic thief?" Tristan asked with interest, setting down his goblet. He, too, gestured for more ale, and a servant hurried forward.

"She would sew his coin into his seams, good sir," Lettys answered promptly. "If he was going someplace disreputable by himself. Or, if she was with him, she might take the keeping of the purse into her own hands."

Tristan nodded gravely. "But what if he has need of his money?" he asked. "Would it not be most inconvenient to try to retrieve it?"

"Oh no, sir," Lettys replied. "For what manner of man don't have a pen knife about him? 'Tis a matter of mere moments to unpick."

Julia yawned ostentatiously, but between them, Guy and Tristan endeavored to keep Lettys's flow of conversation steady. She told them all about the whimsical tales the minstrel had regaled them with. Of fantastical creatures and heroes and villains of unsurpassed bravery and beauty. It crossed Guy's mind that he should take Mathilde to the fair come spring. She would doubtless enjoy the spectacle, and he would enjoy taking her there. He imagined her pleasure and smiled in anticipation of it. Perhaps the four of them could go together as a party?

After supper, he made for his study and immersed himself in the estate business he had been neglecting of late. He worked until past midnight, and the candles had almost all guttered. Light was failing as he closed his last ledger when a knock on the door heralded the arrival of a servant with fresh candles.

"Don't bother," Guy barked at the tread on the floorboards. "I am done here for the day."

When he looked up, however, it was his steward who stood hesitating in the doorway. "Firmin," he uttered in surprise. "I thought it was someone come to light the sconces."

"Nay, Guy. May I enter?"

Guy waved a hand in assent as he locked his account books in his drawer.

"You are going to the lodge?" Firmin asked, pursing his lips.

Actually, he wasn't, but that was not his steward's business. "What if I was?" Guy pinned him with a level gaze.

"I only thought—that while we have our honored guests, you would refrain from such...*sport*."

Guy froze in the act of slipping his key around his neck. "Firmin," he said with ominous quiet. "Do not go too far, my friend."

Firmin flushed. "I meant no offense."

"Then be careful not to give it," Guy recommended. "I cannot speak now," he said shortly and turned resolutely away from his crestfallen steward.

Climbing the stairs, he reflected on the matter. He had always had the highest opinion of Firmin as both a servant and a man. They had fought together side by side during the war. Firmin had served Guy's father before him and given many years of good service. But Guy was not about to let that sway him when it came to the respect due him. He did not keep servants to safeguard his morals. *He* was undisputed master here of Acton March.

No doubt, Guy thought as he performed a short strip-wash, Firmin's ideas of etiquette were offended. He, like most hereabouts, heartily lamented the fate of the Kerslakes. It was not as though Guy would ever forget that his closest friend, Miles, had been killed in battle and his neighbor's estate leveled to the ground. That did not mean, however, that he would blindly pander to Miles's brother and sister's every whim. They were afforded his hospitality whenever they asked of it. But he was not about to dance attendance on them.

It had almost seemed to Guy for the last week that Julia and Tristan *enjoyed* playing the role of tragic figures. He shook his head slightly as he flung his discarded clothing onto his chair. He could scarcely believe he was entertaining such harsh thoughts about them, but there it was. They did not even live in the north anymore, he thought with impatience. Just showed up once a year, inflicting themselves on all their old friends and

254

neighbors, raking up the war and harping on about past injustices.

To top it all, he had to host a damned banquet in their honor the day after tomorrow. Julia had alluded to it several times over the last few days. Probably that was what Firmin had wanted to talk to him about, he thought irritably. At least it would be enough to keep his steward occupied the next couple of days with the drawing up of various lists of refreshments. It ought to keep Julia busy too and keep her from springing out at him at every opportunity with her annoying topics of conversation. The thought cheered him considerably. And once it had been hosted, then the Kerslakes might finally start to think about leaving.

24

Mathilde sighed dreamily as she brushed her hair and gazed at her reflection in the glass. Guy had said that her hair was not too short now, but shoulder length, though in truth it was a little short of that. Perhaps she should try wearing it up again, though the idea of getting much of a braid out of it was a little ambitious. Only that very day, Guy had bought her some very pretty hairpins that had caught her fancy from a street trader in Wickhamford. She tried braiding a side section and then pinning it away from her face, then turned this way and that to consider the effect. Perhaps if she tried the same arrangement also on the other side?

Guy had told her that he would not return to the lodge that evening, and though she was disappointed, she was a little tired after such a long day. Of course, it would have been nice to fall sleep in his arms, she thought wistfully. Perhaps when she returned to Acton March with him, to take her rightful place at his side, whenever that would be. He had made no mention of it since she had moved to the lodge, but surely it would be soon. They were growing closer by the day. She was sure of it. She yawned and, glancing over her shoulder at her bed, thought how inviting it looked about now. After all, she had risen early that morning and that seemed hours ago. She heard a soft tap on the door.

"Come in!"

Mathilde told herself she was a fool when her heart leaped. Of course, it was only Prudie with a jug of warm water for washing. She placed it on the side with a clean washing cloth, then banked the fire.

"Can I get you anything else, milady?"

"No thank you, Prudie. I think I'll to bed. I'm really quite tired."

"Not surprised, milady. Not after your busy day." The maid hovered, and Mathilde looked up expectantly. Prudie took a deep breath. "I expect you'll be wanting an explanation," she said and turned rather pink.

Mathilde blinked. "An explanation?"

The maid squared her shoulders. "For Waldon turning up this morning like he did," she said, folding her lips resolutely.

Mathilde cast her mind back. "Oh, er, well." She hesitated. "I did notice the salt box was full," she said tactfully.

Prudence bit her lip. "Yes, I thought you might." They both lapsed into silence.

"I take it Waldon came to visit with you, then," Mathilde ventured. "You are—friends?"

Prudence dragged one toe across the rug. "I don't know as I'd say that precisely," she mumbled.

"He is wooing you, then?" suggested Mathilde gently. At a guess she would say Prudence was in her midthirties, and Waldon looked to be late thirties if not early forties.

Prudence's shoulders rose and fell. "As to that, milady…I can hardly say." She huffed out a breath. "I've not—much experience." She looked as if it pained her a little to admit it. Suddenly, Mathilde's heart went out to her awkward maidservant. In this respect, they had something in common. "Sometimes I think he is. He'll call me lass and tip me a wink, but then other times…" She frowned. "I don't think he can have any partiality for me at all. He's hard to read."

257

"The important thing is, do you want him to woo you?" asked Mathilde directly.

Prudie looked as if she would vehemently deny it for a moment. Then she gave a quick nod of her head.

"Yes," she all but whispered. "But I've got no clue how to bring him up to scratch," she admitted wretchedly. "For my mother died when I was only knee-high, and I am not close to my stepsisters."

"So, you've come to me?" asked Mathilde, vastly flattered to be considered an authority on men and courting.

Again, her maid nodded, looking so pathetically hopeful that Mathilde was touched.

"Do you read?" she asked suddenly.

Prudie nodded. "Aye, when I've the chance."

Mathilde stood up from her seat and went to her chest before she could change her mind. Drawing the scandalous book from its recesses, she thrust it into Prudie's hands. "Read the first chapter at the very least and see what you think. You will have to be bold indeed if you choose to take it for instruction, but…" She took a fortifying breath. "It worked for me."

Prudie gazed down at the book and then back at Mathilde. "Very well, milady," she said with a spark of hope kindling in her eyes. "And thank you, milady."

"See how you get on with it," Mathilde recommended. "You may find it's not for you." She cringed a little, remembering some of the illustrations and how stern Prudence seemed sometimes. Hopefully, it would not turn her hair gray with shock. That might be hard to explain away in the morning.

After the maid left, Mathilde undressed and washed. She knew Guy was not coming, so she kept on her shift and climbed into bed wearing the thin white robe. For ten minutes or so she lay staring at the ceiling as her eyelids drooped. She thought of her mother, and Nurse and dear Fenella, Gordon, Piers, and Willard. Once she was installed at Acton March Manor she would write to her friends and to her mother and let them know that all was as it should be.

But until then…until then, her position was precarious. She could imagine her mother demanding her return. Lady Doverdale was an important woman at court, after all, and Mistress of the Queen's Robes.

Mathilde yawned and rolled onto her side. She longed to feel secure in her position as Lady Martindale but…how could she when no one had even called her by her title since she had arrived? She frowned over this until sleep overtook her. Somehow, she had managed to push that fact resolutely from her mind, but it was still a little disquieting when she remembered it.

When next she woke, she found a large arm wrapped around her waist. Momentary startled out of her wits, she gave a muffled yell.

"It's me," rumbled a voice behind her. She breathed out again in relief and sagged back against him. "I didn't mean to frighten you," Guy muttered. "But you were sleeping like the dead when I arrived."

"I was so tired," Mathilde mumbled. She glanced toward the window, but all was still in darkness.

"Go back to sleep."

She let her eyes drift shut again before a thought occurred to her. "How did you get in?"

"Your maid is in the kitchen, reading by candlelight."

"Oh." *Oh.* She almost asked if Prudie had a shocked or horrified expression on her face. Then she decided against it and dropped a hand to rest on his, which was lying against her belly. "I thought you weren't coming tonight."

"I thought the same."

She smiled into the darkness. "I'm glad you changed your mind."

"I don't want you getting cold in the night," he said gruffly.

"I won't now," she said appreciatively and wriggled against his big, warm body. She heard him catch his breath.

"Go back to sleep," he growled. "You're tired, remember?"

"I am," she agreed softly. "You won't run off before I wake, will you?" Her voice was sleepy yet anxious. When he didn't answer, she twisted her head back over her shoulder to look at him.

"I mean to leave early," he admitted. "I have been…neglecting my duties of late." He cleared his throat. "I won't be able to come for a couple of days."

"Oh, but…"

"I'm just here to sleep, Mathilde."

Maybe she shouldn't have lent that book to Prudie, she thought vexedly. Not when she still clearly had need of it herself! Then he squeezed her hip. She realized what it was that was resting against her bottom. He was hard. *Oh.* She relaxed back against him. Perhaps she had no need of the book after all. He was genuinely being considerate of her, not disinterested. With a soft sigh, Mathilde drifted happily back off to sleep.

25

When next she woke, Mathilde was once more alone. She rolled onto her back and sighed, wondering what business Guy filled his days with at Acton March. Estate business, no doubt, as by all accounts the estate covered an exceptionally large area. She cast her mind back to her brief visit to his ancestral home. A very grand residence it had been too, fit for his station.

Should she venture to ask him, she wondered, when he would take her back to his official seat? Her instinct urged her to wait. To wait for the moment when he would tell her they would return together as man and wife, and he would introduce her to his household. Her heart swelled at the idea, and she clasped her hands over her chest.

The fact that he had come to the lodge last night merely to cuddle with her must be a positive sign surely?

She wriggled her toes gleefully at the notion he wanted to spend time in her company. Firmly, she put from her mind the last four years she'd spent unclaimed and shunned, a wife in name only. She did not want to dwell on the barren beginnings to their union. Instead, she wanted to concentrate on the life that had sprung forth from such unpromising origins. Respect, liking, and dare she even hope for true affection from her spouse? It had not been very heartening being the scorned wife whose husband never laid claim to her.

Oh, she had known what people said about her in corners where her mother would never hear them. She had been sheltered but not deaf. That she was a poor little creature, a pathetic pawn in her mother's ambitious game. She drew in a breath and exhaled again noisily. No, she would not dwell on it. She had moved past all that. She had taken a flying jump off the chessboard, and landed squarely on her own playing field, which was level and clear, and allowed her to make her own moves.

Rolling out of bed, she hurriedly washed and dressed herself; a glimpse out of the window told her she had overslept, as did the jug of lukewarm washing water. Prudie must have brought it up at least an hour ago. Venturing below stairs, the only body she came upon was Robin's cat, Mabel, who rubbed against her legs. She never had returned to Old Helga, thought Mathilde, reaching down to stroke the tabby. The cat made a little noise in her throat and butted her head against Mathilde's hand.

"Good morning," she murmured, and the cat started to purr.

The sun was shining through the kitchen window, and Mathilde sank down onto the small stool and basked a moment there in the warm rays. Robin and Prudie must have gone to Wickhamford as they had said they would. Briefly, she thought of the carter. They must have put him back in a cell the previous night, she thought with a frown, or he would surely have died of exposure. He would be having a miserable time of it and no mistake. Then she thought of poor Destrian and the many years he must have suffered at his previous master's hands and hardened her heart. Maybe he would learn a valuable life lesson, though in truth she doubted it.

A knock on the window made her jump, and looking up, she saw it was Temur. She gestured to him to come around to the door and made haste to open it. He had a cart with him and seemed to be unloading some apparatus from the back.

"What is that you have brought with you?" she called.

He looked back at her over his shoulder. "Wait and see!"

She watched as he slung two pieces of a large wooden frame over his shoulder and picked up a sack. It was a tapestry loom! Mathilde clapped her hands together. "Where did you get it?"

"Guy sent me to Helesport to buy it for you. He wanted the absolute best money can buy." He swung the bag he carried up in the air. "All the threads are in here. Every color you can imagine."

Mathilde caught it clumsily. How thoughtful her husband was. He must have bought it to keep her busy while he could not visit her.

"Where do you want it set up?" Temur asked, looking about him.

"Not down here, it's far too big," said Mathilde. "The sitting room upstairs would be better suited."

He nodded in agreement and carried the two pieces he had up the stairs. "I'll be back down and collect the other parts next," he called over the banister at her.

"Can I help carry anything in?"

"No!" He shook his head. "Guy would have my guts for garters!"

He ran back down the stairs two minutes later and collected the other pieces. "You can direct me how to set it up though," he said, scratching his blond beard. "It looks a lot more complicated than the one Lettys has at home."

"Yes, of course," enthused Mathilde, following him back up the stairs. It didn't take them long to set up the loom in one corner of the room.

"It's a fine one," she said admiringly and peered into the bag of threads. "You really did get every color."

"Where's young Robin?" asked Temur, looking about him.

"He's gone into Wickhamford to pelt a wrongdoer with rotten vegetables," she admitted. "Do you remember how we told you about the carter who accused us of being horse thieves?"

Temur's eyes grew wider and wider as she told him Guy had exacted his revenge on the previous day.

"He's in the stocks? The man you fought with?" spluttered Temur. "Are you in earnest?"

"Absolutely in earnest," she assured him. Temur sprang up out of the chair he had been sitting in. "Where are you going?"

"To take Lettys to Wickhamford," he told her as he disappeared out of the room. "She would not miss this for the world! It sounds as good as a day at the fair!"

"I'm sure it isn't!" she called after him, but hearing the door slam, she realized he had already gone. She turned to Mabel the cat and sighed. "I may as well sort through these threads, I suppose."

Mathilde spent an agreeable couple of hours separating all her dyed yarn into heaps. Then she fetched a wooden tray from inside the trunk in her room and arranged them into it in a way that she could easily put her hand to the color she wanted. Then, fetching a sheet of paper and a pen, she set about drafting an intricate design.

The picture she drew was a rustic scene of a large hunting lodge in the middle of a green wood. Outside the lodge were five hens, a cat, a boy, two women—one with black and one with short hair—and two horses. She couldn't add Guy, as strictly speaking he did not live there. Then she decided to add Old Helga with her long gray hair and pale blue dress. In order to show she lived nearby she added the plume of smoke from

265

above the trees. Then she had an excuse to add Guy, for Old Helga did not live with them either.

She took great pains to draw out his tall, powerful figure with broad shoulders and long legs, adding in his short black beard to make him unmistakable. Then she drew in Waldon with his slim, wiry frame and hint of gray at his temples, and Temur with his blond hair and youthful face. She would have liked to have added Temur's wife, but she had not yet met Lettys, so she had no idea how to depict her. The design took her the best part of three hours, as she added meticulous color codes for each detail.

Suddenly, a noise below stairs startled her out of her absorption. Mabel perked up and jumped down off the chair she had been curled up in. Mathilde set down her pen and sat up. Could it be Rob and Prudie returned already from Wickhamford? Hastily packing her pen and paper, she made her way below stairs. Finding no one about, she hurried through to the kitchen and came to an abrupt halt. At the kitchen table Prudie was busily chopping mushrooms, but that was not the startling thing. Her maid was not alone. Waldon stood behind her, his arms wrapped around Prudence's waist, nuzzling her neck. Prudie's head was angled to allow him access.

"Oh!" Mathilde started on the threshold. "I am sorry…"

"Nay, don't apologize, lass," said Waldon, taking a step back. "I've to head back to the manor now. Was just taking my leave of this one here."

"Of course!" Mathilde half turned to give them some privacy. She fancied she heard the whisper of a kiss, a murmured promise, and then the slam of the door.

"Sorry about that, milady," said Prudie, who was wiping her hands on a cloth and looking a little flustered.

Mathilde waved her apology aside. "So, you and Waldon?"

"He gave me his vow this morning," said Prudie simply. "We're handfasted."

Mathilde gasped and hurried round the table to embrace her maid. "That was so quick! Why you only read it last night!" she marveled. "What wonderful news!" Prudence was even pinker when Mathilde released her. "Do you have to get it solemnized in a church or any such thing?"

"Round these parts, the country folks just makes their vows to each other." Prudie shrugged. "We haven't told anyone yet," she admitted shyly. "I wanted to tell you first, milady, as you'd been instrumental so to speak." She glanced around furtively. "By giving me the means to snare him," she whispered.

"You mean the *book*? Was it of any use?" asked Mathilde, unable to contain her curiosity.

"Oh yes, milady. Very instructive." Mathilde hesitated, not feeling she really had the right to ask, but Prudie leaned forward. "I went for the easiest one, milady," she confided in a low voice.

"The easiest one?" Mathilde puzzled, not liking to admit she had read only the first two tales. Maybe there was one later that was a good deal less work!

"The lusty landlady one," whispered Prudie. "I wore no undergarments and got him up to my room on the pretext the shelf was broken. Then, when he was examining it, I lifted up my dress and lay across the bed." She turned scarlet. "I told him I longed for his touch, like the landlady did. Waldon took over then." She sounded a little dazed. "For a moment, I nearly lost my nerve thinking he wouldn't react like that Sir Pelomon did. But he only hesitated for the veriest second before he fell on me, exactly like it said!" Her voice was a hoarse whisper now, her eyes very wide. "He didn't even try to resist!"

Mathilde nodded. "Yes, it was the same for me," she confided. "Only I followed the story of the lusty widow."

Prudie's eyes widened. "With the mouse and the tangled hair?"

Mathilde grimaced. "I felt a bit of a fool at the time," she admitted. Prudie gave a startled chuckle. Mathilde bit the side of her mouth. "Truly men are strange creatures," she managed to get out before her own laughter bubbled up. They both laughed until tears rolled down their faces.

"If you don't mind, milady, I'll just hold on to the book for a while to get a few more pointers," Prudie said.

"Oh, of course!" Mathilde was a little taken aback. Clearly Prudie was a much better scholar than she.

"Only it's quite a lot to take in," admitted Prudie. "And Waldon didn't seem to rush on to all those positions same as they did. He was quite happy just doing the first one all night."

Mathilde coughed. "He probably won't expect you to do all the others at once," she said, blushing. "Indeed, he'd probably think it a little odd if you expected it."

Prudie's eyes widened. "Then how—?" She faltered anxiously. "I don't want him to get bored of me, milady."

Mathilde reached across and patted her hand. "He won't," she said reassuringly. "You could always say you had a dream about him doing something to you and you'd like to try it as it felt so nice. Or say you heard some other wives talking about something and you want to know if married couples really do that. Only when you feel ready, mind you," she cautioned. "That book is just a series of adventures, Prudie. Pelomon does not pledge himself to any of those women, whereas you've got your whole married life ahead of you. You're in no hurry." Prudence was hanging on her every word now, nodding.

"Yes, milady," she said. "Thank you, milady."

"You're entirely welcome," said Mathilde, enjoying her role as mentor for once, instead of novice.

"But I don't think you finished the book, milady." Prudie frowned.

"Finished it?"

"For he did pledge himself in the end and settled down into matrimony."

"With who?" asked Mathilde, somewhat startled.

"The original widow," said Prudence. "He went back to her when he realized she'd held his heart all along."

26

Robin returned only just in time for supper, his ears and nose quite pink with cold.

"It was rare sport!" he exclaimed as Mathilde helped him off with his hat and mittens. "I only wish the others could have been there. Will and Piers and Gordon I mean," he added wistfully.

"We must write to them," Mathilde said guiltily. "It's only that things are not yet quite as settled as they should be…" She trailed off awkwardly, but Rob wasn't listening.

"You should have heard how he cursed me when I hit him square on the head with a rotten egg." Robin hooted. "It was every bit as good as that time Gilbert Epsom snitched on me to old Sir Avery, and I struck him that blow in the stable forecourt, and he fell directly in the water trough."

"I'm sure it was a sight to behold," Mathilde replied gravely. Gilbert Epsom was a squire Rob considered his mortal enemy. They were always feuding about something or other.

Robin's high spirits did not abate one whit for the next hour. He scooped Mabel off the chair and began dancing around the kitchen with the cat in his arms. Mathilde shot a look at Prudence, expecting remonstrance, but she was clearly away with the fairies, smiling absently as she stirred their soup. Prudie was yawning a good deal by the time they ate, which they did around the kitchen table together.

"Just lay a place next to mine and Rob's," Mathilde told her. Prudie looked mildly scandalized but was quickly persuaded. "We'll just keep it plain fare this evening and have an early night."

Even Rob's spirits had died down by the time they had finished their simple meal of savory pottage soup and brown tourte bread. "It's his last day in the stocks tomorrow," he said sadly, his thoughts still clearly dwelling on the unfortunate carter. He sighed and dragged himself out of his chair.

"Did you see Temur and his wife in town?" Mathilde asked as she helped him don his jacket again to go and shut up the hens and secure the stable.

Rob nodded. "Oh aye," he said, pulling on his hat. "His aim wasn't as good as mine though." He disappeared out of the door, and she and Prudie cleared the table.

"You go on up, milady. I'll bring up washing water for you presently." A large pot of water was already bubbling over the kitchen fire.

Mathilde opened her mouth to offer to wash down here, but then noticed Prudie's sharp glance at the window. *Ah, she is expecting Waldon's arrival.* Of course she was. They were as good as husband and wife now.

"Thank you, Prudie," she murmured instead and made for the staircase. She was only halfway up when she heard Robin slam and bolt the kitchen door.

"Good night," she called down.

She stifled a yawn with the back of her hand and guessed she would not lie awake for long, but in this respect, she was proved wrong. Despite the fact Guy had warned her that he was not at liberty to join her, Mathilde found herself lying in wait of his arrival long after she had washed and undressed for bed. It was most foolish, but every fiber in her being seemed to leap when a twig tapped against the windowpane or she heard some noise out in the garden, doubtless melting snow falling from the

271

trees onto the ground which her ears mistook for a footfall. He had told her he would not come, but she could not help but remember other occasions when he had said the same thing but still turned up all the same.

She turned onto her side again, hauling the blankets up to her chin, willing herself to relax into sleep that simply would not come. She was just wondering if she ought to rise again and drag out her tapestry design when she heard three loud raps on the kitchen door. Her heart thudding, she sat up in bed and held her breath. Who was that? It surely was not Guy. He had never heralded his late-night arrival before in such a manner. But if not he, then who could it be?

She sat a moment, frozen in indecision, when she heard it again. Another three loud, ringing knocks. Somehow, they sounded ominous, as if they foretold someone's doom. She shivered, even as she heard a tread on the attic stair and realized that Prudie must be descending them to find out who was demanding admittance.

Quickly, Mathilde slipped her sensible green woolen dress over her shift, pulled on her slippers, and poked her head out of her bedroom. To her relief, she saw Waldon was descending the steps behind Prudie. He nodded at her, and Mathilde slipped around the door to join them as they went below stairs. Mathilde halted halfway up the stairs, clinging to the banister as she watched Waldon draw back the bolts and open the door.

Outside, in the cold, stood Old Helga. She wore no cloak and the shoulders of her sky-blue dress were dusted in snowflakes. They glittered, too, in her long gray hair. She lifted one bony hand and pointed past Waldon, to where Mathilde hovered on the stairs.

"I come with a warning for you, little one. You have been betrayed," she said in a loud, portentous voice.

"Betrayed?" Mathilde repeated through numb lips.

Her thoughts flew to her friends Willard, Piers, and Gordon. It would not be so surprising if one of them had been forced to give her away. They would have been under some considerable pressure after all.

"Do come in out of the cold, Helga," she urged. The old woman gave no reaction to this. Instead, she turned over her extended hand and opened her fingers to reveal the shiny black stone from her previous reading.

"By this one," she said croakily. Mathilde frowned, remembering Helga had said the stone represented her enemy.

"But the carter has been punished already," she blurted in confusion.

"Not he," Helga said contemptuously.

"Who, then?" Her mind raced. "I have no other enemy in the world."

Prudie was looking from Mathilde to Old Helga. "You'd best come in, Granny," she said respectfully, pulling at Waldon's arm. "In from the cold." He fell back a step, and Old Helga nodded grimly as she stepped inside.

"Where is Tancred?" Mathilde heard herself ask blankly.

Old Helga shrugged. "He refused to take any part in tonight's doings," she muttered cryptically. "He's stubborn, that one."

Mathilde forced herself to descend the last few steps to join the others. "Waldon, could you please revive the kitchen fire?" she requested, striving for normality. "We could sit in there and have a warming drink perhaps?"

273

"There's a spiced wine I could warm through, milady," Prudie said, hurrying into the buttery.

Reluctantly Mathilde led Old Helga into the kitchen, where Waldon started prodding the fire. She pulled out a chair for the older woman and gestured for her to sit, then took a seat opposite her. The whole time she could feel Helga's gaze trained on her face. At last, she raised her eyes to meet Helga's pale blue eyes squarely. "Should we wait for refreshment, or—"

"Martindale has betrayed you," Helga interrupted her harshly. In the background Mathilde heard a gasp. Then she realized she had been the one to utter it.

"I beg your pardon?" She sat up in her seat, a cold feeling rising up in the pit of her stomach. "I don't think I quite—"

"Even now," Helga continued in a loud, ringing voice, "he sets another woman at the head of his table, wearing a jewel that belongs by rights to his wife."

"No," said Mathilde, shaking her head. "He would not." She could not believe it of him. Not when they were at last approaching an understanding. They were growing closer; she was sure of it!

"Another woman sits in *your* place," Old Helga repeated, her words ringing with conviction. "The place he has denied you time and again. He has set her up in your stead as his false bride. His friends and neighbors all pay court to her. They give her the accord that should be yours alone."

"I don't believe you," Mathilde said, lifting her chin. Her heart was beating now almost painfully in her chest.

Helga reached across the table and placed the black stone between them. Almost against her will, Mathilde found herself reaching for it. Belatedly she remembered that before when the small rock had appeared in her reading, Old Helga had spoken of Guy, not the carter. Mathilde's fingers closed around its rough surface.

"Don't believe or won't believe, little maid?" Helga's voice asked quietly. Under the older woman's steady gaze, Mathilde found her conviction wavering.

"It's not true," she heard Waldon's voice from over at the fireplace. Mathilde turned her head sharply, relieved to find support in an unexpected quarter. The fire crackled behind Waldon as he straightened up. "Lady Julia is a guest in his house, that is all. Nothing more."

Helga gave a crack of skeptical laughter. "A guest!" she mocked. "Is that what he calls her? And what of this little one?" she said, nodding toward Mathilde. "What does he call this one?"

Waldon's lips pressed together, and he flushed. "He does not call her anything," he muttered, avoiding Mathilde's eyes.

"Not wife, then?" asked Helga slyly.

"Wife?" Waldon looked so startled that Mathilde felt all the breath stolen from her body. She squeezed the black stone so hard that its edges cut into her palm. Waldon looked from Mathilde to Helga. "He has given you his vow?" he asked uncertainly, his eyes full of disbelief. Then he shook his head. "Nay, he can't have."

Mathilde swallowed, her mouth suddenly dry. She remembered once more how no one at Acton March had accorded her her rightful title.

"But that is because," she said, trying desperately to rally, "he wanted us to become better acquainted before announcing it." Even to her own ears, the excuse sounded weak. She heard a footfall in the doorway and looked up to see Prudie stood there, grave-faced, holding a jug of wine.

"But Lord Martindale was not at liberty to give you his vow," Waldon persisted gently. "For he is already wed to a southerner."

Mathilde drew herself up in her chair, trying to muster some dignity. At the end of the day, she supposed bleakly, it would always boil down to that. She would forever be a southerner to these people.

"Of course he is," said Prudence sharply. "Just who do you think milady is?" She bustled forward with the wine and slammed it down on the table.

"Then, the Lady Mathilde is—?" Waldon broke off in confusion. "Nay, she cannot be."

"I am the Marchioness of Martindale," Mathilde said with quiet conviction. "And Guy's lawful wife." She looked up again to find Old Helga's eyes watchful, her head tipped to one side like a bird's. Mathilde turned back to Waldon. "There is another lady at Acton March at present?" she forced herself to ask in a small voice.

He cleared his throat. "As I said, a guest of his lordship's—"

"Who is she?"

"More importantly, who *was* she?" put in Helga, holding up a crooked finger.

Mathilde looked expectantly at Waldon. There was a feeling of dread in the pit of her stomach, but she had to know.

"The Lady Julia Allworthy," Waldon answered with clear reluctance. He shot a look of appeal at Prudie, but she folded her arms and glared back at him. "She—in the old days, her family held a neighboring estate."

"Neighbor, was she?" Helga snorted. "And what else?"

Waldon rubbed the stubble on his chin. "They were betrothed," he admitted. "But that was before the war. She's wed now—"

"To a man who lies on his deathbed," Helga retorted. "An old man she left to gasp out his last breath alone."

"I had not heard that," Waldon answered defensively. "She's highly thought of in these parts—"

"Unlike his unwanted southern bride," Helga agreed, "who he stashes in the woods like a guilty secret, while he woos his former love."

Mathilde gave an involuntary cry of anguish as she felt her heart crack.

Prudie rushed forward, slipping an arm around her shoulders. She turned angrily on Waldon. "You should have told me!" she flung at him accusingly.

"I didn't know she was his wife!" Waldon protested. "No one knows!"

Helga nodded sagely. "He has been careful to keep it so."

Mathilde covered her trembling mouth with her hand. "He woos another?" she asked of Helga in a low, urgent voice.

"If you do not believe me," Helga replied calmly, "then there is the evidence of your own eyes."

Mathilde started up immediately from her chair.

"Milady!" Prudie exclaimed in alarm. "Wait! You cannot mean to go there!"

But Mathilde had already rounded the table and was heading with determination for the door.

27

Guy looked up wearily from his plate. The venison and wild boar dishes were being cleared away now, and the musicians were striking up another tune. It seemed there was to be a musical interval between each course. He leaned to one side and signaled for Firmin, who stood on the sidelines overseeing the servers.

His steward darted forward. "Aye, Guy?"

"How many courses are we serving?"

"Seven," replied Firmin proudly.

"A feast fit for a king!" drawled Tristan Kerslake, draining his goblet.

Firmin signaled for Jankin, who was holding a pitcher of wine. He snapped his fingers and gestured to Guy and Tristan.

"Not for me," said Guy absently. His own wine goblet was untouched.

"You do not drink?" Firmin asked in surprise. "This wine was laid down by your father and is of the finest vintage."

"I am sure," Guy replied. "But as host I would rather keep a clear head and remember my duties."

Firmin frowned, but luckily the Courtess of Strethneal was asking a question about the centerpiece of peacock feathers so he was distracted. Guy did not know if he could withstand the temptation to steal away to the lodge after the banquet was done. His head ached from the buzz of conversation and the whining strings of the musicians jarred on him this evening. He drank some ale and leaned back in his seat, frowning at the view of all the neighboring lords and ladies it afforded him.

The atmosphere was not joyous or even pleasant to his mind, but that might have been down to the fact that Firmin had seated Julia at the other end of the table in the hostess's place. Of course, Guy had deliberately left all decisions regarding the banquet to his steward, but this choice was one that bothered him unduly. He knew not why for in two hours' time, the business would be over and done with. That did not stop him from frowning every time his eye fell on Julia in her golden gown and diadem, lording it over everyone like a queen.

It did not help that at her bodice she wore a Martindale ruby which he had been fool enough to give to her as a betrothal gift in his youth. He had almost forgotten he had broken up the set to give it away. It had hardly seemed to matter at the time, but her wearing it now made him acutely uncomfortable.

The ruby was set in the heraldic beast of the Martindales, a large white enameled swan with its wings extended and a gold collar about its neck. It certainly drew the eye, and no doubt all of his neighbors would be aware of who must have given it to her. They could hardly fail to do so, when a huge portrait of his grandmother hung in this very hall, dominating the north wall. The old dowager marchioness was depicted resplendent in the full set of necklace, tiara, bracelet, and brooch.

Guy told himself he was a fool to feel so discomforted that Julia flaunted the brooch now. It was not as though he ever intended for his wife to get her greedy hands on it. Why, then, did he feel almost ashamed whenever he saw anyone's eyes dwell on it now? It was not as though he was saving it for anyone. Unless, a small voice whispered in his ear, he managed to secure that divorce from the present marchioness, then wed where his own choice lay. Immediately a vision of Mathilde rose up before his eyes.

He glanced up at his haughty grandmother and tried to imagine Mathilde dressed in a formal court gown, plastered in so many jewels. He smiled to himself briefly, though it soon faded. How would he answer if she saw the portrait and asked where the missing brooch was? He shifted uneasily in his seat.

He was imagining problems now where none existed! It wasn't like him to be so fanciful. Then he gave a start, straightening in his chair. Emerging from the shadows, as if he had conjured her from thin air by the power of his thoughts alone, came Mathilde. He stared. Surely his mind was playing tricks on him, but no, other heads were turning now

The musicians faltered, their fingers stalling over their instruments. Guy found himself unable to catch his breath. He felt frozen to his seat as he saw her cross the room like a sleepwalker, the expression in her eyes wounded. The room fell deadly silent, and almost as if on cue, the conversation died on everyone's lips. People gasped audibly at the appearance of this stricken-looking stranger.

Mathilde's gaze went from him to Julia, and then he watched in horror as they dwelt on the portrait and then back to Julia. Her cheeks flushed hot with color. She walked up the long table in her simple wool dress, past all the guests in their fine silks and velvets, and finally arrived in front of him, coming to a halt. He swallowed and tried to fight down the irrational guilt that engulfed him.

Julia Allworthy's voice rang out authoritatively across the whispers. "Mistress, you forget yourself!" she said in a loud, stern voice. "Your kind are not welcome here at Acton March!"

Guy started, the harsh words shocking him out of his stupor, but even as he opened his mouth to refute them, Mathilde's expression altered to anger.

"Sweetheart," he said hoarsely, and at his word, she stiffened, drew back her hand, and delivered a stinging slap across his face. It rang out so loud that it silenced all the muttering.

"How *dare* you…" she uttered in a low, trembling voice. He reached for her hand. It had to smart from delivering that blow, but she snatched it back before he could massage her little palm. "You *faithless* man!" She pronounced the word as if it hurt her throat to speak it.

He stared at her, his own face fast draining of color. "Faithless?" *Never that.* Her breast rose and fell with emotion. "Mathilde…"

Her servant, Prudence, emerged from the crowd. "Come away, milady. Come away from this wretched place!" she urged, grabbing for her arm. Mathilde turned toward her, almost blindly, allowing her maid to lead her stumbling away. Someone else detached themselves from the crowd and took her other arm. Guy thought for a moment it was Waldon.

"Wait!" Guy called hoarsely after her.

She didn't even pause, gave no acknowledgment she'd even heard him. By the time he'd managed to stagger out of his chair, she was almost across the other side of the room. Instead of detaining her, not one of his idiot household had even lifted a finger to stay her. Instead, they had fallen back from her fleeing form, giving her a clear path of escape through the Great Hall.

"Mathilde!" he roared. He felt unsteady on his feet, short of breath, sick at heart as he started after her.

"Well, well," he heard Tristan Kerslake drawl into the stunned silence. "No one told me that Lady Martindale had finally come home."

Guy turned his head over his shoulder to stare at him. Shocked murmuring broke out afresh at this, rising to an almost deafening babble. *Lady Martindale?* What the hells was Kerslake talking about?

At his incredulous look, Tristan shrugged. "Her disappearance is the talk of all Aphrany." *My gods.* He could not take this all in right now, only that she was fleeing from him.

"Stop her!" Guy roared as he staggered across the hall. His servants and attendants milled about in consternation and panic. "Where is she? Do you have her?"

He burst out into the corridor outside where the air was fresher and filled his lungs with it. Firmin's face wavered before him, ashen and grave. Then Temur and Lettys were pointing toward the door, and Guy looked up to find Mathilde being hustled back through it by two of his men.

"Be careful with her!" he bellowed and hurried forward to relieve them of their burden. She struggled a moment, her fists raining fierce blows on his chest, then as he swept her up in his arms, she fell suddenly still and limp. Guy cradled her to him as Waldon and Prudie burst through the door.

"What are you doing with her, you wicked man?" Prudence shrieked. "Won't you be content until you've killed her stone dead?"

"Hush love, hush!" Waldon caught the distraught servant to him, and she burst into noisy tears.

Feeling eyes on him, Guy swung around to find a crowd, including the Earl and Countess of Strethneal, peering at him from the doorway of the Great Hall.

"It's a misunderstanding only," Guy found himself saying angrily. "Return to your seats."

No one paid him any heed, their eyes all fixed on the small still figure pinned to his chest. Tightening his grip on her, he strode toward the staircase, pale-faced servants scattering before him.

"Guy, what can we do?" Firmin called after him in an anguished voice.

"Send everyone home!" Guy flung back at him over his shoulder. "The spectacle is over for this evening. I can scarcely be expected to provide any more entertainment," he added bitterly.

28

An hour later, Guy reentered the hall, his expression haggard. Mathilde refused to speak to him, or even acknowledge his presence. Her expression stony, she had turned her face from him and looked as though she were fiercely willing him from her presence. She would not listen to reason or assurances, and finally, realizing she was utterly exhausted, he had left her—he hoped to sleep—and posted a servant at the door to make sure she did not abscond. He could tear his own hair out at how things had transpired. For the life of him, he was unsure how things had blown up so badly in his face. Firmin hovered anxiously on the edges of his vision, but he ignored him.

"Where's Kerslake?" Guy flung out aggressively. Only a few servants remained clearing away the last of the abandoned feast.

Firmin cleared his throat. "He, er, retired along with all the other guests," he said miserably. "I believe he repaired to the south-facing sitting room. I sent along a bottle of wine for him there."

Guy paused in the act of turning around to head for that room. "And his sister?" he asked coldly. He didn't want to stray across Julia's path if he could possibly avoid it.

"She has taken to her bedchamber," Firmin answered. "The lady was most distraught at the unfolding of this evening's events."

Guy stared at his steward. "What the hells has she to be distraught about?" *How typical of Julia to try to make everything about her*, he thought caustically.

"I believe there were one or two pointed comments directed her way," Firmin said awkwardly. "The general feel of the room was not kindly toward her. The, er, Countess of Strethneal was quite scathing about Lady Julia's conduct under your roof." Firmin scratched his jaw. "It was unfortunate she chose tonight, of all nights, to wear that Martindale ruby."

Guy snorted. "Unfortunate, is that what you call it?" He left the room abruptly and headed for the sitting room Firmin had mentioned. He soon found his quarry. Tristan had made himself comfortable, lolling on one of the cushioned benches. He had unbuttoned his doublet and cuffs and was tossing back the last of his wine when Guy entered.

"Mine host!" Tristan greeted him jocularly.

Guy threw himself down in the seat opposite. "Explain," he said tersely, "your remark at supper." Tristan set his goblet carefully on the windowsill behind him. When he was not quick enough to speak, Guy added, "You identified her as my marchioness. How and why. Tell me now."

"I identified her because I was eminently in a position so to do," answered Tristan calmly.

"You have met her before?" Guy barked.

"Allow me," said Tristan, raising his hands placatingly, "to explain."

"I am waiting," Guy said shortly.

Tristan hauled himself into an upright position. "I have never met her, not formally. You are quite right in thinking it is highly unlikely that I should have done so. I have never set one foot in the Argent King's court, as you know. But my travels do take me down south quite frequently, having no fixed abode of my own." He cut short a regretful sigh, seeing Guy narrow his eyes.

"I have a friend in Aphrany," he said swiftly. "On some occasions we have ventured to watch the public lists. I saw her there, at least twice, in the royal box. She was pointed out to me as a figure of interest, my friend knowing our families are connected. I must say," he added thoughtfully, "she looked a little different in those days. Like a little doll, wheeled out to a formal event. She certainly did not wear her hair curly and loose. I fancy," he mused, "she wore both jeweled headdress and veil."

Guy let out a puff of air. His head was reeling. "And you are sure it is she? The same female?"

Tristan eyed him curiously, then nodded. "Oh yes, there can be no mistake," he said simply. "Even in peasant's garb, it was she. I never forget a face."

Peasant's garb?

"You said her flight was the talk of Aphrany," Guy prompted him stiffly.

"Well yes," Tristan admitted. "Even in such unfashionable quarters as my friend inhabits, the story was spoken of. How she had tricked her nurse and escaped her mother's clutches dressed in her page's clothing. They switched places, apparently."

Tristan looked highly diverted at the retelling, but all Guy could think about was that everything she had told him was true. Here then, was the explanation for the boyish clothing, the savage haircut, the lack of traveling companions.

She had run away. To him.

His mouth was dry. And he had not believed her. Cynic that he was, he had thought the whole story was a lie. He passed a shaking hand over his brow.

"It is a wild tale, is it not?" said Tristan with such insightful sympathy that Guy flinched. "Have you been keeping her as your mistress this entire time?"

Again, his tone was light and amused. Guy flashed him an angry look. He was not about to discuss such things with Kerslake. Swiftly, his houseguest rearranged his face to one of solicitousness rather than diversion.

"I can see that might lead to some awkwardness," he said with the understatement of the century.

Luckily, Guy was distracted, remembering Mathilde's odd comment at the marketplace that she did not think she should have been in her nurse's charge for as long as she was. Then, too, there had been that rambling story he had not been paying much heed to. Something about her nurse's old tales of…Lord Matty and Lady Tilda, he remembered suddenly and swore. That only made sense if her name indeed was Mathilde. How could he have missed that? He was a damn fool.

"Doubtless, she would not have been impressed finding Julia sat in her place," Tristan mused with a lack of sensitivity that almost took Guy's breath away. "Where did you have her stashed away? In the village?"

Guy glared at Tristan, whom he'd never particularly liked. "Of course not," he retorted. "And I'm not taking you for a confessor either."

Tristan laughed. "Can't say as I blame you," he said fairly. "I doubt it's a role I'd play well. Though you may have to attempt to smooth my sister's ruffled feathers."

"Why the hells does Julia think she's any right to feel hard done by?" he demanded.

Tristan sighed. "After all, she enjoys the status of returning northern heroine in these parts. She'll not be happy to relinquish that coveted role for the unenviable one of scarlet woman."

"Julia knew I had a wife," Guy answered shortly. "Just not one in residence."

"True," Tristan conceded. "And at the end of the day, your behavior has been exemplary. Why, you even secured her a chaperone while she was under your roof."

Guy grunted. It wasn't his conduct toward Julia Allworthy that troubled him.

"Cutting up rough, is she?" Tristan tutted.

Guy didn't bother to reply. Even in the current dire circumstances, thinking of Mathilde in terms of his wife gave him a warm feeling that made it easier to breathe. *She is my wife!* If he focused on that, it made it easier for him to bear this present catastrophe. How could he have already been the possessor of everything he ever wanted and not be aware of it? It defied all logic. She would have to forgive him for his monumental stupidity. She just had to. Wearily, he clambered to his feet. He wasn't so foolish as to think of sleeping beside her in his bed tonight. He would sleep in a guest bedchamber close by.

"Things will doubtless look less bleak in the morning," Kerslake murmured with a breezy assurance Guy found himself envying.

"You can tell you've never taken a wife," Guy responded heavily.

Tristan smirked. "I doubt it would suit me."

Guy was inclined to agree. As far as he was aware, Tristan's income derived from leeching off his brother-in-law and various friends and acquaintances. He had no estate, for it had been claimed by the Crown after their castle had been razed. He eyed Tristan with a faint curiosity. He knew for a fact that his older brother, Miles, Guy's closest boyhood friend, would never have borne such a life. What would Miles have done had he survived the war? Guy liked to think he would have helped his friend establish himself somehow. Should he have done more for his younger brother? he wondered now. He was sure that several of the northern lords had stood as Tristan's sponsor at some point or another. How else could he live such an indolent lifestyle?

Tristan yawned. "I think I'm for bed too; it's been a long day."

It certainly had, thought Guy grimly. And he needed to muster his energy for the battle ahead.

29

The next couple of days were hell on earth. Guy set about putting things to rights with a vengeance, but Mathilde refused to meet him even halfway. Prudie guarded her mistress's door like a tigress, baring her teeth at any intruders who dared to darken it. In the end Guy felt compelled to have Prudence sent back to the lodge. Waldon had been strangely disapproving about the whole thing.

"Damn it, man, what is it?" Guy had snapped in the end. "I can't have maidservants barring me from my own bedchamber!"

"Who's to fight in her corner with Prudence gone?" Waldon had asked with a stubborn look on his face.

"I'll fight in her corner," Guy had replied. "Now and always."

For a second, he had thought a scathing retort had hovered on Waldon's lips, but whatever had sprung to mind, he managed to swallow down in the face of Guy's narrowed eyes.

"I'll take the lass back, then," he mumbled.

"Aye, you do that," Guy glowered.

"I'd better check on the boy, in any case."

Guy glanced at a movement in the window. "Don't bother," he said shortly. "For he's here."

They watched Robin dismount and head toward the house. Guy, remembering the lad's previous behavior, steeled himself for a confrontation. However, to his surprise, Robin seemed to be the only one who did not consider him a villain.

"Was she sat at your knee?" he'd asked bluntly.

"What? Who?" Guy had been momentarily at a complete loss.

"This other woman."

"Of course not!" Guy had spluttered.

"So, there's nothing in it, then," Robin had said, and his calm tone had been such a relief after Waldon's indignation and Prudie's outright hostility that Guy had relaxed enough not to shout.

"Nothing at all," he had rumbled.

"That's alright then," Robin had said easily. "Why don't you tell my lady that?"

If only it was that bloody easy, Guy had thought grimly. He'd tried again, only that morning, and made no dent in her defenses. He sighed and rubbed his eyes. When he looked up, he found Robin's gaze fixed on his face.

"You had better set things to rights with her," Robin said, giving him a level look. Guy paused, wondering if he was imagining the air of significance to the boy's words. "There's four of us," he added suddenly.

"Four of you?"

Robin nodded. "Me, Willard Peyton, Piers Winstanley, and Gordon Fairfax. But I'm closest to her."

Guy waited, for he could tell there was more to follow. Sure enough, after a few moments the boy continued.

"She does things for us, and we do things for her. At court, I mean."

Guy's eyebrows snapped together. "What sort of things?" he found himself asking, remembering Mathilde's words about her friends over that card game. It seemed weeks ago.

"Binds our cuts, mends our clothes. Helps us write our letters home," said Rob vaguely. He rubbed his nose.

"I meant, what do you do for her?" Guy said pointedly.

"Teach her things about life. Useful things," the boy replied. "Her mother keeps her so hemmed in she can't hardly breathe. Her old nursemaid still follows her around like she's an infant. Luckily, the old thing's almost blind. She never even had any friends until she met the Countess Vawdrey."

Guy felt his face harden at that accursed name. She was friends with a Vawdrey? He'd have to coach her not to mention the fact in these parts.

"It's not her fault," Robin added quickly, misinterpreting the source his disapproval. "She didn't know any better. Once we started showing her the ropes, she soon caught on."

Guy shot him a look of misgiving. He didn't know what to think about four young squires tutoring his wife into the ways of the world.

"I need to have some speech with her," he had concluded abruptly. He'd have to pursue this conversation at some future point in time. "Waldon is taking Prudence back to the lodge now, so you could either go back with them, or stay here if you prefer." Leaving it up to the boy to decide, he nodded at Robin, who cautiously returned the gesture, then strode from the room.

"I need you to talk to me," Guy told the huddled lump in the bed. "We need to…explain to one another. I need to explain." *Nothing.* He reached out and grabbed the sheets, dragging them down to her waist.

She looked pale and wan, lying there in her shift. "Leave me be," Mathilde said wearily.

"I did not betray you, Mathilde," Guy insisted. "Julia Allworthy is a guest in my house, nothing more."

Mathilde turned away from him to face the wall. If she would only cry or scream at him, it would somehow be better than this, he thought.

"I'm not giving you any more time to grieve yourself about this," he said tersely. "You've had two days, and you'll get no more."

"I can go home?" she asked in a small voice he barely recognized as hers, so lacking in spirit was it.

"You are home," he said uncompromisingly. Did she mean the lodge or worse? He refused entirely to acknowledge the possibility of the latter. "We can visit the lodge together at our leisure, but our place is here." She gave no answer to that. "I'm sending Lettys in to attend you and help you dress."

"I want Prudie."

"Well, you're getting Lettys," he snapped. He regarded her a moment, his brow furrowed. "When you're up and about, we'll talk more," he said in a stilted manner. "I have much to speak of."

Her listless reception of this disturbed him more than he could say. She seemed to have passed the distressed stage and reached some place he could not touch her. And he did not like it. Not one bit.

On his way back below stairs, a frightened-looking servant approached him. "My lord, a visitor awaits you below."

"I'm not seeing anyone," Guy answered, practically grinding his teeth. No doubt it was some prying neighbor who had attended the feast and wanted more salacious details about the state of his marriage.

The servant turned pale. "It's, er, well, it's, er…"

"What?" Guy barked. "Oh, never mind, I'll tell them myself!"

He didn't care if it was the Earl of Strethneal; he'd send him away with a flea in his ear! However, on reaching the hallway, he found it was altogether a different class of guest.

"Mistress Helga," he blurted, seeing her upright figure stood just inside the doorway. "I did not realize it was you."

He glanced about wondering where the servants were cowering. Staying out of his way no doubt. He came across them in small huddles, whispering to each other and glancing at him askance. No wonder that fool had not wished to turn her away. Didn't have the guts to.

"Come through," he invited in a weary voice. "I'm sure we can find you some refreshment."

The large black raven on her shoulder croaked. "Be quiet, you," Helga muttered, sounding annoyed. "Who asked your opinion?"

Guy shot her a startled glance.

"Tancred and I are not on friendly terms this morn," she said by way of explanation, following Guy down the corridor. "He says

295

I do not deserve to break my fast." She sighed. "It's a hard life when one's actions are judged so harshly, is that not so?"

The topic of conversation struck a chord of fellow feeling, and Guy found himself concurring. He felt very ill judged at present. Even Temur's wife, Lettys, his previous ally, had looked at him beadily when he had told her she was now to wait on his marchioness. He was quite sure half of his staff thought him an unprincipled lecher who had used his wife very ill.

"Tancred does not appreciate my methods. But I always tell him, the end justifies the means, do you not agree, my lord?"

They had reached the Great Hall now, and Guy led her to a wooden bench and gestured for her to be seated.

"Quite," he murmured distractedly. He caught sight of a shadow lurking beyond the door at the far end of the room. "Hie! You there, fetch us ale and oatcakes," he ordered briskly. Hasty footfalls told him his orders had been received. "How can I help you this morning?" he asked politely as he considered his next move in the campaign to break down his wife's defenses.

Suddenly, it occurred to him that Mathilde had a fondness for the old witch. Maybe he could recruit her to his service? After all, the old crone must know he was quite innocent of any wrongdoing, other than his failure to trust his own wife. When he turned his head to give the old woman a considering look, he was startled to find himself being eyed in the same appraising nature.

"Maybe 'tis I'm here to help you?" she suggested slowly. "Ever considered that?"

"I was just entertaining the notion," he admitted grudgingly. "I find myself in need of an advocate at present. How do you fancy the job?"

296

Footsteps approaching forestalled the old woman's immediate response. A tray was borne in with the ale and oatcakes he had demanded. Drinks were poured and a platter set down between them. Helga helped herself to an oatcake as Guy took a swig of ale.

"Let me guess," she said, tapping her chin. "Your task for me is to try to weasel your way back into your wife's good graces?" she suggested.

A dull flush rose in Guy's cheeks. "Am I so easy to read?" he asked, glancing away.

"All too easy," she scoffed, offering the cake to her bird. Tancred resolutely turned away from her peace offering and she sighed. "Besides," she added loudly, "how can I plead your cause, when it was I who denounced you for a traitor in the first place?"

Guy wheeled around. "What? What do you mean?"

"It was I," explained Helga impassively, "who told your wife you entertained another in her place. In short, that you betrayed her." At his incredulous stare, she nodded her head gently. "Yes, I confess it freely."

"Why?" he thundered. "Why would you do such a thing?"

She drew herself up. "It was necessary," she said in her portentous voice. "I am not one to shirk my duty." Tancred gave a loud croak.

"You try my patience, old woman. A vastly pretty husband you've made me out to be!"

Helga looked at him thoughtfully. "Think," she said sternly, "of the results of my ploy. Your people pity the wronged wife who walked into your fine banqueting hall and found you carousing with another woman sat at your table, dressed in splendor and jewels."

Guy gripped his cup. "I was not carousing!"

"No one," Helga interrupted him loudly, "even mentions that the wife was an outsider, a hated southerner in the retelling." She paused, letting this significant fact sink in. "They whisper of her peasant garb, her bare feet, her sweet little pregnant belly…"

"She wasn't barefoot!" snapped Guy. Then his head whipped up. "Pregnant?" he echoed. "Nay…"

"They recognize the old story," the woman carried on, ignoring his words and nodding her head. "*The Wicked Lord and the Other Woman*. Their sympathies lie firmly with the abandoned wife, humiliated and scorned…"

"I didn't abandon her!"

"You denied her her rightful place," she said firmly.

"Because I didn't realize—" Guy scraped his fingers through his hair in frustration. "I can't forget the look on her face," he said, passing a shaking hand across his face.

Helga leaned forward and patted him on the shoulder. "Take heart." Guy mopped his brow. "This way is far better," Helga persisted. "So, your tenants will eye you askance for a few months. They'll whisper you're no better than you should be. What would you rather? Mathilde endure twenty years of being shunned as the enemy of your people? Would you prefer your tenants threw dirt and stones at her when she was unaccompanied? Called her 'the southern bitch' behind your back? Rued the day you were forced to wed her? For them to tell each other the Kerslake girl was your true love?"

"No!" Guy burst forth. He looked appalled. "Is that—?" He hesitated. "Is that what would have happened?" He felt sick.

Old Helga's blue eyes turned dreamy. "It's what I foresaw lay ahead for you if I did not act."

Guy broke out in a cold sweat. "Then you were right to do what you did," he said hoarsely.

She nodded gently. "Well, I thought so," she murmured. "I know the little one, she suffered, but it was a fleeting pain, not to be sustained. You'll find she is surprisingly resilient. The important thing is that a true understanding of heart and mind is established between the two of you."

"How am I supposed to achieve that?" demanded Guy bleakly. "Any understanding between us has been shattered. She trusted me, and I—" His voice lowered. "I broke that trust."

Helga nodded her head sagely. "Now you have smashed the rotten foundations, you can start to rebuild."

"Rotten?"

At his angry tone, her eyebrows rose. "Do you deny this match was entered into in the wrong spirit?"

"There was nothing rotten about our beginnings, nothing at all!"

"Your hand was forced," Helga reminded him. "You did not want her."

"I don't care! She was meant to be mine," vowed Guy vehemently. "It was fate. If it hadn't been this way, it would have been another."

Helga looked pleasantly surprised by his words. "Well, well," she murmured. "Almost, you impress me." He scowled at her. "Think of it this way. Your foundations were mostly sound, but one tower was built on a cliff edge that would erode in time. Seeing this, you dismantled this tower and rebuilt it on firmer ground." Guy considered this a moment. "Does that sound any more palatable?"

He gave a short nod and cleared his throat. "Aye. I'll consider it that way."

"Excellent." She shot him a sidelong glance. "Shall I tell you the fate I told your father would befall you?"

He was startled but did not hesitate. "Tell me."

"That you would fall deeply in love with your own wife, a southerner. And that if you managed to earn her love in return, all would be well at Acton March."

Guy flushed. "That was it?"

"It was."

Tancred gave another croak. Helga gave a wintry smile. "Oh, you will, will you?" With a deft movement of her hand, she tossed an oatcake up into air. It was caught in a large black beak and consumed with ruthless efficiency. "I accept your apology," Helga added coolly.

Guy wasn't sure if she was talking to him or the bird.

30

"Come in," Mathilde called out listlessly in answer to the light tap on the door. She already knew it wasn't Guy from the lightness of the rap.

She was sat bundled up on the window seat, a woolen mantle over her shift, and her hair in a messy mop of curls. She had washed but hadn't bothered to so much as drag a comb through her hair. She would have to use his if she did, she thought, looking around the large bedroom in a desultory fashion. And she didn't want to touch anything of Guy's. It was curious to think she would have been so happy to have been set up in his rooms only three days ago. A blond head peered around the door. *This must be Temur's wife*, she surmised. She was young and fair and carrying a bundle of clothes in her arms.

"Good morning, my lady," Lettys said, gazing about her in open curiosity. She shut the door behind her. "I have some of your clothes here brought over from the lodge."

Mathilde eyed the scarlet dress on the top of the pile with disfavor. Prudie must have repaired it. She certainly wasn't wearing that! Seducing Guy was the last thing she wanted to do.

"My green wool gown will do very well," she answered with obvious disinterest.

"Begging your pardon, my lady, but his lordship has had that given away."

"Given away?" Mathilde was momentarily startled out of her apathy. It was the only warm dress she possessed. Certainly, the only one that covered her charms adequately.

"A woolen dress is not fit for a marchioness," Lettys informed her firmly.

"Well, he seemed to think it appropriate when he gave it to me," Mathilde answered tartly before she could stop herself. Lettys's eyes widened.

"It little matters," she continued quickly. "As I have no inclination to venture below stairs."

She turned her face away from Lettys's curious gaze. The young woman shrugged and placed the pile of clothes down at the foot of the bed, opening and closing drawers, tidying her things away. Mathilde fought down a wave of annoyance at the way her own wishes were being so ignored.

"Where is Prudence?" she asked pointedly.

"She's returned to the lodge," Lettys informed her cheerfully.

Mathilde sat up in her seat. "Returned to the lodge? Without me?"

"Which one does your ladyship wish to wear today?" asked Lettys brightly. She held up the scarlet or her sapphire gown.

"When did she return?" Mathilde persisted. "I did not give her leave to return."

Lettys nibbled her bottom lip ruminatively. "If I tell you, will you oblige me by picking a gown?" she cajoled before adding hurriedly, "your ladyship."

"It little signifies," Mathilde sighed. "And please stop calling me 'my lady,' I am not accustomed to such considerations. Call me Mathilde."

Lettys looked gratified. "I'm by way of a cousin of yours through marriage," she said eagerly. "I'm called Lettys. I believe you know my man, Temur? Temur is a second cousin of his lordship's. On his mother's side."

"I'm pleased to meet you, Lettys," Mathilde found herself murmuring, unable to ignore societal politeness. After all, it was not this young woman's fault that Acton March was the last place on earth that she wanted to be right now, and its master the very last person she wanted to see. Seeing Lettys take up the scarlet dress in the face of her silence on the matter, Mathilde was forced to speak up. "Not that one," she said apologetically. "It has…associations. I'll wear the sapphire blue."

Lettys likely thought her a contrary and difficult woman, Mathilde thought forlornly as she laid out scarlet stockings for her and yellow garters.

"I believe there is a pale cream underdress," she forced herself to say. Perhaps if she wore that under the low-cut gown, it would give her some modesty. "It is of samite. If you could find it for me, I would be most grateful."

"I think I remember seeing that," Lettys said obligingly and went back to one of the drawers. "Ah yes, here it is. What lovely fabric."

Together they managed to get Mathilde dressed and looking halfway decent, but when it came to her hair, Lettys looked less confident. Lettys's own hair was worn in a braided coronet wound about her head.

"What do you normally do with it?" she asked, sounding perplexed. "It's far too short to braid."

Mathilde glanced over at the looking glass and found her hair stood up almost on end like a dandelion clock after Lettys's brisk brushing of it. "Um…" She reached up and tried to smooth it down. "I may need to apply a little water," she said distractedly. "It's most strange, when it's long it has a wave, but not curls like this."

"Were you ill?" asked Lettys sympathetically. "My sister had scarlet fever and they had to cut all her hair off. It took an age to grow back."

"I'm afraid it's rather complicated," answered Mathilde, not wanting to go into the whole story.

Lettys nodded. "She had complications too," she said breezily. "But it grew back in the end."

"I'm so glad," murmured Mathilde, slipping on the garters over her stockings.

"So was Gladys. When Erik saw the state of her, he vowed he wouldn't marry her for a herd of heifers. Not when she looked like a plucked hen."

Mathilde paused. "And did she? Marry him I mean?" she asked in spite of herself.

"Oh yes. And they'd not been married a twelvemonth when Erik's own hair started to recede. You may be sure she flings it in his face when it suits her. 'My old plucked cock' she calls him. 'Never mind your field of heifers,' she says. 'What about my fine prize bull?'" Lettys laughed heartily and picked up the comb again gamely. "Let's see what we can do."

It was somehow impossible to stay disinterested and apathetic in the face of Lettys's lively conversation. Still, Mathilde felt an emotional wobble when Lettys pronounced her ready to precede her downstairs.

"I want only a quiet sitting room where I won't be disturbed," she reiterated nervously. She was not up to any confrontations with her husband again so soon. Not now she knew what lay behind that handsome face—betrayal.

"Aye, my lady," Lettys assured her. "All is in place."

"Mathilde."

"Mathilde," Lettys corrected herself, shutting the door behind them. "His lordship specified you were to have the best blue sitting room at your disposal."

Mathilde pulled a face. It was a little late, she thought, hardening her heart against him, for him to be rolling out a warm welcome for her in his home.

"We won't find his other guests there?" she ventured sharply as they descended the staircase. Again, her thoughts strayed to *that woman*, with her golden gown and jewels and her cultured voice, and she felt a tremor of anger reverberate through her.

"The Lady Julia has been locked in her bedroom in hysterics this last two days now," Lettys told her, clearly seeing through her query. Mathilde bit her lip, determined not to betray herself further.

"His lordship relieved me of my duties, chaperoning *her* about," sniffed Lettys. "And a good thing too, for she was a haughty, disagreeable madam at best and resented me something fierce."

"Resented you?" echoed Mathilde, forgetting her resolve to maintain a stony silence on this subject. "Why?"

"On account of she wanted free rein to do as she pleased, but Lord Martindale didn't want her racketing about the place, lording it over everyone."

Mathilde digested this a moment before concluding regretfully that she couldn't take much comfort from this. After all, he hadn't wanted Mathilde to have free rein over his home either.

She remembered her previous visit and the poky little bedroom she had been locked in.

"For all the fine folk about these parts think so much of her," Lettys continued, lowering her voice, "the servants can't stand her. Demanding and spoiled, that's what they all think." Lettys nodded her head. "Her brother directed a bowl of cold water be thrown over her yestere'en, when she wouldn't be quieted. Flew into a passion she did and went at him like a regular she-devil! Caught her by the wrists he did, by all accounts. 'That's enough, my girl,' says he. 'You'll not be sharpening your claws on my face!'"

Mathilde's mouth fell open. "Her brother is here too?" She hoped she managed to mask her astonishment. Was it usual for a man to house his mistress's brother also?

"Oh yes, for they come every year to visit the neighborhood of their birth."

Mathilde lapsed into silence. She didn't want to hear about it after all. Still, at low moments, she couldn't help herself from thinking of that ruby set in a swan brooch the other woman had worn. Mathilde may have only been wed by proxy, but she knew very well the crest of the Martindales, the gorged swan with wings outstretched. In four years, she had received no token from her husband, but perhaps after all, that wasn't so surprising if he had given them all away to his various mistresses over the years. In spite of her resolve, she smarted at that thought and had to hold her head higher to hide the fact.

Her every feeling was raw and bleeding. How right Old Helga had been to identify her true enemy as Lord Martindale and not the carter. The carter could never have inflicted this amount of pain on her, for all he had trampled and kicked her. Guy had dealt her a far more grievous blow, even though, she remembered dimly, she had been the one to strike him. In front of an audience too.

No doubt the servants whispered she, too, was a vicious woman and cruel. She remembered indistinctly that the people who sat at the table had been fancy in raiment—no doubt Guy's friends and neighbors who she would never win over now. The visiting gentlefolk, too, would have no good opinion of her after the show she had put on.

What did it matter? she asked herself wearily as Lettys led her into a well-appointed room with large windows flanked with blue velvet curtains. A servant was busily laying logs in the fireplace. To her surprise, she spied her new tapestry loom had been set up in one corner. Set next to it was the lift-out shelf from her trunk at the lodge which contained all her threads. Mathilde flushed at the idea of people going through her things, but then she remembered Prudie still had the scandalous book and calmed a little.

Spotting a piece of parchment, she recognized it was her design of the lodge and its inhabitants. Her lips twisted bitterly to think of how differently she had felt when she set that scene out. It had been a few days merely.

Walking over to the loom, she picked up the design and let her eyes travel over it a moment. Her first impulse was to tear it up and cast it into the newly lit fire. But, after all, she was badly in need of a distraction if she was to tarry here awhile. She eyed the drawing and felt a pang when her gaze fell on one figure in particular. Well, she would omit him from the tapestry altogether, she resolved.

She must get word to Robin. He would help her plan her escape from this accursed place if Guy refused to see reason and release her. But first, she must bide her time awhile until she was sure of the lay of the land. From the impassioned

307

interviews she had with him thus far, Guy had every intention of keeping her here, ironically, now she no longer wanted to stay. Well, she thought, stung, she would soon change his mind about that! She had no intention of playing the role of his marchioness, a role he clearly had always thought her unfit for.

Her chest heaved. Her mother had been right all along, she thought bleakly. She was not equipped to deal with the harsh realities of married life. Men were faithless beasts who could not be trusted.

She seated herself at her loom as Lettys gave some instruction to the servant for refreshment. Mathilde cared not; she had no appetite. With unsteady fingers, she selected the materials she needed from her wooden box and set about starting her tapestry.

31

Guy eased the door open and nodded to Lettys to make herself scarce. The lass was quick-witted enough to catch his meaning and made her way lightly over to him.

"Wait until I call for you," he said in a low voice, and she nodded and left.

He closed the door behind him and stood on the threshold a minute, contemplating the picture Mathilde made as she sat absorbed at her tapestry loom. She ought to look rather lost, her small figure in the midst of its large frame, but she was clearly mistress of it, for her fingers moved over it lightly and confidently. He cleared his throat, and suddenly she was sat stiff as a board, her back straight and her cheeks suffused with an angry flush.

"My lord—" she started.

"My lady," he replied, looking up at her, fully aware it was the first time he had addressed her as such.

She was quiet a moment. "What are you about? I believe I told you that I have no desire to hear aught you have to say."

"And I told you I still have much to say on the matter."

She gave a determined shake of her head. "'Twould be pointless," she insisted. "We—we do not suit each other, sir."

"That's a damned lie."

"You do not want me here. You never did."

Her voice was suddenly so quiet, he had to strain to catch it. "I always wanted you," he said abruptly. "I just didn't know it until recently."

She didn't even pause. "You love another," she said in a wobbly voice.

This accusation stunned him so much, he had to grope a moment for his answer. "What the bloody hells are you talking about now, woman?" he growled.

"Waldon told me about Julia and your first betrothal. I deserve a husband who can give me his whole heart."

Guy reeled. *What?* "Waldon was talking utter nonsense!" he roared, then noticed the tear that was tracking down her cheek. *Damn it!* He was making a mess of this.

"I don't love anyone but you!" he bellowed. No doubt the whole damned household had heard that, but he was past caring.

"I don't believe you," she said, sticking her little button nose in the air. Gods, she was obstinate and pretty and *infuriating*.

"Did you hear what I just said, Mathilde?" he asked, drawing in a steadying breath. "I have never spoken of love to a woman before in my life."

"You didn't just now," she said, rallying. "You flung it in my face like an insult."

He blinked. *Well, she might very well have a point there.* "I love you," he said blankly.

"Well, I don't love you," she said, but the fact she sobbed it softened the blow.

"I'll make you," he said resolutely.

Strangely enough, speaking the words made him feel somehow better. With each second that had passed since he made his declaration, he felt stronger, like some weight had lifted from his shoulders. The terrible ache that had filled his chest was abating, though not gone completely. Still, her expression was wooden, unbending.

She opened her mouth, but before she could even speak her unforgiving words, he said, "I never loved Julia Kerslake. It was just a passing boyhood fancy. I admired her looks when I was too young to notice her personality."

This made her fall silent, but her expression was still unutterably hurt. "I lied," she said sadly, robbing him of all breath. "I loved you as soon as I clapped eyes on you. You were everything I ever wanted in life."

His heart swelled, though his mind boggled at the fact he could ever have been anyone's romantic ideal. Then the past tense of her statement filtered through the glow. *Were?*

"I still am," he said belligerently. "Or I'd better be." She said nothing, and he took a deep breath. "Mathilde?" She gave a slight shake of her head. "I'm not giving you any more time to yourself," he growled. "I'm never making that mistake again." She closed her eyes, and he walked unsteadily forward.

"Please, don't—sweetheart, I can't stand it. I won't."

This isn't working, he thought wretchedly. He needed to take a different approach. Hauling her out of her seat at the loom, he half dragged her over to the window seat. He saw her seated and then knelt at her feet. It was the only way to bring them onto a similar level.

"When I first saw you," he said desperately, "I wanted to shelter you, from the law even. And I didn't even know who you were then." *No reaction*. He continued. "Then when you revealed yourself, I was so angry, so very angry." He swallowed. "But still…I felt this—this strange urge to protect and…" *Own you* would sound wrong. *Take ownership of you*. No, that wasn't right either. "I wanted so badly to…" *Join my body with you?* "Be with you," he stammered.

Gods, he was bad at this!

"I didn't trust you, but I wanted you so, so much. And that threw me too, because in recent years I felt I disliked and mistrusted women. But you were so beautiful and so different from what I knew and what I thought I knew. I just couldn't stay away from you. Not if my life depended on it. I wanted to possess you utterly."

He winced at his crudeness. He'd be lucky if she didn't run screaming from the room at this rate. He fell silent waiting for some sign from her that his words had registered. When she did speak, it still took him by surprise.

"My first husband was seventy-nine years old," she said in a quiet voice, and he clenched his fists until his short nails bit into his palms. "I only met him twice. My second husband I met once on his death bed."

He nodded, managing to stop himself from denying anyone was ever her husband save himself. It took an effort though.

"Aye," he said roughly. He wanted her confidences, for her to talk to him. Just not about other men in her life.

"I didn't know anything about…husbands or the marriage bed," she said, refusing to look at him.

He cleared his throat. He already knew that. "I don't understand how—" he started hoarsely, but she cut him off.

"I was twenty-four years of age. I still had Nurse, although there was no more story time. It wasn't needed anymore. My mother had successfully maneuvered me through three political marriages, yet I had never left her side. I had never run my own household, had never held a child of my own in my arms..." Her voice cracked.

"Sweetheart..."

She turned her face away again. "It's too late, Guy. You have broken my heart."

32

Mathilde spent a melancholy, but quiet, afternoon at her tapestry. She got a goodly portion of it started off and felt quietly pleased with her progress, though in all likelihood she would spend the rest of her life trying to forget everything that had taken place at the lodge. Her insides still felt lacerated though. If she sat very still, and quiet, she told herself, then there was a chance she would not fall completely apart.

In an odd way, it reminded her of her old life, back in the days when all she had wanted was to go unnoticed. How she would have loved to have sat at such a loom in a beautiful room like this away from all the intrigues at court! Lettys had picked up on Mathilde's desire for silence and asked for leave to go and fetch a basket of mending from her own room. Mathilde quickly assented. It would be peaceful for the two of them to sit industriously occupied for the afternoon. With a bit of luck, she would not need to speak more than a handful of words between now and bedtime.

She sank into silence, and when the door creaked, she did not turn her head at once, imagining it was Lettys returning. A small cough sounded, and Mathilde turned to find a good-looking man with copper hair wearing a fine burgundy doublet hovering in the doorway. He looked strangely familiar to her. Frowning slightly, she turned back to her task, guessing he had taken a wrong turn. She had no desire to speak with him. After a moment, the door carefully closed, but the sound of a throat being politely cleared, made her turn back again.

"Lady Martindale," he said, presenting her with a very elegant bow. "I trust I do not intrude?"

She gazed at him wordlessly. What could she answer to that when plainly he *was* intruding in the worst way? His lips twitched, and to her surprise she realized he was amused by her pointed silence.

"I am Tristan Kerslake, your very humble servant. Perhaps you, ah, remember me from the most unfortunate feast two nights ago?" Mathilde's brow puckered. She remembered no one from the banquet save the principal players. "I was the one who identified you as the rightful marchioness," he said with assumed modesty.

"Did you?" Mathilde asked after a small pause.

"Though in truth, you would not remember it, for you had already fled by that point."

Mathilde shrugged a shoulder. He really was very good-looking, she thought dispassionately, though perhaps a little on the short side. Of course, that might just be because she was comparing him to Guy. *Oh dear.* She would always, she realized, for the rest of her days, compare men with Guy.

"I have a friend in Aphrany who pointed you out to me once. You were part of the Queen's royal retinue."

Feeling she must respond at this point to avoid outright rudeness, Mathilde murmured, "I see." He inclined his head. It was at that point she realized she recognized him, though not from a tournament. "I feel sure I, too, have seen you before, sir," she said. "Is your friend a courtier?"

"You flatter me." He smiled. "Alas, he does not move in such exalted quarters and is naught but a wealthy merchant's son. He pointed you out to me at a public event. A tournament, in fact."

No, that wasn't right, thought Mathilde, not that she was particularly interested. She remembered him from court, she

315

was almost sure of it. And for some reason, she *did* associate him with a courtier, and a famous one. In a flash it came to her.

"Lord Oswald Vawdrey," she said aloud and saw him stiffen. "It was Vawdrey I saw you with. I was with his countess at the royal palace at Aphrany, and you were emerging from his office."

His face, she noticed impassively, was flushed. "I assure you, madam, you are quite mistaken," he answered, and though he still smiled, it looked rather brittle and unreal.

She shrugged again, and at this point, Lettys reappeared with her basket. Tristan Kerslake murmured his apologies and retreated, and Mathilde was left once more in silence.

At suppertime, she was escorted to the Great Hall which was brightly lit with candles and manned by many servants who seemed to line every wall, despite the fact that only five places were laid at table. She was led with great pomp to the seat at Guy's immediate right. Temur was waiting at his left and Lettys went to join her husband there.

"We are just family this evening," Guy said. "May I present my steward to you, Mathilde? This is Firmin, who served my father before me."

The older man presented her with an extremely low bow and then drew back her chair for her. She murmured something and sat down. Firmin took his seat to her right and everyone was seated as the first course was served.

Mathilde was glad to find she felt pleasantly numb and quite divorced from proceedings as she sipped her vegetable soup out of convention more than hunger. She made no effort to join in the conversation that struck up as the fish course was served and soon, when she did not respond to any lures, they began talking of business and the estate and Mathilde was able to sit in utter silence.

Again, she was reminded of her previous life as the timorous Lady Martindale at court. Then, whole conversations would be carried on around her without her being expected to participate. *Perhaps it would not be that surprising*, she mused, *if I were to slip back into that previous role of mine?* After all, it had not been so very long ago. Perhaps she could not escape her fate as the meek and unassuming Lady Tilda.

"Mathilde?" With a start, she found she was being addressed by her frowning husband. She raised her eyebrows at him eloquently. "Do you have no opinion to put forth on the subject?" he asked challengingly.

She opened her mouth to explain she had not been listening, but for some reason other words entirely tumbled out. "It is no concern of mine," she said coolly instead.

A spark kindled in his gaze. He sat back in his seat, regarding her. "No concern of yours? What an amenable wife you shall be," he mocked.

"Aye, but not to you," she answered crisply. "For presently I shall return to court and request the King finds me a fourth husband who may be more suited to me."

"Don't!" he said sharply, but it was the note of pain in his voice that halted her. She lapsed into silence, acutely aware of the startled eyes of the other diners riveted on them.

"How long?" Guy rumbled, not even attempting to speak quietly. She did not answer. "How long are you going to punish me?" he asked hoarsely. "I make no complaint, you understand. I just need to know my suffering will be finite."

"How about four years?" Mathilde heard herself ask in a clear, concise voice. "How does that sound? The amount of time I waited in vain for you to send for me." You could have heard a pin drop in the Great Hall.

Guy did not answer a moment, then he cleared his throat. "That sounds fair," he said at last, and not one more word was spoken between any of them for the remainder of the meal.

As she climbed the stairs for bed, Mathilde realized with shock and a certain amount of grim satisfaction that Lady Tilda had left for good. There would be no sinking back into her previous life. What, then, would become of her? The future stretched out before her, strange and unknowable.

Should she seek out an audience with Old Helga for guidance? She felt a strange reluctance to, after the painful interview a few nights previously. Her memory was hazy as to when the old woman had left them that night. She had definitely been leading their way through the woods as they had set out for the manor house. But when Mathilde had mounted the steps to the main door, she did not remember Helga being present.

She would not send for Helga, she resolved as she brushed her hair before bed. Indeed, she had the strangest feeling that no messenger would even find her cottage unless Helga wished it to be so.

She was washing before bed when she noticed the large carved wooden box that had been placed at her bedside. Lifting off the lid, she found it full of precious jewels. She recognized the rubies set in enameled swans immediately. Only the brooch was conspicuous in its absence. Quietly, Mathilde replaced the lid and climbed into bed.

33

The next morning followed almost precisely the pattern of the previous morning, except that Lettys suggested they went for a walk in the gardens instead of retiring immediately to the blue sitting room. Mathilde acquiesced, and they had not walked further than the kitchen gardens when Temur headed them off from the direction of the stables, and Lettys excused herself with an apologetic look and hurried over to meet him.

Mathilde waited a moment, but when they looked deep in conversation, she decided instead to have a walk about the large herb and vegetable beds. Most of the snow had now melted and only the odd patch remained, though it was still very cold out. She could identify fennel, cabbage, leeks, and radishes but not much else. She had not spent much time in the country after all.

She wandered up and down the narrow paths in between the plots, and was just wondering idly which were lentils and which were peas when a quiet voice wished her a good morning, and she looked up eagerly in hopes it might be Robin. To her surprise, she found it was Tristan Kerslake smiling his urbane smile. She blinked at his turquoise doublet and matching cape and wished him a good morning in return, hoping she hid her disappointment that he was not her young friend.

"You are looking rather better this morning, my lady, if I may make so bold," he ventured, casting a quick appraising look at her face. "You have a good deal more color in your cheeks and a sparkle in your eyes."

"Probably the fresh air," Mathilde responded.

Pieces were falling into place in her mind, and she realized now that he must be the brother of Guy's first love. Why had she not properly registered that before? Perhaps because she had flinched from all thoughts that had pained her.

"How is your sister?" she asked dryly. "Is she recovered yet from her shock?"

Tristan gave a startled laugh. "She is fancying herself in the role of the much-wronged, maligned woman," he responded, falling in step beside her. "Alas for Julia, no one else regards her as such. It vexes her greatly."

Mathilde shot a curious look at him. "You are not close to your sister," she said in a puzzled voice. "And yet..."

"And yet I live off the fat of her spoils," he said matter-of-factly. "Oh yes. Lord Allworthy has kindly provided me with an allowance for years. Perhaps you have not heard my own tragic tale?"

He sighed heavily and cast her a sly look beneath his lashes. Against her better judgment, Mathilde was diverted. Mind you, any distraction from her current situation was welcome presently.

"I was the younger brother of the honorable Miles Kerslake," he explained. "Miles was your esteemed husband's bosom companion and greatest friend," he continued. "He was killed in battle, defending our family honor."

"During the war?"

"Quite. Typical of Miles to die in a blaze of glory, the Blechmarsh colors clutched in his dying fingers. I never lived up to him in any way," he said ruefully, yet with a hint of scorn. "Of course, by rights I ought to have succeeded him to the baronetcy and the lands but alas..." He heaved another sigh. "King Wymer's forces leveled Kerslake Castle to a pile of rubble for its defiance and rescinded our titles and lands as traitors to the Crown. We were unfortunate that he sent his famous hound of war to deal with us. Sir Mason Vawdrey, perhaps you have heard of him?"

Mathilde gave a start. "Oh yes," she said. The Vawdreys were a powerful family and well-known figures at court.

"Though he is known as Duke of Cadwallader now, for services rendered to the Crown."

"I thought that was by dint of his marriage," Mathilde murmured, but Tristan was not listening.

"It was his brother that you accuse me of knowing," he continued smoothly.

Mathilde looked at him in surprise "Accuse?" she repeated. They had come to the end of the row, and Mathilde turned deliberately back, not wishing to let Temur and Lettys out of her sight. Obligingly, Tristan kept in step with her.

"It is hardly likely that I should be acquainted with the brother of my enemy, now, is it?" he pointed out gently.

Mathilde gave him a thoughtful look. *Now why*, she wondered, *is he so determined to refute all knowledge of Lord Oswald Vawdrey?* In silence, she turned over what she knew of her friend Fenella's husband. He was perhaps the most powerful man at court. The King's chief advisor, and also, it was whispered, his *spymaster*. He must have seen the moment this remembrance flickered through her thoughts, for he gazed at her keenly. She watched the quick play of emotions cross his handsome face. *Annoyance*, she recognized briefly and strangely, *regret*. But why was he regretful?

"Ah, I see that I have merely made things worse," he said with a sigh. "Unfortunate, and rather stupid of me. But you have a far livelier mind that I heretofore suspected." Mathilde frowned.

321

Did her vague suspicions really amount to much? "I am curious about one thing though," he said slowly. "Why on earth does everyone think you such a timorous creature? Are you aware that your misnomer at court is 'Mouse' Martindale?"

Mathilde flushed. "Is it?" she asked before she could stop herself.

He nodded. "Not here though," he conceded. "Here you are the 'southern lioness.'" He made an elaborate twirling gesture with his fingers. "Ballads will be sung in your honor. I may even sing them myself," he added thoughtfully.

Mathilde shot him a look of disbelief. "I hardly think—"

"You do realize," he said wryly, "that the servants hear and repeat every word exchanged between you and Martindale outside of the bedchamber." Mathilde flushed. Guy had not come once to her bedchamber in at least three nights. Of course, she was glad about that. Ecstatic. "Everyone in the county now knows you have the heretofore woman-hating marquis on his knees, begging your forgiveness of his previous spousal cruelty."

"Cruelty?" she repeated, startled. "*Negligence* would be a more appropriate word."

Tristan laughed. "Poor Guy," he muttered. "Almost, I feel sorry for him."

"Almost?" Mathilde glanced around, but Temur had slipped an arm about Lettys's waist and was whispering in her ear. After all, thought Mathilde bleakly. They were still newlyweds.

"Empathy has never been one of my strongest points," Tristan admitted. "Let me ask you frankly, what significance do you think anyone would attach to your claims of seeing me at the southern court?"

"None," Mathilde answered truthfully, but he paid no attention to her.

"Let me put it this way," he continued glibly. "It could cause me some embarrassment round these parts if it were known that I sometimes join the southern king's household. But I could explain it away, at a push." He shot a measuring look at Mathilde, as if to see how she took this.

"I'm sure you could," she said politely. "It is really none of my business."

"If only I could trust in a woman's wayward tongue," he said wistfully.

There seemed no response to this, so Mathilde made none, and they stood in a companionable silence. "Do they really call me Mouse?" she asked at last.

He gave a short laugh. "They do. But they are quite wrong." He paused to consider a moment. "You are more like...a mink. Tiny and exquisite, with sharp little teeth."

34

It was not until that afternoon that Mathilde finally received a visit from Robin. She was back at her loom, but when he entered the room, she was up and out of her seat in an instant.

"Where have you been? I can scarcely believe you have not come to me before this!"

Lettys discreetly excused herself to go and fetch some refreshments.

"I did come," Robin answered with an insouciance that quite took her breath away. "Only you were indisposed, so I spoke with Lord Martindale instead."

"Indisposed?"

"Sulking beneath your bedcovers," Robin elaborated, flinging himself down into a chair.

"I assure you," said Mathilde, drawing herself up to her full height, "I was doing no such thing!"

"In any event," Robin said, waving this aside, "I could not leave Mabel alone, and I had to ensure the hens were tended to. Didacus Eaves sent over that goat I wanted from Little Acton on Wednesday."

"I wonder you have managed to spare me the time now," Mathilde interrupted him sarcastically.

"You needn't think to have me dancing to your tune like everyone else!"

"Rob!"

"It's the talk of Acton Dymock," he retorted. "Even Prudie's climbed down off her high horse now she knows you're making him crawl over hot coals."

"I don't know what you mean!"

"Oh, don't you, my girl!" Rob snorted.

"In any case," said Mathilde, sinking into the chair opposite, "what news of Prudie and Waldon? It seems I have not seen them in an age."

"They're well. Prudie's family all came over to visit her en masse. Probably to hear all the gossip," Rob added darkly. "They were fairly astonished to find she and Waldon are handfasted."

"Oh, of course," Mathilde said. "I hope she extended all the hospitality of the lodge and baked them a cake."

Rob nodded. "Her stepsisters wanted to stay the night in the spare attic room, but Prudie refused them, saying they could not remain overnight without your say-so."

"I should not have refused!"

"I told her as much," Rob said. "But you know what a stickler she is." He delved into the neck of his tunic. "I've had a letter from court."

"Court?" Mathilde sat up. "From whom?"

"Willard," Rob answered, unfolding the paper. "He says your disappearance caused quite a stir." Mathilde winced. "Apparently, he, Gordon, and Piers are celebrities now and have been invited to tell their side of the story to the Queen herself."

"Really?" Mathilde asked faintly. "Celebrities?" She gulped.

"So, the cat's clearly out of the bag about your escape. There's a passage here about Sir Edgar Hill and Lady Elizabeth Coton that I do not quite follow…" He frowned, rubbing his nose. "Apparently they are putting it about that you acted as a cupid to their romance."

Mathilde's eyes widened. Their names did seem familiar though. "Wait a moment," she said. "Sir Edgar Hill… Was that not the gentleman who asked us to deliver that message to his lady love?"

Rob tilted his head to one side, considering this. "The one I told you were a de Courcey bastard?" he asked after a moment.

"Yes, him."

"But you didn't deliver the message," he pointed out critically.

"Well, no, but I did ask Gordon to in my stead. I suppose it's the story that matters." She shrugged.

"You mean, he decided to steal some of the limelight with this tale?"

"It doesn't really matter after all."

Lettys tapped the door lightly, then entered with a tray of fruit juices and honey cakes which she set down before them before withdrawing to the window seat to give them some privacy.

"Thank you, Lettys. I don't suppose," she said, turning back to Rob and clasping and unclasping her hands, "that your letter mentioned aught of my mother or Nurse?"

"Only that Lady Doverdale was mad as fire and sending riders in every direction of the compass in search of you."

"Oh dear!"

"But none have shown up here at any rate," said Rob.

"That's true enough," Mathilde acknowledged. *Thank heavens for small mercies.*

"I suspect her initial enquiry agents weren't searching for two boys."

"Very likely not."

"It's funny, isn't it," mused Rob, "to think of our being figures of great fame at court?"

The thought made Mathilde's stomach lurch with anxiety. She gave him a weak smile. "Yes." She hesitated. "What do you suppose your mother and Sir Avery will think of it all?"

Rob shrugged, not looking much concerned. "I'm not overly anxious to return," he said and did not seem to even consider that she might feel differently.

Did she feel differently? For some reason she remembered Guy's question at dinner the previous night, and her breath caught in her throat. "How long are you going to punish me?" he had asked. "I make no complaint, you understand. I just need to know my suffering will be finite." The thought he might be suffering had not really occurred to her. She had been too caught up in her own pain.

"Why do you think I'm making Guy dance to my tune?" she asked abruptly.

He cast her a shrewd look. "Because he is. Poor fellow is walking on eggshells around you. He doesn't know up from down."

"You don't think he did anything wrong?"

Robin shook his head. "Stands to reason. He never looks at any women except for you."

"How do you know," she persisted, "that he did not do more than look at this Lady Julia, who was his first love?"

"Because I asked him," said Robin simply.

His answer startled her. She crumbled her honey cake. "And what did he say?"

"Denied it, of course," said Rob scornfully. "Think about it. He was known as a woman-hater before you showed up."

"But why would Old Helga lie to me?"

Rob tutted. "Who knows with witches? They have their reasons, and it's never straightforward. Even the best of them speak with a forked tongue."

Mathilde lapsed into a brooding silence. She didn't know what to say. She needed to think. She pushed the plate of cakes toward Rob and turned the subject back to his new goat.

Rob remained for supper, and conversation at the table benefited greatly from his presence. He, Lettys, and Temur kept up a steady flow of conversation, which Guy joined in sporadically and Mathilde barely at all. The same thoughts whirled around in her brain. Could Robin be right when he claimed Guy had eyes for only her? And that Old Helga had, for reasons known only to her, misled her? She went to bed with her mind in a whirl.

35

That night Mathilde slept fitfully, waking groggily in the early
hours to the sound of voices in the corridor outside. She lay
awake, craning her ears, but could hear nothing intelligible.
After a while, the door opened, and Guy entered with a candle.
He came straight to her side of the bed.

"Mathilde?"

"I'm awake," she replied quickly. "What has happened?" He
had not entered this bedroom after dark since she had arrived at
Acton March.

"Messengers have come bearing bad news. They rode through
the night." Immediately Mathilde's thoughts leaped to her
mother, to her old nurse in Aphrany. She sat up. *Oh gods.* "Lord
Allworthy has died," he said flatly.

"Lord Allworthy?" *Oh.*

"Julia's husband," he explained tersely. Mathilde kept her eyes
steadily on him as he spoke. "She needs to return back home."

"Naturally, she does," Mathilde agreed coolly. "One might
wonder at her leaving home in the first place."

She saw a spark of irritation in Guy's eyes. "I need to escort her
back to her husband's estates," he said grimly.

"Why? What of her brother?" Mathilde asked in a brittle voice.

Guy's expression darkened. "He's disappeared, typical of
Tristan. He can never be relied on, and Julia refuses to tarry."

"Oh, does she?" Mathilde said bitterly. "Well, if the Lady Julia
won't wait, then obviously you must jump to her bidding."

"Her husband has just died," Guy gritted out. "Can you not find it in your heart to feel some sympathy for her plight?"

"If she had any regard for her husband, she would not have left him when he was so close to his end!" she snapped, almost shocking herself.

Guy swallowed and seemed to have no answer for this. "What's the point in going over this?" he asked rawly. "It's not for us to fight over. I'm simply doing my duty as a neighbor and host."

Mathilde glared at him. She did not speak the words that came to her lips, though the cynicism probably showed in her eyes. *You have not been her neighbor in years! Kerslake Castle is naught but a few scattered stones!*

"I don't have time to stand and debate this with you," Guy said tightly. "The sooner I go, the sooner I can return."

"If you go…" she started direly.

"Yes?" he said, setting the candle down with a thud and sitting down on the bed. "Let's hear it," he said. As if unable to stop himself, he grabbed her upper arms, yanking her forward so she was practically in his lap. "If I go? What will you do?"

"Don't bother looking for me on your return, that's all," said Mathilde. "For I won't be here."

"You'd leave me? You'd dare to—" He broke off his words as she nodded at him mutinously. He stared at her a moment. "Would you indeed?" he said grimly, and suddenly his mouth was on hers in a punishing kiss that gave no quarter.

Mathilde drew back her hand to push him away, but at that instance, he slid one hand into her hair and groaned roughly against her mouth. She melted. Gods, she had missed this so much. The physical connection with him. Guy shoved her back onto the pillows, dragging her blankets down and bunching up the shift she had taken to wearing to bed. Mathilde gazed up at him, her lips parted, her breathing shallow and fast.

"Tell me now if this isn't what you want," he bit out, but his eyes were focused not on her face, but between her legs. She held her breath a moment. What *did* she want? Slowly, Mathilde lowered her knees. His gaze snapped to hers, and he went very still. "Mathilde," he whispered, and suddenly he was there, pushing her thighs further apart, his mouth between them, hot and ravenous.

Mathilde whimpered, arching her back, grabbing handfuls of his hair as he pleasured her with consuming strokes of his tongue.

"Oh gods!"

He was relentless, using his knowledge of her body to bring her to a shatteringly fast orgasm, and then lapping and sucking her right the way through it, wringing every last drop of pleasure from her. When he sat up, his eyes were glittering. He dragged the back of one sleeve across his mouth.

"Well, that should keep me going while I'm gone," he said shakily. Mathilde lay boneless and limp, surveying from under her drooping eyelids. His eyes, she noticed, despite his words, were roving over her like a starving man. "When I get back—" he started, but Mathilde cut him off.

"I can't wait till then." She held out her arms for him.

He froze. "What are you—?"

"*Please*, Guy. I need you now!"

"What the hells are you trying to do to me, woman?" he demanded, his whole body tense. "You know full well I'm

331

leaving shortly. Even now they're waiting for me in the courtyard below!"

"Then she can wait," Mathilde flung at him, lifting her chin.

Her words seemed to rob him of speech for a moment. "So, that's why you tell me now," he said harshly. "The words I've wanted to hear from you this past week!"

He curled his lip, his tone hard and angry, but Mathilde wasn't fooled. He hadn't moved from the bed, and she could see his gaze was hot as molten lava. She shrugged, lowering her arms, and went to turn from him. Immediately, he pounced.

"This won't be gentle," he growled in her ear. "I'm too far gone for that consideration right now."

"I don't care," Mathilde answered recklessly. His hands were at his crotch, unfastening the ties there, shoving down his breeches. Mathilde sobbed with relief when he slid between her thighs. She clasped him to her.

"Yes, Guy!" she urged him on.

He swore again, and if she wasn't so ready for him, the way he shoved inside her would have been brutal. As it was, they both immediately stilled. "Mathilde?"

"All's well," she panted, grasping his shoulders. "Hurry!"

"Gods," he whispered and started moving. She could feel him struggle to loosen his hold on her hip and shoulder, to pull his powerful strokes, but he was too far gone.

"This won't last long," he gritted out against her neck.

She felt his teeth lightly graze her neck, his ruthless possession of her body. But already his desire was transferring to her, setting her on fire once more with need. She moaned, wrapped her legs around his hips, and dug her heels into his buttocks, meeting his brutal thrusts with her own.

Guy shuddered. "Ah, love," he groaned. "Don't let me hurt you."

"You're not," she insisted breathlessly in his ear, but he paid no need.

"Let me just—" He started to turn his shoulders, as though to roll them, and surrender his dominant position.

"No! I want it like this!" she panted, twisting to resist his attempt to switch. He was so much bigger and stronger than she, she could never stop him reversing their positions if he truly wanted to.

"I'm being too rough," he said, sounding panicked as he continued to thrust into her almost frenziedly.

"No! You're not!" she protested. "I like it. *Please, Guy!* I need it." Mathilde sank her nails into his back like little claws and watched his eyes roll back in his head.

"Ah *gods*!" he groaned. "I can deny you *nothing…*" She felt his body tense, on the verge of explosion, and suddenly his hand was at her jaw, forcing her gaze up to meet his.

"Mathilde?" he said urgently and looked like he was trying to form some other words, before his jaw gritted, and he stopped even trying. His whole body trembled, and she felt her own grip his in fevered anticipation. Suddenly he collapsed onto her with a loud roar. His furious release triggered her own, and Mathilde convulsed around him as he came, and came hard. It rolled over them like a wave, sweeping them under the dangerous current, to oblivion.

She wasn't sure how many moments later he grabbed her nape and mashed his lips to hers in a bruising kiss, which gentled as it went on. Mathilde luxuriated in the feel of his hard body over hers. Never before had he given her his full weight, or the full fury of his lust. Tearing his mouth from hers, he took several great gulps of air before moving to withdraw from her. Mathilde had to stifle her protest as he rolled off her to lie quietly, staring up at the ceiling.

"You little witch," he said thickly after a couple of minutes had passed and they had both caught their breath. "How the hells am I meant to part with you for four days now?" He reached across, tilting her chin so he could look into her eyes. "You're sure I didn't hurt you?" His eyes were alight with concern and something else. Tenderness.

She shook her head, then looked at her own bloodied nails. "No, but I think I…"

He twisted to look back over his shoulder, then surprised her by giving a short laugh. "You've scored my back, little she-cat." He leaned down and kissed her again lingeringly, his large hand at her waist. Mathilde allowed herself to return the soft pressure of his lips.

When he drew back, his eyes were alight again and he looked a different man, refreshed and ten years younger. *Did I have that effect on him?* she wondered dazedly.

"Mathilde," he whispered, "wife." He kissed her again, sweet and gentle this time, his tongue stroking against hers, eager and coaxing.

Again, she allowed it, tangling her tongue against his, letting him draw it into his mouth. His hand slipped around to her back, cradling her to him. Reluctantly, he drew back at last with a soft groan.

"You know I wouldn't go now if I wasn't honor bound." His eyes were seeking something from her. *Permission?* Nay, never that. *Understanding?* She said nothing and saw that pained him.

Swallowing the knot in her throat, Mathilde turned her face away from his searching gaze. Carefully, he cupped her cheek and stroked it with his thumb. She wasn't going to cry, she thought, blinking back tears as he moved away. The rustle of the bedclothes told her he was rising and righting his clothes to leave. Suddenly, she knew she couldn't let him go now without speaking.

"I don't want you to go," she admitted croakily, then took a deep breath. "But if you must, then I want you to take the opportunity to get that jewel back off Lady Julia. The Martindale ruby brooch."

He froze in the act of fastening his tunic and expelled a breath as though astounded by her sheer effrontery. "I can buy you a dozen rubies, Mathilde," he said, his voice hardening.

She folded her arms across her breasts. "And I would refuse them all!"

His brows snapped together. "What did you say, wife?" He took a step toward the bed. "That you would continue to flout me *in my own house*?" His voice rose to a bellow at the last few words, doubtless waking anyone sleeping down this wing of the house.

"I don't want your dozen rubies, Guy," she answered him loudly, her volume rising to match his.

She scrabbled to her knees on the bed to face him. She was still naked but did not care. She could feel her face hot and angry, but for the first time in weeks she felt fully alive and *furious*.

335

For days now, she had felt nothing but crushing heartbreak and misery. Now she felt invigorated and warlike.

"I want the ruby brooch that is mine by right," she announced defiantly. "The one that belongs to the Marchionesses of Martindale, *for that is who I am*!" She struck her fist against the mattress as she yelled the last few words and it felt good. "And I will no longer be denied, *in my own house*!"

He stared at her, his chest rising and falling. "I rue the day that Vawdrey bound me to you," he ground out, his voice shaking. "You, madam, are a merciless, pitiless little bitch."

She inclined her head. "And also your marchioness," she agreed calmly.

He was breathing hard now, his gaze seemingly riveted to her face, then it dipped a moment to her nakedness. Hot slashes of red appeared over his cheekbones.

"We'll discuss this further when I get back," he said in a low, uneven voice.

"If I'm still here," Mathilde interjected, earning an incredulous look from him.

"Are you trying to reduce me to rage, madam?" he roared.

Mathilde had another crazy impulse to fake a yawn and see where that got her. *It could well be over his knee*, she thought, eyeing his rigid stance. *What would that be like?* she wondered and felt herself flush. Was she crazy? Now was *not* the time to find out. With an effort, she pulled herself together. Shrugging one shoulder, she dropped down onto the mattress and rolled into the sheets, away from him. Let him make of that what he would.

Mathilde lay silent, cocooned in the sheets for a long few moments, holding her breath. She thought she could hear his own ragged breathing nearby, and then the door slammed so hard the whole room seemed to shake. Mathilde smiled in grim satisfaction, though her throat burned. She could have sent him away with sweet words and wifely understanding. Instead, she had by turns inflamed and enraged him. Her body ached every place he had touched her, and she was glad because that meant his would too, for her.

Doubtless her scratches down his back would smart on the entire ride to the Allworthy estate, she thought, wiping away a tear from her cheek. Just as she would bear bruises on the morrow from the hard grip of his fingers, so, too, would he wear her scratch marks as a reminder of their tryst. Julia Allworthy would not have one ounce of his attention for the four-day journey. He would be too angry to make polite conversation with her. He would be fuming the entire way.

When she fell asleep twenty minutes later, though Mathilde's cheeks were tearstained, a small smile played about her lips.

36

Mathilde woke late and rolled over, squinting at the sunlight streaming through the window. There would be no snow left in sight at this rate. She hoped Guy's party would have made good progress through the night. A slight knock on the door roused her from her sleepy thoughts.

"Come in." Then remembering her nakedness, she drew the covers up around her. It was Lettys carrying hot water and clean cloths.

She washed and dressed, again using the satin underdress to lend some modesty to the low-cut gown of deep amber she wore over it. She had not worn this dress before and found the skirts rather voluminous, catching them under her feet as she went to fetch her hair comb. Casting around, she saw the dagger on the black leather belt Guy had given her when she first arrived. Snatching this up, she fastened it around her hips, and caught a section of the skirts in the belt, tugging them higher so her feet were not impeded by their length. The satin undergown ensured she was still modest, and Lettys nodded in satisfaction at the overall effect.

Lettys then spent a good twenty minutes pinning a brown velvet toque to Mathilde's head, catching up her hair in sections and tucking and pinning them into place under the toque, giving the illusion that her hair was longer and piled up under the headdress.

"That looks very nice, Lettys," said Mathilde with surprise. Really it was the most respectable her hair had looked since it had been cut! "You have quite a talent with hair."

Lettys blushed. "Thank you," she said, looking grateful. "I always dressed my sister's hair as well as my own. When yours is longer, I'll be able to help you braid it into ever so many styles." She attached a short veil to the arrangement and then pronounced her ready.

Mathilde was just heading for the door when she paused and turned back. "I believe I will wear something from my jewelry box to complete my outfit," she decided.

Lettys helped her select a brooch which had an *M* set out in pearls. She told herself it suited the outfit far better than a ruby brooch ever would have. "Like it was made for you," said Lettys, patting her on the shoulder.

Below stairs, Firmin was solicitous and had a fire lit in the blue sitting room, but Mathilde found she could not settle to her tapestry. Even a walk in the garden did not cure her restlessness this morning. Again and again her thoughts returned to Guy and their enthusiastic reunion the night before. Of course they had parted on harsh words, but to her mind they were a step closer to reconciling. If only he had not had to leave for Allworthy. From what she had been told, the journey took four days there and back in ideal conditions, but in weather like this it would more likely take five.

"I believe I'll go for a ride," she said aloud as she and Lettys neared the stables. "A ride would help clear my head."

"It's bitter cold out!" Lettys protested, shivering and rubbing her mittens together.

"I know the perfect spot," Mathilde coaxed. "Braeburn Heights. It's a sun-trap up there, and there's a good clear stretch, perfect for galloping."

Lettys shuddered again. "I know where you mean, and it's frigid up there even at the height of summer!"

"Nonsense," Mathilde said bracingly. "When Guy took me up there, we basked in the sunshine." She did not mention that she could not feel her nose or the tips of her ears until a full hour after they returned.

"I think a canter up on Braeburn Heights sounds the very thing," a smooth voice interrupted them. Mathilde swung round with surprise. There, leaning against one of the stalls, was Tristan Kerslake; for once he was not dressed in colorful robes but wore simple and inconspicuous black. Mathilde blinked at him.

"You missed your sister's departure for her husband's estate," she told him. "They departed in the early hours of this morn."

He shrugged his shoulders. "Alas," he drawled, "I am out of favor with my sister at present. She has made it quite clear that she does not wish for my company for at least six months." He shot her a direct look. "She thinks I made things worse for her and made her look bad in front of the Strethneals."

"But what of your brother-in-law's burial?" Mathilde said in surprise. "Do you not wish to pay your respects?" After all, he had told her himself that Lord Allworthy had supplied him with a generous allowance for several years.

Tristan pulled a face. "Even your brief glimpse of Julia must have shown you how uncomfortable she can make people when she wishes." His tone was light, but Mathilde still flushed, remembering how the haughty Julia had tried to order her from her own home. "She is quite merciless and would not hesitate to put me to shame before her friends and neighbors by demanding my removal."

He sounded saddened by this, and Mathilde felt a pang of sympathy for him. His sister really was not a nice person!

"That is a great pity," she said gravely.

"I did rather like Cecil." Tristan sighed. "He was a decent old stick and never objected however much I bled him."

"Are you really willing to accompany Lady Martindale up to the Heights?" Lettys asked hopefully.

"Absolutely." He sketched a bow. "I am at your ladyship's disposal as an escort."

Which was rather ironic, Mathilde reflected, when you considered that her husband had been forced to act that very same role to his sister due to his mysterious disappearance. Once they were saddled up and on their way, she asked him where he had been.

"Oh," he replied airily, "I went to visit with some wholly disreputable old acquaintances. No one that Julia ever knew."

"And you returned this morning?"

"That's right," he answered easily. "We were out carousing all night."

"How exactly," Mathilde asked, "does one carouse? I've always wondered."

He laughed. "Well, for my part it usually entails large quantities of wine, women, and song."

"I see," she replied, feeling if anything even more curious than before. Experience told her that he would not give her any more details. "And what of Guy?" she asked.

"Guy?" He looked startled. "Nay, he did not accompany me." He hesitated. "He was never much of a one for carousing, even before the war."

Mathilde flushed slightly. "I meant, does he know these disreputable types with whom you associate?"

"Ah," said Tristan. "I see." He shook his head. "Guy and my brother, Miles, were always more serious-minded than I. We did not move in the same circles. Still don't."

Mathilde considered this a moment in silence. They were nearly upon the Heights now. The only downside to her elegant toque was that her hood kept slipping down over it. No doubt her ears would be quite pink again by the time they rode back, she thought. There was barely a trace of cloud in the sky, and Sabrina was in high spirits as they galloped along the newly thawed ground.

"Did Guy show you the caves?" Tristan called as they rounded the tor. Mathilde shook her head. "They're well worth a look," he suggested, pointing to their shadowy depths in the bare rock.

Mathilde glanced at them doubtfully. *What was it Guy had said about them?* "Aren't they rather dangerous for strangers?" she asked.

"Ah, but you have an expert guide with you," he answered swiftly. "I know them like the back of my hand. A misspent youth," he added at her quizzical look.

Without waiting for her reply, he rode toward the caves and dismounted, tying his horse to a nearby tree. Mathilde followed his example and he tethered Sabrina there too. The sun had disappeared behind a cloud now, for all the sky had been clear only moments before.

"What is it?" Tristan asked, taking her arm and drawing it through his.

She shook her head and Tristan led her up the steep incline to the nearest cave entrance. When they reached it, Mathilde felt her first real prickle of alarm.

"It's very dark," she commented with misgiving.

"Lean on my arm," he offered easily. "It's only this first part that is narrow and dark. It opens out once you get inside."

Mathilde took a tentative step inside. "Is it damp?" she asked anxiously. "Only I shouldn't—"

Tristan took a firm grip of not only her arm, but her waist and hauled her inside. "Walk before me now, if you please," he said in a calm voice of authority. His tone was flat and lacked its usual teasing quality. For some reason, all the fine hairs on the back of Mathilde's neck rose up in warning. Her mouth was dry.

"I can't really see where I'm—" Mathilde broke off as they came to a section where the roof of the cave was missing and light streamed in. The floor was flooded with water, likely melted snow. Mathilde looked back over her shoulder at Tristan, but what she saw was far from reassuring. His expression was grim, and even though they had momentarily emerged from the darkness, somehow, he still seemed among shadow.

"This cavern is flooded," she pointed out. "I think we should turn back."

He did not answer, just gave a shove to her middle back, propelling her forward. Mathilde drew a sharp breath as she negotiated the slippery rock floor. *Something is very wrong here.* She managed to come to a stop before the next gaping

343

hole in the rock face, but then he was behind her, forcing her to continue through it into the pitch blackness. Her hands groped around on the walls blindly as she stumbled along.

"I wrote to Lord Vawdrey," he said, his former light and breezy manner returning. Somehow it seemed rather chilling to hear it now in the darkness when his presence was so menacing in every other way. "I told him that my position had become...sadly compromised."

"Compromised?" she repeated through numb lips. "How so?"

"Keep walking," he ordered sharply, then sighed. "Let us have frankness between us at this point, Mathilde. You have fathomed out, have you not, why it was you saw me issuing forth from Vawdrey's study?"

"I am persuaded I must have been mistaken that time, as you suggested," she said and leaned against the wall of the cave. "Please," she begged. "Let me only catch my breath a moment."

"You were not mistaken," he said heavily, and his hand landed on her shoulder, making her jump. "Walk," he said abruptly. "Now. There's a good girl. I won't tell you again."

Mathilde gritted her teeth and carried on further into the caves, sealing her own doom. *I will never find my way back out of here*, she thought despairingly. Was he going to retreat into the shadows and leave her here? To wander around in the dark, getting increasingly more and more lost? She had remembered now what it was Guy had said about people walking into these caves and then never walking back out again.

"Lettys knows we have come here together," she reminded him and was surprised to hear how calm her voice sounded. "She will tell Firmin and the others that you have ridden out with me."

"What of it?" Tristan answered coolly. "Do you really think me incapable of spinning some yarn to satisfy them? Perhaps you will be wrested from me by a band of villains, robbers, and thieves. Yes, I rather like that. I struggle, of course, valiantly, but in vain. I stumble back to Acton March on foot, but by that point you will have been at their tender mercies for a matter of hours. Who only knows what will have become of you? I will be distraught at your cruel fate, of course," he added as an afterthought. "But since the war, there *have* been some desperate, dispossessed men who roam the countryside, looting and taking what is not theirs. The story will have a ring of truth to it."

Would it? wondered Mathilde. After all, the household at Acton March were loyal northerners all. They would probably take the word of one of their own trusted countrymen. Except possibly for Prudie. Prudie was loyal to her. And Robin, of course.

"What are you thinking?" he asked with an idle curiosity that disconcerted her.

"I'm wondering what everyone will say," she answered truthfully, "if you return without me."

"Precious little against me, I assure you. People are rather stupid like that."

She thought back to his expression that day when she had thoughtlessly remarked she had seen him at court. He had denied ever setting foot in the southern court. But he had lied. At the time she had been so distracted, she had not really thought through the implications of this. It had not really seemed her business. She had been heartbroken, forlorn. She had cared nothing of what he was about. But this one comment it seemed had sealed her fate. She remembered his look of regret. At the time it had struck her as strange, but now she realized he had contemplated this moment. This moment where he was going to have to do away with her!

"I don't understand," she said through teeth that chattered slightly—and not just from the cold. "How can you be in the employ of Lord Vawdrey? You are a northerner."

"I am," he agreed. "But there are always traitors, on both sides."

Traitors? Mathilde's blood ran cold. "I am sure you are not that!"

"Oh, but I am," he said. "I am the ultimate traitor. For I am in the pay of both the north and the south." He gave a soft laugh. "As dear Julia noted only the other day, I have no loyalty whatsoever."

Mathilde gave a muffled gasp, as yet again, he shoved her forward, and she half stumbled over a loose rock before righting herself. "B-but what is that to me?" she asked. "The war is over now. I lost no kin. I bear you no grudge."

He was quiet for a few heartbeats. "You don't understand. It is more what could fall from your lips at any moment that concerns me. I must silence that pretty mouth forever, you see. Although you may not care, there are many in Karadok who would kill me as easily as draw breath for the role I have played over the years. You must not think," he added in a kindly tone, "that it is in any way personal. I like you, Mouse. You are refreshing, quite wasted on all these grim northerners. In truth, I like you far better than I do my own flesh and blood."

Mathilde's heart began to beat louder as she came to the horrible realization that though Tristan *liked* her, he was going to *kill* her. That was why he had looked that way before, so regretful. He had known then that he was going to have to do this, to take this dreadful step to ensure her silence. She felt sick as her brain scrambled to cope with these terrible facts.

Her thoughts turned to Guy's blade she wore at her hip. It was wickedly sharp. Did she really have what it took to stick a knife into a man? A man she liked? For the awful thing was, she did like Tristan. But her every instinct shrieked at her that he was not only a traitor, but a killer. From the casual way he talked about it, he had likely killed before and would again. Being fond of her, even regretting the necessity, would not stop him.

She swallowed as she thought of Guy, her friends, Robin, Fenella, Prudie, and her mother even. *I have people who love me*, she thought, feeling her resolve stiffen. People whose lives would be affected by the discovery of her dead body, perhaps years from now in this secluded cave

And what of Guy? What would he think after their argument the previous night? That she had been fleeing him and had a foolish accident? She turned cold all over. He would blame himself for her grisly fate.

I have to fight, a small, cold voice told her. The dagger she wore was not the same as a necklace or some other decorative ornament. It had a purpose. It was there for her defense—not decoration.

They had come out into an open area again; a section was missing from overhead and the light streamed in. She watched as Tristan approached her with feigned casualness. It was the way you would approach a skittish animal to win its trust. She had to fight him. But her body was small; she definitely did not have the strength to go toe to toe. Which meant she would have to use cunning.

347

"Please, Tristan," she said in appeal even as she discreetly dropped her hand to her knife. "I won't tell anyone. You can depend on my silence."

"Ah, Mouse," he said sadly, drawing closer. "I wish that I could believe you. But depending on the word of a woman, in my experience…" He let his words trail off. "Even if you did not intend to let it slip, at some point you undoubtedly would."

Swiftly he closed the gap between them, his eyes boring into hers, not noticing her hand as it unsheathed the dagger beneath her cloak and held it pointed toward him. Instinctively she took a couple of panicked steps backward as he loomed over her, his hands seizing her upper arms in a painful grip, his eyes blank and expressionless. Somehow in this moment, he no longer looked like Tristan at all, but some frightening stranger who wore his semblance like a mask.

Then she felt a sickening give in the tension between them and something was running down her hand and wrist. Something warm and forbidden. She looked down, and all she could see was the hilt of the blade and her hand covered in blood. She stared a moment, and then looked up in dawning horror. Tristan was blinking at her, his own expression returning to his face. He was looking down too, in disbelief.

"My gods," he whispered. He sounded utterly astonished. Then thrust her away from him and staggered back, falling against the rock wall. Mathilde released the knife with a stifled cry as he sank down to the ground. She covered her mouth with her hands, then realized she was getting blood smeared on her face. *His blood.*

"You've done for me," he said accusingly, looking up at her. "Why?"

"Because," she said in mounting panic, "it was you or me! Wasn't it?" Panic clawed at her throat. Had she misread the signals? Had she willfully murdered him? *Oh gods!*

He watched her a moment, and then a look of wry amusement passed over his face. He raised one arm and let her see the blade that was concealed at his wrist. "It was," he admitted. "But I was going to slit your pretty little throat. I wasn't going to give you a mortal wound and then let you bleed out for hours."

"H-how kind of you," she stammered, dashing the back of her hand across her eyes. Tears were coming thick and fast now. She had been badly frightened for a moment there.

"Come now, don't cry," he tutted. "You've defeated the nasty wolf. Now is not the time for tears, my brave little mouse!"

"But your wound!" she wailed.

He glanced down at it. "There's nothing can be done about that," he said regretfully. The dark red stain had spread out across his entire stomach area. Extracting his own knife from his sleeve, he flung it away from him. The thought crossed her mind that he could very easily have chosen to throw it at her. She suspected his aim would be lethally accurate.

"No point crying over spilt milk," she said shakily through numb lips.

He grinned, though he was quite alarmingly pale. "Sensible girl," he said bracingly. "Now pick up my knife and put it in your sheath, so you feel safe."

Mouse stared at him before retrieving his dagger and slipping it into her black leather sheath. She did not test the blade, for she already knew it would be very sharp. "Men are always giving me knives," she said with a small sob.

349

"Is that so?" He sounded genuinely curious. "Who else made you a present of one?"

"My first husband," she said through chattering teeth. "M-my friend Willard, and then—then Guy." Her eyes returned to Guy's knife which still protruded from Tristan's gut so horribly.

"And now me. How many benefactors can one girl have?" he drawled with a wan smile. "We doubtless all thought you defenseless and in need of protection."

"Really?" she quavered. "Even you? Even though I—"

"Mouse," he cut in sternly. "Do not disappoint me now." He beckoned. "Come sit down next to me." He winced as he adjusted his position to pat the ground.

She dropped down onto her heels next to him. "Should we try to take it out?" she asked hesitantly, pointing to the knife.

"Not unless you wish to hasten my end," he said cheerfully. "Pass me a twig or a sharp little stone. Something good for drawing with." Mouse scanned the floor of the cave and passed a few such to him for his inspection. After casting away her first two finds, he settled on a piece of flinty stone. "This will do." Then he started drawing in the dirt.

"What are you drawing?" she asked, though she suspected already.

"The route you must take to get out of these caves," he explained. Mathilde closed her eyes a moment. When she opened them, he was watching her. "You must not mind overmuch that you were the cause of my demise," he said. "It was bound to be someone, sooner or later. I would rather it was you than any of the others. At least you I like."

"I don't understand how you can—"

"I know." He sighed, forestalling her. "I think," he said ruminatively, "that there is a piece of me that is either broken or perhaps missing altogether." He turned his head to look at her. "Please don't trouble yourself over it. I would only ask that you try to remember my good points and not the bad." He looked at her thoughtfully. "Or is that asking rather too much?"

She shook her head. "No. No, it's not."

"Will you be sad when you think of me, little mouse?" he asked, sounding strangely wistful.

"Yes," she whispered. "Because I liked you. Even now."

He smiled, his lips looking rather pale and bloodless. "That's nice," he said. "I feel the same way. Or..." he added conscientiously. "As close to such a sentiment as a cold-blooded creature such as I can achieve." He held his hand out to her, and she took it, clasping it firmly. It felt cold to the touch. "You must follow this route," he said, gesturing to his diagram with his other hand. "It will lead you out of the caves. Then you must head down southerly, retracing our steps. You remember where I tethered the horses?" She nodded. "Now study the drawing until it is imprinted on your memory." They sat in silence awhile as Mathilde's eyes traveled over the lines and squiggles in the dirt. His head jerked up. "Have you memorized it?" he asked.

"Not quite," she prevaricated, clinging tighter to his hand.

"I don't believe you," he said sternly "Not after seeing that intricate tapestry pattern you devised " She did not answer. "I do not want you to sit here in the cold, standing vigil and waiting for me to die, little mouse." His voice sounded thick and like it was forced.

"I don't want to leave you alone here," she admitted.

He was silent a moment. "Think of it this way," he said at last. "The sooner you get back, the sooner you can send help to find me."

They both knew he was lying through his teeth. By the time a search party was organized and rode forth from Acton March, he would be dead. Mathilde ducked her head and took a shaky breath. "Very well."

"And don't go telling any lies," he said. "Trying to defend my honor, or some such nonsense. If you tell them we were set upon or attacked by robbers, you'll get some poor tramp or traveling tinker hanged." Mathilde swallowed and nodded. "We both know I don't give a damn about my sister's feelings on the matter." With a great effort, he pulled his hand away and shoved at her shoulder. "Go!"

Mathilde climbed stiffly to her feet. "Tristan," she said in a wobbly voice.

"Go!" Wearily, he leaned the back of his head against the cave wall. "Hold!" he said suddenly, seeming to change his mind. "Let me fix you in my mind a moment." Then he smiled at her. "I have you. Leave now."

Mathilde nodded. "Goodbye, Tristan," she said in a choked voice.

He did not speak, but let his eyes drift shut, still smiling. Then, turning on her heel, Mathilde fled.

Quickly, she traversed the narrow tunnels, following Tristan's directions until she found herself in the flooded chamber. She was forced to wade through the cold waters, feeling them seep into her ankle boots. Finally, she caught sight of the shaft of light that marked the entrance. With a muffled sob, she plunged through it and started running down the slope on legs that shook. She didn't even notice the collection of figures that had arrived and were looking over their horses. A tall figure detached itself from the rest and stepped quickly forward, just as Mathilde realized she could not slow down and cannoned into him.

"I've got you," said Lord Oswald Vawdrey, catching her in a surprisingly strong grip. Mathilde's legs gave way, and she sagged against him, winded as he said, sounding relieved, "I was just starting to get seriously concerned about your welfare."

Mathilde lifted her face from his shoulder. "Please, you must help him!" she said in a low, urgent voice. For the life of her, Mathilde could not fathom why the King's chief advisor should be here at Braeburn Heights, but for the moment, she just knew she had to get help. She clutched at his hands and tried to hold back her sobs. "He—he's dying! I've killed him!" She could hear the note of hysteria in her voice, even as she sought to suppress it. She heard some startled murmurings from the group of men behind him.

"Calm yourself, dear Lady Martindale," Earl Vawdrey said soothingly. "I'm sure all will be well." Then he checked his words, and Mathilde saw the direction of his gaze. Her cloak had fallen back, and he was following the bright red bloodstains that streaked down her skirts. She covered her mouth with the back of her hand and concentrated extremely hard on not screaming.

"Do not say any more just now," he said in an urgent undertone. "Let's get you to this tree trunk and sit you down." Mathilde found herself deposited carefully onto the large trunk of a fallen tree.

Oswald Vawdrey knelt down before her, his compelling gaze trained on hers. She wanted to look at who was with him but could not quite tear her gaze away.

353

"Kerslake is up there? In the caves?" he asked quietly. She nodded, her eyes brimming with tears. "But you are not injured?" She shook her head. "Can you check for me now?" Mathilde gazed at him a moment and then looked down at herself. Her skirts were rather a blood-splattered mess.

"It's not my blood, you see," she whispered. At last, he gave a swift nod and straightened up. "Anderson, you will lead a search party up to the caves to recover him," he said. "You two, go with him. Kerslake is injured," he said briefly.

Mathilde looked up quickly. "They'll get lost; the caves are very treacherous for strangers."

"Anderson is from around these parts," he assured her with a quick smile. "You must not fret, Lady Martindale. All is well now."

But how could all be well? She gazed up at him hopelessly, and then to her consternation, burst noisily into tears. A man had died by her hand.

37

It was not until they were halfway to Woodcote House, where it seemed Lord Vawdrey was staying, that she thought to ask why he had not taken her back to Acton March. No doubt the entire household would now be looking for her return. She was mounted on Sabrina, but Lord Vawdrey rode close by, and bringing up the rear were two more men who he had not left at the caves.

Oswald Vawdrey had looked apologetic at her enquiry. "You see," he said after a moment's hesitation, "there is a concerned party at Woodcote that needs to be assured of your good health."

"A concerned party?" Mathilde asked in bewilderment.

"Yes. And one or two others who are merely consumed with vulgar curiosity," he said wryly.

Mathilde was too exhausted to react properly to this news. The ride had taken longer than she had realized, Woodcote lying some seven miles to the west of Wickhamford. She felt annoyed with herself that she had allowed herself to be shepherded away like this when her guard was down. But then, she thought, suddenly stricken, perhaps Lord Vawdrey was looking to prepare some charge against her for her crime? After all, she thought wearily, had not Tristan confessed to being some agent of Lord Vawdrey's? Indeed, she rather thought that he had mentioned something about communicating with Lord Vawdrey only recently. She eyed the earl warily, but he was smiling affably back at her.

"I do not think I shall allow you any visitors until you are rested," he said with sudden decision. "It would be a mistake, I think, to deliver you up to them while you are vulnerable."

"Deliver me up? To the authorities, you mean?" asked Mathilde dully. She gripped her reins very tightly.

"The authorities?" A startled expression crossed over Oswald Vawdrey's handsome face. "Dear me, I seem to have expressed myself very ill, my dear Lady Martindale. I am here, I assure you, purely out of concern for your continued well-being." He paused. "I am not sure it is advisable to discuss recent events at this present moment. You are wearied and in much need of a bath and then bed." His eyes tracked back to the men following on behind them. "I would rather discuss such things when we are assured of privacy. You understand?"

Mathilde gazed back at him miserably. *Not really.* She inclined her head in acquiescence all the same. What else could she do?

"Fenella," he said, speaking his wife's name in an abrupt change of subject, "will be overjoyed that you have been recovered none the worse for wear. She charged me with several messages for you and sent several parcels and letters. She would have come herself if she could have persuaded me, but we have recently discovered she is expecting my heir."

Mathilde looked up quickly. "Oh, but that is wonderful news! Fenella must be overjoyed."

"We both are," he said firmly, and she could not mistake the pride in his voice.

"I am very happy for you," she replied before allowing her head to droop forward again.

How tired she was. And how she longed to get out of her horribly stained gown. Before they had mounted their horses,

Lord Vawdrey had whipped out a kerchief and scrubbed efficiently at her cheek. It had only occurred to her afterward that there must have been dried blood from where she had touched her face with bloodstained fingers. She shuddered now to think of it. What must everyone have thought when she shot down the hill like that toward them, covered in blood? "None the worse for wear," Lord Vawdrey had said, and she marveled at his word choice. Still, he was a politician, and everyone knew they expressed themselves differently from most people. Oh, whatever would everyone at Acton March think when she did not come home?

38

What would everyone think when she did not come home? The words reverberated through her mind as she woke with a gasp four hours later. The room was dimly lit, and by the door, a quiet, mature-looking woman sat with a distaff, winding yarn. She nodded gently when Mathilde sat up, placed her spinning down on her chair and poured a cup of water, which she brought over to the bed for Mathilde to drink.

Mathilde took it with thanks and drank it down as memories of this woman helping her undress and bathe flooded into her mind. She had not spoken once before tucking her into the comfortable bed. At the time, Mathilde had been profoundly grateful that no explanations were needed for her gory dress or monosyllabic conversation. Her eyelids had been drooping the entire time she had sat in the tub.

"Thank you for all your help," she murmured now as the lady fetched a brocade robe for her to slip over her clean shift and then buttoned it from neck to hem.

Mathilde stood obediently as a child as soft slippers were placed on the floor in front of her. Feeling as though she were in a dream, she stepped into them, and then the woman took her hand and led her across the room into a dark corridor and down it to a small room where Lord Vawdrey sat writing at a desk. He looked up at her and smiled, placing down his pen.

"Ah, I see you look a good deal recovered," he said with satisfaction. "If you could be so kind as to have our supper brought into us, Mistress Bassington?" The woman smiled and nodded and left the room.

"Do take a seat, Lady Martindale," he urged her, gesturing to one before the fire. He stood up and came to join her there. "You slept well, I trust?"

"I, er, yes," Mathilde agreed. "This is a very comfortable house." She wondered who the large country property belonged to before deciding shrewdly that in all probability, it would be the Crown.

"Yes," agreed Lord Vawdrey. "Alas, the Bassingtons did not prosper. That lady who attended you is that last of that once proud family."

"The war?" Mathilde guessed with a sinking feeling.

Oswald smiled thinly. "Quite so. Mistress Lucy Bassington remains on here as caretaker."

"Her home confiscated?" Mathilde ventured in dismay. Oswald inclined his head. "Can she—? I mean—"

"Her tongue was cut out," he answered. "By her own brother, who considered her an informer to the southern forces."

Mathilde's hands grasped the arms of her chair. After a moment she said slowly, "The war took a considerable toll here in the north. There are many scars, some you cannot see."

"That is a very good way of putting it." Oswald said gravely.

"Was she an informer?"

Oswald's eyes flickered. "If she was, she was not aware of the fact."

Mathilde looked at him. What a tricky man he was. *How did Fenella ever know where she stood with him?*

Just then, Lucy Bassington returned with a young girl, both carrying trays of food which they set on the table against the wall. Mathilde watched the older lady's faded blue eyes. She would not have willingly betrayed her kin, she felt sure of that. She must have been tricked, poor thing, by some man in all probability. Perhaps a charming, unscrupulous man, she thought, like Tristan Kerslake. Or Oswald Vawdrey.

"Let us sit to the table for our meal," he suggested, rising from his seat and holding out his hand to her. "You will need to build up your strength for the morrow."

Mathilde's gaze darted to his as he pulled out a chair for her. "Tomorrow?" she repeated nervously. He nodded and made his way to the seat opposite. "My husband will return the day after tomorrow," she added, not really sure why she felt the need to say that aloud.

Lord Vawdrey paused in the act of pulling in his chair. "You need have no concerns on that score," he said. "If that is what worries you."

He was spooning some vegetables onto a plate of fresh lettuce and cabbage leaves served in a vinegar oil dressing. He slid it over to her and she took it with wide eyes. What did he mean, she "need have no concerns" about her husband's return?

"Let us eat first," he said contritely. "We will talk afterward. In the meantime, I will try not to make any more cryptic remarks."

Mathilde bit her lip and did her best to force down the light supper of salad and fish served with fresh baked bread. She drank sparingly of the watered wine and surprised herself by making a rather decent meal of it.

Lord Vawdrey made light conversation and they progressed to a second course of cheese and candied fruits. Mathilde was just nibbling on a sucket of orange soaked in syrup when he mentioned the popularity at court of the tale of her escape dressed as a boy. "Doubtless there will be poems and, dare I say, plays written in your honor." He grimaced at the word *play* and Mathilde's memory was jogged.

"Did Fenella manage to suppress that play?" she asked on impulse. "The one she was so worried about?"

To her astonishment, she thought Oswald Vawdrey colored ever so slightly before her eyes. He gave a small cough.

"No, she did not," he said ruefully. "She discussed that with you, did she?" He shot her a swift, appraising look. "I wish I had managed to inspire her confidences to a similar degree. I made rather a mess of that whole episode, I'm afraid."

Suddenly, it hit Mathilde with clarity why his manner seemed so strange. He was speaking to her as if she was an equal, she realized. She didn't think a courtier had ever done that to her before. Except for Fenella, of course.

"I'm not sure what it is about wives that can send a man into a perfect frenzy of idiocy," he continued with a sigh. "But I acted like the greatest fool on earth. Mercifully, Fenella is the best of all women and has forgiven me."

"And everything is well between you now?" pressed Mathilde a trifle anxiously. Fenella was the sweetest and kindest person Mathilde had ever met, and Lord Vawdrey...was not.

He smiled, and Mathilde blinked. She didn't think she'd ever seen Oswald Vawdrey smile quite like that before. Suddenly, he looked a good deal more approachable.

"Oh yes," he said with a satisfied assurance that spoke volumes. "And I mean to spend the rest of my days making sure it remains that way."

361

Mathilde released a relieved breath. "So, what will you do about the play?" she asked curiously.

Her dear friend Fenella had become a patroness to a playwright with disastrous consequences. He had decided to capitalize on her notoriety by releasing a play about her disastrous first marriage, divorce, and subsequent remarriage to Lord Vawdrey, under the thin guise of a tragedy.

Lord Vawdrey waved a negligent hand. "It is dealt with already. I met with the playwright, a Mr. Entner—perhaps you know him?" Mathilde demurred. She was not a patroness of the arts, having a lively horror of speaking to artists and practically anyone of consequence at court. "A most enterprising fellow," he continued smoothly. "I persuaded him that extensive rewrites were in order. My assistant, Bryce, has uncovered a heretofore unsuspected talent for literature and helped in the redrafting. It is now ready to tour the provinces with a revised title and ending. *The Tragical History of a Woman Most Foully Betrayed* has now become *The Husband Tamer: A Play in Three Acts.*"

Mathilde's mouth dropped open. "*The H-Husband Tamer?*" she stammered.

Oswald's smile grew. "Yes. It is no longer a tragedy, but a farce. When it was originally performed in the Great Hall at Aphrany, everyone was most underwhelmed by Mr. Entner's ending. Now, instead of perishing a tragic martyr, the Lady Mawby ends the play triumphantly leading her adoring spouse, the Lord Orlando, about by the nose."

Mathilde gasped. Lady Vyella Mawby was a thinly disguised caricature of Fenella, and Lord Orlando of Oswald himself. "And you don't mind it ending that way?" she asked tentatively.

He shrugged. "Not at all. My self-esteem is quite healthy, I assure you. Fenella was more horrified than I, but then, she has no notion that it was changed at my instigation." A smile spread over his face. "Naturally, I enjoyed her indignation on my behalf. She has been most solicitous to ensure my feelings aren't hurt by this new turn of events and has forsworn playwrights altogether."

Mathilde's expression wavered. "You will not tell her it is at your instigation?"

Oswald's eyebrows rose. "Good gods no! She would insist that it was rewritten again, with me as a shining beacon of virtue. It is much better this way," he said with calm assurance. "I predict Entner has a great hit on his hands. No doubt it will be touring for a good few years and finance his prodigious offspring."

Mathilde considered this a moment. "I do hope it comes to the north," she said wistfully, and Oswald leaned back in his seat and laughed.

"You mean to remain, then?" he asked, leaning across and refilling her goblet.

Mathilde gave a start. "Of course," she said with a frown. "Really, I need to return home forthwith. My husband will doubtless be most concerned if I am not awaiting his return."

Oswald looked unconvinced. "I don't think that's going to work," he said regretfully. "You see, I am in possession of some facts that you are not."

"What facts?" asked Mathilde in alarm, lowering the goblet she had been raising to her lips.

He looked apologetic. "The Queen and your mother are also put up here at Woodcote House."

Mathilde's heart thudded. "My mother?" she repeated in startled accents. *Oh no.* "Why is the Queen this far north?"

"To see you," he said frankly. "You do not seem to realize the stir you have caused at court, my dear Lady Martindale. The whole place is in uproar over it."

Conversation was stalled while the table was cleared, and they returned to the seats set in front of the fire, Lord Vawdrey settling back in his with a sigh.

"I feel I must apologize," he said. "You see, I did not realize how perilously close to the edge Tristan Kerslake had grown, playing his dangerous game. The letter he sent alarmed me greatly. Thankfully it reached me, although I was already en route."

"You were already coming north before you received his letter?" Mathilde asked.

"Yes, or I would not have been in time," he said. "Though, in truth, you were forced to save yourself in the end. I simply helped pick up the pieces."

"But why?" Mathilde persisted. "Why were you already headed north?"

He was silent a moment. "I'm not sure if you have been in communication with anyone at court recently?" Mathilde almost folded her arms. Oswald Vawdrey seemed to ask more questions than he answered. He gave a small smile, as if aware of her thoughts. "You see, it had finally been confirmed that *this* was where you had flown to."

"Oh." She digested this a moment in silence. "So, when you spoke of 'delivering me up' to 'a concerned party' you meant…" Her words trailed off in dismay. "To my mother."

"I think on the whole, it would be better for you to see them on the morn, when you have had a good night's sleep."

"Oh, I agree," said Mathilde fervently.

She shuddered to think of her old nurse putting her to bed again, but the awful thing was, she had been so tired earlier that no doubt she would have allowed it. She definitely needed to be on guard around her mother and Nurse, or they would be eager to resume their time-honored roles in her life as her custodians. She could allow no backsliding now she had finally achieved independence.

"Whereabouts in the house are they?" she asked with misgiving. She hoped there was no chance of stumbling upon them unexpectedly in the corridors.

As if he guessed what she was thinking, Oswald Vawdrey smiled. "They are in the east wing, so you need have no fears on that score. We are in the west."

"And my mother does not come around to hound you daily about your progress?" she asked shrewdly.

"I have been most careful to curb such behavior," Lord Vawdrey said with what Mathilde could only suppose was massive understatement.

Mathilde frowned and leaned forward in her seat. "I, um, I don't suppose there will be any need to divulge what happened today," she said hopefully and fixed him with an appealing look. "You see I dread to think what Mother would say if she knew I allowed myself be led into a dark cave by a treacherous spy. No doubt lots of scathing things about my naivety. That and my being quite unfit to leave her side."

Oswald Vawdrey gave a small cough. "Even if she knew that only you walked out of the cave alive?" he asked.

"Oh," said Mathilde, considering this. That aspect had not quite occurred to her. "She would probably still think, quite unfairly, that the north is a nasty, dangerous place," she concluded with a sigh. "And that I should return to the palace with her."

"I am guessing," said Oswald good-humoredly, "that the account of your adventures you regale the Queen with will be highly edited. No mention for instance of Wickhamford jail." He shot her a sidelong look, and she gave a violent start.

"You heard about that?" she asked, alarmed.

"I did." He inclined his head.

"Is it too much to hope that no one else has?" asked Mathilde, biting her lip.

"Well, not from me," he said with a smirk. "But if you take my advice, you won't give them too sanitized a version of your travels. After all, you mean to prove you have found your feet, do you not? And besides," he added dryly, "the Queen will be satisfied with nothing less than high drama."

Mathilde turned this over a moment. "What about the Kerslakes though? Would not their name be dragged needlessly through the mud by a frank retelling?"

Lord Vawdrey gave her a considering look. "It might be as well not to mention that part," he conceded. "Though we may be forced to admit the truth to a select few."

"What, um…" She swallowed. "What *were* your instructions about…the body?"

Oswald looked startled at the directness of her question. "It was to be recovered and taken away," he admitted after a pause. "I have not yet decided on the best course of action. Perhaps, in a few days' time, it will be found at the bottom of a cliff. Kerslake will have had an unfortunate accident and broken his neck in the fall."

Mathilde fidgeted in her seat. "Tristan said he did not care about preserving his good name, but…I am not so sure."

"You are generous," said Oswald heavily.

She brushed this aside. "Though he was a little concerned that an outcast might be blamed for his death." Oswald's eyebrow arched skeptically, though he did not comment on this. "If I spend the day tomorrow with my mother and the Queen," said Mathilde, "then will I be permitted to return home to Acton March the day after in order to wait for Guy's return?"

Oswald hesitated. "Let us see how things go with the Queen," he prevaricated. "After coming all this way, I do not think she will allow your reconciliation quite so meekly."

Reconciliation? Mathilde looked up sharply. It was a strange word to use, unless… Unless he had heard about the way she and Guy had been carrying on these last few days. Her color rose. But surely, he could not be informed on such matters?

"Come now," he said quietly and rose to his feet. "You must be tired. The hour grows late, and you have a big day ahead of you tomorrow, persuading your mother and the Queen that you are a vastly contented wife."

Mathilde glanced at the window and guessed the hour must be around midnight at the very least. She rose to her feet. "You are probably right," she admitted distractedly.

He took her hand and, bowing over it, regarded her thoughtfully a moment. "I am starting to suspect you are quite the husband tamer yourself," he said with a quirk of his lips. "I begin to pity Martindale quite sincerely."

Mathilde looked up at him, startled. "Pity him?"

"He must be harried to death, poor fellow. And when he finds out how close to death you came this day…" He sighed. "It would be kind of you to take some pity on him."

39

Two Days Later

The wind whipped the pavilions and Mathilde could barely hear herself think above the chatter of her teeth. Where was Guy? Lord Vawdrey's men had reported his return to Acton March two hours ago. She was going to freeze to death out here before he came to claim her!

Her mother was approaching from the royal tent. She came to a halt beside Mathilde's chair. "Daughter, I really think we should ask permission to go back into the house. You will catch a chill and—"

"Nonsense, Mother!" She had to yell to be heard above the howling wind. Willard sat to her right, snorting with laughter, and she noticed Gordon and Piers nudging each other. She supposed she did sound rather rude and ungracious. "Queen Armenal herself instructed us to wait here," she added, glancing back at the Queen, who was sat nearby on a scarlet dais under a golden canopy. For all that she was under cover, she did not look much warmer than they. The Queen's lips were tinged blue, and she clutched her furs around her tightly. The ideas of tents and pageantry in such weather was the height of folly. The snow had now melted, it was true, but it was bitterly cold and the bare trees stripped of leaves shook in a gale force wind. "Guy will doubtless be arriving shortly. He must have received the Queen's invitation by now," she added.

Her mother hesitated a moment, but then stiffly inclined her head and retreated back to the Queen.

Mathilde realized she had shocked her mother a good deal the previous day with her tales, though Queen Armenal had been agog. Strange to say, the one who seemed to grieve Lady Doverdale the most was Mathilde's confession that she had sulked when Guy had departed to escort Lady Allworthy back home. Her mother was incredulous that Mathilde could have behaved with such a lack of wifely dignity. "Lord Martindale was acting under obligation, rather than personal inclination," she had pointed out in shocked accents.

Of course, Mathilde had left out certain factors in the recap, but more had slipped out than she had intended. The business of the brooch, for instance. "That would be vexing, of course," her mother had conceded. "But to have demanded its return like that was vulgar in the extreme, my child!" The Queen had loved it though and vowed that if Lady Allworthy did not return the ruby, then she would give to Mathilde her own ruby brooch which she had brought with her from the Western Isles.

The Queen had fussed over Mathilde almost as much as Nurse had and bestowed on her a fine gown of rose damask and a cap of pearls to wear over her curling head. She vowed she had been sorely missed at court and acted as though Mathilde had been a feted favorite rather than a sad failure. Really, the whole thing had been most peculiar! Nurse had shed tears over her and her lost hair, and Mathilde had allowed it for an hour or so and then gently detached herself.

"All is well, Nurse, and how it should be" had been her refrain whenever Nurse had started fretting. The old woman had been sadly bewildered but resigned to the fact her charge had moved on.

Anxiously, Mathilde scanned the horizon. *What is that?* She sat up straighter. One dark figure appeared on horseback, then, two, four, six…? She heard a stirring behind her and the clash of steel against armor. The Duke of Cadwallader loomed behind her seat, barking orders, and pointing to the company of men the King had sent to accompany the Queen north. He had seen the riders too and did not sound happy about their number. Mathilde twisted in her seat to see Lord Vawdrey walking across to his brother, the duke. Normally, Mathilde was terrified of Mason Vawdrey, Duke of Cadwallader, but this morning she found herself almost in sympathy with him. He, too, was extremely frustrated with the Queen's notions of meeting on an open field and negotiating Mathilde's return to her husband. No one, not even Lord Vawdrey, could convince Queen Armenal otherwise though. She was determined to have her sport.

"Why are there so many of them?" Mason barked at Oswald. "I recognize some of these colors. Strethneal, Kirkland, Osbeck. Have you forgotten that I led the forces that defeated these men in battle?" he demanded tersely. "I razed Kerslake Castle to the ground. I defeated Strethneal's nephew in combat and imprisoned Kirkland's only son."

Oswald tutted. "War is a brutal thing, brother," he murmured. "If I have my way, Karadok will never be plunged into such dark times again."

"This is no time for your politicking! We could be plunged into battle this very morn! And look at us with naught but a handful of men and a bunch of mere babes!"

"Hey!" objected Piers. "We happen to be Lady Martindale's personal guard!"

Mason ignored him, drawing his sword and stepping level to Mathilde's seat, signaling to the other guards to advance and stand beside him.

Mathilde saw the approaching party halt and confer. She could make out people now. Guy was there at the head, with some noblemen she recognized vaguely from the night of the feast.

She could also see Temur, Waldon, and even Firmin. She swung around to address the fearsome duke hotly.

"Why have you drawn your swords? My husband will surely think you are hostile!"

He answered her grimly, "There are twice as many of them as us, and they have no women or children to hinder them."

"Personal guard," muttered Gordon. "Not children!" The boys murmured resentfully between themselves.

Then Will sat up. "There's Rob!" he yelled. "Hey, Rob!"

Mathilde could see Robin among their number now; he looked startled to see his fellow pages sat in matching red tunics on golden seats. He gave a tentative wave, and the other three waved enthusiastically back.

Oswald clasped his brother, the duke, on the shoulder. "Look at his face, Mason," he said in a low, compelling voice.

Mason Vawdrey hesitated and scanned the party opposite. Mathilde followed suit. Guy did not look well. Even from this distance she could see the purple smudges below his eyes. He looked like he had not slept in a week.

"What ails him?" Mason asked after a moment.

"He doesn't give a fuck that you're his hated foe. Look where his gaze is trained." Mathilde noticed both brothers were now gazing at her. "Mason, she's his Linnet," said Oswald softly.

Mason looked up sharply. "Do not say such things lightly, brother," he said warningly.

"I would never," Oswald answered him gravely. "I recognize the symptoms having suffered from them myself. So can you if you look closely." Mason seemed to take another considered

372

look at Martindale, and then after a long moment, sheathed his sword and flagged a hand for the soldiers to follow suit. "Good man," Oswald commended him, clapping him on the back. Mason merely grunted.

"What's causing the delay, my lords?" called Queen Armenal from her seat. "Bid Lord Martindale to approach us."

Mathilde could have sworn that Mason muttered an oath under his breath. Oswald smiled his blandest smile and walked forward looking for all the world as if he was taking a morning stroll. Mason gave a short laugh. "He's a cool devil, my brother, I'll give him that." Oswald held one hand up in welcome and stopped a short distance from the others.

"I can't hear anything," Gordon grumbled. Willard was cleaning his nails with the jeweled dagger she had given him.

"They'll surrender shortly, you see if they don't," said Piers, nodding his head. "Cos *we've* got something they don't. A hostage," he said, glancing furtively at Mathilde.

"She's not a hostage, you dunderhead," sighed Willard.

"What is she, then?" asked Gordon.

Will shot a look at Mathilde. "She's the hero," he said simply.

40

Guy stared across at the man who had forced him to sign the marriage contract four years ago. Oswald Vawdrey looked just the same. *One untrustworthy bastard.* The whole day was starting to take on the properties of a nightmare, unreal and bizarre, with the same underlying feeling of dread that one experienced in the throes of one.

The entire ride home, he had been dogged with unnamed fears and a terrible sense of foreboding. He would never forget his feelings on returning to Acton March, when asking for his wife, and Firmin, ashen-faced, had presented him instead with a royal summons. *Please gods let her be returned to me.* He asked for nothing else. He *cared* about nothing else. Not anymore.

Vawdrey led him to a green-striped tent and bade his men to wait outside. Once they were alone, he had turned to him and asked coolly, "Give me one reason why I should allow you to take her back."

Guy glared at him. "Who the hells do you think you are, Vawdrey?" He seethed. "To stand between a man and his wife?"

"You seem to forget," Oswald said mildly, "that it was I who gave her to you in the first place."

"In name only!" Guy fired up.

"True… She gave herself to you in person and found herself rejected."

"That's a damn lie!"

"Indeed?" Oswald's eyebrows rose. "And yet, I have heard," he continued with infuriating calm, "that you withheld the protection of your name. That she was known as your mistress at Acton March and kept in a separate household to your own."

Guy's face flamed. "I—that was only at the first," he protested, feeling winded. "I never meant for that to continue."

"You intended to wait and see if she would catch for a child before bestowing your name on her?" asked Oswald with interest.

"No!"

"Apparently she is not with child," carried on Oswald as if he had not heard his objection. "So you may be easy on that score."

Guy ground his teeth. "It makes not one whit of difference to my wanting her return."

Oswald shrugged. "Doubtless you are ill suited in any case. I should never have matched with you with such a shy little mouse. She would only need to see you roar once and would scuttle back to her home."

"This is her home!" Guy burst out. "And she's no mouse," he added bitterly. "She's heard my roar a hundred times without so much as turning a hair."

"I confess, I have heard some very strange tales from this neck of the woods," Oswald murmured. "But in truth, a good number of them sound most unlikely. Especially about so meek and timid a woman."

Guy snorted. "None of you know the first thing about her nature."

"Until the day she ran away to be with you, she had never done a bold thing in all the years I've known her."

Guy thought of Robin's words about Mathilde never having been permitted to live her own life. He remembered Mathilde saying she had barely met either of her previous husbands. Oswald was quiet for a moment.

"What if I said I could get the King to sign a divorce, quietly and painlessly, granting your freedom from this dissatisfactory wife of yours?"

The only thing that kept Guy calm was the fact Vawdrey had acknowledged Mathilde was his lawful wife. "I would not take it," he ground out furiously. "Not for a thousand gold coins. Not for ten thousand. Not for all the gold in Karadok."

Oswald gave a thin smile of amusement. "Indeed?" he said. "But I have heard you northerners prize gold and a strong sword arm above all things."

"Not all things," Guy said, not trusting himself to say more for the moment. "Not this northerner."

"Not more than a loyal wife?" asked Oswald quietly.

"Is she loyal?" Guy barked with a bitter crack in his voice. "I hadn't noticed. Last time I checked, loyal wives didn't up and leave their husbands."

"You'd still want a disloyal wife?"

Still want her? He stared at Oswald. "She's mine, and I'm having her. I don't give a damn if she's loyal or not. I won't give her the chance to be otherwise."

Oswald gave a dry smile. "Her loyalty will never be to the north, of course. But you might have had it if you'd treated her with a bit more consideration."

"I don't give a shit about the north anymore!" exclaimed Guy, stung. "I've never raked any of that business up between us!"

376

He gazed past Oswald through the opening in the tent to the fluttering pennants, the royal pavilion. "If necessary, I'll pledge my loyalty now to the Argent Queen," he said. "On bended knee."

"Armenal would doubtless like that," Oswald mused. "But I don't think your wife would like to see you humbled in front of your men."

"I would not give a damn." Guy shrugged.

"Lady Doverdale," Oswald began, his tone casual, "wants to negotiate a separation with you and take her daughter back to Aphrany on the morrow."

Guy was immediately livid. "I won't permit it."

"Despite your dislike of southerners and your vow of allegiance to the Blechmarsh line?"

"I renounced that fealty years ago," Guy reminded him. "There's only one vow I care about now."

"Oh?"

Guy glared at him, feeling frustrated and entirely out of his element. What did this man want from him?

"Can I take it," Oswald elaborated painstakingly, "that the vow you speak of is the one I extracted from you so deviously? Your wedding vow?"

"You can!" Guy muttered the words angrily.

Oswald sighed. "I need to hear from your lips, Martindale, that you prize her and mean to treat her well."

Guy stared at him. How the hells was he supposed to vocalize such things to this man, his enemy? Then he took a deep breath.

"I'd do anything just to receive her smile, her good opinion," he said gruffly and felt his face turning hot. "I cannot tolerate the thought of returning home without her. My life would be empty. Desolate. *Worthless.*"

"And if she said she wished to spend half of her time at court?" Oswald speculated.

"Not without me."

Oswald's eyebrows rose. "You would come to court? You? To wait on the Argent King and his Queen?"

He didn't even hesitate. "Aye, I would. Anything."

Vawdrey was silent for a moment. "You poor bastard," he said. "I promised my wife I would make you suffer a little for what you'd put Lady Mathilde through, but if it makes you any easier, I am deriving little joy from it."

"Well, you can tell her I'm suffering the torments of the damned, if that will make her happy!"

Vawdrey arched a brow at him. "It wouldn't," he said. Then added curiously, "Is it really as bad as all that?"

Guy clenched his jaw. "I need to speak with her!" he burst out rawly. "You don't understand, Vawdrey. Before we parted—" He broke off wretchedly at the throb in his voice. "I said some things…" He found himself unable to continue.

"And, if you had some speech with her?" Oswald prodded gently.

"I can make things right," said Guy hoarsely. "Give her my vow, plight my troth anew. Whatever she deems necessary."

378

Oswald nodded. "There is also another matter, Martindale, that I must have some speech with you about," he said cautiously. "One that, I confess, I bear some blame."

Guy tensed. "If you're trying to claim there was aught amiss in our vows…"

"Nothing of that sort," Oswald hastened to assure him with a flicker of a smile. "No man has ever escaped a legal document I've drawn up. You were locked in tight, never fear."

Guy relaxed. "Then whatever it is, it makes no difference to me."

"Kerslake was a double agent," said Oswald smoothly. "He operated both for the north and for the south. Always has."

Guy stood very still at this astonishing piece of news. Tristan Kerslake was a traitor? Then he swallowed. "Karadok is united now," he said at last with a quick shake of his head. "This is no concern of mine."

"There are still certain…factions rumbling away that would seek to depose King Wymer if they could."

"I'm not among their number. Not anymore."

"Oh, I know that," Oswald agreed blandly. "You take your vows very seriously." Guy stiffened, but it seemed Vawdrey did not mean to cause offence. "There is also the fact Princess Una refused your attempt to free her three years ago at Sandysford," he carried on casually. "Yes, I know all about that."

"How?" Guy licked his lips. "The princess told you?"

Oswald shook his head. "You do her a disservice. It was Kerslake that told us. He had a firsthand account."

"From Ulverston," guessed Guy. He was silent a moment. "Tristan told you that, knowing he could have got us all hanged as traitors?" He could hear the disbelief in his own voice.

"Oh yes," agreed Oswald with a nod. "He told me that and a lot more. Every time a northern lord drank a toast to the imprisoned princess, every treasonous remark, every half-baked plot. All the northern nobles held him in such high esteem," mused Oswald. "He had all their confidences. After all, he lost everything in the war, did he not? His birthright."

Guy clenched his hand. "It wasn't his birthright. He was the second son. If Miles had ever known he was capable of such perfidy—" *Miles would have struck down his brother himself.* Still, he thought, swallowing down the bitterness, he had other aspirations now.

"All this is nothing to me," said Guy harshly. "I don't care if Tristan is a spy. I've nothing to hide."

"Well, he'll be doing precious little spying in future," commented Oswald wryly. At Guy's questioning look he carried on a little ruefully. "After you departed, Kerslake decided to rid himself of a loose end." Oswald shot a glance at Guy's frowning face. "You see, one time at court, your wife saw Kerslake in my company. I did say, did I not, that she is a particular friend of my countess?" Guy struggled to focus on what exactly he was being told. "It is common knowledge, I believe, even this far north, that as well as chief advisor to the King, I am also his spymaster?" Vawdrey continued calmly.

"Aye," Guy rumbled. "What of it?"

"It would seem Kerslake did not feel easy in the knowledge that the Marchioness of Martindale could let this slip at any moment, shattering the confidence so many held in him in this part of the country. He wrote to me. And what he wrote alarmed me so greatly that I thought it expedient to come north immediately."

Guy's heart clenched. "You mean—?"

"He attempted to take her life two mornings ago." Guy took an involuntary step forward. "Unsanctioned, of course. I would never have approved such a course of action."

Guy struggled with his reaction of alarm and panic. His gaze shot over Vawdrey's shoulder, seeking out her figure through the opening in the tent. "She's not hurt? She—?"

"Defended herself very ably," Oswald continued smoothly. "With your dagger, or so she tells me. He did not emerge from the encounter with his life."

Guy paused, turning cold all over. "You mean…" He focused on that small figure again. It was the only way he could keep his calm. Tristan Kerslake had waited until he had left home and had then attacked his wife? "Nay."

Oswald smiled thinly. "I think I probably spared you a good deal, being the one to come across her running down from that mountain, her skirts covered in blood."

Guy thought of the baby Helga had spoken of and swayed. Vawdrey stepped forward sharply to grab his arm. "It was not her blood," he assured him. "But still, it was not the sort of sight a husband would relish overmuch."

"I need to see her, Vawdrey," Guy muttered hoarsely, his fists clenched. "Tell me now what I can say or do to make that happen."

Oswald looked thoughtful. "Believe it or not, I am fully alive to your plight," he said sympathetically and let Guy absorb these strange words before continuing. "If I were to arrange a meeting between you now…?" He let his words trail off.

"I can give the assurances she needs," Guy practically begged. And he wasn't ashamed to do it. "Then after to the Queen, her mother, whoever."

"Very well, then," said Lord Vawdrey. "Allow me to retreat and confer with Queen Armenal. I shall return forthwith."

41

Mathilde hurried in Lord Vawdrey's wake; it was so cold it was almost painful to breathe, and she was suddenly filled with horrible misgivings. Did Guy even know that his best friend's brother had died by her hand? As she approached the green-striped tent, she saw the northerners there all give her their bows and call her name in greeting, although she did not recognize them all. Then she realized they were all calling her Lady Martindale. She threw them her most dazzling smile.

"Good morn," she called warmly. "Good day to you all!" At the opening, Lord Vawdrey threw back the curtain and bowed, allowing her to enter ahead of him. She barely noticed when, instead of following her inside, he simply fastened it shut behind him.

As soon as the tent flap closed, Guy was upon her, a desperate look of entreaty on his face.

"How dare you leave me?" His harsh words were counterbalanced by the fact he sank onto his knees before her, wrapping his arms around her, pressing his face against her skirts. "Mathilde." She barely heard him speak her name, but his voice sounded anguished.

Mathilde felt her frozen heart stutter and then start to pound again. "I did not expect you to discover I was gone so soon," she lied. What was she saying? It seemed pride was dictating her speech. "You must not have stayed at Allworthy for very long."

"I did not even stay one night," he responded grimly. "And my homecoming was to discover you gone and the house in chaos."

Mathilde placed her hand on his thick black hair. "I did not leave you, Guy," she said softly, but he wasn't listening.

"I did *nothing* with Julia Allworthy, save listen to her histrionics until I was sick to my stomach. I swear it. You have to believe me, Mathilde."

He looked up at her, and his expression was so earnest that it took her breath away. Swiftly he came to his feet, gazing down at her, and Mathilde was so caught up in savoring his nearness that his words took a moment to register with her. He took her hands in his.

"Even when I did imagine I cared for her," he continued doggedly, "it was all very shallow. It was never real. Not like you and me. I could never touch her now. I don't even like her hand on my arm."

"Oh, I know that," Mathilde assured him. "I knew you would not look twice at Julia. Not after my send-off."

He blinked. "Your send-off?" he repeated uncomprehendingly. Then, apparently, he recalled their frenzied coupling the night he left and reddened. "Then… *Why?* Why did you leave me?" he demanded in bewilderment.

"I didn't." Mathilde sighed. "Please, Guy, let us take a seat."

She gestured to where two cushioned seats were set out. Guy hesitated for only a split second before walking toward them, still holding her hand. With some reluctance, he released her and sat down. Instead of taking the seat next to his, Mathilde settled herself on his lap. Automatically his arms closed around her, though his gaze was wary. She looped her arms loosely around his shoulders and gazed at him, biting her lip.

"There is something I must tell you. It is very terrible, and I want you to—"

384

"I already know about that bastard Kerslake," he interrupted her.

Mathilde's eyes widened. "Y-you do?" she stammered. He nodded tersely, and she felt the tension running through his whole body. "I'm so sorry, Guy," she began. "If I could only—"

"Sorry?" he burst out incredulously. "If he was still alive, I'd kill him with my own hands!"

Mathilde's jaw dropped. "But...what of Julia?" she forced herself to say. "Now, she's lost not only her husband, but her brother too. You know I don't like her, but—"

"I don't want to talk about Julia or Tristan Kerslake," Guy interrupted her in a growl. "Miles was the only decent one of the whole bunch and he's dead. I don't care if I never set eyes on a Kerslake again. In fact, I'd prefer it."

Mathilde tried to push down the ignoble elation that rose up in her at his words. "I shouldn't be glad about that," she admitted. "But I am, because I don't like her!" His lips crooked a little at that, but he turned serious again almost at once. "I'm also wildly jealous of her," she admitted in a small voice and felt him relax the tiniest bit.

"You've got no cause to be, Mathilde," he told her shakily. "She can't hold a candle to you. Since I've known you, I've barely spared her a glance. Every word she speaks grates on me. I had no time for her as soon as she showed up at Acton March. I never should have let her stay, but gods forgive me, I've been punished for that stupidity tenfold. I'll never do anything to upset you ever again."

A dimple appeared in Mathilde's cheek. "I expect you will," she said frankly, and when he went to argue, she leaned forward and lightly kissed his lips.

"What if I make you a vow?" he asked her with steady determination. "A blood vow. To swear I was never untrue to you and never will be."

Mathilde shuddered. "No, thank you. I've gone off blood and knives recently." At the haunted look in Guy's eye, she decided to try to lighten the mood. "Willard told me you can swear an oath with spit and it's almost as good."

"Spit?"

She nodded. "We did a disgusting spit handshake." Again, the faintest glimmer of a smile and then it was gone. "But perhaps we could kiss? In any case, I don't need you to swear a vow, for I believe you."

Once more, his hold on her tightened before loosening again. "I want to kiss you very badly, right now," he said uneasily. "But I know I won't be able to think straight once I do, and I have so many things I need to say to you." He took a deep breath. "Will you introduce me to these friends of yours? Willard, Gordon… What was the name of the other one?" he asked gruffly.

"Piers. And yes, of course I will."

He gazed at her intently. "I know they're important to you, which means they're also now important to me."

"They're the ones who are here dressed in the same colors as me. It was Queen Armenal's idea. I think she reads too many romances."

"Mathilde…" he said gruffly, interrupting her.

"Yes?"

"I need to know you can forgive me. In time."

She frowned. "For what?"

At her words he shook his head. "Being the worst husband in the kingdom," he forced out.

"You weren't! Guy, those things I said... I never meant them. I was just striking out because I was so terribly hurt."

He closed his eyes. "I hate that I did that," he muttered. "And ruined *everything* between us."

"You didn't!"

"Things were so perfect between us at the lodge, I didn't want to put an end to it. But I should have set you in your rightful place weeks ago," he said ruefully. "I was just so happy. I'd never been so happy in my life. I selfishly wanted to cherish what we'd built together, and instead I...I tore it apart."

Mathilde sat up straighter on his lap. "You'd never been so happy?" she echoed. "But it was the same for me. Oh Guy!" Her eyes filled with tears. She dashed them away. "Oh, *why* did you not say *that* to me after the banquet, you great oaf!" She swatted him on the shoulder.

He pulled her in closer, hugging her tight. "Would you have forgiven me quicker if I had, sweeting? Nay, I don't believe you." He cradled her face gently. "You were so determined to make me suffer like the damned. Like I deserved."

"Guy..."

"I should have sent for you," he said fiercely. "Come to court and demanded you, years ago."

Mathilde caught her breath, feeling a rush of emotion at his words. How could he possibly know the exact right thing to say? It was like he was drawing out a splinter from a wound that had festered for years.

"Guy," she said again weakly. *If only he knew what a terrified little mouse he would have found if he had!*

"I was not ready for you then," she said truthfully. "It took degrees for me to come into my own. First my friendship with Robin and the boys, and then Fenella." She paused. "That was when I dared to hope for more from life. When I began to long for you."

At the catch in her voice, he drew her closer. "You longed for me?"

She nodded. "So badly. And then when I met you…it became even worse. Ten times worse. I never knew I could want something so much."

He drew a shaky breath. "If I'd had any damn sense, I'd have come for you," he insisted. "Gods, when I think about those *wasted* years…" His words trailed off as he gazed down at her. "If I'd only known what was waiting for me there, I would have battered down the doors to get to you."

Mathilde gurgled with laughter. "Likely the King would have thought the north was rising up against him if you had."

"I'd wage a war for you," he said seriously. "I still might have to if your Queen doesn't turn you over to me."

"It's not the Queen you need to worry about," she said seriously. "It's my mother."

He blinked at that. "Which one was she?"

"The grim-looking one in purple. Stood next to the Queen."

He shrugged. "She can't be any fiercer than you." She gave a startled laugh at that. "I still can't believe you're being so forgiving," he admitted. "You refused to give me any quarter last time. I alternated between anger and black despair. And *still* you held firm." The look in his eyes was so admiring that it took Mathilde's breath away. "My magnificent wife," he said with feeling.

"Well, but it wasn't your fault Tristan tried to kill me," Mathilde pointed out.

"I should have been there to protect you," he insisted. "Instead of on that fool's errand."

"That's true enough," said Mathilde, and looked at him sideways to see how he took that!

He gazed back at her, a little wary. "If I ever do anything so stupid again…"

"You could swear your oath on it now, with a kiss," she suggested hopefully.

He drew a sharp breath. "But first," he said huskily, "I need to apologize for those words I spoke to you that night we parted. *Gods*, Mathilde, if you only knew how much they've haunted me." He swallowed. "As soon as I left you that night, they started eating into me, and causing me pain. They were the first thing I thought of when I woke, and the last thing I thought of before sleep. They were with me every second of the day and they weighed down so heavy on my soul that I felt like I could barely—"

"Guy," she broke in frowningly. "Do you mean when you called me a pitiless, merciless bitch?"

He flinched at her words. "Aye," he said hoarsely.

"Then I can honestly say they hurt you far more than they hurt me," she said firmly. "In truth, I've not dwelt on them at all."

"You swear it?" He looked so pained that she tightened her arms around him.

"I do."

"I struck out at you because I was feeling guilty and miserable, and I suspected that I was acting like a damn fool. I also didn't want to go, which made me angry with myself. I thought about you *constantly* while I was away. I was terrified I'd get back and find you'd left me. Then, when I did return home and found you gone…" His voice thickened with emotion.

"Oh, Guy…" She leaned forward, pressing her forehead to his. "I didn't leave you," she said, stroking his cheek. "After Tristan…" She swallowed. "After what happened in the caves, I was so disoriented and…distraught. Lord Vawdrey found me and bore me away. It didn't dawn on me until it was too late what conclusion you would draw."

"Vawdrey said he found you covered in blood," he said starkly, his gaze bleak.

Mathilde winced. "Yes," she admitted. "It's strange, but after I…" She swallowed again. "Once Tristan knew he was done for, he was so kind to me, Guy. Even though he was going to kill me, he bore no actual malice toward me. He—he said he had a part of him that was missing. And that I shouldn't feel bad about what had happened." A tear rolled down her cheek, and Guy rubbed it away with a swipe of his thumb. "I know it doesn't make much sense, but I vastly preferred Tristan to Julia," she confessed in a rush. "I still do." Guy made a choking sound. "But then, he never tried to take you away from me like she did."

390

"Maybe not, but he tried to take *you* away from *me* permanently!" Guy growled.

"I know," she whispered. "It was when I thought of what you'd do, if I was discovered dead, that I knew I had to fight. I drew my dagger," she sobbed. "The one you gave me, but I never deliberately struck at him with it, Guy, I swear. He came at me so fast, and he did not see that I had the knife—" She broke off, wiping her eyes.

"Mathilde," he said shakily, drawing her against him. "My brave girl." He kissed her forehead, then her nose, then her chin. "My brave Mathilde. I'd have *died* if anything had befallen you. I just couldn't have gone on. Knowing how badly I'd treated you, how I'd left you unprotected and alone."

She raised her head. "But you didn't," she pointed out. "That dagger was the first thing you ever gave me. You gave it to me the very night we met. And I used it to protect myself."

"Thank the gods you asked me for a knife," he said. "And I was unable to deny you anything you asked for, from the very first."

"And looking back now," she said, drawing a steadying breath, "I *can* see how my sudden appearance must have seemed very suspicious to you, so it's little wonder really that you acted the way you did…"

His grip on her grew tighter. "Don't make excuses for me, my love. My actions were disreputable and deplorable. I knew I wanted you from the first. And I didn't give a damn about wrong or right, or my honor, or any consideration save getting you for myself. Old Helga warned me not to squander my Yuletide gift, and I so very nearly did. I can't *bear* to think of how close you came to death.

391

"I don't deserve this blessing," he said seriously. "But I'll give thanks every day from this day forward that you're mine. I'll never forget how close I came to losing you, Mathilde. Never," he swore.

"It's not just you who behaved badly," Mathilde said in a pained voice. "I did not respond as I should have when you told me you loved me. And when I said it to you, I phrased it in such a way that you could take no pleasure from it."

"I did not deserve any pleasure at that point. You have nothing to reproach yourself with," he said vehemently. "The fault was mine."

"Can I tell you now?" she asked in a hushed voice. He swallowed and gave a quick nod. "I love you, Guy," she said in a low, tremulous voice. "I love you so very, very much."

He uttered a brief exclamation, and then as if unable to help himself, leaned down to tenderly claim her lips.

Moments later, when he raised his head again, Mathilde wondered at how much happier he looked. As though some great weight had been lifted from his shoulders.

"I told you that I loved you from the first," she murmured, a little shyly. "But when did you fall for me?"

"From the moment I saw your bruised little feet," he rasped. "My heart flew right out of my chest."

"That was early," Mathilde marveled. "So then—"

"I lied," he said, cutting her short. "It was before that. Long before that."

"Really?" She caught her breath. "When?"

He gave a mirthless laugh. "I don't know. When you told me you wanted your knife."

"Oh, then—"

"No!" he burst out frustratedly. "It was before that too."

"Guy?" She gave a gurgle of laughter.

"When you stepped forward and whispered you were my wife. I felt it right here." He pressed a fist to his chest.

"Instantly?"

"Aye. I knew that you belonged here. With me."

She continued to stroke the back of his neck in a calming fashion. "I understand why Temur and Waldon came with you, for I have a personal bond with them. But how did you persuade the Earl of Strethneal, Lord Wallace, and the others to accompany you today?" she puzzled. "They are staunch northerners, are they not?"

"Aye," he agreed. "But it seems when Julia used to complain other women did not like her, she spoke true. The Countess of Strethneal and Lady Wallace put fleas in their husbands' ears after that night. They were as appalled as everyone that I had not given you your due. And it seems Kirkby is a romantic. He should get on well with your Queen," he grumbled.

"How do you mean?"

"Seems he heard some ballad he took a fancy to. About my wronged wife kicking my arse and throwing my leman out on her ear."

"What leman? Julia? I bet she's spitting about that."

"Oh aye, she's furious her sainthood's been revoked," he agreed dryly. "Kirkby's very much looking forward to meeting my warlike bride. And they all agree the Crown should return you to me, if I vow to treat you right."

"You do treat me right," she said staunchly.

"You're too good to me, my love," he said frankly. "I have your jewel by the way. It's in the case back home with the rest of them. She wasn't happy to relinquish it," he said grimly. "I was forced to be quite blunt."

Mathilde forbore to answer, remembering her mother's words. "Lord Vawdrey told me you'd suffered enough, and I should go easy on you," she said instead. She, for one, thought they had dwelt quite long enough on Julia.

"He did?" Guy sounded startled.

She nodded. "I know you don't like him, but—"

"He brokered our marriage," he interrupted her. "So, I already owe him a considerable debt. And if he asked you to look kindly upon me today, then it seems my grudge against him is long past."

"Truly?"

"Aye."

"That's good," said Mathilde earnestly. "For Fenella, his countess, is very dear to me and has written that she hopes our children will grow up to be close friends with theirs." Guy's eyes widened at the idea of future Randalls being friends with Vawdreys, but he managed a murmur of assent.

"If that's what you want, then they will be," he vowed.

"What do you think of the name Leander for our firstborn son?" she asked musingly. "Leander Randall, Marquess of Martindale."

Guy's expression wavered a moment, then he swallowed and nodded. "Aye, love, it sounds…very well."

"Really? You didn't look too sure."

"Quite sure," he insisted, and when she continued to look unconvinced, he coughed and added, "I was only thinking that young Leander would have one of my lesser titles until the time comes for him to inherit mine."

"Lesser titles?"

"Probably my secondary one—Viscount March."

"Viscount March?" Mathilde sat up. "Leander Randall, Viscount March," she pronounced with satisfaction. "Oh, I *do* like that."

"Wait a minute." Guy frowned. "Vawdrey said you were not yet expecting…?"

"Oh, well, I'm probably not just yet," Mathilde agreed. "But even if I'm not already, I'm sure I will be before long."

Guy breathed out noisily. "Aye."

She nodded. "I should have told you I loved you before you left for Allworthy, but I didn't want to fling it in your face as a reason for you not to go…" She bit her lip and lowered her gaze, ashamed. "I know I acted very badly that night, but even I was not quite up to that."

"Mathilde." He enveloped her in his arms. "This Queen should not be expecting you to sit out on a hillside in bleakest February. Are you cold, my love?"

"Not anymore and I never will be again." They both sat a moment deriving comfort from their embrace.

At last, Mathilde drew back with a small sigh. "Guy, can I just say that when I said what I did about divorcing you that night at dinner…I was not in earnest. I have been angry with myself, remembering those words. I want you to know I spoke false."

"They did not hurt me as much as they should have," Guy admitted now apologetically. "For I knew I would never permit it, not while there was breath in my body." He hesitated. "Then there was the fact you were so angry about Julia…"

Mathilde groaned. "Is that your tactful way of saying I acted like an extremely jealous wife?"

He definitely smiled at that, though it quickly died away.

"That was the only thing that gave me hope," he confessed. "You were so cold to me, but when it came to her, you grew hot as fire."

She watched his eyes darken. "Are you thinking of that night?" she asked awkwardly.

He nodded and cleared his throat. "Constantly," he admitted. "You were so—"

"Guy…" Mathilde squirmed, feeling herself blush.

"Demanding," he finished. "I loved it."

"Really?" She exhaled.

"But I'll only be gentle now," he said, tightening his hold on her. "Until you're fully recovered from your ordeal."

"Oh, but I am fully recovered," Mathilde assured him hurriedly. "I was the moment you returned to me."

"I still want to be tender with you," he said gruffly. "Until I'm assured you realize how much you mean to me."

"Well, gentle is good too," Mathilde said, placing her forehead against his. "But what if I want you rough again?"

"Then you can scratch your nails down my back, and I'll be as rough as you like," he promised in a low, intimate voice. Mathilde sighed happily, and he laughed before gazing down at her face. "I hope you are with child," he said. "Not just for my sake, but 'twould be a factor for winning over your mother. I would have an ally in her camp," he said. "Leander will be her first grandchild."

Mathilde laughed. "It could be a girl."

"And what would her name be, I wonder?" He looked, she thought, a little nervous.

"I thought perhaps…Heloise?" she ventured.

"The honorable Lady Heloise Randall of Acton March," he said aloud and nodded his head. "I like it." She smiled. "There's just one thing I still don't understand." He frowned.

"Tell me." She stroked his chest encouragingly.

"How the hells can people think you timid?"

Her hand halted a moment. "You don't find me timid?"

He snorted. "Hardly. And it doesn't sound to me like you ever were."

She frowned and leaned one elbow on his shoulder. "You mean because of my daring escape from court? Or because…of Tristan Kerslake?"

His arms tightened around her. "Because," he said with deliberation, "nervous little virgins don't dream about marrying great ugly brutes like me."

"You're not ugly," she said indignantly.

"I'm not the stuff of maidenly dreams."

"You have no idea what maidens dream of," she pointed out with a smothered laugh.

"That may be so," he conceded. "But dreams are dreams, and you, madam, seduced me."

"I?"

"You," he said firmly.

"I did, didn't I?" she whispered. He nodded, his eyes alight with admiration. "I should probably warn you," she said, biting her lip, "that after your audience with the Queen and my mother…"

"Yes?"

"I'm going to do it *all* over again."

He groaned, tipping his head back to rest on the chair. "You little witch," he complained. "How am I supposed to concentrate now on the task at hand?"

Her eyes danced. "You'll manage." She patted his shoulder. "I have *every* faith in you."

42

Her mother had been shocked, and the Queen delighted, when the Marquess of Martindale had gone down on one knee before them, humbly appealing for the return of his wife.

"She has put you through the mill, this one, I think, no?" the Queen had speculated, her eyes gleaming. "And brought this proud warrior to his knees?"

"Once proud, Your Majesty," Guy had corrected her heavily. "She has all but destroyed me. My pride lies in tatters."

Mathilde could remember her mother's astonishment and the Queen's high glee. "But yes!" Queen Armenal had breathed, clapping her hands. "This is very satisfactory. But very satisfactory to me!"

"I would face any challenge," he had declared. "Swear any vow to ensure her return."

"But I haven't gone anywhere!" Mathilde had pointed out and been ignored.

As the interview had continued, Mathilde had realized with dismay that the Queen fully intended promoting her to a position of eminence among her ladies. "Oh, but Your Majesty—" she had started to protest, but Guy had squeezed her hand and given the tiniest shake of his head.

"But how can I spend time at the southern court?" she had demanded in an indignant whisper. "When I have no intention of leaving your side?"

He had smiled at her words and then in a low voice responded, "My love, there is no southern court, there is only one royal court these days. And if you're there, just where do you imagine I will be?"

That had brought her up short. "You wouldn't," she had answered uncertainly. "Would you?"

"I would," he had answered firmly. "You're going nowhere without me."

Later that night, they had lain together in one of the guest bedrooms at Woodcote House.

"You did not mind," Mathilde said anxiously, "that the Queen wished for us to remain one night here before returning to Acton March?"

"Nay, wife, I care not where we are, so long as we are together."

"Tell me about Prudie, and Destrian, and the hens," she had demanded after they lay in the afterglow of their lovemaking. Guy had been as good as his word. First, he had been painstakingly tender and slow and taken great care with lavishing his every attention on her, whispering sweet nothings and praise in her ear the whole time. Then she had sunk her nails into his back, and he had responded every bit as ferociously as she could have wished. She watched the rise and fall now of his hairy chest as his labored breathing returned to normal.

He did not seem to have heard her request, for he turned his head and swiftly kissed her shoulder. "Mouse indeed," he mocked. "If only they knew."

"Someone once said I was more like a mink," she admitted. He lifted his head at that and frowned. "Small and exquisite, with sharp teeth."

"Who the hells said that?" he asked, sounding annoyed.

Mathilde thought a change of subject might be expedient. "Tell me about Prudie, Destrian, and the hens," she insisted.

His hand rested at her hip as he considered this with a pucker between his brows. "Prudie and Destrian are well, as are the hens. Waldon and Rob are here so you can ask them in the morn. Now tell me, who said that to you?" His expression was foreboding in the extreme. Mathilde reached up to brush the fall of dark hair back from his brow.

"No one you need worry about. How long do you suppose it will take before my hair grows back?" she asked. "Mother said I look more like a pageboy these days than a maid."

"I know what you're doing, and it won't work," he growled, rolling onto his side and looming over her. "Distracting me," he elaborated in answer to her raised eyebrows.

"Tristan said it," she admitted softly. She looked away from Guy's intent stare. "I think he rather liked me, despite everything." She looked up sharply at Guy's muffled exclamation. "I daresay I'll always feel guilty over what happened. I wish it could have been resolved differently."

"It wasn't your fault, Mathilde," he said tightly.

"I know that really, but I can't help feeling badly about it."

"I'll fill your belly with babies to stop you getting such foolish ideas."

Mathilde considered this. "How many?"

"Dozens," he replied without pause. "One after another. 'Til you're past bearing age. But I'll plough you even then."

"I want you to grow your beard back longer," she replied, supremely unconcerned by this glimpse of a future filled with incessant childbearing. She tugged on the short black bristles. "It was longer on that first night I met you." He grunted. "Will you?"

"Aye. Anything. Whatever it takes."

"To what?"

"Keep you contented with me."

"You do and you always will," she assured him confidently. "Now, let us think about names for all these children."

Guy groaned.

Epilogue

Six months later

"Guy!" Mathilde lowered her letter from her friend Fenella, her face flushed. "Only fancy! Twin boys!"

Guy lowered the cloth he was scrubbing at his neck with. "Twins?" he repeated and frowned.

Mathilde nodded eagerly, returning to her letter. "They have called them Nathan and Stephen Vawdrey. Is that not terribly exciting?"

If anything, Guy was silent a moment. "And she is well?" he asked in a low voice. "After birthing them?"

He cast down the cloth and made his way over to the bed where his wife was reclined having an afternoon rest. He edged his way up onto the mattress next to her, resting a palm on her pregnant belly.

"Oh yes," Mathilde assured him quickly. Just lately, Guy seemed to have fallen prey to anxiety around any accounts of labor or pregnancy. "Fenella writes she is very well and enjoying a period of rest at their new town residence." She read aloud from the letter. "The boys are healthy and hearty. Nathan is the elder by a quarter of an hour." She lowered her letter again. "I suppose that means he will bear his father's lesser title for now—Baron Vawdrey. It's funny to think of a baby being a baron, is it not?" She thought briefly of all the barons she had known, who had mostly been bluff old men with booming voices. "I think perhaps we should have Heloise now," she said, resting her hand on top of his. "And have Leander as our second child."

403

Guy looked startled at the postponement of his son and heir. "And why is that?" he asked in bewilderment, raising his head from the pillow to squint at her.

"Because then Heloise can marry Nathan or Stephen and ally our two families," she pointed out reasonably.

A slight frown passed over Guy's face, and Mathilde wondered if he had entirely accepted Oswald Vawdrey as an ally. He had been wholly impressed with his countess, Fenella, when they had met and had told Mathilde that she was free to visit Acton March whenever she pleased, but he still seemed to have a few reservations about Earl Vawdrey.

"If our daughter marries a Vawdrey she'll marry the future earl, not the younger son," he said with feeling.

"Nathan, then." Mathilde nodded. "I shall write back to Fenella."

"I don't think we should be overly hasty to enter into any betrothals for our children," Guy said. He shot her a sidelong look.

"Oh, but I think it is quite important that there is not too much disparity in age, Guy," she said earnestly.

Immediately, he was contrite, and she realized he knew she had been thinking of her own previous marriages. "Of course," he muttered soothingly. "But Strethneal has an infant son, don't forget. Heloise will have more than one opportunity to be a countess. And if she marries Strethneal's heir, then she would live awfully close to us after marriage."

Mathilde's eyes widened. "That is a good point," she conceded. "I had not thought of that."

"Of course, if Heloise is an unspeakable brat, we could send her down south without any compunction."

"Guy!" He laughed and turned to kiss her lips. "I thought perhaps we could bring my old nurse back to Acton March with us to help with the baby when it comes," Mathilde said tentatively. "Mother doesn't know what to do with the poor old thing these days and I'm no longer worried she'll go back to cossetting me now I've found my feet."

"I don't know about that." He frowned. "She must be blind as a bat to have mistaken Willard for you."

All three boys had been to stay at Acton March, and Guy had spent some considerable time befriending them all. Mathilde had been very touched by the efforts he had made. As for Robin, he never had returned to old Sir Avery, but had stayed instead as part of Guy's household, officially as his squire. He and Mabel the cat shared quarters now in the west wing. His hens and goats had been moved up to the manor as his personal pets.

"I don't want her mistaking a piglet for our son and heir."

"Well, she's not likely to make that mistake!" Mathilde pointed out with a giggle.

"And what about our daughter, the fair Heloise?" he continued. "What if she tries to mold her into a perfect Lady Tilda?"

"We'd never let her!" Mathilde said, impressed he'd remembered the tale she'd told him. "Fancy you remembering that."

"I remember everything you tell me," he said smugly.

"You're very good," she agreed with a sigh. "But I've thought of a counter for that. How would it be if we made Old Helga one of Heloise's godparents?"

Guy went off into a coughing fit. "Gods, Mathilde!"

"She'd be perfect," she insisted.

"Perfect?" He looked skeptical. "I've only just forgiven the old crone for causing all that discord between us six months ago!" he said sternly.

He had told Mathilde the whole conversation that had passed between himself and the witch, including her prophecy of his southern wife. Mathilde had freely forgiven the old woman for her interference, for it was clear to her that Old Helga knew what she was about. Guy had found it a little harder to let bygones be, but he was getting there.

As for Mathilde's mother, Lady Doverdale had stayed with them on a month-long visit. She and Guy had clashed a couple of times as both had strong opinions, but Mathilde had learned to simply take a step back and let them argue. It soon passed, and on the whole, she did not think they thought any the worst of each other for it.

"Have you finished with your letter?" he asked, eyeing the missive she still held loosely in her fingers.

"What? No, why?" Mathilde took it up again. "There is something really astonishing as a postscript, which you will hardly credit, Guy. Now, when we went to court in the spring, I do not remember, did I introduce you to the Lady Eden Montmayne?"

Guy whipped the letter out of her fingers and threw it over the side. "Who?"

"Guy! I meant to read it to you!" she said in exasperation. "You won't believe this, but apparently Lord Vawdrey's youngest brother, Roland, has eloped with her!"

Guy rolled his eyes. He muttered something she did not catch, which sounded suspiciously like "not more Vawdreys." Then carefully he pinned her arm above her head and kissed her collarbone.

"Well, yes," she said breathlessly, "but the astonishing thing is that Eden is so very proper and a real stickler for decorum, whereas Roland Vawdrey, is decidedly *not*... It's such a very strange match. Almost as strange as ours."

He paused at that. "Our pairing is not strange," he said firmly. "It was foretold in the stars."

"Is that what Old Helga said?" Mathilde was startled. She did not think she had ever heard the old woman speak so fancifully.

"As good as," muttered Guy.

His lips traveled down, and Mathilde's inclination to talk court gossip diminished rapidly. After all, they would be returning to Aphrany in the winter, and she could catch up with everything then. Just then her eye fell on the large tapestry she had created for the bedroom wall. It depicted the lodge in all its cozy familiarity. Perhaps she should have shown a starry sky above the timbered building?

"Guy," she said, running the fingers of her free hand into the dark hair at his nape.

He lifted his head, his eyes a little unfocussed. "Yes?"

"Let's go to the lodge next week for a few days. Just the two of us."

He gazed down at her blankly. "The lodge?"

"Yes, the lodge."

"And why, my love," he asked carefully, "all of a sudden do you want to go to the lodge?"

"Because," she said wistfully, "it would be so nice if it was just you and me for a while. After Mother's four-week visit, I mean. I can boil you eggs to eat. We can play cards, and there is a book there that I particularly wish to reread."

His lips curved into a grin. "Well, that all sounds very nice. Let's do that. Now, may I return to my explorations? At this precise moment I have an inclination to keep you flat on your back."

She laughed. "Very well," she conceded with a happy sigh. "But after I've read my book, there may be some other positions we could try."

But Guy wasn't listening. He was otherwise occupied, and Mathilde was just fine with that. She would surprise him with some new ideas about that next week. Surprising her husband was one of the many, many delights of her life. And life right now, she thought, really was delightful.

THE END

If you want to read more about Karadok, then the next book in the series is Lenora's story:

The Unlovely Bride

Lenora Montmayne leads a charmed life as the most beautiful woman at King Wymer's court, surrounded by admirers. And then disaster strikes. The red pox sweeps the summer palace at Caer-Lyonnes, and Lenora's fair face falls victim to its ravages. Without her looks, what does Lenora have left to her?

If ever there was a knight the crowd loves to hate, it's Garman Orde. Even his own family despises him. Then one night a heavily veiled lady offers him an extraordinary bargain. And he finds out that Lenora Montmayne was never just a pretty face.

The Consolation Prize

Princess Una harbors no illusions about her claims to Karadok's throne. The days of the royal house of Blechmarsh are done. The last of that ill-fated line, she is just grateful she emerged from the dark days of war with her head still on her shoulders. Now if only she could stop these rebellious northern lords from plotting to overthrow the King and set her up in his stead!

When her royal cousin bids her to join him at court, Una is eager for the opportunity to publicly renounce her rights. After three years languishing under house arrest, she is keen to start her own life afresh, hopefully in relative obscurity.

Little does she realize what manner of husband fate has in store for her...

If you enjoyed this book, please consider leaving me a rating on Goodreads, Amazon, Bookbub or wherever else you leave your reviews. I would be very grateful.

You can find my website at: www.alicecoldbreath.com where you can sign up for my monthly newsletter and find out what I am up to.

Also, please do check out some of my other stories!

Many thanks, Alice.

The Vawdrey Brothers Series:

Book 1: Her Baseborn Bridegroom

Book 2: His Forsaken Bride

Book 3: An Ill-Made Match

The Brides of Karadok Series:

Book 1: Wed By Proxy

Book 2: The Unlovely Bride

Book 3: The Consolation Prize

Book 4: Her Bridegroom, Bought and Paid For

Book 5: An Inconvenient Vow

Book 6: The Favourite

The Victorian Prizefighter Series:

Book 1: A Bride for the Prizefighter

Book 2: A Substitute Wife for the Prizefighter

Book 3: A Contracted Spouse for the Prizefighter